A SENSE

First published in 2001 by Matthewman Books

In this work of fiction, the characters, places and
events are either the product of the author's
imagination or they are used entirely fictitiously.

A SENSE

Published by Matthewman Books

Copyright © Richard Matthewman 2001

Richard Matthewman asserts the moral right to be identified as the
author of this work

Cover design by Trevor Laming, Faversham

ISBN: 978-0-9928971-0-9

Printed in England by BookPrintingUK, Remus House, Coltsfoot
Drive, Woodston, Peterborough PE2 9BF

richard@rmatthewman.wanadoo.co.uk
www.richardmatthewman.com

A SENSE

Part I

Chapter 1
(Friday, Day 1 - May 1992: Kent)

AROUND THE CHURCHYARD sun glinted through trees and distracted her from the words being spoken, made her blink and cast her eyes away to the grass and the darkness that lay beyond it. How could this be done with such ease, something so terrible carried out with such calm; how could they all be so calm?

She peered again around her at those in the churchyard, for whom it seemed the funeral of David Whellans was as peaceful and as loving an occasion as could be wished for - all that was needed to say farewell to the great man and to settle the past. Again she looked around. Still they were all so calm; and yet her own emotions were as far from calm as they could be.

Now it was movement - the sway of the vicar's cassock beside the untidy violation in the earth and the twitch of the hems of coats of those who looked on - that distracted her. Her eyes flickered around the faces, then back to the grass at her feet. Beside the bones of his ancestors, where a new stone would stand, David was now buried

She had to get away. As the notion settled in her mind, she looked up to see her son edge towards her, as if he sensed her need. Taking her arm, he walked her away from the crowd. 'I think father would have approved, don't you? I think it was as good as it could have been.'

Content to be led, she walked with him. How strange that people could adapt so quickly. 'Yes, I am sure you are right, Jonathan; I am sure it was perfect.'

As he steered her around the church and away from those who gathered at its entrance, past the millrace, across the bridge and along the bridle-path beside the river, she gripped his arm and, throwing back her head, let the sun warm her face. 'Thank you for taking me away; I'm not being very good am I?' she said.

Turning to him, she watched him shrug a reply. *Must think I'm pathetic, no longer* compos mentis. The notion made her smile and, summoning her energy, she said, 'I think I will have to get away from here now; I don't think I'll be able to stay close to all our memories.' And stepping away and dropping his arm, she wondered if she was being overly negative. *Yes, of course she was.* Glancing across at him, she said, 'How foolish we were to stay here for so long.'

'You'll have to give it time, Mother.'

'Time, Jonathan? No, I don't think time will help. We've been robbed; your father had so much to do. I don't think time will help me now, however much we have.' To let her mind settle, she stopped. 'That's not the problem: it's me, just me. I have to get away...' and with that admission, she closed her eyes, cast her head back and breathed in deeply.

'It's been a shock to us all,' he said.

With eyes still closed, she nodded and then, turning back to him, caught his look of bemusement. 'Of course it has; a shock that has taken everything away... I know you think I am mad, but the shock - if that is what it was - seems to have wiped my brain clean, left me with a mish-mash of feelings that aren't thoughts at all, just images, ideas at the best. It reminds me of what your father always said: *Don't think too much or you'll forget what you were thinking about.*'

'Hm, he was good at saying things like that, wasn't he?'

Taking his arm again, as he steered her round the pot-holes, she swayed in the rhythm of their steps. 'My brain is clear now, really, but I have no interest in anything; just vague impressions.'

'It's early days, Mother; let's wait and see,' he replied, seeming to want, but failing, to console her.

As they walked on beside the river, she nodded: 'Yes, it's early days. We lived such peaceful lives here, your father and I; he loved it. All he wanted was a place of solitude, so that he could look beneath the surface of his thoughts in harmony with his environment, and create music.'

Slowing again, and stumbling over the rough surface of the track, she stared ahead. *What was there in a place? This wasn't her place. She belonged where her heart was, and it wasn't here.*

Almost in a whisper, she said, 'This was the place for your father, not me,' and she looked to see if he understood. 'Although I was born here and we stayed here together, it was he that loved it, not me. Now I will have to go; the village holds nothing for me now.'

'No, Mother,' he said, and laughed, 'this is where you belong.'

'*Belong* Jonathan? No, it was your father who belonged here. Except for being with your father, I have never belonged here.'

Again, he said, 'Just give it time...'

'Time. Yes, I do need time, though now it's to be nearer to you and Anna. I wish you were not so far away.'

He laughed. 'I think I will come back soon.'

Yes, poor boy, now his father had gone he might return. 'I do hope you will.'

They turned to retrace their steps. 'I hope you don't think I'm sounding too selfish? I know you have suffered too.'

AT THE CHURCH, Alexandra Whellans and her son led those that still remained there back past the weeping willows and into the garden of the cottage, a house she had known since childhood, only a stone's throw from the church and from the house where she was born. Most people stayed for lunch, content to spend the afternoon at the place where David Whellans had lived so long.

She surveyed the scene; *just look at them, voyeurs into my life.* She looked at everyone: family and relatives, friends, neighbours and the retinue of colleagues and acquaintances that David had inspired or encouraged in their work. *Just look at them.*

A tall woman of her own age who she had noticed earlier at the graveside caught her eye. *Who was she?* She looked at her and then away. *Should she know her? Surely she knew everyone there.*

'Who is that, Jonathan, the woman with the red hair?' She nodded in the woman's direction.

Jonathan followed her gaze. 'I haven't seen her before; do you want me to find out? Anna might know.'

She shook her head. 'No, it doesn't matter.' The woman looked over again and then away.

'They're all staring at me,' she muttered to herself. 'And who's that Jonathan? The big man over there.'

'Ah, now that's Major James Fenton; I was talking to him earlier; said he knew father during the war.'

'Oh, I don't think I've ever met him...'

When the first round of drinks was served and everyone had a plate and napkin in their hand, she slipped away, back along the lane and towards the churchyard. Where she sat beside the grave, the grass was dry.

'This happened too quickly, my love,' she muttered to the air around her. 'You left me too quickly.' And, kicking off her shoes, she rubbed her feet in the earth.

'How stupid: you've taken my life,' she whispered. 'We met in this church when we were six or seven years old and singing in the choir, just as the children today. Now it is finished.' Her toes dug into the grass and made holes through the turf.

'*My God*,' she murmured. 'I've been so naïve. What shall I do now, now that you've left me, now you are only in my thoughts?' She closed her eyes and continued to think and, with head bowed, said, 'I was here only for you and now I don't belong here anymore.'

Tears pricked her eyes and, letting her head roll back, she breathed in, then held her breath: 'Hm! You dreamed, and from your dreams, made music. What of me?' She looked into the grass and then again closed her eyes.

The cycle that had started in the church those many years ago neared completion: David had gone. A mile from where she was born, next to the new grave of her husband, she continued to sit. Something had stopped - the silence after a scream, when people wait and the mind freezes in stillness ahead of the crash.

Swans flew overhead and roused her. *The guests! Better get back.* Hopefully most would have gone; Paul and Colette would still be there.

Pulling herself to her feet and starting towards the cottage, in the shadow of the grand church and at each twist of the path, she lingered, reminisced beneath the trees, asked herself again, what should she do now?

Chapter 2
(Easter, 1934: Kent)

IT WAS EASTER and that morning he was out with his friend Paul Spiers west of the village in the hills towards the coast where it was like being on a roof, with nowhere higher to go than the sky. Where the brow of the hill appeared ahead of them, between trees silhouetted against the clouds, they ran along the rise of the Downs. To the east lay a mosaic of fields, some ploughed and pock-marked with chalk, others pasture with sheep, that swept away into a hazy distance where patches of woodland roughened the landscape. From across the fields, drops of rain gusted towards them.

At a farm gate, to catch their breath, they stopped. 'We must be half-way now,' he said and, recovering from the pull up the hill, wiped the water from his eyes.

'More than half way, I should think,' Paul replied, his breath coming in gasps as he flexed his calf muscles and kicked mud off his shoes. 'The railway line was six and a half miles according to the map.'

He looked at him, at his sharp features and the deep, far away eyes. He was a great musician and, although slight in build, he knew he was strong. But still he felt concern. 'Are you alright?' he asked.

'Mm, fine,' Paul replied, now flexing his shoulders.

They were doing a half marathon, but he wondered if it was too much. 'The pace is good,' he said, still unsure of his friend's stamina. 'There's no hurry...'

Paul arched his back. 'You're not running away from me, if that's what you mean? Yes, it's fine.' And now he looked up and stared at the sky. 'Look,' he said, 'the moon - it's still there. I've never seen it like that before.'

A half-moon clung to the morning sky, ghostly pale, as a wisp of cloud against the blue. He followed his friend's gaze. 'Odd, isn't it; I think it's often there somewhere in the sky in the daytime, but we don't see it because the sun's too bright.'

Paul nodded and, aware of his interest in sources of inspiration, said, 'Did you know the moon is where some of our rhythms come from?'

He glanced over at him. 'No, - which rhythms?'

'I'm not sure, but I know that rhythms come from the moon, and maybe from the stars and planets too. We are influenced by them.'

For a moment he continued to stare into the sky. *Rhythms!* He turned to Paul again. 'If there *are* moon rhythms, do you think we can detect them?'

Paul shrugged: 'Animals and plants cycle with the moon. Women - you know, the twenty eight day cycle - are in rhythm with the moon. Feelings change in the cycle; highs and lows. Men might have cycles from the moon too.'

'Could that be the source of some of our music do you think?'

Paul nodded. 'It could well be, in the same way you listen to the woods,' - and now he parodied what he had once said: '*The silent, damp and dark, mysterious music of the woods...*'

He laughed. 'Did I say that? It's true though, I have tried to write *damp and dark*. Could you play *damp and dark* on the violin?'

Quick to take up the challenge, Paul said, 'Yes, - probably I could.'

He laughed again. 'You can show me next time I'm round...'

Paul shivered. 'Okay, I will. Come on, though, I'm getting cold now.'

He nodded. 'After you,' and, waiting for Paul to leap the gate, he followed as they started off again. 'We circle the woods and then go down to the river and along the track,' he said.

On they ran across the Downs through rain that now fell more heavily. Mud spattered with each step on the track and, as they traversed oak woodland, exertion was stretched another mile, until the river opened before them. Like the river's flow, the rhythm swirled through his mind. Rain added colour; each drop rippled and then shattered under another drop on the river's surface. The sensation of rain and the rhythm of running, the inter-play of responses to the dripping world, played in his mind.

In silence they continued and finally ran past the church and into the village where he caught a glimpse of Alex Morton as she dashed into its porch to shelter. He waved but she didn't see them. Along the street the gutters flowed in streams.

'Tomorrow at the same time, then,' Paul said, offering his hand as they parted.

'Yes, see you tomorrow,' he replied.

They had run thirteen miles. Once back in the house, soaked and dishevelled, he sneaked to his room and, while he dried off and changed, let the rhythms from the hills and the rain settle in his mind.

ON A GREEN CARPET at an angle to and a little to the side of the window a grand piano filled the central space of the room. Next to a music stand, a violin case lay open on the floor. Beneath the window stood a desk. All else was minimal: a bed, a bookcase and a chest of drawers. In one corner an amateur radio set lay assembled on a small table.

The window opened onto a view of the hills and when he looked out, the moon had disappeared, lost in the brightness of the day. But the rhythms remained and for an hour, at his piano, he made them into music.

Afterwards, looking relaxed, as she arranged a cloth of lace in the centre of the table, he found his mother in the dining room. Wearing a flowered dress of roses on blue and green pulled tight at the waist with a bow at the back, she turned as he entered. 'Hello. I heard you playing; how is it going?'

He pondered. 'Moon struck.'

She gave a puzzled look: 'Mad, dreaming, still asleep?'

'Dreaming, maybe. The moon was up when we were out; one of those late winter moons. Paul talked about it and I've been playing with his ideas.'

'Ah, I didn't see it. Anyway, it's spring now, not winter.' She gave a bright smile. 'Winter has gone; it's past the equinox. Isn't it warm when the sun comes out? You're sure you have everything you need?'

He watched her: she treated her sons in the same way she treated plants on the veranda. Edwin, the eldest, inherited his father's practical mind, whereas he, he knew, as a musician, took after her. She always said it made him more temperamental than Edwin. Different plants have different needs and different needs needed different treatments, and so she watched over them as a gardener tended a garden; no need to pester or pamper, just watch and do what was required. He smiled at his thoughts about her.

'What are you smiling at?' she said.

'Just you. No, everything's fine,' he said, and gave the slightest of nods and another smile to please her. 'Now that it's been enlarged, the window is much better,' he added. 'I can see more and the room is brighter.'

Finishing her arrangement of daffodils in a vase on the dining table, she asked, 'Do the trees still get in the way? We could thin them if it will help. I'll talk to your father. You will try to relax a little, won't you?'

Between the dining room and the conservatory, he stood by the door. 'Of course I will, don't worry. I'll be out each day with Paul.'

She left the arrangement of flowers and, giving him a peck on the cheek on the way past, went to the conservatory. Light shone through her hair that flowed over her ears into waves and curls that tumbled down. The sun lit her shoulders. 'But I do worry; what were you dreaming about?'

'Where our rhythms come from; do we get them from the moon?'

She smiled: 'You see, that is why I worry.' Re-arranging pots on the ledge, she moved the cane rocking chair beside them.

'It's a real question; are they in us, or do we make them? If we have them, where did they come from?'

She smiled. 'Yes, I know, they are good questions. But they can drive you mad, as well.'

'Like the moon?'

'Yes...' she said, with a vigorous nod.

Absorbed by her movements, he watched her, and wanted to tell her of a new idea, but continued to wait. She collected leaves that had fallen to the floor from a plant on the windowsill.

He needed her help: 'I have a plan to write an overture during the Easter holiday; I'll need to be alone.'

She listened, her smile coming easily. 'That also is what I'm worried about, but then that is you, isn't it?' And she widened her eyes at him.

He nodded and returned her look.

His father was less easy and expected him to join in his activities. He coaxed him, tried to lure him away fishing. He remembered his words. *You need a change from the books my boy. Come to the Wye Valley in Wales. You'll enjoy it; I'm sure you will.*

He had declined and now explained his ideas for an overture to his mother.

WHEN HE WAS younger it had been different. At thirteen, at the same time as he practised for a role in Hamlet at school, he had written two anthems in a week. He had done it in a rush of nervous energy, with boyish enthusiasm. Now, while in many ways no less a boy, he needed to know he could write at a more measured pace.

His perspective was broad: the violin, the piano and the organ in church. Then there was has father's love of jazz which he often played on the gramophone and which seeped into his consciousness alongside music from the church.

Paul Spiers was the opposite: focused and brilliant. He played the violin and his feel for the instrument was what every teacher hoped to find in a pupil: nervous linkages complete, a brain able to handle the thread that tied emotion to musical creation, the ability to strive to perfection and struggle with each phrase and nuance. Paul had them and attained the perfection everybody expected from him.

Like Paul, since an early age, perhaps when he was five or six years old, he had known what he wanted: quite simply, to write songs. That was what he told people when they asked: like the choir master, I want to write songs, he would say. It was an innocent but clear ambition, one which he had never lost and one that with age had grown and widened. Now he would say he wanted to find music within himself and in the world around him and turn that music into notes on a page. He still wrote songs, but more and more he composed music. At seventeen, that was the pursuit that gave him reason.

Childhood influences were the orchards of Kent and the sea and the coves of Dorset in the summers. Now he sought to express more complex ideas. As a boy he pestered his mother: come and listen to this, he demanded after an hour of commotion from the drawing room. It's a song I've made from my poetry book. Or else, I've written a prayer for you to sing.

She sang his songs at soirées hosted for her friends. At nine he wrote an *Anthem for Christmas*, which he handed to the choirmaster and said he would like to be performed in the service. The choirmaster humoured him: Certainly David, he had replied, and, with only minor alterations, included it.

His mother arranged lessons in composition. He wrote music for a nativity-play that year and set poems to music. *The Stour Suite*, written when he was twelve for a string quartet of two violins, viola and cello, was performed in a competition. He used Haydn and Brahms, which his mother loved and had taught him, for inspiration. At the Canterbury music festival he met Ronald Gudge and, at the age of thirteen, started composition lessons with him. At the Choir School, as a day pupil, more and more time was devoted to music. He rejected the suggestion that he should board and resisted all efforts to persuade him. His ability and inspiration were cradled by his home and the village he lived in. And - he had to admit it - also by Alex Morton. She lived there too and now crossed his mind. Later, he would go to see her.

THE NEXT DAY, as they set off through the orchards and up the rise to the Spinney, he laughed and said, 'So England won the rugby then.'

Paul cast a sideways glance: 'You knew they would. I heard the report on the radio; France had a chance, but they lost it in the second half.'

Their own game was one in which each took the lead, so that balance rested between them. Paul used it to clear his mind; he to gain ideas. The analogy was with the flute and oboe that wrapped melody around and between them, to and fro. For a while the game enticed them. They left the village and headed for the Downs.

It was the village of Maklam that nurtured his music. The vision, the decisions, the toil and the elation were all part of the village.

Looking back as they climbed the hill, he saw the church and the houses that nestled in the bend of the river, and drew comfort from the sight.

When they slowed down to mount a gate, Paul turned to him: 'You're not making it to choir much these days.'

He shook his head: 'No, it's such a distraction. The music stays in my mind and I'm thinking in rhythms and melodies of hymns for hours; sometimes even for days.'

Paul nodded: 'I know what you mean; it's the same for me. The Germans call it an earworm. *Ohrwurm!*'

As they ran on, he raised his eyebrows.

Along some stretches, the rhythm becoming hypnotic, they progressed in silence. Sometimes they just let the rhythm carry them, disturbed only by the calls of lapwings that circled the fields, or the cries of rooks in the trees at the edge of the woodland.

The stillness could be like a meditation that appeared in the flow of steps. Beneath and behind it, the nebulae of responses wove into notes in his mind.

In the lead, his feet light on the ground, Paul pulled them on. 'No moon today,' he gasped, as they entered the village again.

'No, but today I can hear other rhythms.'

'They might come from the moon...'

'Yes, they might,' he said.

Chapter 3
(Day 2 - May 1992: Kent)

IT WAS DAYBREAK, the first end of dark and the first show of light, when the vixen re-traced her trail through the lanes, when lives realigned. The day did not break, nothing cracked and no pieces were left behind, just a trick of light when it was no longer night.

She watched the vixen jump the fence and run across the lawn. Seeing her, it ran on. Since before dawn she had been in the garden and did not notice the change; at some point it was light. With her back against the wall, sitting on a cushion on the grass, she moved only to ease the numbness.

Now it was finished and the time for grieving had come. The loving friends had gone, taken their kindness and thoughts. Grieving came as an unread book on a shelf, or as a cove along the coast never visited, as a surprise. After a lifetime shared, she was alone.

Barely a sound disturbed the space around her. Something in the noiselessness made the air appear unused, as new notepaper or the surface of a pond. Her mind mirrored it, noiseless, only part engaged. Soundlessness focused on her, like the girl on the train who tells a friend the secrets of her new romance, the intimacies, holy privacies, and then looks up to find all eyes on her, the weight of attention draining into her.

Perhaps because of its fragility, perhaps because of the effortless way things had been destroyed, she was not easy with this new silence. Perhaps it was novelty that enabled her now to hear what she had not heard before, the almost inaudible voices in her, vibrations that impinged on her consciousness.

Anna was the only one in the cottage, asleep and, she supposed, not knowing what to do. Already Jonathan had departed to return to his work in Mali.

She knew what they would do when they met: look only, half smile, hug, say nothing; Anna knew to say nothing. She watched her now, like the vixen, cross the lawn, approach from nowhere, then crouch, put her arms around her neck and look into her eyes, rest her forehead on hers. She tried to smile and, almost to herself, said, 'Don't sneak up on me, like that.'

'I knew you were here, heard you come down hours ago, saw you from the window. I've been working all night, getting on with the paper. You look so pale.' For a minute she did not move. 'I made some tea; shall I bring you a mug?'

She nodded, her voice almost inaudible. 'Yes, please.' It was the least line of resistance; 'no' could have been misconstrued. *Working all night; did she never stop?*

'Okay. Stay here,' she said, and slowly walked back across the lawn.

Her small smile forgave the humour; she was not going anywhere. Not yet, anyway. Nothing changed inside her; her urge to get away, to disappear and have nothing to do with her past or present, still remained. The walk into the garden a few hours earlier was part of that need. Would it be different anywhere else? Where could she go that would be different? The questions nagged at her. She must go - but where?

Anna placed a mug of tea on the grass beside her and again squatted on her haunches, clasped her own mug between her hands and waited.

'When are you going to go? You don't need to stay any more,' she said.

A wariness coloured Anna's voice. 'I think I'll stay a little longer. I don't know what I can do, what you want, but anyway, I'll stay a little longer. Nothing will waste at home; they will understand.'

Go home and leave me alone, she thought. 'You can't stay forever...'

'True, but you won't need me to stay for ever, will you?'

'I don't see how tomorrow will be any different from today. Can you see anything changing?'

Anna squeezed her mother's hand. 'I don't know, Mummy. I don't know what the days will bring, but it's time to stop this. It doesn't matter what I can see changing; I'm happy to stay. I'm not giving you a choice. Let's wait and see.'

No, some things, like the sunrise, would never change. She had not noticed how they had broken the silence. Not noticed the sounds that had crept into the air around her. Funny how with one event, everything could change. Now she didn't fit anymore.

Picking up her cup, she turned to Anna and, looking into the distance behind her head, knew that it wasn't just her who was in need; Anna had lost her father. 'I'm alone now; do you understand that Anna? I never questioned our lives. Just went bulldozing on, never knew the real reason I could do it. *Mother is a tower of strength*, you said. And all the time it was not me that did it; I leant on your father. Now he's gone and there's nothing left for me here.'

'Of course it was you, Mummy. That's what partners are for, to support each other. You just didn't register how much. Anyway, you were the same before you were married, weren't you?'

She pondered for a moment and then said, 'Maybe, yes, there was a time when I didn't need him. But no, Anna, even then I had your father. When I wanted him after the war, he was there. That's just it; I have always relied on him for his sense of belonging.' She stopped, and for a while let her thoughts wander through the lost and hidden times. Now she hesitated: 'There are things I've never told you - about those times. I just got on with life, as I'd been taught; worked and did my duty. When I needed him, your father was there for me. All through the war he waited, though I hardly contacted him for years.'

Anna listened, and then said, 'What did you never tell me?'

She paused. 'Just things...' Her mind wandered again. 'I will tell you one day.'

Anna didn't push her. 'You're just a good woman,' she said, and poured the dregs of her tea into the grass.

'I need to do something...'

'Yes, of course you do. So, well, as you always say, find the door that opens for you.'

'Do I say that? Hm, yes, I suppose I do.'

'Where does it come from?'

The phrase brought back memories of France and of a church on a hillside that she'd come across, which she had never been to before, but had always known. 'It's a French saying, I think.'

'Is it? Was it something Grandma said?'

'Not that I can remember; no, I once saw it over the church door, but I knew it before I saw it there, the church as well.'

'How do you mean?

'I knew the place, but I'd never been there, or read about it or anything else.'

'That sounds a little odd?'

'I know; anyway... something will happen.'

'Yes, something will, but it's not the time to think about it now, and you can't just sit on the grass in the garden. Come in and I'll make breakfast; I'll call Max and see how things are at home.'

Anna left her, so that again she sat alone, her back against the wall, her head against the rough stone. Only the pain finally made her move. She had to get a grip and, dragging out the words, muttered to herself, 'This has to stop; take your own advice - pull yourself together.'

With her face buried in her hands, she shook her head and closed her eyes. 'Urghh...'

Chapter 4
(Easter 1934: Kent)

THE STONE building that housed Maklam library contrasted with the weather-boarded constructions on the rest of the High Street. A heavy atmosphere greeted him when he entered, disturbed only by the creak of polished boards. With her back to him at the far shelves, Alex Morton's appearance, in a calf length dress the shade of pine needles, for the first time he could remember was not of a girl but of a woman. She had always been part of his life and yet, despite his knowledge of her, now seemed less familiar, as if she had shed earlier versions of herself.

At the desk he handed in a book from his mother and then returned his gaze to Alex. With hair combed back over her ears and turning into her neck, at her jaw-line she twisted a few strands of it in her fingers. As she turned to see who had come up beside her, a hint of chestnut and French blood from her mother showed in the complexion around her eyes and temples. She resembled a sister more than a friend.

Trying to speak in a whisper, he said, 'Hello, Alex. Haven't seen you for ages.'

She smiled: 'No, but it's you who's missed choir for weeks.' Her voice was round, whole syllables, minims and crotchets of modulated middle-English. She reminded him of his mother.

'Yes, I'm sorry; I arranged for a stand-in for the organ...'

'Shh,' she said, and put a finger to her lips.

'...I've got a lot to do.'

The woman at the desk looked over.

'I thought it was your holiday? What do you have to do, work in the orchards?' She teased him and knew he would not work there.

'Yes, as it happens,' he said, and grinned at her.

'Shhh,' she said again, and her eyes opened to a stare. She emphasised her whisper: 'Well that's impossible; there is no work this early in the season, except raking out around the trees. I was offered a job myself.' She searched for the right place, and replaced a book. 'So what is it you have to do?'

'I've been writing...' he said, still making an effort to whisper.

Now she smiled. 'I guessed it would be something like that; how is it going?'

He tried to sound blasé. 'I'm happy with the results so far. The ideas have grown since Christmas.'

'That's wonderful; what are you writing?'

'An overture...'

'Hm. Impressive. When will we hear it?'

'I wish I knew,' and he laughed. 'That's the frustration; writing is the easy part. But I will give you a preview. In a few weeks we are going to have another musical evening. Come, and I'll play it for you then.'

'Thank you, I'd love to,' she replied, and continued to smile. 'I'll call on your mother.'

He walked past her and looked along the shelves. What was *she* doing now? 'Are you here over Easter?' he asked.

She nodded. 'Yes, I have to keep going.' In her voice, he heard the sound of drudgery. 'There is so much I need to catch up with; I just have to keep at work.'

At school she could not do all that she needed to study medicine and so her parents agreed to private tuition. Her father pushed her to succeed.

'Is it going well?' he asked.

She nodded. 'Yes, of course. I just can't wait to finish and get away from here. I find the village so claustrophobic.'

He shook his head. 'I love it here; I'm surprised you don't.'

'Well, I don't,' and she pulled a face of disdain. 'The village leaves me cold. It's like a place I might visit once and never know anything about. It's all so bland.'

Opening his eyes wide, he just stared at her. 'No, - that's not true. I love it here; I know every lane and path, every tree and hedgerow - for miles around.'

'You're lucky...' She gave him a teasing stare. 'For me, the village is just somewhere to live.'

At the prospect of her leaving, panic rose in him. She was so focused on her work, the peak that stood higher than all the rest, pushed up in the process of things. 'Would you like to do something together?' he asked.

'Come round and we will...'

So they parted and, with two science-fictions and one detective novel clutched under his arm, he left the library.

Outside, an unfamiliar sight for the middle of the day greeted him as his father's car approached along the lane. Theodor Whellans - Theo, to everyone but his wife - was a partner in a business that his father had founded called *Whellans and Whitlan*. They made glass for high precision optical instruments and specialised tools. His father alleged that they made the strongest glass in Europe. A firm in America sent samples they said were harder and his father's firm made some even harder and sent it back; and so on and on. *Almost as hard as diamonds this*, he once said about a small piece of glass he took from his pocket. He always tried to look impressed.

'Hi,' he said as they met in the drive.

Theo slammed the car door. 'Hello, to you too.'

He took his father's bag.

'I just saw Alex along the road,' his father added.

The image returned of her in a green dress. 'Yes, I saw her in the Library. She told me there's a fête somewhere.'

'Ah, that's right, an open day at the Manor. Pity we won't have time to go; so much to do for tomorrow.'

Through the wrought-iron gate and ducking to avoid the arch he entered the garden near the side door of the house. The day would be unsettled. To please his father, he would have to stay around. Inside, his elder brother Edwin greeted them and asked about a fly rod. His mother, after her *Hello Darling*, asked about wisteria.

'Affirmative to both; got 'em!' Theo replied. 'Hello Elizabeth,' he said, and embraced his wife. 'They're in the boot, Ed; be careful of the dirt on the wisteria.'

Theo announced that he had invited his colleague and wife for a pre-lunch drink and that they would arrive in half an hour. In the evening the Whellans expected other friends for supper.

As an aside, his mother whispered: 'We'll have a peaceful week with your father and brother away. I've set myself a challenge too - the herbaceous borders.'

ON SATURDAY his father and brother departed by train for Wales to spend the week fishing in the borders. Quietness settled on the house and, as he started to listen to the sounds and rhythms in his mind, provided a mental lift. The overture progressed. After three days, thirty pages of score were completed. Another few days would see it finished. That would take him to Good Friday.

On awakening the next day, while he adjusted to the sounds around him - doves cooing and blackbirds singing - he lay and mused. The house was quiet and he knew he would not see his mother until later. In the garden, as the sun rose behind trees, he searched for the crescendo to the overture and focused on it. As everything seemed to wait for the day to begin, birds disturbed the stillness.

Over the lowest trees, rays from the sun broke and lit a corner of the wall above the greenhouse. Over the glass pitch of the roof a tiny fragment of warmth appeared and, as he watched, this tiny focus of light expanded. He imagined the forces of the universe that caused the flicker of that tiny flame. For the morning it was a first sunbeam of warmth; for his overture a finale fanfare.

In his room he worked for three hours until the work was completed. Then, exhausted, he went to see Paul. 'It's finished...' he said, and let the comment hang in the air between them as he stood at the door.

Paul paused to acknowledge: 'So, the supreme moment...'

It was, but he didn't reply.

'Is it - as you hoped?' Paul asked, and waited for some response from him.

He smiled. 'I think it's fine, but I look forward to hearing what you think, as well.'

'Come in; if father hadn't finished the whisky last night, I'd offer you a glass to celebrate. You'll have a sherry instead? He won't mind.'

'Thank you.'

'Are you feeling, err...' Paul searched for a word, '...released - now that you have completed the work?'

'I'm not sure; - relieved perhaps,' and although he wanted to talk about the piece, he hung back, needed first to become more familiar with it, so that he could describe it in his own words. 'Many of the nuances that I searched for I think I've managed to find,' he said.

'Even better, then; finished, and also, complete.'

He sat on a chair by the window. 'I wouldn't go as far as to say that...'

'No, I guessed you wouldn't. Cheers, anyway. So, when will I get to hear it?'

'Later, I think? Tonight, tomorrow?'

Paul let it rest. 'Alright,' he said, and then, with a questioning raise of his eyebrows, asked: 'What about Alex, these days?'

'What about her?' he replied.

He returned his glance. 'Just curious; wondered how were you getting on with her? I thought she might be source of - *inspiration*?'

He rose to Paul's quizing. 'She might be; I did once try to write some songs for her. Maybe I'll finish them now.'

Saying nothing more, Paul agreed to meet later to play through the overture. 'I'll bring the pieces I've been studying, too. They are modern and I think you'll be interested in them.'

The place where he lived provided the security and inspiration for him to develop. Paul Spiers, the ideal companion, and the church choir master, the faultless role model, supported and motivated him. And, yes, Paul was right, in the village, Alex, the female companion and reluctant muse, danced on the edge of his mind. As he walked back through the village, he smiled.

VOICES FROM the drawing room attracted his attention. The younger voice he recognised as Alex's and, absorbed by the pull and push of his responses to her, he listened. Perhaps Paul was right and, in silence, he laughed. With the overture finished, he would try something new, weave in descriptions of her.

In the afternoon, after he played part of his new overture in the drawing room, he searched for his mother in the kitchen. In a voice that was almost a whisper, he asked her what she thought.

She turned and, resting her hands on the edge of the sink behind her, smiled. 'I like the feel of the middle section. It's the most, well, delicate part I think. It flows well. You said it was about the village; does it have the river in there?'

'Yes, it does. I must be improving.'

'Hmm,' she nodded. 'Despite the contrasts, or even because of the contrasts, I like the melodies and energy. I think you will have to see what happens.' She invited him to go to a concert with her in London. Yehudi Menuhin is playing Elgar's Violin Concerto,' she said.

He accepted.

'Isn't it wonderful to have such a genius for inspiration, who's just a year older,' she said, referring to Menuhin.

'Particularly for Paul,' he answered.

'Yes, true; would he like to come too? Ask him? Such a loss to music,' she continued, referring to Elgar's death. 'I was so sad when it was announced. You know, when he died he had an unfinished symphony, an unfinished piano concerto and an unfinished opera of all things.'

'Yes, I know...'

'On Sunday, Alex has invited you to go out with her, to roll eggs on the green, apparently,' she said, 'and she's asked if you would like to help her organise the event for the children.'

Event for the children? He nodded an *alright*.

'I'll call her and tell her you'll go then, shall I? I have to call anyway.'

He nodded again.

GOOD FRIDAY arrived and, to show his father when he returned, he had an overture and the beginnings of a more modern piece. Paul had mastered the first part of the overture and played it through. They discussed long into the evening.

'The beginning is great; the build-up perfect,' Paul said.

'I'm astonished how well you interpret the music; I could never play with such clarity, even though I wrote it. You add to what I've written.'

'In a number of places there's much feeling that comes through.'

While he admired his mastery, Paul played on. He really did seem to sense the images when he played.

'You're such a perfectionist; you make it sound so easy.'

Paul seemed pleased. 'I think I understand what you are trying to say. After all, I must have run most of this music with you, over the Downs,' he said.

He laughed: 'Hmm, I suppose you have. That would make a good title: *The Downs Overture*, wouldn't it?' He looked at Paul. 'I'm thinking of another modern piece; this time for you.' *And Alex*, he thought. 'I can hear you play it. You gave me the idea when you said that you were optimistic for the future. Something triumphant with clashing cymbals, I thought.'

With a grin, Paul encouraged.

So he continued to compose.

The next evening, as the heat vanished from the sky, his father and brother, with ruddy faces and in high spirits, arrived home. While he listened to them talk of the rivers and streams of Wales he brought them cups of tea and helped sort the tins of fishing paraphernalia. With his mother he indulged them in their tales.

Theo was exuberant: 'What would have interested you, David, was the music down at the *Abbotsweir Inn*.' He looked at Elizabeth: 'Had to go down quite often, as you'll understand.' And to David, said: You would have enjoyed the music, wouldn't he Ed?'

Edwin nodded.

He raised his eyebrows, and asked, 'What sort of music was it?'

His father pondered. 'Traditional tunes, I suppose you would call them, as far as I could discern. I haven't heard anything like it before. And some singing; Welsh, but up-dated if you know what I mean.'

'Sounds interesting…'

'There's music in some of the pubs around here,' his father said. 'You should search it out.'

AFTER HE had done as much as he could to show interest in the trip, he went out and, walking past the church and up the hill to a lane that was perhaps the prettiest in the village, where the grass verges were as well tended as the gardens behind them, he approached Alex's house. Cherry trees with the first splash of white and pink blossom, like confetti on their boughs, lined both sides of the lane. They caught the last rays of the evening sun, and now, in the declining light, as the air turned cooler, he stood outside and looked at the house. Orange magnolia and yellow forsythia bloomed at the gate and ivy clung to the walls and overhung the porch around the front door. Opening it, she invited him through to the living room, where a fire burned and drew him in. A dozen or more painted eggs adorned the large dining table. She showed him and let him inspect the patterns.

'No more to paint?' he asked.

'No; I only said that as an excuse. I did enough this afternoon. I just wanted you to come round. Mummy and Daddy are out.'

With her beside him, he sat on the couch. 'What are you working on now?' she asked.

Propping himself up with a cushion, he said, 'Something lively; something for you. I've just started to have ideas.'

'You're so clever, David.'

'Mother said something about helping you organise egg-rolling competitions tomorrow afternoon on the green.'

'That was just an excuse too; but I'd love you to come.'

He reached for her hand.

While her smile lingered, she did not move, and now he leaned towards her.

She held back.

'You being coy?'

'No...' She smiled at him and, coming closer, sank back into the couch and pulled him to her.

They laughed together and the evening slipped away.

Chapter 5
(Day 2 - May 1992: Kent)

MORE BECAUSE it seemed ridiculous to sit there anymore, she gave in and abandoned the wall. Yesterday the garden had been full of people and the scene, it seemed to her now, had been of some sort of celebration - of things that had come to pass in peoples' lives - the passing of a great man.

Once inside, the stillness of the cottage folded around her and then, in her bedroom, she looked from the window over the trees as far as the river. By the time Anna came she was seated, with her eyes closed, on the edge of the bed.

Without speaking, Anna rested her hands on her shoulders.

'I'm not going to do anything; I'm just going to stay here,' she said.

'That's okay; you can be alone as long as you need to be.'

Later Anna brought drinks and then, untouched, took them away again. She switched on the record player and asked what she should play.

'You choose...'

Anna played Berlioz and Vivaldi and then the Edinburgh Chamber Orchestra that performed her father's Sonata, *A Scottish Summer*, and his violin concerto, *Themes of a Nation*, which were some of the first well-known pieces he had written.

On the cover, she read what it said about the composer and about the village of Lochinver on Scotland's west coast: *Lochinver enthralled the young composer and sowed the seeds for this composition that evoked origins and the spirit of the sea that lay deep in the people there.*

Where was Lochinver, she wondered. She had not visited those parts and David had never returned. Now her attention was drawn to the small print of the music. 'Is there something I should remember here?' she muttered to herself. The morning passed and at three o'clock she was alone. Anna had gone for a walk, taking her book and her diary with her.

Thank you for reading '**A Sense**', which I hope you enjoy.

For me to be able to improve the book, I would be grateful for your comments. All feedback will be useful, so please be honest.

My address is: Richard Matthewman, 25 Southdown Road, Halfway, Minster on Sea, Isle of Sheppey ME12 3BG

If you would like to email your comments you can do so via my website or email address:

www.richardmatthewman.com

richardmatthewman@outlook.com

Comments

Thank you. Richard

'She doesn't know what to do,' she muttered to herself.

Yesterday the weather had been warm; today it was warmer. Then the garden had been full of people; today it was empty. The changes had come too fast. Now there was just Anna, being there, with her. Over the village, the heat of the day rose to a haze.

Near the laburnum tree that overhung the front gate, hearing something above her, she looked up into the sky to see a hot air balloon rising over the trees, menacing her with its size. The burner flared and she waited to see if more would appear. As a leaf, wafted on water, progress was slow. She gazed at its flight. 'Balloons are fine for floating,' she murmured. 'I'm not floating.'

Alone with its muddled messages, as it dipped out of view, she sighed. *Floating!* No, she was not floating; released into a new medium, perhaps. Back to the wild, yes. Now she understood more of what David's struggles had meant, the ghosts he had to lay. But she was not floating. Why did all this matter now? Her thoughts cascaded to the time when they met again after the war, after all the tragedy of those years.

She walked away, along a track that meandered by the river where she had walked with Jonathan just two days before, to a bridge where she crossed and started to climb the hill until she could see the lakes in the distance amidst the trees with the river below. How was Jonathan, she wondered. The poor boy had never seemed to find his place.

The view of the river brought other images to her mind, of meadows with flowers and trees beside another winding river and a stone wall with cows that grazed to the edge of the water, which seemed to blur with the scene below her now. If she closed her eyes she could travel over the mysterious landscapes. And in her mind she spoke French, with images of France and her grandmother's voice and images of hills with flowers and farms.

Before starting to return and retrace her steps along the river to where a gate opened into the bridal track, she stared long at the scene. 'This is no good,' she muttered, and started back. When she was almost there she saw Anna approach from the opposite direction and they met outside the shop.

Anna smiled. 'How are you, Mummy?'

She fiddled with a teasel she had picked along the way. 'There's no answer to that, my dear.'

'No, I suppose not,' Anna said, and looked up at the sky. 'Did you see the balloons?'

'I saw one, a white one with grey stripes, but I didn't see any more.'

'Oh, I saw three; aren't they amazing; so incredible at close quarters?'

'I thought how aimless they were,' and she avoided her daughter's eyes. 'I'm not seeing things very clearly at present; my mind is playing tricks with me.'

Anna nodded. 'No, I'm sorry, I shouldn't try to make small-talk. Forgive me,' and she hugged her mother.

'I love you Anna.'

'I know you do, Mummy. I love you too.'

'Yes, I know too, but sometimes I wonder why it is so easy with you, and yet so hard with your brother, why he is so difficult. I was just thinking about him, now that your father is gone.'

Anna shook her head and, taking her mother's arm, walked with her back to the cottage. 'I'll make us a cool drink. Why don't you go and sit in the garden.'

Doing as she was told, letting her daughter nurture her, care as only a daughter could, she retreated to the garden. Then, later, she lay down and slept, curled on the floor of the studio, head on a cushion. When she awakened, while the darkness fell and enveloped her, she sat alone.

Anna came to her. 'Come downstairs and let us talk,' she said, and rested her elbows on the back of the armchair that her mother now nestled in, and tried to coax her out of her reverie. The panes of the studio windows, which almost touched the floor, seemed to absorb light and spread a glow into the room. 'Isn't it beautiful in here.'

'Hm. Part of the beauty is in the memories of music.' Now what she heard was music that David had written in France, in the summers he spent there in the fifties. She looked at Anna. 'All the music is trapped in this room. I'll always be able to hear echoes of it here.'

'Mm, so will I; it has a lovely feel. I'm sorry: I shouldn't disturb you.'

'It's hard to disturb someone who isn't really doing anything,' and she smiled again. 'Yes, I'll come down.'

In the living room, Anna cleared away her work, all the photocopied papers and books that still cluttered the floor and table. 'Are you cold?'

'Hm,' she nodded.

Sitting together on the couch, she wrapped her cardigan around her.

'You haven't eaten all day; no wonder you feel cold.' She waited, then said, 'So what do you think you might do?'

'Really, I don't want to do anything; I don't even want to talk. I know you think I should do something; I actually want to flee. Yes, that was really what I want to do.' She felt her daughter's eyes upon her. Had she been so disconnected, just lived day by day all this time? For a moment, her eyes returned to Anna, then away. Yes, that was just how they had been, David and her, caught up in their lives, missing the greater picture. That's what had happened: at least for her, that was sure.

Anna waited and, when she looked at her, returned her gaze. David had gone, and in the space and silence that remained, she saw and heard something new around her. She tried to give Anna a smile: 'It feels as if I just need to get away. As if there are things I need to do. Find the door that opens, as you said.'

Anna snuggled up to her mother. 'You seem to have withdrawn more since last week.'

She pulled Anna to her. 'Last week it had taken me by surprise. I must have been suffering from shock.'

Anna nodded. 'I'm sure you were.'

'You shouldn't worry about me so much though; you have yourself to think about.'

'Yes, but you are my first concern.'

Trying to look at Anna, she said, 'I thought I might write something, as you do.' Her words sounded hollow. 'As a form of desperation activity I suppose. What do you think?'

'Sounds a brilliant idea.' Anna looked up to give her a smile. 'What will you write?'

'I thought I would do one of those mind-map things of reminiscences - to level out my thinking... I feel such a long way from where I've been; a long way from where I was last week...'

'Well, that sounds just the job.' Giving encouraging nods, Anna continued to look at her mother. 'I think mind-maps and reminiscences are different things though.'

'Oh, - don't worry about that. I've never done any of that sort of thing anyway, and I hate writing.'

'Would you like a glass of wine?' Sitting up, Anna reached for the bottle on the table. 'I can't drink all this by myself. It's dry; you should like it. Very expensive; Max bought it.'

She did not reply and, pouring herself another glass, Anna snuggled down again. 'It's taken its toll on you; people noticed yesterday. You appeared more than upset. People said you looked haunted.'

'*Haunted?* I think I am; by memories and doubts. You know how they say, when you are in great danger your whole life flashes before you, well, when they told me your father had had a heart attack, and that it didn't look very good, my life did flash before me. And you know, what was most acute was that I felt guilty that I had wasted it.'

She tucked a cushion under her head. 'Questions surfaced from long ago about your father during the war, and before. My mind kept coming back to that time. He would never talk about it and I had not pushed him to tell me about it. Then, when they told me, memories of those early years, returned. They asked me if I wanted a cup of tea, thought I was taking it badly, which of course I was.'

Anna smiled and turned to look into her mother's eyes. 'But why do you feel guilty; why should you have doubts? As long as I can remember, you've always been so sure.'

She laughed. 'I don't know why; I suppose, because I'm not sure now - not sure of anything. I can't even think straight.'

'But why? What has changed?' Anna slid down onto the floor beside her mother and put her arms around her. 'What has changed, other than father not being here?'

She felt for her. *Other than father not being here.* 'Hm; good question! Now it seems there's no past. I just got on with life. It had been easy, clear-cut,' and she thought how she had always had a job to do that nobody could argue with, and did just get on with life.

Anna waited for her to continue.

'I was here with your father. This is where my life happened; except for a few years, has always happened. I worked, and that was all fine, the same as you, on and on; research, cure for cancer, on and on. At the moment they told me he'd had a heart attack, everything changed, as if a blindfold was removed. That is how it is now.'

Nodding and smiling, still she looked into her mother's eyes. 'It does sound as though you've lost yourself.'

Now she became irritated. 'No Anna, it's not like that; you make it sound so trite.' She shook her head and closed her eyes. 'No, I'm sorry, I didn't mean that...'

'No, it's okay.'

She waited until she calmed down, then said, 'Your father once told me that it would take a lifetime to understand his life and where his creativity came from, what his intuition meant. I think over the last few years he began to make it and felt more fulfilled. He often told me he lived in patterns of the past.'

Anna leaned back against the couch. 'Yes, I know; he often said that. Why does that make any difference now?'

'I thought I knew what he meant. His soul was locked somewhere in the past. I always lived for the present. Now I am cast into doubt, as though somebody turned the lights on in my head so that I can see what I couldn't see before. It's something about me, yes, that I need to understand.'

She stopped and for a few moments just lay there beside Anna.

'I feel so hollow, as though my knowledge of who I am has been deleted. Now I want to get away from here, as if I need to find something I've lost, get back to something I've left behind. I've never been settled here; you know that.'

Anna regained herself and nodded. 'I know; you have often said that. But so what? This is your place. You've been here all your life.'

'Yes, but that's just it; this is not my place. It's David's place; not mine. I never enjoyed it here, even when I was a girl.'

Anna shook her head. 'I'm sorry, I'm getting confused. You're from here, the same as him, as I am. I don't understand.'

'I know: I'm confused too. When I close my eyes, I see images that have been with me forever. They are of a landscape, but not one from round here.'

'Yes; and…?'

'I don't know. Today, as I was walking, in my mind I was speaking French and had images of France and my grandmother's voice in mind. There were images of hills with flowers and farms and, would you believe, a strong urge to make cheese. Quite bizarrely, I was thinking about making cheese, but I've never made cheese and never had any inclination to do so.'

Anna smiled. 'Yes, that sounds odd; must be you remembering France from when you've visited.'

'No, I've seen these images all my life, long before I went to France, but they have all sprung to life again.'

'But anyway, well, I'm pleased you've decided to do something to occupy your time. Time will help.'

'That's what Jonathan said, dear boy. He'll be back in Mali now. I do hope he's alright.' She closed her eyes and thought of him, so different to Anna and so much harder to be close to. Time only numbed the memory. It didn't let her forget; and she didn't want to be numb.

Anna nodded. 'Shall we leave it until tomorrow?'

She nodded as well.

Later, in her room, taking off her clothes and putting on her night dress, she was in no hurry to go to bed. Downstairs Anna worked on, and it was past midnight when she came in to say goodnight.

'I could see the light under your door.'

'I know: I can't sleep yet.' She stared through the window at the night sky.

Still whispering, but with excitement sounding in her voice, Anna said, 'I've almost finished the paper. It looks good.' And then, standing and bending over her mother to give her a kiss, she said, 'I hope you manage to get some rest.'

She had been awake since before dawn and now, as the flimsiest design for the days to come began to emerge, she gave in to sleep.

Chapter 6
(Spring, 1935: Kent)

ALMOST A YEAR to the day after he started to compose the Downs Overture its first public performance took place. The concert involved the work of four young composers and organisation for the overture began on the evenings before Christmas when the players practised in the church hall. Preparation for the concert demanded more than the writing, and success came as much as anything from the efforts of Ronald Gudge, his tutor, who, until the final rehearsal on the Thursday of Easter week, inspired the composer and musicians to work together.

It had been a hard winter in the south, the cold lasting longer than usual. Snow came at Christmas and people pulled together through the weeks when the land froze hard. Muffled in their coats, the musicians found it difficult to play.

In the concert, his overture was the longest piece and he conducted it himself. Although he heard every blemish and weakness, afterwards his spirits were high. Attendance had been good and the Gazette report was favourable. Paul Spiers led the small ensemble and his mother kissed him and said it was wonderful. The performance even heartened his father, who invited everyone back for drinks.

Between rehearsals he had written a song sequence about winter. Then after Easter, having been offered a place at the Royal College of Music, anxiety about the future held back his creativity.

News came that, in order to start the final preparation for medical school, Alex would leave within weeks; she would stay in London and continue private tuition there. Consumed by her effort, he could find no opportunity to see her. She had been accepted at the Royal Free Hospital, or, as she reminded everyone, the London (Royal Free Hospital) School of Medicine for Women. He would never forget the celebrations at her house on the day of her acceptance.

For him the thought of leaving the village caused distress. He knew that whenever he had gone away in the past he had not been able think as clearly as he could when at home in the village. The uncertainty of new places, where the strand of creativity was more elusive, inhibited him. He clung to the stimulation of his home and of the village and tried not to think about the future

A FEW WEEKS after Easter Alex announced her departure. In the spring of 1935, the peace of the village contrasted with turbulent events in Europe - the rise of fascism and murmurings of nationalism. In the hills above the river it was difficult to reconcile emotions that arose from the upheavals in Europe with the simplicity of the countryside around him.

The cries of nationalist struggle rang in one ear and the harmonies of rural life in the other. Somewhere between them music emerged that he began to sketch, music both descriptive and reflective from within and without him. From what little he knew of the cauldron of British politics it seemed that in the past mind finally had ruled over emotion. Was that true? Aggression had been defused and democracy evolved. Elsewhere, power-struggles fostered the ferment of nationalism.

For once his views agreed with those of his father, who asked, 'What did you think of the news this morning David?'

'Quite ominous: what everyone talks about - instability and the threat of war - seems ever closer. The trouble is, nobody believes it.'

'I read in the paper that the government has released plans to expand the armed forces. Did you hear that?'

'Yes. Britain's great stance for unilateral disarmament failed there.'

'I have to agree with you...'

He changed the subject: 'How would you define folk music?'

'Folk music?' Theo thought for a moment. 'Well I suppose it's traditional music that's performed by the local folk; things such as *Green-sleeves* and *Early One Morning* that your mother sings. Music that is passed down by word of mouth?'

He mused: 'It must be a pure form of music then, would you

say?'

'Hm, in some ways, that must be true.'

HE FOUND Alex studying at home.

'It's nice of you to come round,' she said.

'I had to; you'll soon be gone.'

'I know; I'm sorry, but what can I do? I am glad to be getting away to London, and you will be coming soon.'

'Yes, well, in September; but I can't say I'm looking forward to going; for me, nothing will be the same.'

Alex softened her voice. 'You'll get used to it and we'll meet up; there will be so much to do.'

He gave a resigned shrug: 'Maybe we will...'

'Of course we will.'

But the thought of writing music and the fine balance in his mind that he needed to be able to do it brought a sigh. 'I just think it will destroy everything...'

'I do understand what you mean: you write so well here, but of course it won't destroy everything; don't be so pessimistic. You'll see, it will bring new ideas and new experiences to weave into your music.'

'Yes, of course - that's what everybody says...'

'David, stop it; you're making me sad,' and she took his hand. 'Come on, let's go out.' She stood up and dragged him to his feet.

They walked by the river in the afternoon and in the evening he stayed for supper. Those hours together felt like a beginning and an end.

Chapter 7
(Day 3 - May 1992: Kent)

AWAKENING TO a bright room, and outside no haze in the azure sky, she knew what she would do. Although the air was dry, at midnight there had been lightning which she had watched from her window. Anna had said a storm was forecast; perhaps it would come later.

When she was dressed she drove to the Downs. It was Sunday and her first willed action. Not aware of a reason, from waking her mind harboured images of rolling landscapes, a water-colour-wash to her thoughts: a sense of something within her. Through domed tunnels of trees that canopied the lanes, she drove towards the coast. Sun shone through leaves and, responding to a goose flesh of suggestion that had been there when she went to sleep, she progressed towards the light.

Gentle hills.

Something unfolded: maybe a need for open air, space to earth her energy, to lose her spirit in the hills and let it fly as ashes in the breeze, to blow away her dismay and sorrow. At the foot of a ridge, on an impulse she stopped her car and walked to a cluster of rocks at the top from where she could see to France. What should she do now? Shout out loud, quote Shakespeare or lines of poetry, see lights flashing?

'Alone on a hillside,' she muttered. 'No-one knows I am here; I don't have to go anywhere or do anything. Why have I come, drawn by images of hills?'

She sat on the rocks. 'I'm so confused,' she shouted, and glancing towards the road saw a man and a woman, other early risers, walking towards her. They nodded as they continued along the ridge.

Did they hear her ranting?

The gorse bloomed yellow. From this rise on the Downs she could see the Channel that lay between her and France. The colour of the sky reflected in a shimmer of greens and blues that calmed her spirit.

Quite beautiful. Anna! She should call her. Eight thirty her watch told her. Without wanting to wake her, she had escaped the cottage, but suspected that she had heard her start the car. She had left a note to say she would be back before dark.

Call her now! She searched for her mobile phone.

Anna's voice had an edge to it. 'Of course I heard you go, you know I did. Where are you?'

She closed her eyes. *Where am I; what am I doing?* 'I'm along the coast at the moment.'

'Are you alright?'

'Yes. I just need space; don't worry about me.'

'Of course I'll worry about you; tell me you are alright.'

'Yes, I am. I feel better this morning. Really, don't worry. I'll call you later...'

'Okay, see you later...'

FOR AS LONG as she could, she sat, then drove on along to the coast and back inland towards the Downs and stopped again and peered at the views around her. *How stupid just to sit there.* She took out her notebook.

Not knowing what to write or even why she should write it, she started some edited highlights of the good and the bad times of her life with David. Then stopped and threw down the pad. That was impossible. She put down her pen, picked it up again and forced some words onto paper. In the jumble of cameo glimpses that she produced of her past, patterns emerged.

These are my memoirs... David's crises were frequent, she wrote and in writing, realised that she had derived benefit from those crises. 'I imposed my help on you,' she said, aloud to herself.

'Your moods so frustrated me and I needed to know the causes,' she whispered. 'We had known each other for twenty-one years before we married. You were my childhood friend.'

The words began to help, but it only took a flicker of reality to re-enter her thoughts for panic to rise again. She should go home; lie down and be normal.

Setting off again, she stopped at a petrol station and started to fill up. Next to the pump in front of her stood an old friend; his face lit up as he saw her.

'Alex, my dear, hello, God-bless you.'

'Oh. Hello, Gilbert.'

He replaced the petrol cap. 'I read the obituary in the paper, but I apologise that I could not come on Friday. I had duties to attend to here.'

Other funerals no doubt. 'Gilbert, don't worry,' she smiled. 'Thank you for telephoning anyway.'

He came over to her car. 'And how are you now, my dear?'

Familiarity broke some of her reluctance to talk. As she squeezed the nozzle, the words tumbled out. 'Terrible, absolutely terrible: no, I'm sorry, it's not as bad as that.'

'Tell me about it.'

'It's impossible to say.' She hesitated. 'I have lost everything. Every ounce of interest I ever had in anything. It's worse than on Tuesday when you called.' She replaced the nozzle. 'I am so agitated: empty and agitated.'

He turned and waited for her. 'You are empty, certainly half-empty. You lost your lifelong partner; half of you has gone.'

Vicars, they're all the same. 'Yes, I know, but I feel a failure too, as though - I let David down, as if I didn't take enough notice of him.'

Gilbert led her towards the station shop. 'Well, that sort of feeling of guilt is unfortunate, and very unjustified.'

'It's more than that, but I am not explaining very well.' She stopped, put her fingers to her forehead and shook her head. 'I have this thought that there are things I need to do.'

He put his hand on her shoulder. 'Then search them out my dear.' He smiled and spoke slowly. 'That is all there is for it.'

Find the doors that open... 'Yes. I am trying to; thank you Gilbert.' She nodded as if everything now was clear to her. 'But I do feel so empty.'

'You are changed, Alex, but you are not empty. You have just not become used to the change. You have to reinvent yourself.'

But I am empty. 'Gilbert, I feel so useless, so...'

He waited. 'Otiose is the word you are looking for, but you are not.' Gilbert narrowed his eyes and focused on her. 'God wants us to be empty sometimes. You cannot be filled until you are empty. Start with that thought and see where it leads you.'

Empty, lost, what was that about though? 'I have always been strong.'

Gilbert was quick with his answers. 'I should say that you have been granted many gifts Alex. In some ways they have served you well. In others, maybe they have made you close your eyes to important things, made you complacent.' He paused. 'Maybe you need to look to the source of your gifts'

She looked at Gilbert and resisted what he said to her. 'You know I don't agree with all that stuff Gilbert.'

He tilted and nodded his head in recognition of her frankness. 'True, I do know how you think, but I know also that God can take away the gifts that he has granted. It seems to me from what you say that God has taken away one or two of yours now. But I may be wrong.'

You are. 'I am sure you are right,' and she sighed.

'Listen to your thoughts and respond with honesty to them. You will not go far wrong if you do that.'

I know. 'You are very understanding, Gilbert. You make it sound so easy.'

They paid for the petrol and went out again to the forecourt.

'I have to get to my other parish now,' he told her, 'but do come to chat again. Telephone and let me know how you are doing. You look well though, I must say. A little pale perhaps, but well. You defy your age.'

Her face softened to a faint smile. 'Thank you Gilbert, but don't exaggerate.'

'No, I don't. You do.'

After he had gone, for showing her feelings, she reproached herself. Why should she talk to people such as Gilbert; what did he know?

Chapter 8
(May 1939: London)

AFTER EASTER, when his Overture had been performed and write-ups appeared in the local press, he spent four years in London. For three of those years he attended the Royal College of Music, where he studied composition.

Echoes of his uncertainties about the move remained through the first months. As he looked from the window of his lodgings, gas lamps outside the house cast shadows on the walls. His thoughts wandered beyond the streets and he imagined that if he could go high enough he would see Kent and Maklam village beyond London's edges.

Soon, he moved to Hampstead nearer to Alex and for the first months, lodged with a new friend, Douglas Cameron, who was from Arbroath in Scotland. Douglas was a fine tenor. May 1939 was a crossroads.

At the end of Broadacre Street he stepped into the gutter to avoid a woman and small child. Despite early reservations, he had adapted to the urban environment, and found his walks a source of inspiration. He turned left into Crayburn Mews.

What did the future hold? The advantages of remaining in London were many. He could stay and wait, or perhaps follow-up an opportunity to go to Durham, to be an organist at the Cathedral and have time to compose. His aunt lived there and he had visited and met people at the cathedral. Or he could return to the village.

As he crossed over to catch the last evening rays of the sun, at the edge of the park the familiar cry of kestrels came from the top of a horse chestnut tree, which was one of their favourite places to sit before they flew to their nest on a nearby roof. Often he watched them there.

His recent move to the flat in Hampstead, two minutes from the heath and the nearest thing to the Kent Downs, helped him make the decision to stay for a while longer in London. The street, a three-storey terrace built in grey and silver brick that was all windows and doors with patches of grass or flagstones at the front just large enough to take two deckchairs in summer, satisfied his need. He lived in the one off-beat construction of the row three doors from the end and called *The Tower*, jammed between the houses in an architectural clutter that resembled a children's play-block creation and seemed could only have been achieved by using giant hands.

Although Alex had lived only a few streets away, in truth he had seldom seen her. To begin with, in the first year, it was different, and they had met often and maintained the thread between them. Partly her prediction had come true; they did venture out together into London society. And just to see her, released his mind from London and sent it spinning back to the lanes and orchards of Kent. Alex, the village, his music, all were part of the same tangled continuum of familiarity. Then she left London and moved to a hospital in Birmingham. Her commitment to medicine reduced their contact. *That is how medical students are,* she told him. He wrote to her, but received only brief replies; often none at all.

What London had done was make a composer of him, but still he had little reward, still had written nothing of even modest consequence.

Leaving the park and kestrels behind, three roads further on, turning into Pulleaver Street, he approached the Argyle Hotel which stood back from the road. Over the mirror in the foyer hung a stag's head with spread antlers.

As the rendezvous for London's Scots émigrés and known locally as the '*Highlanders Inn*', the Argyle attracted Scots from all over London. A braid of green tartan flounced the reception desk and two bone-handled shepherd's crooks leaned in the hat stand.

There, at a Burn's Supper some months earlier, accompanied by her father, Iain, and brother, Gordon, he had met Helen Strachan. Invited to play a medley of airs, sometime between eulogies to the haggis and the lassies being toasted, he was awarded due place in the gathering. An honorary Scot someone commented. *Even for an Englishman, laddie, ye play a fine fiddle and ye ken yer airs,* droned a kilted Scot. He had learned them from his friend Douglas.

Helen, her head flung back into the cavernous chair in which she had chosen to seat herself, hands splayed on each arm, was twisting her head to stare up at the stag when he walked in. She turned and smiled while she looked him up and down.

'Lovely to see you, David,' she said, and now pulled herself to her feet, an even broader smile lighting her face.

'Hello, Helen.' Beneath the stag he sat down and looked around the decorations. 'Has a feel of ancient Burn's Suppers,' he said, and, surprised how his memory had faded, now he studied her. Something was different; she must have cut her hair. She was very dark and, with an air of confidence and of going places, her eyes smiled.

She nodded and, raising her eyebrows, said, 'Almost four months; you never did get back to me.' Her accent, though still with a lilt, lacked the roll of the Scots' tongue that he associated with the language and that resembled French in its superb tones.

'True but anyway, here we are; you contacted me.' He suspected that Helen was not the drinking type and so asked, 'Shall we stay in the Argyle or do you want to find somewhere else to have a drink?'

She rose to his challenge. 'I could do with something, not a whisky though, and so somewhere else might be a good idea.'

Two streets away they entered the Duke of Wellington. In good humour, and encouraged by his reaction to Helen, he relaxed. To his question about a drink, she replied, whatever you are having, and, as they settled down into neutral lines of conversation, accepted a beer and sipped it. He told her about his minor achievements and her eyes grew wide.

'Sounds exciting; you have to start somewhere.'

'I know, but I have a friend, Paul Spiers, who now plays in the Hallé' and is making rapid progress with his career. My mother feels I am being left behind.'

'So where *are* you going with your career, then?'

'Who knows? I've just finished work for a film company, the scores for two films, and more, I'm sure, will come from that.'

Again, she raised her eyebrows. 'That sounds exciting.'

He nodded. 'Hm, - to create music for a story, I found an interesting challenge.'

'How do you find London?'

'It's grown on me, sure enough. I hated it at first, but, well, I'm beginning to enjoy living here. Films and radio are part of London; you need to be here to make them. Sometimes, though, I feel a little lost. At home in the village I knew how I felt... Anyway, I need a change.' As she tapped the beer glass in front of her with her finger nails, he continued to look at her. 'Is the beer to your taste?'

'I could get used to it... What sort of a change are you looking for?'

He hardly knew. 'I have written pieces that I have been dissatisfied with though other people congratulated me about them. Then other times quite the opposite; pieces that seemed to float out of me in response to London and which created the whole picture, no one thought anything of at all. I need to continue the search for *sources of inspiration* that I can respond to.'

'Well, if you need something to do while you're searching, why don't you come to Nairn with me and play in the festival?'

For a moment, his brows furrowing, he paused. 'Nairn?'

Now she hesitated and he watched a look of nervous uncertainty cross her face. 'Yes, where I come from... Then there are Inverness and Fort William and maybe even Ullapool. You would be very welcome to stay with us. My grandmother lives in Nairn. In fact, that is what I had wanted to talk to you about...'

Helen held ambitions to become a journalist and worked for two magazines. She told him that one editor, because of her Scottish links, wanted an article about summer festivals and she had made contact with numerous organisers. Now she had put strands together in her mind, arranged to visit the festivals and written him into her plan.

He frowned. 'What do you mean by, *that was what I wanted to talk to you about?*'

'Well just that: music is your *forté* and so I thought I would invite you up to Scotland.' She smiled. 'We could do the festivals together; you play and I'll write.'

While he contemplated, he went for another two beers and brought them back to the table. 'An important question, is, who will pay?'

Helen seemed to have that one sorted out. 'I think we could arrange a fee for performances. I know the organisers in Nairn and we could try to get something arranged with them. Do you like the idea?'

In truth, except that Douglas, his close friend from College came from somewhere in Scotland, he saw little merit in the proposition. Would a link-up be possible, he wondered. 'Where is Nairn?'

'On the Moray Firth near Elgin.' She looked for recognition. 'Almost at the top on the east side between John O'Groats and the bulge of Grampian.' She drew it on a scrap of paper. 'It's very quiet and there are few people. Not much changes from year to year, a smattering of tourists in the summer, nothing in the winter. It has a small harbour.'

He sat back. She was being very bold and he couldn't help admire her nerve. 'Sounds interesting,' he replied. Now he watched her more closely. Was she *too* bold for him? And what about Alex? It wouldn't go down well with her that he'd just cleared off to Scotland. 'What's the festival about?' he asked

'It starts in the middle of July and goes on for two weeks with concerts, traditional dance and music and some international artists.' She pushed the small of her back into the chair. 'Then Ullapool is another good centre. There is Oban in August, but that might be a step too far away. Then there is Shetland; again, a longer trek, but there are plenty of options to choose from.'

The names meant nothing to him. He nodded. 'Where's Ullapool?'

'Further up on the west coast, in Ross and Cromarty. It's beautiful there: pure wilderness, a last wild place; otters and wildcats. Ullapool is about fishing. It's on the edge of Loch Broom.'

'I have a friend from Arbroath. Is that anywhere nearby? He sings. Maybe we could meet up with him.'

Helen grasped the straw. 'Great, yes, why not? Arbroath is before Nairn, not too far though, further south on the coast near Dundee. He could come and stay as well.'

The suggestion made his eyes widen. 'Last year we played together in the Barcelona Festival and the year before in Salzburg.'

Helen looked impressed.

'It was great to travel. I wrote a suite for flute and violin for Barcelona. We played together and performed again with the BBC Singers.'

She maintained her round-eyed stare. 'Well I am sure Scotland would be as stimulating; and fun, as well.'

Maybe it was the beer, or maybe Helen, but something started a light to shine for him. 'I think what would most interest me, while I would be happy to play in the festivals, would be to learn about traditional music, to learn something about the folk traditions.'

Helen went with this drift to the conversation. 'That would fit in very well.'

'Would it?'

'Yes, it would. I could write an article about traditional music, and you could play it; we could work together.'

After two hours, he was ready to pack his bags and go. 'I'll send Douglas a telegram to see if he is free and sort out some music. He will master them with no problem.'

It was dark when they left the pub; Helen took a taxi and he walked. The streets had a backstage-feel when everybody has gone home before the caretaker douses the lights and bangs the door shut. He skipped along and laughed at the turn of events.

Chapter 9
(Day 3 - May 1992: Kent)

SHE SLEPT in her car in the sun and, at half past four, awoke to an afternoon with a post-crescendo feel about it. As she got out to stretch her spine and relieve the strain, she looked across the Downs. *What she should do now?* Call Anna! If I could click my fingers, she mused, and be anywhere, where would I be? The pictures in her mind were of places she did not know, looking out over wide expanses: hills somewhere.

In her car she sat and, opening the notebook, closed her eyes and tried to focus: Of the time before Anna and Jonathan were born, she wrote, I have vivid recollections. At the Royal Free, David visited and sometimes stayed in the flat when I was doing nights; that was after the war...

She stopped and closed the book. It was hopeless; this was not the answer. And starting the engine, she pulled off along the lane. The Downs lay ahead and glimpses of the scarp appeared in the dips between the trees as she progressed northwards. Maybe she should just keep driving; it was as good as anything else and the views were pleasant and enough to keep her occupied. She passed through villages of wood-veined Tudor cottages and glitzy pubs with boards that advertised beer gardens and bar meals.

A mile or so before the village she turned off, got out and walked along a footpath at the edge of coppice woodland. She had known the meadows as long as she could remember. There were fields with horses and sheep and today a chestnut mare flicked her tail at the fence. Everything was so familiar, but none of it mattered. She was not part of it anymore.

Her conscience pricked: poor Anna waiting at home. She called. 'Hello, Anna, I'm on my way; I'll be home soon.'

Anna's voice sounded defeated. 'Where are you?'

She glossed over the truth: 'Somewhere on the Downs.'

'Oh, get back quickly now. I'll make supper.'

Her voice went limp. 'Yes, okay.' She smoothed her irritation. 'I haven't eaten all day.'

Anna tutted. 'Alright, I'll get a salad ready. How long will you be?'

'About half an hour I should think.'

'See you soon, then.'

She clicked off the phone. Why did she tell lies?

Not wanting to go home, to waste time she walked along the river and stopped to watch the water funnel over the millrace. Small fish tried to swim against the current and splashed down with a flash of silver undersides. Brown trout circled at the bottom and pied wagtails flitted over the surface to catch flies. Between each burst of activity, they settled on rafts of weed. *The greater picture.*

Looking across the race, she remembered where the flourmill had been. It had all gone; the bridge as well that led to the island between branches of the river. She watched it as she had done before: sounds and sights that were old to her since childhood. What was her *greater picture*?

'Must get back,' she muttered. Poor Anna. As she parked her car, she saw her at the kitchen window. They both waved and, smiling, Anna opened the door. 'You were a bit longer than half an hour.'

'I know,' and she lied again. 'I went into evensong.' She threw her fleece onto the banister.

Anna frowned. 'I've made you some pasta and a salad: courgette and mushrooms.' She picked up the fleece and hung it in the cupboard under the stairs.

'Hmm, smells delicious; even salads have an aroma when you are famished.'

Anna laughed. 'You *must* be hungry. I bought one of those elder flower wines that you said you might like to try. Would you like some now?'

'When I'm ready, please. I'll just clean up.'

When she came down again, Anna was laying the table.

'Tell me what you have been doing all day?' Anna crunched a mouthful of courgette. 'I'm intrigued.'

'Nothing really: just wandering about. I did nothing. I tried to write.' She pushed the mushrooms around her plate. 'But it was no good; I couldn't do it.'

'You must have done something.'

'I saw Gilbert Brockington. He preached to me in the petrol station... The salad is delicious; thank you.' She changed the subject. 'And what have *you* been doing all day?'

'I did some clearing out for you.'

'Oh, you didn't; I asked you not to.'

'Yes, I know, but Daddy's old gardening jumper that was full of holes and covered in bits of clay and sawdust, I thought that could go. I cleared out the rubbish from the shed. Three pairs of boots, all with holes in as well. So much junk...'

'It makes no difference.' Did she really care? 'You can't make judgements now. I would prefer you just to leave it.'

'They were only old clothes and boots...'

She brought her hand down on the table and the force of the impact knocked a side plate over the edge. 'I don't care,' she said as the plate fell and shattered into pieces that flew across the floor. A look of shock came over her face. 'Oh, I'm sorry,' and she began to laugh, but it was a precursor to tears.

Anna hesitated, but then stood up and put her arms around her and for a while they remained still like that together.

Wiping away her tears, she laughed again. 'Yes, you are right, they were only old clothes. I don't know what came over me.' She gave an involuntary shiver. 'I really don't care...'

'It doesn't matter Mummy.'

'I really think I am losing my grip, I really do...'

'Nonsense. It's taken it out of you that's all.' Now Anna changed the subject. 'Anyway, my good news is that my paper is finished. I'll be able to send it off tomorrow.'

'Oh, well done. Which journal?'

'National Immunology, I think.'

'That's the best. Shouldn't you be getting back to Cambridge?'

'No; no-one there is bothered. Olly can carry everything and she's pleased I'm writing the papers; saves her the chore.'

The release of tension helped, so that she began to relax and started to recount her day to Anna. They stayed at the table until darkness fell.

'There must be some midges about.' She scratched her ankles. 'I'd better close the windows.'

While she did so, Anna talked. 'Remember I told you about the obituaries in the newspapers last week. I've collected them and checked the newspapers each day. I have kept one set of newspapers and taken another lot of cuttings. They are all in this folder. Do you feel up to looking at them?'

She shook her head. 'I don't think so, Anna. I looked at one. It was awful. I think it can wait.'

'Of course; some are a little superficial, but two are good.' Anna put the folder on the table next to her mother. 'I've put them on top. Take them and look when you feel up to it. I know you cannot be bothered with the nitty-gritty, but I do think you should get ready for the solicitors tomorrow. You remember, I made an appointment?'

'Oh, Yes, I'd forgotten. I suppose I should. I'll call first thing.'

They lapsed into silence.

'The rain's here,' Anna said and stood up. 'We'll have a downpour tonight. I'll go and close the summerhouse windows.'

Distracted now, she picked up pieces of the plate from the floor.

Later, after they had said goodnight and before she went to sleep, she opened the folder, took out the top newspaper cutting of an obituary to her husband and started to read. Thomas Sperring, the director of the Royal College of Music and a man she had met often over the years, had written it. Much was as she had expected, a well-rehearsed account by a man who knew and respected David. Thomas was not one to be flamboyant and yet the words mystified her. Often she did not recognise the person they described. When she had finished she was trapped in a parcel of words. *David Whellans would be remembered for the clarity of his vision into the soul of the age and for the way he transposed his cultural heritage into music and verse that could be understood by others.*

Words; just words.

She read the rest. They were the same. Most were less well informed, but all in their way described someone she found hard to recognise: *a composer caught in the mystique of resonance between the reality of his present life and the senses, memories and knowledge of his forebears and landscapes of his ancestors...*

Who was this?

And another: *a man who was able to listen to the innermost*

thoughts and nuances of his subconscious and transform them into remarkable music of such vividness...
Still more confused, she fell asleep.

Chapter 10
(May 1939: London)

AFTER THE evening with Helen in the Duke of Wellington, he slept well and awoke in the morning to a new feel. He was not sure what it was; something had finished, but he was not sure what had begun. What was this plan about Nairn?

No curtains hung at the kitchen window of his flat and bright morning light flooded in. His littered room was more of a workshop than a bedroom. He would go to see Taylor and talk over plans for the future. Martin Taylor, his former tutor at the Royal College of Music, could always be relied on to give advice.

In the kitchen, which was no more than a few shelves with a cooker and sink behind a gingham curtain, he put an inch of water in the aluminium kettle. The shop across the street sold milk and, at seven o'clock every morning, he bought some and a newspaper. A letter - written as a diary while he drank his first cup of tea, ten minutes at the most - he sent home each week.

That morning the headline in the paper read, *Uncertainty about war. Germany signs 'Pact of Steel' with Italy.* The Pact obliged Germany and Italy, in the event of war being declared, to aid each other. It ensured that neither country would be able to make peace without the agreement of the other, and was made on the assumption that war would occur within three years. The talk on the street was of conflict sooner than that.

With the letters to his mother he sent his latest manuscripts. She kept everything he had ever written. To Martin Taylor also he gave copies of his main works. *Someone had to know*, he told them.

As was his usual routine, work on his current composition was followed by a practice: an hour of each. Today he needed advice and as he looked out of the window saw Mrs Barclay walk past. Must be ten to eleven, he thought. He checked his watch; it was. In London, even after four years, he felt like a small boy on his first day at school, bewildered by the newness of it.

Taylor would understand. What *was* Helen's idea about

Scotland? Something good might come from it and Taylor's views would be helpful. He took a tram and then walked to the Royal College of Music. At half past eleven he climbed the staircase to Professor Martin Taylor's room and arrived at the large oak door, knocked and went in. As he looked out of the window, Martin Taylor stood with his back to the door.

'I knew it was you,' Taylor said, as he turned. 'You are the only person who does not wait; you never did.' He smiled. 'Come in; how are you?'

'Good, thank you,' and he slung his duffel bag from his back and hung it on a chair. 'I'm letting the sands settle.'

'That sounds positive. Are they settling well?'

'I think so.' He accepted the offer of a seat and as he sat down his bag slipped off and fell to the floor. 'Sorry,' he said, and picked it up. 'I have a piece of work with a movie company and have a commission for theatre.' He watched his mentor move away from the window towards him.

'That sounds promising.' Taylor sat down as well. 'So what brings you to see me?'

He started to relax. 'Ideas, I suppose, is the simplest answer. I would be grateful for your opinion if you've got a few minutes to spare.'

Taylor wore his academic gown from his morning lectures, which gave him the appearance of a Boys Own Annual school teacher. He stood up and, taking it off, looked less imposing. 'I was just going over some details in my mind for a rehearsal later this afternoon; nothing important. These days people come to see me if they have a problem,' he shrugged, 'so ideas will make a refreshing change.'

'There is no saying you will approve of them.'

'Fire away anyway. We can go down and have some lunch later.'

'That sounds a good idea, thank you.' He lent back. 'I'm contemplating a trip to Scotland to look for material: folk themes and traditional arrangements. I wondered what you thought about the idea.'

Martin Taylor stood up and turned to the window again. 'Who can tell?' His voice offered the confidence of a lifetime's experience. 'You could do many things to develop your career. You are a good musician and as likely as not will be a lousy composer: most are. You turned down a major offer from the London Orchestra. But you have made your decision, had some successes and that is about the long and the short of it, is it not? It has gone on too long now, so my advice is to give it the best you've got. Follow your instincts; if inspiration is what you need, go and find it.'

'Thank you.' *At last, some encouragement.* 'You are the first person who has actually said that to me.'

'My only advice is this.' He looked at him and spoke slowly. 'Be ever vigilant, set one task at a time, think long, talk long, then go ahead and don't look back; head for the horizon. Finish what you start and then move on. Build up your experience and confidence. It's a rocky road.'

He could only nod. Taylor turned back towards the window and looked down on the street, on its crowds. 'Look at all those,' and he pointed down into the road below.

From the window they watched a crowd of people pass by. He thought he saw Helen Strachan amongst them, but maybe it was his imagination. Taylor continued. 'Only a fraction of those people will ever achieve anything of greatness. And do you know why, they don't have the personality for it. They may be brilliant, but they lack that vital flair. That is what you will have to find in yourself.'

'Ah, well...'

'Yes, flair...' Taylor repeated.

Above them in the room, as a constant presence in a lustreless painting, Handel looked down on them. In his lifetime he probably sat in this very room and gave advice as Taylor today, but now was just a picture on the wall. He looked up at the man that had charmed Queen Anne and tried to imagine his genius. Taylor turned round and saw his expression. 'Yes, it's difficult to focus on him. The picture needs attention; these old oils become so black.'

How often had he looked at the painting? 'I wonder about him - as a musician, as a composer.'

'Ah, yes, you have to work hard to catch him in the blur of time. We are too far removed from his time now and too much has happened since then to understand or draw a parallel. We move too quickly. The future is worse. As many options but nothing has been written or done yet. There are no flags or markers.' Taylor raised his eyes to the painting. 'In 1712 Handel was a pioneer. Who can predict outcomes.'

He looked out of the window again. Was he up to the challenge, he wondered, and said, 'Handel did have the flair, though, didn't he?'

'He did! Come on, let's go to have some lunch.' Taylor swept him from the room. 'Tell me about your recent compositions.'

They descended to the basement canteen and for the next hour chatted as old friends. He recognised the compliment that Martin Taylor had paid him; he had moved on from being a student. For all his help, Taylor was still a traditionalist. He erred on the side of caution and steered him towards the influences of the great composers, rather than away from them.

'Oh, and by the way,' Taylor ventured as they parted, 'give it a try, but I think you will find that little mileage remains in the traditional folk theme approach you suggest. You had best think of something new. Seek your vision of the age and transform it into as remarkable music as you can achieve. There are many that masquerade in the pretence of having found something new under the canvases of the gypsy caravan. Why not have a deeper look at Wagner?'

The sting in the tail. 'I will remember that; thanks for your advice, and for lunch. I will let you know how Scotland goes.'

AT HOME, a note from Helen, hand-delivered, lay on the mat. She had been there. In it she listed concerts and venues where he could play and addresses he should write to for confirmation. She said she had contacted them already. Was this moving too fast? His note in reply gave a time to meet at the Duke of Wellington.

Over the next few days, pages of sheet music - hundreds that he had extracted from the College archives - became dispersed on every surface in the room. He worked on pieces that took his interest, mainly original folk tunes, for eight or ten hours each day, noted forms and arrangements and composed short studies that he blended from his responses.

Excited, prepared to risk an adventure into the unknown, though there was nothing clear about the route and not even a goal, he decided to follow his intuition. The future was staked on an idea, on an impulse - to search for contrasts in music to those which he knew already. It was all up to him.

His mother's reply arrived the next morning and gave the gossip from the village: the vicar had retired; a swan had wandered around the lanes for two days until somebody caught it and took it to the river; they were having the outside of the house painted. Then she asked the question: Was he sure he knew what he was doing, staying in London to compose. And what was this about going to Scotland?

It was May 1939 and changes loomed in a turbulent Europe. He could go to the United States; Paul Spiers had decided to go. Surely many people must have had this problem. Like Van Gogh: the urge to paint was hard to pin to reality; one day, brilliant pictures: the next day he was drunk. Van Gogh did not have enough information either; though Van Gogh did have flair.

'SO, FORT William's off,' Helen said, and put down a letter. 'Ullapool is a possibility and Lewis also. We'll have to investigate those options.'

He listened. 'How's the beer?'

'Good. I've begun to get used to it.' She up-dated him with progress: 'My contact is the editor of the Nairn Telegraph, a man called Gavin Brink. That's who the letter's from. I asked about the Nairn Festival and he has put me onto some people and knows people in Ullapool and Lewis.'

In part at least he felt more amenable than at their last meeting. 'So it looks spectacularly promising.'

'Don't be sarcastic...'

'No, I'm impressed; you are a great organiser. Thanks for your effort.' The idea that Helen had brought to him, to go to Scotland, was the firmest ground beneath his feet since graduation. Though some doubts remained, her confidence was reassuring.

'The trip will work out fine.' On the table, she put her hand on his. 'We'll find musicians and hear plenty of music to inspire you, I am sure of it.'

After she had taken it away, he felt her hand there still. 'Look,' he said, trying to smile, 'this plan is rather involved and I don't know how it will work out. We might run into trouble...' He stopped and thought what to say. 'Do you think we could talk about the mechanics, as it were, before we go any further?'

If Helen felt the ground give a little under her feet, she did not show it. 'Yes, of course. What do you mean by, the mechanics?'

What *did* he mean? 'Well, for a start, you will be very much in charge. We will be on your territory and stay with your family - your grandmother. I'm not very good at communal living, or being toted around. I need time to myself...' He paused: *and then, of course, there was Alex.*

Helen seemed to sense that he had not said what he meant to say. 'If that is all you are worried about, the answer is easy. I will take double care to ensure your privacy and that you have time to yourself.'

Alex, where was she? What was she doing these days? She did not reply to letters. It was not her style, but her neglect left him without encouragement. They'd had little contact. He'd started to forget what she was like. Though none of the threads had been broken, that was what she was becoming, a memory. Should he tell Helen about her? Would she care? Alex was too vague. Maybe there had never been anything in it.

'What else?' Helen asked.

He shook his head. 'Oh, that's all. Tell me more about Nairn.'

By offering to keep an open mind, she secured a compromise, selling him the idea to make a short visit to Nairn over a weekend in two weeks' time. She would pay the train fare (or her Grandmother would) to Edinburgh and on to Inverness. They would leave on a Thursday and return on a Monday. He could see Nairn for himself and make up his mind. If he liked it they would arrange a longer trip in July and August. She would go anyway.

So there it was; the decision was made.

Chapter 11
(Day 4 - May 1992: Kent)

WITH THE FOLDER of obituaries on the table beside her, she lay in bed and read. It was that time of stillness between waking and moving when the calm of night remained unbroken. Downstairs a noise, Anna in the kitchen, had awakened her.

In sleep she forgot. By not moving or thinking, she had learned to extend the minutes of no memory, when she could listen and lie on into the sequences that brought her thoughts back to those of the previous day. Was it depression she now felt, an imbalance in her mind that hitherto had been unfamiliar, or was there more to it than that? She wanted to leave the cottage and village. Whatever her mind alighted on, she rejected. It was simple; she had to get away.

Against oak beams that held the trusses, the ceiling ducked into the eaves. White walls intensified the light. The brightness, which was positive when the mind was positive, now threatened. She had come to the hardening phase, the clench fists and grit the teeth phase. 'I can do without this,' she muttered to herself.

Outside her room, as she walked along the landing to the studio, the floorboards creaked. On the wall hung a painting of a town, *Senlis*, not far from Paris where her grandparents and her ancestors for centuries before, came from. Cobbled streets and houses with shuttered windows in the picture evoked the music David had composed there all those summers ago. She looked at the grand piano, with its top closed, that she had known since her childhood, but which she would never hear played again in the way that she had heard it all her life.

She continued downstairs. Half-opened curtains in the kitchen revealed a tangle of creepers that had not been cut back since last year. The blackbird that had its nest above the window pecked at the earth amongst the shrubs in the border. From the still hot teapot she poured a cup and then went out into the garden.

Anna sat in the first rays of the sun and turned towards her. 'Hello Mummy, how did you sleep?'

She hugged her and gave her a kiss. 'A little better. I know what you are going to say.' Her eyebrows floated up her forehead and she gave an accusing look. 'Don't ask me what I am going to do.' *Though I do know I have to do something.*

Anna peered into her mother's eyes. 'Why shouldn't I ask you what you are going to do?'

'Just don't,' and she pulled a face. 'Really Anna, I cannot have you coaxing me. It's no good.'

Anna had been out for a jog, a habit gained from her father. She wore trainers and a mauve tracksuit, her hair tied in a knot with a scarf. 'Well, that's alright. Why don't you try to do a few odd jobs around the garden?'

'Anna, I mean it...' and as she turned back towards the cottage, watched her get up to follow her in.

'I'll see,' she said as Anna came up behind her. She rearranged the vases on the window ledge. 'Anyway, I did read the obituaries last night.'

Anna put her arms around her. 'Oh, you did? What did you think?'

'I didn't think anything. Except that I didn't know the person they were written about.'

'In what way?'

'About the sort of person your father was,' she said, and reaching over while still in Anna's grip, dropped the previous day's newspapers in the wastepaper basket. 'I never knew him like that.'

'They are only generalisations, Mummy. They feel they have to say something.'

'Yes, of course, but it's what they say. I knew your father better than anyone.' She stopped and sighed. 'He was my...' she hesitated, '...you know, lover, friend, source of joy and happiness. None of that is in the newspapers.'

Anna brought her arms up and round her mother's neck and hugged her. 'Would you want it to be?'

'No, I suppose I wouldn't. That's not what I mean though; it's the person they do describe that I never knew. I have lost him and yet everyone else claims him as if they knew him well. Things such as, *He was always so concerned about social issues...* How do they know?'

'I know what you mean; they do seem - a bit distant.'

'I knew your father most of my life...' She turned away and walked towards the French windows. 'It seems they knew him much better than I did. I am just an appendage. They even know things about him that I don't know, particularly about the early music. How do they know all that?'

Anna followed her and wrapped her arms around her and held her. If she had any idea of an answer she did not make it. 'What you know is much more important,' she said.

THAT MORNING, while Anna worked at her table in the living room with books and papers opened all around, she telephoned her solicitors.

'He will be round at 11.30,' she reported.

Anna raised her eyebrows: 'Oh, yes, good.' She took off her spectacles and rubbed her eyes. 'Sorry, I was miles away. What does he say needs doing?'

'He wants all the information about the estate. He'll bring the Will...' She bit her lip. 'Your father left everything to me and I did the same. We wrote our wills together.' She closed her eyes and sighed. 'I can't cope with the organisational details at the moment.'

'It's normally your *forté*. I'll help. It has to be done, so the quicker the better...' She jotted a sentence in the margin of her article.

Giving in to Anna's suggestion that she should find something to do in the garden, she pottered around the pond. After clearing weed and algae, it was with wet hands that she greeted the solicitor when he arrived and ushered him into the living room where he settled himself on a chair in the sun that streamed through the window.

It took him the best part of an hour to complete his business. 'To fulfil all the legal requirements, Mrs Whellans, I need you to provide me with a full account of the value of all of David's estate, so that we can apply for probate. That will include all bank details, savings and the like and any valuables kept with the bank. I notice that the Will mentions these, but let us come to that. Also the value of property: if everything is in joint names, it shouldn't be too much of a problem.'

She listened while Anna made some notes.

'Would you like a sherry?' she asked when he had arrived at a suitable resting-place in his explanation.

'That would be very kind.'

She poured him a glass.

'The Will...' he now became very business-like, '...is relatively straight forward, as I am sure that you are aware already. Most of Mr Whellan's estate is left to you Mrs Whellans, but there are a number of small exceptions...'

He went on in this way for a while.

'To you Mrs Weaver, your father has left all his early manuscripts and the first recordings of his music. You will be more familiar than me with the details, but there is a long list of material that is described as, pertaining to the period of Scottish composition and that of the war and early post-war years. I remember your father writing this part of his Will when he informed me that you had a particular love for these pieces of his music. He made a special point to include it.' He looked at Anna with the satisfaction of one in the know.

'Did he; that's interesting? I learned to play some of the pieces when I was younger...'

'Some manuscripts are in fact held in the vaults of your bank. Not all, as I understand.'

'I think that most of Daddy's things have been stored in the roof,' Anna said. It sounded trite. 'He was meticulous of course and kept everything straight. I will start to go through it if that's alright with you, legally I mean and with you, Mummy?'

She waved her hand. 'Yes, of course. Please sort it all out, but do not throw anything away.'

'A number of items have been left to Jonathan. These are mainly pictures, some water colours I think you will find, that David valued and wished him to receive.'

She listened and nodded. 'Yes, I know David wanted that. The paintings in the studio were his favourites. Jonathan says that anything David left to him can stay here.'

'Yes, quite. I have written the details in this letter,' he said, 'which explains what needs to be done.'

The solicitor departed.

THAT AFTERNOON she began to gather the information that was required. To begin with it seemed an awesome task, but once she started she finished more quickly than she expected.

While she did that, Anna went into the roof. There were three trunks and four military-looking wooden boxes that contained some of her father's archived possessions. It was to these that the solicitor had referred.

Anna asked the neighbour to help bring them down. 'We can put them in the studio,' she told him, 'that will be the best place for us to go through the contents.'

Downstairs in the study, mesmerised by the years of accumulated paperwork, progress was made. 'I've found the bank statements and all the details I can of our savings,' she called out to Anna, and threw the wad of papers onto the kitchen table. 'I really don't know what else I can do.'

'No, that's fine,' Anna consoled her, coming down from the studio. 'I am sure you have done enough. I'll take it in for you.'

She nodded while Anna went into the kitchen to wash her hands. 'Let me show you what I've found before I go,' Anna called over her shoulder. 'Some of father's things from his visit to Scotland, all from 1939 just before the war.'

Taking her upstairs to the studio, where seven trunks were stacked below the eaves and pushed beneath the grand piano, she picked up a bundle of papers she had found that were of interest. 'Look at these, they're photographs taken at a festival of Daddy playing and people he was with on a boat. Going to the Isle of Lewis, it says on the back. Then there is another of him with a woman. Do you know who she is?'

She glanced at the photograph. 'I really have no idea.' She took it from Anna's hand.

Then Anna gave her more and also envelopes she said contained leaflets and other bits and pieces. 'I'll go into town now and take the items to the solicitors; then he'll have it for tomorrow. I have to go into the library, so might be a while. Can I take your car?'

'Yes, go ahead.' She followed her into the drive. 'See you later.' She watched the car disappear.

When she stepped back inside, the cottage had a feel of autumn and, starting to recognise the signs of depression that settled on her as shadows down her spine, she shivered. Alone, emotion rose in her, and tears welled in her eyes. 'No, I can't give in now,' she muttered. Through the tears, she saw herself as someone else might see her, and the present she began to view with detachment as a reminiscence. She'd moved on, was not part of this anymore.

The cottage took on the feel of the house of a neighbour, only partially known. She walked through as if it were an auction room. Every drawer she looked in and each cupboard she opened wrenched her heart, but she didn't want it anymore. Her cheeks and eyes throbbed.

Picturing the trunks in the studio and feeling anxious at the thought of going through David's possessions she hesitated. The collection of envelopes that Anna had shown her was on the floor. Next to the grand piano she sat down and looked at everything. Then she emptied the contents of an envelope onto the carpet.

She frowned, had never seen any of the items before and cast her mind back to when she was at medical school and remembered how, when they were first married, David had spent hours recounting his tales to her. Then she muttered, 'Why have I never seen any of these?' She studied a photograph of people on a boat, a ferry, like the one to the Isle of Wight, with David in the middle of the group. It seemed that she looked into a hole in her past. The group was of people that she did not know, four men and two women, at the rail of a boat with the sea behind and land and hills in the distance.

Was her restlessness rooted here? And who was this, a tall woman at the edge of the group? She seemed familiar.

Associations came to her, images of hills and how she had been drawn to them the other day. Upland fells rose behind the group and disappeared in the over-exposed sky. Their remoteness eclipsed the laughter on the boat and the smell of sea air that came to her. She remembered Birmingham and London that summer, the heat and the ambulances at the hospital gate, felt the roll of the boat and the breeze, could hear the voices as the action moved on. The group reformed at the bows for the next photograph; now three men and three women. Another woman, who she assumed had taken the other photograph, stood with them next to the tall woman who now ducked in front of the rest. The next was a photograph of David with his arm across the shoulder of the dark-haired woman. He smiled and she caught the laughter and the mood, and continued the journey with them on the swell of the sea. Then there were photographs of the people taken from behind, in groups, as if the photographer were snooping on them.

Where were they going?

On the back of one photograph it said, *To the Isle of Lewis, August 1939*. There was nothing written on the others.

The Isle of Lewis: she had never been that far north. Although she thought she knew everything about him when he was in London, she knew nothing about this. He made trips to Spain and Germany too, she remembered. What was it like for him then? What did he do?

The photographs were more than remnants of someone's past. They resembled forgotten pictures of herself that awakened memories of lost times. Her mind went back to something David had said before he died, about wanting to tell her something. The photographs recalled her past, as if she had forgotten how she had been, how she had looked. They reinforced the memories that returned when David died and the questions that surfaced from long ago. They reminded her of the war and the years before, and how he would never talk about that time.

The hole in her past widened and, to the sad clutter of David's possessions on the studio floor, she said, 'I must do something.'

Chapter 12
(June 1939: Nairn)

EVERYTHING HELEN had told him about Nairn seemed to be true. The light came as a shock of static in the dawn, ice-bright, even on that summer's morning, sharp and raw.

The train journey had not been long, but the distance that it transported him from all that was familiar to him was vast. Ancient walls at York and the Cathedral in the hook of the river at Durham, no more than hints of interiors to places and lives, made him realise how little he knew about other places. The images that logged on his retina were of an opening countryside with fewer people. Mile after mile the landscape emptied. Compared with this, London was full and the patchwork of Kent, of hop gardens and orchards, thatch roofs and oast houses, was tame.

After the bridge at Newcastle the effect telescoped and each mile took him further from previous experience. The shimmer on the water of the estuary of the Tweed at Berwick, the Northumberland coast, the bend into the Firth of Forth at Dunbar, all signalled a diminished pull of the south. When, after ten hours, they arrived in Edinburgh, it was with a sense of trepidation that he stepped from the train. There would be a wait before the final leg to Inverness. 'Shall we go to look at the castle?' Helen asked. 'We just have time if we are quick.' They ran up the Mound and stood on the ramparts at the edge of the esplanade that faced north across the river and to the hills of Fife. The fire of the sun as it set in the west enhanced the view in the early evening. He felt the northern chill and buttoned his coat.

As dusk closed, the train crossed the Forth and by the time they reached Perth it was dark. The station bustled with activity. *Ginger Beer*, a boy cried at the window. *Tea and Cakes*, another shouted with his tray slung around his neck. A tricycle-trolley edged nearer along the platform, pedalled by a man in a white apron: *Hot Mutton Pies*, he shouted through the open window, and some of the passengers bought them. After Perth, they were on the old

Highland Line. Pitlochry was a station in the night and Inverness a silhouetted town behind the station wall when they arrived at midnight. Helen's grandmother had booked them into the Station Hotel, *all round the best thing at that time of night,* she had written in her letter. 'More for her own benefit than ours, I'm sure,' Helen said.

When, next morning, the train left Inverness, he began to understand Helen's enchantment with Nairn. 'This is superb,' he said, wanting to convey his optimism and smiled as they sat back for the short journey. 'Here's to the dawning of our day.'

Helen's response was guarded. 'Hold your judgement until you have met Gran and seen where we will stay.'

As an ice-flow from the landscape beneath the train, the Moray Firth spread before them. He cast his eyes across the estuary. The northern shores appeared in the lens of the train window.

Where was this? Iceland, Norway? As they unfolded, his imagination mingled with the new scenes. 'Look at the view,' he muttered to himself. They were as near to images of such places as expectation could have prepared him: a foreign land. What clarity touched the light; how sharp the feel to the air. What a difference to southern England.

At the garden gate of Coulter House Helen's Grandmother waited and met them as they walked towards the grey stone dwelling. 'Hello, Helen my dear.' She bobbed towards them with open arms. 'My, you do look well.'

'Hello, Grandma. It's lovely to see you,' Helen said, and hugged her grandmother. She wore spectacles that poked out from beneath grey hair swept back from her forehead to a clasp at the back.

Turning towards him, she said, 'And you are David, just as Helen's letter described.' She looked him up and down. 'How do you do. I'm Hilda Strachan; welcome to Nairn. Do come on in.'

He admired the front door that led into a vestibule and then another door with stained glass that opened to an airy hall with a high ceiling and elaborate plaster cornices with stucco-work around the light. The floor of polished tiles sparkled and reflected in the gilt-framed mirrors with lilies painted on them that hung side by side before the drawing room door.

Hilda wore her apron and had traces of flour on her hands. 'I have done everything I could think of to make you both comfortable,' and she looked at them as if trying to discern what she might have forgotten. 'You must let me know if there is anything else you need.'

'I am sure everything will be fine, Grandma,' Helen replied, and took her Grandmother's hand. 'I know my way around enough by now to sort things out.'

Hilda clasped her hands in front of her apron. 'My, it seems no time since you were here last year Helen.'

Along the hall, past the drawing room door, they entered the back parlour, which led into the kitchen and to the door in the scullery that opened onto the garden. Hilda took them through and put on the kettle. 'Go out and have a look at the garden if you've a mind.'

The garden sloped up a small bank and they climbed steps along the path that snaked through the middle to a brown painted door in the rear wall. Except for roses, the shrubs on either side were unknown to him. Together they looked over the wall towards the town. 'What do you think then?' Helen asked.

'You'll have to give me more time to answer that.' Dropped into a fictitious place, he thought. 'I'm impressed by the houses; they are large, aren't they.'

Helen beamed at him. 'Yes, this one has a good feel. I knew you would like it.'

'The stone is magnificent.'

Back inside, Hilda Strachan made a cup of tea and showed them their rooms. 'You are both at the back, so you have a view of the Firth. Your room is rather small David. It is off the half landing and once was the maid's room, when we had one.' Hilda's voice softened the more she spoke. 'Look, you can only just get a bed in it.'

He eyed the room. 'Don't worry Mrs Strachan, it's perfect.'

'Call me Hilda, please. Someone from the Nairnshire Telegraph came round to say he would come to see you. He said you had written to him.'

'Yes. He's my contact, Gavin Brink.'

'Aye, that's the one. Well, he knows what is going on around here. He is well known.' Hilda sounded pleased with herself. 'I have chatted with a few others and told them of your visit.'

Helen gave her Grandmother a warm smile. 'That's very good of you Grandma. Thank you.'

'Mr Brink said he would come at around eleven o'clock this morning, on his way to Elgin he told me.'

Despite the fuss she made, Hilda was very helpful. Her network of friends was able to dig deep into the fabric of local society to find people for them to contact.

'Alright, we'd better get a move on then,' Helen said, and started to take control. 'We only have a few days.'

While Helen stayed to talk to her Grandmother and bring her up to date with family news from London, he went out and walked along the lane at the back of the garden towards the Firth. When he returned, she was giving presents from her mother. 'I will call them later when we go out and let her know we arrived safely.' There was no telephone in Hilda's home.

At eleven o'clock the front door resounded under the weight of the knocker. On the doorstep, with hands pushed into the pockets of a woollen cardigan and a beret pulled down over her forehead, stood a young woman. Bunches of straight red hair flowed out from either side over her ears to her shoulders. 'Hello. I'm Nonie Sinclair,' she said to Helen, who opened the door.

'Hello, I'm Helen. Do you want Mrs Strachan?'

'No, no,' Nonie smiled, 'I think it's you that I want.' She looked at Helen as if she knew her. 'I work with Gavin Brink. He sends his apologies. He had to leave early and asked me to come instead. I hope that's alright.'

'Oh, of course, I'm sorry,' and Helen brought her hands to her mouth to hide her surprised smile. She asked Nonie in. 'It's very good of you to come. This is David; this is Nonie,' and she looked back at her.'

It was hard to think of words: stunning.

In common with Helen, she wore no make-up that he could discern, but now there was perfume in the hall. Her skin was pearl and her eyes blue. He offered his hand. 'Hello, pleased to meet you. No-nie,' he said. 'What a lovely name. I have never heard that name before.'

'Thank you,' she said. 'Yes, No-nie.'

Her arrival threw him a little and, not ready to engage with someone else yet, he said, 'Look, why don't I take another stroll while you discuss business.'

Despite Helen's glance, he made for the door.

'Alright, we'll see you later. Get back soon though,' Helen called as he went through the gate. Closing the front door, she took Nonie into the parlour to become acquainted and exchange journalistic notes.

For ten minutes he walked through the granite streets down to the quayside where strong odours of fish hung in the still air. At the harbour, thirty or more fishing boats were moored side by side to capstans on the quay. He read their singsong names: Clever Lassie, Alice Eniluce, Cawdor Castle, Maggie Bella, that each held its own charm and superstition. Many, he noted in his book. The noises were of gulls, crates dragged on the cobbles and the cleaning of decks. The main work of the day had finished. Fishermen and fish gutters, blue-jerseyed and black-shawled, in small groups, ambled away from the harbour. Feeling conspicuous, he moved along the pier to the edge of the harbour, where the square ruggedness broke off into a lower sea wall and then to the beach of the estuary. He stared after them, at the tired gait of the men and the sway of the women's skirts.

For a while he stood and, across waters that rippled towards him over pebbled sand, he looked inland to the west. The estuary was calm, its force and power held under leash. To the east an expanse of pool-broken sand and inlets sparkled in the sun. Then, his senses heightened to the sea and the vastness of oceans, he looked north into the firth.

Through the narrow streets that led from the harbour between close-built dwellings that housed the fisher community, he walked, stopping often to stand and stare. Women draped nets across the narrow alleyways and dragged others into tall wooden-shuttered sheds. Crates of fish, stacked from the morning's catch, waited at a building with a sign Barron's Salting Yard. Then he passed a shed that left no doubt about its function, for the rich aroma of smoked fish filled the air around it. Passing a cooper's yard and peering through the gates, he watched men hammering oak shingles into place.

Back at Hilda Strachan's house, Helen ran through the plan that she had mapped-out with Nonie and her Grandmother's help. 'What do you think?' she asked.

'Looks daunting; can we get through all that?'

Helen nodded: 'With Nonie's help I am sure we can.'

With a reassuring bob of her head, Nonie echoed Helen's confidence.

'How is it for women going into the taverns around here?' he asked.

'Not really the done thing,' Nonie replied.

'Just that it occurred to me while I was down at the harbour that we might get into one or two to meet the fishermen?'

'Well, with Gavin and you it shouldn't raise too many eyebrows,' Nonie said, and raised her own. 'We could go down tonight. I'll ask Gavin.'

He looked to and fro between the two. 'The programme looks good to me; I'll take-off by myself in the lulls to see the countryside.'

Helen eyed him. 'There won't be too many of those...'

'No, I suppose not...'

Nonie excused herself and said she would be back after lunch.

Ambition drove Helen and already she traded opportunities with Nonie for collaborative ventures. While they ate lunch in the parlour, they talked. 'Nonie could come to London for an exchange visit,' she told him, 'and bring news of Scotland to the metropolis and news of the metropolis to the readers of the Nairn Telegraph. She has agreed to help me with an article about woollen crafts in these parts for our Women's page.'

He laughed. 'Sounds a little like cheating, if you ask me.'

'No, we just share information. It was her idea; she has done an article herself that appeared in the Inverness Times. And what about you: penny for your thoughts so far?'

'Well,' he paused to consider, 'I am glad you persuaded me to come. I must admit that I was in two minds when we met and you first sprang the idea.'

Hilda brought in the desert and left them alone again.

'I was nervous about asking, you can be sure,' Helen admitted.

'Your Gran seems to like me I think and so that's a plus.'

'Feel quite relaxed then...'

'Hm. So far, so good...' In truth he was enamoured by Nairn, its *tranquil mien* as he had read somewhere. It was new, with few reference points.

Helen seemed to be unsure about the overall aim of the trip. 'Are you going to be, er, inspired?'

'Don't worry about that; just give me time.'

She nodded, and dipped into her egg custard. 'How was the walk?'

'Very revealing: the harbour is an interesting place.'

'And how do you find Nonie?'

He laughed. 'Wouldn't you like to know; that wonderful hair, so Mary Magdalene.'

Helen allowed herself to rise to the remark: 'Don't let your imagination run away with you.'

'No, I won't. Some of the fishermen in the harbour are more northern, I noticed, not red, but fair and Nordic.'

'Hm, the Fisherfolk; they're a different race, for sure. They speak a different language. Nairn is divided into the upper town and, around the harbour, Fishertown, where they speak a Gaelic language.'

'When I walked back through there, I felt out of place: they stared at me.'

She turned to look sideways at him. 'You'll have to make yourself more Scots, then.'

'It appears that the men and boys go to sea and the women and girls do everything else.'

'More or less,' Helen said and, standing up, went to her Grandmother's bookcase to find a book about Nairn and gave it to him. 'The women mend the nets and keep them in good shape. The men go off to the Brackla Canteen and smoke and get drunk.'

He laughed. 'That was what I meant.'

Helen folded her napkin: 'Nonie will be back at two. She'll take us to meet a woman called Sarah Fraser and her husband John. Sarah plays the button accordion; some people call it a melodeon. There is a bus that leaves at quarter past two.'

SO IT STARTED: information flooded in for Helen while he stood back and observed from a distance. She talked and listened, gathered the facts; he heard the undertones. Together they delved into musical traditions. The jewels were the songs and tunes they heard along the way.

That evening at dinner with Hilda they reminisced about Sarah Fraser, whose melodeon tunes - that she played for more than two hours - provided him with ideas. She provided a wealth of information about music in those parts, so that, already, they both felt they had done enough to justify the trip. He sought Hilda's opinion: 'I was surprised to find that women play the melodeon. I'd the impression it was a man's instrument.'

'No, no; not here it's not.' Hilda spoke with the authority of a local. 'Men and women play melodeons. Probably more men play the piano accordion though, because of its weight.'

'We told her we might go back on Sunday morning.' Helen took the optimistic approach. 'She invited us with such enthusiasm. If not, we will visit when we return in July. She is such a lovely woman and so knowledgeable.'

'So, I shall expect to see you again, will I?'

'I am sure you will Grandma, but we will go to other places as well, such as Stornoway. We have a contact there through Gavin. You will be the first to know our plans.'

Smoked haddock, poached in milk and onions, was on the menu that evening. In the knowledge that Gavin Brink had agreed to meet them in the Shore Inn at the harbour at eight o'clock, he enjoyed supper all the more.

TO HIS EYE, accustomed to London pubs, the bar at the Shore Inn looked freakish, as though, rather than being an authentic drinking house, it was mocked-up for a theatrical production. An atmosphere of smoke, beer and maleness greeted them. Until he arrived, Gavin Brink was the odd man out at the bar, neater and trimmer than the bearded men of the company. At eight o'clock there were no women and Helen's arrival turned heads, as did that of Nonie a few minutes later.

'Glad you arrived before me,' Nonie said to Helen as she

surveyed the men who stared at her from the bar.

Helen raised her voice. 'It's a one-off; we're visitors, so we can break the rules.'

'I'm not a visitor,' Nonie said, and laughed and looked at Gavin. 'I just have to accept the bad reputation that my male colleagues bring upon me.'

She said hello to Gavin, who was affable and at ease with the locals, and bought the first round of drinks. He gained the impression that what Gavin did not know about the underworld of these parts was not worth knowing. He introduced the new comers to the men around the bar and told them about their interest in local music. He also told them he was a violin player. Then he was left to sip beer at the bar and to listen to the talk around him. He pulled his stool next to Nonie.

A rugged hulk of a man, about thirty years of age, pitched in and questioned him on his music playing: 'Fiddler are ye, laddie? Saw you down the harbour this morning. Wouldn't have guessed you were a fiddler; an Englishman, yes, but no a fiddler. You haven't brought yer instrument with you, then, I see?'

'No, I didn't, I'm sorry,' he said, and remained cautious. 'It seemed too much to carry on the train. Do you have one here by any chance?'

'Joseph,' the man shouted over his shoulder, directing his words to a wizened grey beard who sat away from the bar, 'Laddie here says he wants a fiddle. Joseph'll sort one out.' Five minutes later he was presented with an instrument that, though well worn, was playable enough. 'How's that for you?' asked the fisherman, whose name he had ascertained to be Drew Duggie.

He plucked the strings: 'Sounds a fine instrument.'

'Good enough to fiddle a few tunes, then?'

He looked at him, and helped himself to a good pull of his beer. Running his fingers up and down the strings to get a feel for the instrument, he launched into some slow airs. He was, to his surprise, a little nervous.

'Feels a little like bringing coals to Newcastle,' he said when he had finished the first set.

'Or herring to Nairn,' Nonie replied. She pulled her stool nearer. The men crowded round. Mastery of the fiddle gained the indulgence of those at the bar. After a few minutes everyone had an ear to the music and tapped their feet, some adding the odd yeeha at significant points. Having passed the test, he was expected to play for the rest of the evening. A double whisky sat next to his glass of beer and it promised to be a heavy session.

Turning to Drew, he said, 'You looked as though you had a good catch this morning.'

'Season's good so far; no the height of the herring yet, but fair enough.' Drew was happy to chat. 'Been some good shots caught and landed: forty crans in one boat, thirty in another, but nothing like the old days when they fished up the coast and over around Wick; could earn a year's wage in six weeks in those days.'

'What's the problem now?'

'Fish not there: who can tell?' Drew pulled his stool round. 'Was the beginning of the herring fishing here a century ago in the Firth when they started salting and exporting to Russia and all over the world.'

'Russia?'

'Aye, St. Petersburg; down to Leith and then shipped all the way to St. Petersburg. Then the fishing was good: a hundred boats.' He nodded to himself as though remembering back to those days. Drew turned his attention to Nonie: 'And you on the Telegraph as well, then?'

'Aye, two years now: have you no read my articles.'

'I don't read the women's pages,' he replied, and laughed at his joke.

'Did you read about the problems with the new harbour wall down here in Nairn?' Drew nodded. 'I reported on that. I reported the sinking of the 'Shonmora' along the firth as well, so you might have read more than you thought.' Drew offered to buy her a drink and she accepted.

The owner of the fiddle played some reels and he listened. 'You don't mind if I write down the tunes do you.' He jotted down melody after melody, some, with the help of the fishermen, to which he was able to put names. They were not the only musicians. Another man pulled out a mouth organ and played *Bonnie Mary of Argyle* and another sang songs when the fancy took him and he thought people were listening. He could not decipher many of the words, though again he jotted down the melodies.

They continued to chat about the town and its folk: 'You mentioned the new harbour,' he said to Nonie. 'When was it built?'

'Only a few years ago: they began in 1931. The old harbour on the other side of the river - Telford's Harbour - was dangerous and silted up. So they decided to build on this side. It's smaller, but there are fewer boats now anyway.'

'How many fishermen?'

'Fishermen? Oh, hundreds,' Nonie said, hazarding a guess. 'How many fishermen here now, do you reckon Drew?'

Drew stroked his beard. 'Hundred families,' he replied. 'Must be more'n two hundred fishermen these days...'

Nonie continued. 'In 1860, at the height of the herring fishing, there were more than a hundred boats. Zulus, they called them, long and fast, with the shark fin sails. There are still some here now.'

Again, he looked impressed. 'You seem to know plenty about fishing.'

'I wrote an article about it last year, about the decline and how the fishermen moved away, down to Dunbar and Yarmouth and round to Kyle.'

'How many boats now?'

Drew calculated. 'About forty, I should say. Twenty or so Drifters, and the rest Zulus.'

'Drifters are the new steam boats,' Nonie added.

They chatted on and he played more tunes, but, at ten o'clock, his keenness to stay did not stop Helen drawing a close to the evening. 'I promised Grandma we would be back early to allow her to get off to bed. She insisted that she would stay up and since this is our first night, we should try to be good guests.'

He acquiesced and, feeling mellow, noticed that his friends appeared the same. Outside it was not only the shock of clean air that struck them, but the still light sky: the prolonged twilight of the northern summer. Out past the harbour in the firth, lights shone from boats.

Gavin shook his hand. 'Thank you for playing.' He opened his car door. 'It was a pleasure to listen to you. We will see you both in the morn, then,' he said, and opened the door for Nonie to climb in.

'Goodnight to you both.'

'Yes, thanks to you too,' Helen said, and went round to Nonie's window. 'We'll see you tomorrow.'

Declining a lift, through the deserted streets, they walked in the direction of Coulter House.

Chapter 13
(Day 4 and 5 - May 1992: Kent)

ON THE STUDIO floor in the cottage, the old trunks had become the focus of her attention. Hundreds of manuscripts and notebooks, all labelled and sorted, lay around the piano and underneath it. Anna had found her father's first whole composition, written when he was twelve, in fine black notation, and she took her time to read through the work.

'I've found more about father's time in Scotland,' Anna told her and - containing more scrap-book items similar to the ones she had seen before, of festival programmes, posters, poems and newspaper clippings - she handed her a bundle of envelopes.

She sat at the kitchen table and looked at them until she felt she knew every detail. Some of the poems were signed Douglas Cameron, a name she had faint recollections of. The name occurred in some of the concert programmes, Douglas Cameron, tenor, one programme proclaimed, about a concert in Nairn and another in Stornoway. The name was on some of the photographs, with more people and more names. Most of the other poems were attributed to someone called Malcolm Ross. While she recognised the name, it meant nothing to her, but some phrases of the poems she recognised as words that David had put to music.

They must have been the originals. It felt as if she had found the secret panel in a desk that concealed an ancient document, as if she snooped into privacies that were off-limits for her, that she invaded, as a voyeur. Moving away from the table, and leaving the papers littered there, the collection of images, pictures in her mind, remained as she walked into the lane. Her nerves jittered and, for a while, to let them settle, she walked around the village and mused as she moved along. *How long would it take to get to those parts of Scotland?*

At the moment the solicitor was leaving she walked back through the front door and only when she saw him remembered the appointment. 'Oh, I'm sorry,' she said. 'I became carried away by all those photographs and forgot our appointment; how stupid of me.'

'Don't worry,' Anna reassured her, 'we have done everything. Mr Inglis has arranged for an evaluator to come and all the rest is dealt with.'

'Oh, good. I don't need to be here for that, do I?' and she squinted at the solicitor.

'No, not at all, as long as somebody is,' he reassured her.

A look of concentration formed on her face and, as she watched Anna, who raised her eyebrows, she twisted a lock of hair at her jaw-line. 'So, can I assume that everything that needs to be done is done and that I don't need to do anything else?'

Inglis clicked his briefcase shut: 'Yes, I think we can say that is true. There is nothing for you to sign, if that is what you mean and I think I have all the information required. So everything is complete.'

'Good - in case, if I am not here for the evaluator, it might be worth your while to take a key. You can arrange with my neighbour to turn off the alarm. He knows all about that.'

Inglis looked the model of compliance. 'That will be perfectly alright.'

Anna frowned.

'Good,' she repeated, and bid him farewell.

Nairn... She remembered the gleam of sun on water in the photographs and the names of places on concert leaflets. *Could she find them for herself?* Could seeking the unknown past that had emerged, be a way to settle her agitation? The pointers began to converge; she would follow them, go to Scotland, take the boat to Lewis and see for herself.

LATER THAT evening, after Anna had worked on her next paper, starting all over again with more results from on-going research, she watched her give up and switch off the computer.

'I am tired,' Anna said, pulling herself to her feet. 'I can't concentrate anymore; I'm going to get ready for bed.'

'You should have given yourself a break after the last one; it's too soon to start again; you're doing too much.'

'Yes, I know, but, well, life in the fast lane and all that. You know what it is…'

'Quite,' she said, and then had to think. 'Well, no; I wonder if I do any more.'

Fifteen minutes later Anna came back and sat down; she had an inkling of what was to come. Sitting cross-legged on the couch, Anna smiled at her. 'Something's going on, Mummy? I sense a plot.'

She did not reply, knew the streak in her that rose like the hair on a cat's spine when she was cornered.

Anna waited. 'Well?'

She tried to be gentle and softened her voice. 'I need a break, Anna. I need to get away.'

It was not good enough and Anna pursued: 'Yes, you've said that, but what does *get away* mean this time?'

'I've decided to go away for a while.'

Anna's impatience welled to the surface. 'You know I'm worried about you; don't just tell me you are *going away for a while*.' Her eyes glistened and she hugged her mother. 'What do you mean, need a break; where will you go?'

'That is all I know, Anna, that I need to get away. I don't know. Really, since your father died I have felt…' and she struggled to express her feelings.

'Well, where will you go? You must have some idea, a plan.'

To France… 'Anna, I'm not sure; to Scotland, perhaps? I might go to Lewis.' Her voice became surer. 'I think I have made up my mind and now I am clear about it.'

For a moment Anna seemed resigned. 'It doesn't sound all that sure…'

'Well, you know, sometimes you need to just go on a hunch.'

'Yes, I suppose I do understand; sometimes I feel the same as that myself, but…' and stopping, seemingly also unable to express her feelings, she gave a look of resignation.

Yes, she would go, and in Anna's pause, she said, 'I think I will go tomorrow…' Like the morning mail dropped through the letterbox onto the mat, the words slipped into the conversation.

Anna's control slipped away. 'What?'

Now she had said it, she felt resolved. 'Yes, there is no need for me to be here now; I need to get away and so I can drive. That's not a problem.'

'But you can't just go off by yourself,' Anna stammered.

'I'll be alright.' Her voice grew firmer. 'I'll go to Jenny first and then on. There are plenty of B&Bs. It should be no problem at all.'

'B&Bs? How do you know there are plenty of B&Bs?' There was something that seemed to make her worry, and she grasped at straws. 'Would you like me to come with you?'

As upset as Anna sounded, she continued: 'No, no, Anna, I want to go alone.'

'Isn't this all a little precipitous?'

On this point she was sure. 'It may seem like that, but I've had this urge to get away for days. I've told you. I think I can see a path ahead and I need to take it.' She turned and took Anna's hands in hers. 'I can't stay here. I'll go crazy. I'm sorry my dear. I do know that you are worried, but please understand, I must go.'

While she continued, Anna remained silent. 'This satisfies my needs to get away.' Her tone softened. 'Gilbert said I should listen to my thoughts and respond to them. That is all I'm doing, Anna.'

'Oh, Mummy, are you sure? I'm so worried.' A wave of loneliness seemed to wash over her.

No, she wasn't sure. 'I know darling; believe me, I'm not ignoring you or your concern.'

'Sleep on it and see what you think tomorrow.'

'Alright, but it's not so much, what I think, but how I feel. I will just call Jenny now to see if she's there.'

Anna looked at her mother in desperation: 'Isn't it a bit late?'

'No, I don't think so.' She smiled and thought of Jenny. 'No, she won't mind.' She stood up and went to the telephone. 'Even if she's in bed, which I doubt.'

THERE WAS nothing Anna could do, and the next day she departed. The M2 at three in the afternoon was quiet. The outside lane of the M25 at Reigate bumper to bumper with three litre saloons that flashed their head-lights, was hellish at four.

It was a release. The tension of the wheel took over: foot on the accelerator, back pushed into her seat, she let the car ride and felt the small hairs stand up on her neck. For a while, in the aerosol of adrenaline that filtered into her blood, emotions levelled. She had to put this behind her - ride on, out of it. Putting her foot down, she manoeuvred through the flows.

'I've concentrated too much on getting from A to B...' she said to herself. 'Maybe I've missed the point.' *All alone on the road; all alone at the wheel. Only me now.*

Headlights flashed behind and she pulled away, then slipped into the middle lane to let him pass and looked across at the driver. 'Same to you,' she mouthed; then drove on through the maelstrom, slowing only when she caught sight of a police car trailing behind.

At six o'clock, in a village near Oxford, she stopped outside a modernised block of flats. Her friend Jenny was in the drive before she had turned off the engine.

'Alex, welcome, you made it so quickly. I saw you from the window.' In leggings and a floppy jumper, Jenny hovered by the car door. Her silver hair, which retained hints of its original fair hues, was tied in a black scarf at the back.

She got out and gave Jenny a kiss on both cheeks. 'I know. I drove far too fast; charge of the light brigade.'

Jenny giggled. 'You always did drive too fast: such a lovely car.'

'It's so frenzied on the motorways, but at least it's quick.' She looked at her friend and her voice became serious. 'It's lovely to see you; you don't know what a relief it is for me to be here.'

Jenny took her by the arm and the two women walked towards the entrance. 'You're very welcome. Come in and tell me how you are.' Continuing arm in arm, Jenny led her up the two flights of stairs to the flat.

As she went inside, she breathed a long sigh of relief: it would be plain sailing from now on. The flat was ultra chic, not an antique in sight, unless the art deco period counted. She looked around: 'The flat's lovely, Jenny. You have such a flair for style.'

'Not much else though,' Jenny replied. 'Thanks anyway.'

'It's so light. I love the lamp stand.'

'Hmm, Rennie Mackintosh; take a seat,' and she slumped down in her big leather armchair. 'How's Anna?'

'Oh, thanks for reminding me, I must call her.' She rested her hands on the back of the armchair. 'She's been brilliant: stayed for the last two weeks and has done everything. In truth I couldn't have managed without her. Now I've gone off and left her all alone. I've been awful to her. Can I use the telephone and let her know I'm here?'

'Sure, go ahead.'

'I love this mirror; it's new, isn't it? Very twenties?'

'Yes, it is; thank you.'

While she sat at the far end of the room and called Anna, Jenny finished a glass of gin and tonic. She kept it short: 'Anna sends her love,' and she sat down on a small cup-shaped chair with lemon upholstery beside Jenny. 'She's going home to Cambridge tomorrow.'

Jenny acknowledged with a smile. 'I can't be bothered to cook, so I thought we would go up the road to the Bull and have a bite there.' Her eyebrows raised in expectation. 'They do interesting snacky things.'

She smiled and nodded, knew Jenny well; anything to get into the pub. 'Suits me fine...'

They walked up the road and entered the Bull. 'I had to get away,' she said, 'thanks for agreeing. I have such an odd feeling about the cottage. It has no purpose for me anymore.'

'Well, I guess we are all different.' Jenny ordered them a drink each. 'I stayed on here after the divorce and that was twenty years ago. Been here ever since and never looked back.'

'You are much more like David than I am. You're from near here, aren't you; and you're a loner like him.'

Jenny put on her mocking authoritative voice. 'I'm from near here, but David was never a loner.'

'Of course he was; he didn't want to get married. If I hadn't come back into his life, he would have stayed a bachelor all his life. He was always a loner at school.'

Jenny tutted: 'He was independent, I agree, but I would never have called him a loner. That was his *artistic* side. He was with you long enough.' She was halfway through her gin and tonic and took another long pull. 'Well, anyway, we are meant to be talking about you now. How are you going to get to grips with yourself?'

Starting to relax, she replied, 'I feel that, in a click of the fingers, forty five years have been written off and I missed much it. David's death woke me up. I seem to have got it wrong and now it's a bit too late to be realising. Do you see what I mean?'

Jenny rolled her head. 'Well, no, not exactly, but I'm a good listener. Keep going and I'll nod at the appropriate places. What's all this about you having to come to terms with yourself?'

She appreciated the humour, but shied from the direct question. 'Who knows? I just feel I've been set adrift with questions and no answers; but, well, I must admit, the questions aren't all new.'

'If I didn't know you better, I would say it was the usual shock and denial syndrome. But I do and so there must be something more.'

There was more. 'I am sure there is some of that. I'm not immune to normal feelings. But, yes, there's more as well.'

'You'll feel frustrated because you can't focus and get on as you used to. It's only been two weeks, so give it time.'

The old *time* thing: 'Don't you start, Jen; anybody would think I was a nineteen-year old. That's what everyone keeps telling me. *Just give it time.*'

'Partly right though, but sorry, yes it's a silly platitude.'

'You'll be telling me I'm pining next.'

'No, I don't think so. Well, are you?'

'Of course, but it's more than that.'

'So, well, what do you have to come to terms with?'

'Okay, you're a psychologist and a bit of a boffin. Maybe you have some thoughts. It's something to do with David, or something to do with me: maybe both. The mind can be an odd place. I always loved him, maybe I am romanticising. I grew up with him. It was so easy for me to love him and because it was easy, I now see I took him for granted.' She stopped and contemplated, knitted her brow.

'Go on.'

'Yes, there's so much. You know, it's just occurred to me that I might have been the loner all along. You may be right. I just got on with my work all my life. David helped me along and still found enough solitude to work himself. God, *he* was the balanced one and I was using him for support; not the other way round.' She made an amazed face.

Jenny looked puzzled. 'I'm not quite sure what you mean.'

'Well, I've always thought of David as being the temperamental one, when in fact it's me that has been agitated and on the move and never settled. Now that he's gone, I feel very unsettled. With his death, it's as if my cover has been blown and I've suddenly been exposed for the fraud I have been.'

Jenny looked sceptical. 'An interesting idea: you haven't moved very much though.'

'I know, but I wanted to. David was happy to stay in the village forever. He kept in touch with his family roots and the place of his ancestors, with the genes and knowledge of the place of his origin, if you see what I mean. I lost both of those connections. The village was his place of fit; it was not mine. I stayed there with him because he gave me security, he was someone I knew there and was familiar, but I did not fit. I fit somewhere else, have connections with ancestors somewhere else and with knowledge and memories from somewhere else.'

Jenny sat and listened.

'It's like an ecological niche, somewhere that a person fits best, is adapted to the characteristics of...'

'I think you might be getting into the realms of fantasy there.'

'Well, all animals and plants are adapted to their place, so why shouldn't human beings be; but what is the human niche? We've adapted to every sort of environment. But there might still be the remnants of *our place*, which we are better fitted to and which makes us alien to another? Don't you think?'

'Who knows? Have you spoken to anyone else about this?'

'No, just been thinking over the past few days. Now that my mother and David have gone from the village, the feeling is so strong, there's nothing left that I'm fitted to. Even my father wasn't from there; he was from London. I'm as unsettled as I've ever been: lost who I am, or, maybe that's the same as saying, I never fitted, and am just realising it.'

'So you are going in search of yourself then?'

Hm, sarcasm; must be the effects of the gin. 'Don't mock or I shan't continue; but yes, both, I suppose.'

'No, I'm not. Let me get another drink: same again?' While she enjoyed anonymity in the corner of the lounge and felt herself begin to unwind, Jenny went off to the bar.

Thumping more glasses on the table, Jenny sat down and said, 'To get away for a while, seems a good idea to me.'

She brought her mind back. 'I've given myself the next couple of weeks to think about things, that's all.'

'You could stay at home to do that.'

'Yes, I know.' She still wondered. 'There's something about David's music, something about Scotland, something about things that happened there. Before he died he was going to confide in me, then he got cold feet and I didn't push it. It was something about the past. I thought I would satisfy my curiosity. It's the best I can do.'

Jenny nodded and sipped her gin and tonic.

'There's much more though. This getting away to Scotland is just because I found some old photos in a trunk. My mind has been occupied with other things, almost from the moment of David's death. It was as though something was lifted from my brain and all these hidden thoughts emerged, quite clear, like memories that I had forgotten about: hills and fields and speaking French.'

Jenny's eyebrows raised. 'Speaking French I can understand. What have the hills got to do with it?'

'Mystery to me,' she shrugged. 'In those still moments that we all have, I hear the breeze on hillsides.'

Jenny gave a mystified look. 'Not in Scotland, though?'

'I think they're different. I don't know; it sounds silly. I just need to know why I feel what I feel. And I want to know about Scotland, I want to know why I have this unsettled feeling. It's all so jumbled. That's what I was going to ask you; David always talked about having knowledge of the past. Do you have any ideas about that?'

'Seems plausible to me. When does a foetal brain start to think and does it have any memory? Good question.'

She shrugged again. 'I think I might be following my secret memories.'

Jenny echoed the shrug: '*Secret memories?*'

'Hm,' she nodded: 'Memories that come with your genes.'

Jenny's look was more of sympathy than understanding. 'Well, tomorrow you can start to find out can't you.' She swirled the last dregs of her gin and tonic. 'What's the plan?'

She thought ahead. 'David spent time on the West Coast, in Lewis, and in Nairn on the east. So I will go there. Tomorrow my destination is Loch Lomond. I'll stay in the Youth Hostel would you believe? Anna telephoned this morning and booked me in. I have to join as well.'

Jenny's nod showed amused surprise.

'Then I will go to Fort William and on to Mallaig and across to Skye. We worked out the route this morning.' She concentrated while she tried to remember. 'From Skye I'll go to Lewis then back to Ullapool and over to Inverness and Nairn.'

'Quite a trek.' Jenny looked impressed. 'Are you up to it?'

She nodded and raised her eyebrows. 'I've brought some of the photographs and concert programmes.' She showed Jenny.

Jenny turned them over and squinted at the people in the groups with David. 'The artist as a young man,' she said. 'I'm jealous. It sounds as if you'll have a great time. Will you come back this way and tell me all about it?'

She smiled. 'Let's wait and see.'

Chapter 14
(June 1939: Nairn and London)

HILDA STRACHAN rose early and was about her first chores
when he awoke. He heard her downstairs and they met in the
parlour as she laid the table: 'Well, good morning Davy,' she said,
and spoke with the usual cheerful ring to her voice. 'I didn't expect
you this early. I hope you slept well.'

'Very well, thank you, Hilda. Waking to the view was a treat.'

Giving it a glow that he had not noticed the previous afternoon,
the sun lit the parlour. Over her shoulders Hilda wore a black
shawl. In the morning light, she looked more frail and he saw her
limp as she moved around the table.

Speaking as if she did not want to disturb the silence, she said,
'If I know Helen, she'll be a while yet before she rises.'

'Yes, I think so,' he replied, careful not to sound too sure. He
prepared to excuse himself. 'I thought I would go out for a run
before breakfast. By the time I get back, maybe she will be up.'

'Oh, by all means. Just as you have a mind. Will you go out by
the scullery door? The front door's locked and bolted still.'

At the harbour, their shawls pulled close, crews of women and
girls waited for the fish to be loaded into gutting boxes. He went
along the shoreline, edged by green rocks that the Moray's water
lapped at high tide.

Was he panicking? Was too much happening? Helen was
business, not his sort at all. Was he getting drawn in? He ran on
along sandbanks to the east until he came to a road that looked as if
it would lead to the town and crossed the river into Bridge Street
and arrived at the golf links where the firth opened as a panorama.

From there he looked into the estuary's distance to a scene that
was wilder and more resonant than views of the sea in the south.
On the other side, in a line along the water's horizon, the cliffs of
the Black Isle rose, and to the left lay the entrance to the Cromarty
Firth. He could see oat fields to the side of the town and the golf
links that sloped down to the beach with pinewoods next to it. The

colour of the sea changed in the sunlight and with the shadows of the clouds. As always, running loosened his thoughts. As far as music was concerned, the visit was going well: melodeons in the afternoon and fiddles in the smoky tavern the previous night.

Hilda Strachan had promised porridge when he returned at seven and she was good to her word. Helen was up and looked ready for the day, even boasted about having rinsed her smoky clothes from the previous evening. With a starched cloth and spotless cutlery, Hilda had the table laid for breakfast. There was home-made marmalade and butter in pats, and she brought in toast and hot bread rolls, porridge and Arbroath Smokies. 'The baps have just been delivered by Mr Asher,' she said. 'They're still warm.'

'That looks lovely Grandma, thank you,' Helen said, and, as Hilda went back out to the kitchen, she turned and smiled: 'How lucky we are; everything has turned out well, don't you think?'

'I'm finding it difficult to keep up with you but don't worry, it's fine. It's a boon to have Nonie and Gavin to help us?' He blew the porridge on his spoon: 'Just need some space, that's all.'

She smiled. 'Good. What about the music?'

'Enchanting! What we heard yesterday was new; I need to let it settle.'

She had her diary beside her: 'Alright, today might allow that, but there will be more music, and lunch is planned for the Royal Marine Hotel where they have a ceilidh-band this evening. If we wish we can go to that or do something else.'

'Keep an open mind, I think...'

'Before lunch we are going to visit one of Gran's friends, Jeanette Sangster, for more music?'

'That sounds fine.'

AN INAUSPICIOUS cottage in the middle of a terraced row of three, that looked from the outside as if it might fall down at any moment, was where they met Gavin and Nonie. Gavin described the terrace as fishermen's cottages, but they were not the same as those in Fishertown. He gesticulated towards an outside stair that led up to a door on the first floor. Above the red tiled roof, in full song on the chimney, sat a starling, its neck feathers quivering. As they climbed the stair, the door opened and they were greeted by the broad tones of a woman's voice. Jeanette Sangster welcomed them in. 'Very good of you to invite us Jeanette; the baking smells good, too,' said Gavin. 'Have you met Nonie Sinclair?'

'No I haven't, but I have heard about you, my dear. How do you do.' She shook her hand.

'And Helen Strachan, who I think you know, and David Whellans from London.'

Jeanette looked at them, and said, 'Hilda has told me all about you and I must say that I am very pleased to be of any service that I can.' She was a vivacious woman with hair that was almost black except where grey strands had begun to intermingle. He watched her as she made them all sit down. Pulling a chair round for herself, she sat and folded her hands on her lap, and said, 'I call myself a social historian and specialise in local traditions, of which musical ones are a very important part.'

He sat beside her.

The flow of articulated words captivated the listeners, still more the pictures that she painted of life in Nairn. 'The language of these parts is called Erse, a sort of Gaelic, and the music and songs have been influenced by this.' In a circle around her, her audience listened until, suddenly, she stopped: 'My goodness,' and looking at the clock that ticked on the mantelpiece, she said, 'You've been here twenty minutes and I haven't offered you any refreshment.' She went to the kitchen and put the kettle on the stove.

It was during this interlude that there was a rap on the door knocker. 'Ah, that will be Isobel Hunter I shouldn't wonder,' said Jeanette as she went to open it. A small woman in her mid-thirties, with fair hair, wearing a black coat and carrying a bulging leather case in front of her, peered in through the door. When she swung it through, issuing greetings as she came, the case seemed to be as tall as she was. Everybody stood up and, helping with the case, Gavin gave a warm greeting to the woman. 'So this is your plot Jeanette,' he said, settling himself down again. 'Not only a seminar on local traditions, but a special treat for us, as well.'

'That there is, Gavin,' and she turned to introduce everyone. 'This is Isobel Hunter everybody, who is one of our two local *clarsach* players.'

Helping Isobel again, as he did so, Gavin explained: 'With a friend of hers called Corrine Lambie, in a duo called *Clyack*, Isobel plays the Highland harp - the clarsach.' They placed the instrument, which was the colour of oak panels and with the 'S' shaped front standing as the prow of a ship, in the middle of the room. Jeanette poured tea and, fresh from the oven, offered them cheese scones. Isobel prepared to play.

The music from the thirty five strings resounded through the cottage and filled every crevice. Notes flowed as the ripples of water that ran from the gullies on the hills. Helen caught his eye and smiled. Isobel played and Jeanette talked until well after they had expected to leave. It was Gavin who intervened and organised the close to the morning. Thrilled by the meeting and with both the entertained and the entertainers in good spirits, they departed from Jeanette's cottage. For a late lunch, Gavin drove them to the Royal Marine Hotel.

Afterwards, relieved when Helen suggested that she would go with Gavin alone to meet his acquaintances that afternoon, he returned to Coulter House. They all agreed that in the evening they would go to the ceilidh.

WHILE HILDA Strachan weeded the flower beds, he wrote tunes from the melodies he remembered from the morning and previous day. Then in the evening, the ballroom in the Royal Marine Hotel was the centre of attraction.

Gavin led them in: 'It's the same every month - always a good turn out.' Finding a table for them, then, as was his way, he went to buy the first round of drinks. As the floor filled with kilted men and tartan skirted women, the five-piece band started with a Strathspey reel.

He looked around the room. 'No wilting wallflowers here then,' he said to Nonie.

'Certainly not; come on,' and she led him to the floor. For those who knew the dances, the whirl and twirl of the ceilidh were a delight. Helen knew most and Nonie filled in those she did not. Together they tutored him. 'It's good for a musician, not only to know the tunes,' she said, 'but also how to dance them...'

Despite his implicit agreement with the sentiment, while Gavin and Nonie danced on, he sat at the table and exchanged banter with those beside him.

'Did you hear the news today?' someone asked.

'No. What's the latest?'

'Thirty or more IRA bombs in London and elsewhere; in post boxes this time. They also bombed Hammersmith Bridge.'

He shook his head: 'If it's not the Third Reich threatening us, it's the IRA. We can't win.'

'We might win against the IRA, not the Third Reich.'

He grimaced and Helen looked at him. 'That's my next trip: to Germany,' she said. 'I've started to discuss the prospect with my editor and hope to get her to agree. Events have moved apace and there's so much we don't get to hear about.'

As he sat down again, Gavin mopped his brow. 'Germany, you say? You'll be lucky: it's all very restricted these days.'

'Oh, well, we'll see.' Jumping to her feet, she said, 'This is a Gay Gordons, it's very easy,' and she led him to the dance floor.

WHEN HE MET her in the parlour the next morning, as usual before his run, Hilda had a Sunday subduedness about her. They had agreed to go to church at nine o'clock. Then, with the proviso that they would meet Gavin and Nonie in the Shore Inn that evening, they had made no plans for the rest of the day.

After lunch they walked to Culbin Sands, a local beauty spot that Nonie had recommended, and let the afternoon roll away.

What was it about her? Nothing pretentious, just as she was delivered, newly unpacked. It was all there, like the jumbled letters of an anagram that made sense as a word appeared. The breeze ruffled her hair.

'You are all unbrushed,' he said.

Until they went to the Shore Inn that evening, their reflection continued.

AT HALF PAST eight on the train the next morning, Nairn receded into the distance behind them. Helen followed his stare from the window: 'You would have liked to stay longer wouldn't you?'

He knew that until now she had not relaxed, but as the train rattled its way south, she seemed to apply her brakes and slow her pace. With eyes fixed on the window, his affirmative was a vacant nod.

'I noticed your melancholy at the station as we left,' she said, as she gazed at him. 'I'm sorry; I've been too pre-occupied.'

'No, no, you've been fine; it suited me well in the end.'

To catch her thoughts, Helen's notebook lay open on her lap. As the train hissed through Speyside, between hills that were a pastiche of brown and green, grey rock outcrops and screes that flowed like lava to the foot of twisted gullies, they reflected on their stay in Nairn: 'I've been thinking about the sorts of people we met and the sort of music we've heard, about the patterns in it all,' he said, and looked out of the window trying to draw her into his thoughts. 'A bit like the patterns on the hills up there.'

She turned to peer through the train window and let her eyes survey the landscape. 'Go on,' she encouraged.

'There are patterns in people, as those on the hills, which we can see if we have the right eyes.' He pointed to the hillside where the colours blended like a Cézanne landscape. 'These hills are as beautiful as anything we've seen...'

Clasping her notebook on her lap, Helen raised her eyebrows in anticipation of his further explanation.

'In the people we have met, there are patterns that we can't see. We have to fathom them out in some other way.'

She waited and again appeared to be unsure what he was trying to tell her.

He looked back into the landscapes of Scotland. 'The patterns are caught up with people's pasts, which are otherwise forgotten. People in a certain place may share the same pattern.'

The train was quiet. In his mind he held impressions folded to the flimsiest of whole shapes. They were swirls of ideas, of people and places, Nairn through the streets and across the Firth, shades of light and sound.

Helen had not moved and continued to look at him. 'I'm still listening,' she said. 'How would you describe the patterns?'

'In truth, I'm not sure.' He tried to describe his ideas. 'People anywhere are like this year's water in a stream that has run for thousands of years and will run for another thousand. In patterns of knowledge from earlier times, in behaviour and language, and in music, they carry the past with them.'

Helen nodded and settled herself and seemed to adjust to his change in mood.

'You can hear the past sometimes as well. There must be communities that have come down unaltered, that we meet every day on the streets, but in which we don't recognise the links with the past. We see the superficial part of the mixes of knowledge and culture that stamp people's identity...'

Helen listened to the ideas.

'Our patterns fall through history. It's something we can't avoid.'

The train slowed into Newtonmore and stopped beside logs piled by the track to await transport. The Guard's whistle blew and the rails replied.

Helen waited until the train was on the move again. 'How do you find out what the patterns are, Davy?'

'You can see them in yourself. They are what you feel without words. It's like a *seventh sense*; you have a sense within you of the past.' She nodded and raised her eyebrows. He kept talking. 'In other people, I suppose we can spot the patterns in looks, language and character, in a sort of montage and in the music and songs, the melodies and rhythms that people play and sing. They are the fingerprints of the people, part of the pattern. That's what I am looking for.'

He paused again to let his mind chase the ideas.

'Some strands probably change very little, so their patterns are almost the same now as they were in the past. We might meet people who are almost identical to people say two or three hundred years ago. They might have the same language, much the same knowledge and social behaviour and live in similar conditions now as they did then. So that if you could travel back in time you might find that some people now are almost the same as they were then.'

Helen caught the threads. 'You will have to tell me how you make these ideas into music. I can't imagine how you do it.'

He nodded. 'One day I will. I don't really know myself. First you have to hold the pattern and the ideas of the music, then transpose them. Much of it is about how you listen into your own head, into your subconscious. It's a sense of what is locked away from the past.'

Helen pondered for a moment. 'I have three articles to write from my head.' A hint of excitement entered her voice. 'I think it will be quite easy.' She looked at him.

He turned and forced the smile to return to his voice too. 'I'm glad you have done what you needed to.'

'Yes, I have, and am doing. Only three days and everything went so well. Now I need to get back to the office to start writing.'

'It's going to take me days to get back into a routine in London. I have noticed it before. It's like being set adrift. You start to tune-in with where you are and then you move on. I'm getting better at being in new places.'

Helen seemed to narrow in on his view of the world. 'It's because you live in your mind so much, you know. I am back in London with my notes and information and you are still in Nairn with your thoughts.'

'It's just that I had started to hear things, to tease out a strand and now we have left it all behind. I will have to rely on my memory. You have plenty of notes and hard facts.'

'Next time we'll stay longer, I promise, and we'll make sure you find what you want.' Helen planned ahead. 'When should we come back? I need only a week or two to write my articles and when that is done I will be ready to be off again. When do you think?'

He had no doubt and now he smiled at her: 'As soon as possible for me.'

'Alright. What about in three weeks' time; that will be the end of the first week in July. Let's plan to stay as long as possible. Through August if that suits you, and into September; I'll write my articles up there. I would post them back.'

'Good idea. Where could we stay when we're in the west?'

'Leave it to me.'

He saw her start to make a mental list of jobs that needed to be done. 'You know, I do believe your Scottish accent has grown stronger in the last few days.'

After Edinburgh, there was no peace on the train. The rattle of the rails made a terrible noise and a stream of cold air hit him on the back of the neck from the window that would not close. Before they set off that morning, he had looked forward to the journey. Now he stared at the picture of Scarborough above the seat opposite and, while the carriage rattled and rolled and passengers swayed, Helen managed to do some work. The hours passed and nothing changed. He could not settle; he just waited to be back in London and for time to level again.

What form would the compositions take?

The period of agitation produced two answers. He would write a sonata, a three part description of Nairn entitled, *A Northern Summer* and a violin concerto entitled, *Themes of a Nation*. Even the journey produced a result; now he had a plan.

At King's Cross they parted and a boy carried his bag across the platform. Busy and sultry, as the solstice approached, the streets bustled with expectation. He passed a new poster entitled, *Home Defence Battalion*, that summoned men between 41 and 55 to join up. Helen's enthusiasm was contagious and her parting smile imbued the setting of his thoughts. He held onto Nairn through the adjustment, ready to tap back into the flow of ideas and to sketch compositions.

In a back garden in Broadacre Street, another shelter had appeared with the curved shell of corrugated iron almost finished and covered with earth. It was a joke. His mother was right: how ridiculous to be contemplating going to war. The talk was of the bombing of *Guernica* village in Spain during the Spanish Civil War in 1937 and what it would be like in London if that happened here. *Peril in the streets from the sky* the newspapers proclaimed. As he arrived, the sun beat on the door of his flat and, in the niches of his mind, its brightness helped him to recapture the light of Nairn.

Days of calm followed. He began the sonata and somewhere in his sub-conscious mind laid the foundations for the concerto.

In the flat in Broadacre Street he could block out London and create Nairn in his mind. Even his room began to feel like Nairn. He scored many pages of the sonata and incorporated melodies from the music that Sarah Fraser and Isobel Hunter had played. Even the fiddle tunes from the Shore Inn found a place. He managed to find strands of uniformity in the music from the different people and their tunes that seemed to form a pattern. Rhythms, timing and themes conformed to repetitive patterns that were a stamp of the music of Nairn.

In high spirits and eager to talk to her, after the first few days they rendezvoused. 'I've finished sorting out the concerts,' she said. 'Two confirmed in Nairn, two in Ullapool and two in Stornoway. How's that? Letters were there waiting for me at the office already.'

He leaned towards her, hand clasped round his glass on the table and gave enthusiastic nods. 'Let's just hope we can get Douglas organised now.'

She seemed to be pleased with his enthusiasm. 'We'll have quite a schedule once it's all organised. And, wait for it, I've agreed your fees with the organisers.'

His face lit up. 'Even better; payment gives composing the air of real work.'

Helen's laugh was unforgiving. 'Of course it's real work; get on and write.'

He laughed as well. 'Anyway, I have sorted the programme and I think the selection will work. Douglas is brilliant and a real professional. He knows the pieces; we just need to tie him down.'

'I look forward to meeting him,' and she took out some letters. 'I received a reply from Gavin. He's contacted his friend Malcolm Ross who he told us about, a Gaelic speaking poet.'

He nodded. 'I remember.'

'He lives in Ullapool,' Helen continued. 'We can stay at his house, or at least his mother's, Gavin says.'

'Good,' he replied, and his mind conjured visions of the western isles. 'Everything about the west coast of Scotland seems very romantic.'

'Yes, the people, the history, the countryside, the misty lochs; everyone loves the west. Malcolm will take us to Lewis and help us through the language barrier. He's given me his address and so I'll write to ask if he can arrange places for you to play.'

'MY MOTHER is pining,' he told Helen one day; I need to go to see her. She has asked me and so I have agreed and must let her know when; I'll call her tonight. Have you decided when you can get away?'

She was keen to return and now her enthusiasm showed. 'I'm ready to go now. Why don't we go on the Thursday again, but on the sleeper this time; it arrives at noon on Friday and will be perfect.'

'Okay, agreed.'

Now she seemed to relax. 'Before we leave I thought we might do something special.'

'Such as?'

'The theatre perhaps; would you like that?'

'Would make a change.'

'*The Importance of Being Earnest* has just started at the Globe; we could see that. Shall I get tickets?'

He agreed and Helen booked for the Tuesday of the last week.

That evening, he played through the whole of *A Northern Summer*. The sonata was finished. Its origins lay in the folk arrangements he had heard in Scotland and in responses to the music, the people and the places where he heard it played. After minor adjustments and now satisfied, he closed the manuscript book on the work.

AN EARLY train saw him home and spending the morning with his mother. In town they met his father for lunch, and then toured the High Street shops. Although nothing had changed, she seemed tense with worry about him being in London. 'Why won't you move somewhere else?' she said, as they walked along.

Living in London - cocooned in the flat in Broadacre Street - he heard and saw what was happening, but did not allow the tensions to get to him. While she was in the mainstream of all news, he shielded himself from it. Current events could take over the whole of his creative thought and so he avoided the news.

Now he resisted an answer. *What was the answer?* 'I want to come home, but I think it's too early to make plans,' and he tried to convince her. 'I'm very happy where I am at present.'

'Yes, but I'm not, David.'

Later, at home, while she re-potted plants in the conservatory, they continued to talk. She seemed to try hard to calm herself. 'Have you seen Alex?'

The question stalled in his mind. Alex? Where was she? 'No, though I have tried to contact her. That was months ago; I wrote to her. It must have been in April sometime.'

Agitation got the better of her. 'Do keep in touch with her. It's such a shame since you're both in London.'

He smiled at her concern. 'I do, but she has moved and Alex doesn't write. She's too immersed in her work.'

She agreed. 'Yes, I know; and yes, I knew she moved. I see her sometimes in the village. I met Paul's mother the other day.' She gave him an almost pleading look. 'He has gone to America.'

'I knew he planned to...' And now, avoiding her eyes, he said, 'So has my friend Fabian, who was writing some songs for me. He didn't finish them.'

'Why don't you go?' she insisted. 'You could work there just as well as here. You have that contact in Canada. I do wish you had joined the London Orchestra...' The first signs of desperation entered her voice.

'Mother, you promised...'

'Yes, I know darling, I'm sorry, but it's so worrying. We are having an air-raid practice this weekend.'

He felt her distress, but until now had not felt her urgency.

'I had a letter about it,' she continued. 'On Saturday night between ten o'clock and twenty past. Here, look.' She took a letter from her apron pocket and handed it to him.

'Saturday eighth of July, it says... They'll sound the sirens and all the windows have to be blacked out.... Sounds a little as if they're over-reacting.'

'It's so awful.'

She continued in her spate of agitation. 'And they have appointed Air Raid Wardens. Ours is a woman in the WVS. It's going to be a full blackout between ten o'clock on Saturday night and ten o'clock next morning with sirens on Saturday night to let us know it has started.'

'I can understand in London, but why here?'

'We are in the flight path to London.' She seemed to force herself to change the subject. 'Come and look at the greenhouse.

Your father has extended the back wall.'

It had been so long since he had been there, that he had almost forgotten what the garden looked like. So many flowers were packed in the borders and plants climbed and rambled over the fences. Young starlings fluttered in the horse chestnut tree beneath a hazy sky. The greenhouse provided a distraction. Weariness sounded in her voice when she continued to unburden her concern.

'You seem to have lived in a time when we have been preoccupied with war and now it seems imminent again. Why is all this happening to us, David?' She seemed to be asking for a rational answer, as if he had more information. 'What are they saying in London?'

'You know much more than I do, Mother, but nobody knows and there is much exaggeration. We don't know what will come of it.'

'We have more than a hundred Andersons in the village,' she continued, still with the need to talk about her worries. 'Can you believe it? They build them everywhere. Those awful corrugated sheets. Your father refuses. The government has given free materials to those on low incomes.'

He imagined the Channel; it was forty miles to France. 'I know. They are up all over London.'

'They want me to join the WVS; I said I would think about it. Gisella and Udo have left. Just sold up and gone. It's so sad.'

Seeing the upside, he smiled. 'It's another world in Scotland.'

She stopped and, slowing herself down, said, 'Yes. I'm sorry. Tell me about your visit.' She turned and started to walk towards the house. 'I'm sorry to go on so much about all this worry. Tell me about this friend of yours as well... Helen.'

He talked on, but hardly managed to placate her, and departed from the village that afternoon in an ambivalent mood. The ties of his old home pulled him and he could have remained there. To balance that, the novelty of Scotland lured him.

The next day at Kings Cross they caught the ten o'clock train to Edinburgh and planned to be in Scotland for three months and to use Helen's grandmother in Nairn as their base.

Chapter 15
(Days 7 and 8 - May 1992: Scotland)

EARLY, AT six o'clock on Thursday morning after leaving Jenny's and with the sun in her wing-mirror, she headed north and set her sights on Carlisle. Slowly she watched the traffic diminish on the roads and space loosen in front of her. The countryside could have been New Zealand for the little she knew of those parts. She'd made the break and now she settled in behind the wheel.

It had been Anna's idea to aim for Loch Lomond and to stay in the hostel there. *At least I'll know where you are for some of the time,* she'd said. *Loch Lomond seems a perfect starting point in Scotland as any*, Anna proclaimed. So, Loch Lomond it was.

Despite her hurry, as the miles passed she stopped regularly to adjust to the change of landscape. She was sure she saw an eagle over the fells. It was more beautiful than anywhere in England. Once or twice she got out to stretch her legs and raise her face to the breeze. The Borders between Scotland and England, she thought

In the mid-afternoon, after she passed Glasgow, she drove through hills and left the freight road at Bearsden. Looking across the hills to the right, she pulled off at a suitable place, locked the car and walked up the fells until she could look down and gain a full panoramic view. With the spring of moss under her boots and where boulders nestled in the heather she admired the view north over the loch. Islands were illuminated in the high sun and hills rose beyond them.

As she walked back down to the car, *the cares of tomorrow must wait until this day's are done*, she sang to herself. When she drove on, she listened to David's music, his sonata, *A Scottish Summer*, and then other pieces accompanied her around the southern end of Loch Lomond.

By the time she arrived at the hostel, the air had become chilled and, where it lapped the stones at the edge, the water of the loch lay grey. She shivered and zipped up her fleece. After she had signed-in and done the minimum to prepare for the night, she rested, then, at seven o'clock in the dining area she helped carry plates and dishes from the hatch for the children of the couple on the same table. Afterwards, finding her bearings around the hostel, like pinpricks from the stars in the pitch-black above her, flecks of rain brushed her skin. She zipped her fleece tighter.

Only loneliness, as cold and hard as the stars, remained. *Loch Lomond; why was she there? Had David ever been to Loch Lomond?*

THE FIRST real day in Scotland opened with a breeze of excitement. The bed in the dormitory had not been so bad and, under a bright sky and beneath heather on the slopes above her, she manoeuvred along the loch-side. With sunglasses, and a headscarf tight around her hair, she hit the low road that cut along the foot of the hills at the loch's edge. It twisted, and seemed to want to tumble in at every bend. The going was slow and she viewed the scenery with ease.

Rachmaninov's Piano Concerto was in the glove compartment and she gave herself over to the music, letting the car swing round the bends to its rhythms. It was as all days that began with no memory of night; life seemed a little better. The sun shone above the hills, reflected in ashen water, rippled by a slight breeze. All movement of the night had gone, smoothed with no trace, so easy, as her past had disappeared. She felt like the sole survivor of an earthquake who walks away from the tragedy, everything behind her, only her own future ahead. *How strange.*

At the northern end of the loch, when she turned back to look, she remembered being told to watch out for Ben Lomond and now saw the peak in the sunlight above the hills. A vestige of snow clung to the top. Along the shallows, a wind-surfer leaned back into the breeze and almost touched his hair in the water. She watched him float across the surface, balanced on air as he defied nature's forces.

'Floating,' she said to herself, and remembered the hot air balloons that floated over the cottage in Maklam.

On along an empty road she went, which was so unlike England.

Blanks on her map filled themselves with the colours of spring heather and the silvers and greys of the wide loch. And yet it was not easy to keep a balance. The bubble of calm, which had held her earlier, burst. To protect itself from changes and the challenges that might come, her mind hardened. Panic rose as she forced the car on; she felt she needed to stop and talk to Anna, but kept driving.

Soon she was in Crianlarich and then did call Anna. 'Hello, darling, how are you?' She strained to hear on the line.

'I'm fine Mummy; what about you?' Her voice showed concern. 'Where are you?'

'Darling, I feel I am driving into the unknown. You were right; this is crazy.'

'Yes, but where are you?'

'I'm driving towards Glencoe.'

'That sounds exciting; how is it?'

'It is really beautiful, everywhere.' She wanted to tell Anna everything she was seeing. 'So peaceful and yet also foreboding and unspoilt. I'm frightened though; it just goes on and on. Where will it lead to?'

Over the miles, Anna cast her caring arm around her and tried to comfort her. 'Just stop and think for a while, Mummy. Then call me back when you've settled down a bit.'

'Alright, yes that's a good idea. I'll do that.' With the unanchored tag on her mind flapping in the wind behind her, she drove on, north and further north, edged on through the pass at Glencoe and to Fort William. Her mind seemed as empty as the hills she had passed through on the way and her mood deepened with the miles.

At Fort William she wanted to stop, needed relief, but pressed on. There were hitchhikers. She passed the first two youths that looked all eager and chisel jawed, but stopped for a young woman who stood ahead in the assumed queue at the roundabout. As she bobbed up and down to attract attention, she could not resist the girl's smile, though the rest of her looked rather dishevelled.

She pulled over and shouted, 'I'm going to Mallaig.'

'So am I,' the girl nodded frantically.

'Okay, get in.'

She wrestled her rucksack into the back and got in. 'Hi. I'm

Jodi,' she said, with a large grin on her face.

'Hello. I'm Alex.' They shook hands. She relaxed and shivered away more of her tension as she set off again. To find the right road out of the town was easy and soon they headed west along the northern shores of Lock Eil. 'I'm going to catch the ferry over to the Isle of Skye,' she said, looking at her new companion.

'Oh, me too,' Jodi said, and, taking off her woollen hat revealed a plaited confusion of hair with beads and dreadlocks all over the place.

'That's lucky then,' and she felt pleased she had had the courage to stop.

'Yeah, sure is.'

'I like your hair.'

'Thanks. Do you travel around Scotland a lot?'

She shook her head 'No, not at all. Once I spent a weekend in Edinburgh, that's all.'

'I come from near there; it is nice, isn't it?'

'I don't know.' She cast her mind back. 'It was February when I was there, just before the war.'

'Oh, I see. It must have changed a lot since then.'

'Yes, I am sure it has. We stayed in a cold hotel on George Street, I think it was, and I shared my friend Jocelyn's tooth brush and other things because I lost my bag on the train. We just went up on the spur of the moment, six of us. It was the sort of thing expected of students, even in those days.'

'What were you studying?'

'I was a medical student. We took off for the weekend for a break. It was so intense. Other than that distant memory, Scotland is only a catalogue of place names to me.'

Jodi settled deeper into her seat. 'The west of Scotland is the same for me. That's why I applied for a job in the hotel, to get to know the Western Isles better.'

She looked at her, snuggled down now with her arms crossed. She wore baggy orange trousers that were frayed and muddy at the bottom and with large pockets down the sides. 'That sounds interesting. Which hotel is that?'

'In Broadford on Skye,' she said, controlling her hair as best she could. 'I'm going to work there through the summer.'

'That sounds nice. It's a bit early for summer though, isn't it?'

'Yeah, but I'm taking a year out. I've been in France for six months and then this job came up and so I thought I'd take it now.'

'Very wise. A bird in the hand... My mother was French.'

'Was she? You don't look French.'

'Don't I? No, well, my father was English... So, you haven't just left school, then?'

'No. I worked on the cross channel ferries for a while as a stewardess. Then I decided to go to college. I sang in a band for a while and I even travelled in India for three months.'

'India?'

'Hmm, it was tremendous. The Indians are such lovely people.'

'They are, aren't they? How adventurous you are,' and she let her mind wander for a moment; she had worked in India once, a long time ago, and the memories sent a shiver down her spine.

'It's nothing,' Jodi said, as she looked over. 'Are you alright?'

'Oh, yes. I'm sorry; just a memory.'

'You looked worried.'

'No, I was just thinking, that's all...'

Jodi continued. 'I loved India, but there is so much to do that I think you get distracted and imagine you have to do it all. There is just as much to do if you stay at home.'

'Yes, of course there is. Which college do you go to?'

'Oh, one in England; I've finished there though. I hated it. Now I'm going to go to one in Edinburgh. I wanted to stay at home, but everybody told me I should go away. Now I've wasted a year of my loan.' She smiled and changed the subject. 'So now you can tick off quite a few place names on your Scottish list.'

She remembered the places she had driven through, and looked at Jodi. 'Yes, Crianlarich, Ballachullish, Fort William and where else? What will you do at college in Edinburgh?'

Jodi gave a shrug. 'I'm not sure yet.' She looked over at her and smiled. 'Well, you will soon have Mallaig and heaven knows where on the Isle of Skye. I love the names of the places around here.' Jodi looked at the map: 'Ardgour, Moidart, Lochailort...'

'Yes, they're lovely aren't they? What did you study before?'

Jodi's voice sounded unenthusiastic. 'It was a teacher training course.' She sounded unsure. 'I would like to go to university, but the course is four years and now I can't afford it.'

'What would you do at university?'

'Psychology is my first choice. They also do para-psychology.'

She gave an encouraging smile. 'Funny you should say that. The friend that I was with yesterday is a psychologist.'

'Really?'

'Hm.'

'They've offered me a place, but I think I will have to do another three year teaching training course. My Mum and Dad don't have much money and so I would have to work as well. Accommodation is more expensive in Edinburgh.'

She nodded. 'Hmm, it must be difficult. I hope you manage to work it out.'

Jodi looked unhappy, but seemed to snap out of it, and, casting round eyes across the dashboard and then up at her, she said, 'It's a nice car.'

'Thank you.'

'I love the breeze and the open top. What sort is it?'

'Mercedes 350 SL...'

'Must have been expensive...'

'Hmm, cost a bomb, and goes like one too.'

'I imagined you were an actress when I saw you: so posh...'

She laughed.

TWO HOURS later they stopped in Arisaig and walked on the beach. While she crunched through broken shells and shingle, Jodi ran to the shore. Dragging her feet in the swathes of dried seaweed, Jodi searched for stones and gnarled driftwood. She wove a piece into her hair. Thrift and orange-blossomed irises grew over the dunes that flounced the beach and red-beaked oyster catchers probed the seaweed between the rocks along the shore.

Across the bay they looked at an island that Jodi said was the Isle of Eigg. It sat on the ocean, sunlit, with its back to the Atlantic.

'It's almost Mediterranean,' Jodi said, casting her eyes to the outline of the island.

'I hadn't seen it quite like that,' and she tried to fit her memories of Italy to the shingle shoreline. It didn't work.

'Oh, it is...' Jodi flashed a dreamy smile at her. 'I spent a summer in Crete. It was just like this.'

'I'm sure you're right.' Jodi's perspective, which was so different to her own, caught her unawares. 'It's always good to see things in a new way.'

'It's the rocky bays and the sun that does it. You can see the bottom.' Jodi sighed. 'I'd love to go again.'

THEY CONTINUED, left the silver shoreline behind, and soon were in Mallaig and as soon again on the ferry, with the harbour merging away into the coastline that diminished behind them.

The sea: I'm on it at last; was this where David had been? She stood against the rail and remembered the photograph of David with his friends. *Would this girl understand?* She watched her as she pulled on her fleece.

'I have my camera,' Jodi said. 'Shall I take a picture?' She was already opening her bag. 'Stay there and I'll take you against the rail.'

'No, really, no it doesn't matter,' but Jodi had taken it.

'I'll send it to you. You must give me your address.'

'Yes, of course...'

Chapter 16
(July 1939: Nairn)

ANTICIPATION, BUTTERFLIES or just impatience: whatever it was, a splash of nervous excitement accompanied David's return to Scotland.

In his lifetime, Helen's grandfather farmed 400 acres to the south of the town where his ancestors had witnessed three centuries of agricultural evolution. They were tenants of the Lairds of Cawdor: crofters at first, then tenant farmers. Now her Uncle Kenneth farmed the land, and Coulter House, where her grandmother lived in Nairn, was part of the farm estate. One day, when their sons took over the farm, her uncle and aunt would live in Coulter House. It was part of the family progression.

Farming ran in the Strachan blood and Helen's roots lay in the land. A restless nature had drawn her father away, first to study medicine in Edinburgh, then, after time in a shared local practice in Nairn, to London. Twenty summers had passed since then, and each year the family had returned to Nairnshire.

As they approached, Helen recounted her earliest memories. The journey reminded her of previous arrivals at the station in Nairn as they were doing today. Memories were of her father and Duncan, the foreman from the farm, as they loaded baggage into the trap. She remembered the ride home to the rattle of tack and the reek of horses, their hoofs, sharp as chisels on the road out to Calder Mains. The strength of the horses, the black and dun, always impressed her, with her brother up beside Duncan, the reins and the whip in his hands, and Duncan shouting, *Whoa there Master Gordon, just show 'em. Ye dinna need to use it. They ken the way home these two and they're sprightly enough.* Her younger sister was wedged next to her mother and her squashed to one side. So much she knew and had known: every station from Perth along the way, stories of the places passed down from her mother, each house seen from the train, each fisher-woman that carried her creel to the farm with fresh herring and on into the hills to earn a meagre living for her family.

Now she arrived again and this time it was Duncan's son there on the platform to take them to Coulter House. Helen saw him waiting beside the dun. 'Josh, hello. Who told you to come? You shouldn't have bothered to drive all this way.'

' 'Twas your Uncle, Miss Helen. Insisted I come soon as Mrs Strachan's told him. Never forgave you last time for creepin' in here unknown.' He stood with his hat in his hand. 'Good day to you, sir.'

'And good day to you, Josh,' he nodded in acknowledgement of the lad.

'Uncle knows how much I love the horses and that's why he's sent Josh and not the car, isn't it, Josh.'

'It is, Miss.'

They climbed onto the trap and drove off. Nairn opened to them in the cool air, then Helen called, 'Josh, please will you take us down the High Street first, so I can buy some flowers for Grandma.'

'Pleasure, Miss,' and Josh flicked the reins.

'You're just like your father, Josh,' Helen shouted through the breeze. 'He's done this all my life. How are he and your mother?'

Josh called over his shoulder. 'Well, Miss. Sent their regards to you, as I was away from the yard. And the Master himself bid me tell you good day Miss and to say he expects you for lunch a week Sunday.'

'Thank you Josh. Please tell him we accept. Is that alright David?'

'Of course. Cameron will also be here by then.'

Helen laughed and shouted as they trotted past St Ninian's and along the High Street. 'Tell him three of us, Josh.'

'Aye, Miss.'

There were other aunts and uncles, all around Nairn. Only her father had moved away. 'I wonder if mother and father will ever return,' she said, and looked at him as she thought aloud. 'I know they both miss their families. Maybe one day they'll come back to Nairn for good.'

LEAVING THEM outside Coulter House with Hilda Strachan holding flowers, the Dun flicked its tail as Josh rattled off along the road back to the farm. With two wicker baskets of vegetables from the farm garden, their bags were beside them.

'It was so good of Josh to come,' Helen said, clasping her Grandmother in her arms.

Hilda nodded. 'You know your uncle would not forgive us twice for not telling him. Welcome to you, David. You must be weary after your journey. Come on in.'

In the three weeks of their absence, summer had settled on Nairn: a balmy season of temperate sun and gentle breezes from the land. 'You're having it warm now Grandma,' Helen said, and turned her face to the blue skies.

'It's been a fine week it's true and plenty of sun we've had.'

He smiled at Hilda. 'London was an oven yesterday. You couldn't escape the heat.'

At the door, like a ballerina, Helen twirled. 'I love Nairn in summer,' she said through her pirouette.

Inside, Hilda sat and listened to her granddaughter while she added rows to the Aran sweater she knitted. 'It's like coming home when I stay here with you Grandma.'

'It seems to me as if it's just two minutes since your father and you all left twenty years ago,' Hilda reflected. 'It's always nice to see you back.'

'The thing about Coulter House that I like so much is that it never seems to change.' Helen smiled at her grandmother. 'I'm glad we have come back every year.'

Helen outlined to her grandmother the plans for the next two weeks. 'I think most of the time David will want to be left alone to work, if that's alright with you?'

'He's most welcome,' Hilda said and, as her fingers moved and she counted the stitches she added to the pattern, she turned and nodded to him.

'You're very indulgent of us, Grandma. David's written something from our last visit already: a sonata. You will have to ask him about it later. It's called, *A Northern Summer* and will be in the concert next week.'

At three o'clock, Nonie arrived and, while she sat with Helen and Hilda in the garden, he walked to the harbour to refresh his memories of the town. A tracery of ideas existed for the concerto. It was to be in three parts, one each for Nairn, Ullapool and Lewis. The first movement would draw on themes of Morayshire, of the sea and the quiet hinterland, of the cultural sliding between north and south. It was to contrast with rugged reverberations in the Ullapool movement and Celtic patterns drawn from the haven of Lewis in the final movement. He would write some songs for Douglas. Malcolm Ross he hoped would provide other material.

IT WAS THE DAY that Douglas Cameron was due to arrive and in anticipation he sat at a grand piano in the ballroom of the Golf View Hotel and rehearsed the first concert.

A varied ensemble of pieces had come together. An introductory nocturne with a light and dreamy evening feel played on the piano, would be followed by a group of songs based on lesser-known Burn's poems that Douglas had selected while at college and he had arranged for him. Then there would be a selection of popular arias from Verdi and Rossini and two music hall pieces to add lightness. The second half they had yet to agree. Plenty of options were available, taken from the repertoire developed at the Royal College, many that were original compositions. Extracts from his, *A Northern Summer*, would be included, which was ready for the concert performance. The melody would be introduced by the fiddle and taken up by two harps that he felt compelled to include. They represented the flowing streams and the racing clouds of late spring. In the concert, Douglas would play the flute.

Through bay windows he looked over the firth and positioned the piano to allow a view across to Cromarty. Outside the window, the reports of balls on rackets and shouts from the players on the hotel's tennis courts could be heard. He left the ballroom and walked to Coulter House and then to Nairn station to meet Douglas Cameron.

IN INVERNESS Helen Strachan and Nonie Sinclair concluded their interview with the Director of the Nairnshire Festival, Angus

Forfar. They had made slow progress but by the end of the morning had wrested from him an adequate, if cryptic, understanding of the festival's history and organisation.

Afterwards they ran to the station. Barrow boys rolled marbles along the flattened kerb stones and fish sellers jostled and shouted at the gates. They dodged the newspaper boys and sweet sellers to get to the platform and made the five o'clock from Inverness with a minute to spare, managing to board just as the guard slammed the doors. His whistle blew as they sat down in the carriage. Opposite them, Douglas Cameron sat engrossed in his book.

'Who's that,' Nonie whispered to Helen and, with a raise of her eyebrows as the train moved off, indicated Douglas.

Helen shook her head and shrugged. For the period of the short journey, Nonie stared into the space above Douglas's head. The book was an anthology of poems by Arthur Rimbaud. 'He must be French,' she whispered. The train pulled into Nairn station where the two women alighted and walked along the platform towards the exit. Douglas Cameron stepped down after them. As they passed under the iron footbridge, Nonie watched him looking around. 'He's got off here as well,' she whispered.

'Who?'

'The man reading Rimbaud; he's coming this way.'

Nonie lingered and, as he passed, she caught his eye. 'You look lost,' she said. 'Can I help?'

He answered not in a French but with a rounded Scots accent that took Nonie by surprise. 'Oh, I don't know,' he said.' Do you know Seasalter Road?'

Nonie laughed. 'Yes, it's quite near. We are going that way. Shall we show you.'

'That's very kind.'

'It's this way.' Nonie pointed after Helen.

'I'm Douglas,' he said, and introduced himself as they walked out of the station yard.

Nonie stopped and Helen turned, both looked and smiled, mirrored their surprise and realisation. Trying to look both ways at once, Douglas stood between them. 'Anything the matter?'

'No, no. Er, Douglas Cameron by any chance?' Nonie asked.

'Yes, that's correct.' Now Douglas looked surprised.

Nonie threw her head back and laughed. 'Well, I'm Nonie Sinclair,' she said, 'and this is Helen Strachan.'

'Ah,' he smiled. 'What a coincidence. Then it is second time lucky for me,' he added. 'I'm pleased to meet you both.'

'You know who we are?' Nonie continued.

'Yes, of course, David's friends and accomplices.'

'That's right; friends at least,' Nonie replied. 'We thought you were to arrive from St Andrews; an hour ago.'

He gave a sheepish look. 'I was, it's true, but I didn't pay attention and am ashamed to say remained on the train to Inverness. As the train pulled out I saw David on the platform in Nairn. He looked unimpressed.'

Helen laughed. 'Nonie Sinclair, since you asked, this is Douglas Cameron,' she said, and laughed again.

Douglas smiled and looked as if he had missed a joke. 'Anyway, pleased to meet you both,' he said again.

Nonie coloured.

'Come on then, Douglas, we'll take you home,' Helen said, and, clasping Nonie by the arm, squeezed it.

CLOSING THE front garden gate, he stepped into the street. Having not checked the time of the trains, at the worst he expected to meet Douglas somewhere on the way to the station, so he was surprised to see the three of them - Cameron in the road, Helen and Nonie on the pavement - already almost home. As he waited and watched their approach, they appeared as a group of old friends. When they saw him, they waved.

The sight took him back twelve months to the scene of their parting at college, a trap in the road outside Douglas's lodgings in Bayswater as they had said goodbye. As the easiest way to earn a living and to bring him home to Scotland, Douglas had taken the post of Lecturer in St Andrews. Now here he was again, open necked and his tweed jacket slung over his father's old leather grip. He grinned as they drew near.

'We found him for you,' Helen said, returning the smile. 'Stopped him going back to St Andrews.'

He was in high spirits. 'Well done. Good to see you for the

second time, Douglas,' and he held out his hand.

'And you as well, David.' Douglas shook his hand, a contrite look the only apology that he made. 'You've arrived north of the border, at last.'

'I promised next time we met it would be on your home ground.' He grinned again. 'You can thank Helen for that. Hello Nonie.' He gave her a peck on the cheek. 'Welcome back, I haven't seen you since Saturday.'

Nonie's eyes were wide. 'Hello David. Thank you for bringing such an interesting and good-looking man to be with us.'

Helen sniggered at her friend's forthrightness. 'Hey, Nonie, not too quickly; be careful,' and she touched her friend's arm.

He laughed too. 'Interesting, I would agree. The rest is the mask of a minstrel, so do not be taken in. When he's alone he takes the mask off. You wait and see; he has an ugly mind.'

'But a lovely voice, so I'm told,' Nonie countered.

Douglas raised his hand in a dramatic gesture. 'Please...' He looked at Nonie. 'Enough or the minstrel will run and hide.'

At his histrionic flourish and catching his eye, Nonie raised her eyebrows.

'See what I mean,' he said. 'Come on Douglas let us show you your lodgings here in Coulter House. Too good for a minstrel though,' he added. 'Hilda's just arrived back, so she'll want to show you round.'

Upstairs at the front of the house Hilda Strachan opened the door of the room for Douglas. 'It's a big room', she explained as she entered the chamber that over-looked the golf links. 'And it's also the best bed in the house.'

He unpacked and then went down to find the others in the garden. 'I think for the trouble I've caused you today, the least I can do is offer to take everybody out for supper.' He sat down on the grass. 'Would that disturb the domestic arrangements Mrs Strachan?' he called to Hilda who knelt to tend her roses. 'I include you in my invitation as well, of course.'

'It won't disturb a thing,' Hilda said, and struggled to her feet with rose clippers in hand. 'And thank you for the invitation, but I won't accept if you don't mind, I have to visit my friend Mrs Sweeney tonight.'

'Is there anywhere we can go then?'

Douglas looked at him, and he proposed the Havelock Hotel.

'Good. That's agreed then and, tonight remember, it's all on me.' Douglas sat centre stage on the grass. 'I have been cloistered like a hermit all year and hoarded like one too. It's time for some small extravagance, I think.'

'Bring your flute Dougie. We can give the town some music as the sun goes down.'

AN HOUR later they took a table in the garden of the Havelock Hotel, and as they waited for Helen and Douglas to return from the bar, Nonie recounted to David the frustration they had experienced that morning. 'The editor was terrible, so unhelpful; he seemed terrified of criticism and, by many accounts, well he should be.'

Helen and Douglas returned each with a tray. In the garden, they sat and relaxed in the still warm sun. 'Helen tells me you had a bad day with the festival director,' Douglas said to Nonie.

'Yes. He was so obtuse: an awful man.'

'His fame has gone before him.' Douglas gave Nonie a knowing glance. 'He's notorious you know. He visited St Andrews to gain support for the festival. I have never heard such a steam of florid and esoteric language like his presentation about the festival. At the time, I didn't give it another thought. Now here I am: part of it all.'

'The wheels of fate,' said Helen.

Douglas's talent for dominating the conversation soon came to the fore. 'So, explain to me your interest in Nairnshire music, Helen. What's it all about?'

'I'll resist the temptation to say that it is to develop my career as a journalist,' and she laid out her plans for the ensuing weeks. 'What it boils down to is the London readerships' interest in all things Scottish. There's good scope for articles about traditional music around the British Isles and so I volunteered to come to do the Nairn festival. Nonie and I had an article in the Review last week that was well received and so we'll continue with local music and the background to the festival.'

'When I was in London, I must say, I didn't meet anybody who showed the slightest interest in anything Scottish,' Douglas said, and maintained a quizzical smile through which Helen seemed to note the slimmest hint of provocation.

'Oh, I wouldn't say that; there's the usual rural attraction. As far as Londoners are concerned, Scotland is a romantic land of mountain glens and misty lochs, a place where politicians go to shoot and fish in the summer.'

Douglas grunted. 'Empty hills of heather you mean; ask them why they're empty. Don't you agree, David?'

'The journey north seemed to bring me to a country a world away from London,' he said. 'I was ignorant except for what I'd read in books.'

'That is correct: a world away and not only geographically.' Douglas emptied his glass. 'An independent, cultural and historical nation as well: it's the people that count.'

'I'll get you another drink; anyone else?'

'Not for me yet, thank you, David.' Nonie shook her head. 'I have never been further south than Glasgow and Edinburgh. I look forward to my first trip to London,' she told Douglas. 'I don't know the first thing about England. It's just the same for us here in Scotland, don't you think.'

Douglas disagreed. 'No. I do not.'

He returned and placed the tray on the table.

'To be quite honest, the English have few if any feelings either way,' Helen said.

'Pah,' Douglas snorted.

'Talking of music,' said Nonie, 'why don't you play something for us Douglas, or sing us a song.'

'Yes, good idea,' Helen agreed.

'Play for my supper when I've agreed to pay already,' he complained, opening the case. He chose a breezy melody, which crept around the garden as mist on a summer's morning. People at the other tables stopped to listen. He held their attention until the last note and faded into the still silence that followed. Everyone clapped.

'That was marvellous,' Nonie said, and looked thrilled.

The air cooled and the light disappeared, but it was ten o'clock before anyone noticed. The music kept more people in the garden than was usual.

'Come on; I'm for an early night,' said Helen. 'We have another day of hazards tomorrow when we see the Choral Society Director. It's on the decline, I understand.'

Douglas pushed back his chair and stood up. 'Good idea.'

'I hope you've enjoyed your first evening in Nairn Douglas,' Nonie said, her voice quiet in the night air.

Douglas turned towards her. 'I have,' he replied, and gave her his best smile. 'I hope we will have plenty more of the same.'

'I stay at the other end of town,' she said to Douglas, 'so I'll see you all tomorrow.'

Douglas did not need a further opener. 'Well, if you have to walk home alone Miss Sinclair, may I offer to walk with you. You can introduce me to more of the town as we go.' Nonie's rate of breathing increased and she seemed to find it difficult to control the sound of her voice.

'Thank you,' she said, the words almost inaudible. 'I'd like that.'

Helen stood behind Douglas, wide-eyed and open-mouthed and when Nonie caught her look, she turned away.

'I'll find my way back, so don't you two wait up,' Douglas said, and waved a nonchalant arm.

'Let me take your case for you, Douglas,' he said, and grabbed the handle. 'Then you'll be unencumbered.'

They parted company and when they were out of earshot, Helen laughed out loud. 'Did you see that; before our very eyes and only hours after they met? She couldn't keep her eyes off him from the moment we got onto the train at Inverness.'

'He's only volunteered to walk her home.'

'I know, but I won't be surprised…'

Tucking the flute case under his arm, he said, 'No, neither would I. Anyway, a perfect match, I should say. Have you ever seen two people so alike?'

Helen's giggle resounded across the street. '*If you have to walk home alone, Miss Sinclair...*' she squealed. 'We didn't even arrange what time to meet tomorrow, Nonie was so flustered.'

'I shouldn't worry. Knowing her, she'll be round at the crack of dawn.'

They walked back to Coulter House.

'It was a lovely evening,' Helen said.

'Yes, it was.' He glanced at her. 'It's all your doing.'

'The visit has its own shape now, hasn't it,' she said, and picked a flower over a garden wall as she passed. 'I can see why you get on so well with Douglas.' She stopped and turned to give the flower to him.

Until now, he had kept Helen on the edge of his cocoon. He took the flower and before it dropped again to her side, took her hand also. It was the act that each had waited for. Helen looked at him and he raised his eyes to hers - all that was needed. As they continued to walk home, she took his hand in both of hers.

AFTER BREAKFAST, as he made his way to the Golf View Hotel, David grinned; there had been no sign of Douglas. In the subdued morning after the night before atmosphere that the ballroom had in anticipation of the sun coming round to the windows, he worked for two hours and then walked back to Coulter House.

In the parlour, not giving the impression of being one who had had an early night, and, in fact appearing to be quite washed out, he found Douglas. It was the look that he remembered from the Royal College when Douglas had played bridge all night.

'Good morning and greetings to you,' Douglas said.

'You sound cheery, enough. Good morning; I hate to say it, but you don't look as though you slept much last night.'

Douglas squinted. 'I didn't sleep well, if that's what you mean.'

He smiled and let the topic rest. 'I thought we could look at the programme for Friday,' he continued. 'At your convenience of course. I will be in the Golf View down the road. Ask them at reception.'

'I'll have a blow along the front,' Douglas said. 'Then I will come along and we can get started. The others are away, are they?'

He nodded. 'Nonie came round early and left with Helen. I'll get back to the Golf View, so come down when you're ready. Anytime…'

Douglas nodded and yawned. 'See you in an hour or so.'

Helen returned early and found him in the ballroom of the Golf View. The spontaneous and unconstrained smile told all.

'Is it telepathy, or just that the message is written all over your face?'

Her words came in a breathless torrent. 'Have you seen Douglas?'

'Yes, for the briefest moment; he hasn't been here and looked distracted.'

'*Distracted?*' Helen shrieked. '*I should say so. They were out all night; Nonie got home at five o'clock.*'

He laughed, more at Helen than the revelation about the nocturnal activities of their friends. 'Douglas just said that he didn't sleep well.'

'At all, more like it. I've come home because Nonie fell asleep at lunchtime.'

Again he laughed. 'I had assumed that Douglas went out for a walk this afternoon, he seemed so contemplative, but probably he's just gone to bed. Come on, let's find out.'

Helen followed him out of the ballroom. 'At lunch, Nonie would not stop talking about him, then just fell asleep. Grandma will know something.'

The result was that four days of practice were squashed into three. Like riding a bicycle, it was not something forgotten and everything they had planned worked well. The two pieces that he had sent to Douglas, he had learned and by Friday evening, they were ready.

THE FIRST arrivals for the concert gathered in the entrance of the Golf View Hotel. They clustered in groups that fused and dispersed as further guests made their appearance through the arched doors. Until that moment the concert had been a notion. The swell and swirl of social groups in the entrance contained the crucial ingredient, which could only be anticipated, not planned: the mix and nature of the guests. From where he stood in the recess near the dining room door, he watched them. With the guests came part, at least, of the spirit of the concert, an abstraction of style and elegance, whispers of approval that set the timbre of the performance. The ballroom, a small and intimate environment of openness and light, was enriched by the audience that became part of the performance. That so many should arrive he found flattering.

'And in such tartan-clad grandeur,' he muttered to himself and brushed the lapel of his dinner jacket.

Loud enough for everyone to hear, as he entered the lobby and removed his top hat, the concert organiser called across the hall. 'Good evening, Mr Whellans. May I introduce my wife to you,' who he chaperoned across the room. 'Janet McDermott. Mr Whellans,' he repeated.

As he shook hands with them both, heads turned. 'A pleasure to meet you Mrs McDermott.'

Henry McDermott adjusted his cuffs. 'I trust you find everything to your satisfaction Mr Whellans and that you are eager to entreat us to your interpretation of the finer arts.'

'I am, and I have not looked forward so much to a concert for a long time.'

While McDermott took him aside, Mrs McDermott was gathered into one of the nearby groups. 'And your colleague, Mr Cameron, he is also, I trust, in high spirits?'

He glanced towards the bar. 'I think we can say that he is.'

'He has not arrived yet?'

He drew a veil. 'He will be here shortly, if not already. As likely as not, he has taken a walk in the gardens to clear his mind.'

'Ah yes.' Henry McDermott smiled a knowing smile and, casting his view over the assembly of Nairnshire society that now found it difficult to move in the entrance hall, he said, 'I had a last minute thought; I should make a special announcement that tonight will witness the first performance of some of your works, those that have been composed and inspired by this locality. What do you think I should say about them in particular?'

'Tell them the sonata is called, *A Northern Summer*, and was inspired by this part of the world and the music found in and around Nairn.' He wrote down a few sentences on a page torn from his diary that McDermott could offer to the audience.

He took it and said, 'Possibly a better title would be, *A Scottish Summer*,' and giving him a quick glance vanished in search of other final preparations over which he could cast his eye and assert his influence.

Possibly it would.

Isobel Hunter and Corrine Lambie, who would participate in the concert, at that moment were making preparations and, having tuned their harps, placed them like resting cormorants on the platform in the ballroom. Douglas Cameron remained at the bar, as anonymous as any other person. They had spent part of the day together at the piano, but since they parted, he had not seen him. Now, as he awaited the commencement of the performance, he anticipated the clarsach introduction and the progression that would be effected from that into his own programme of music.

In the days since Douglas's arrival his mind had been divided between preparation for the concert and writing the first movement to Themes of a Nation. The activities pivoted against each other. Helen was a third focus that seeped through the corrugations and asked for attention. Although he was losing his struggle to separate thought and feeling, his mind remained focused during the three days, between work at Coulter House, at the Golf View's piano and on the shore strand when he let the breeze blow through his thoughts to clear his mind.

After practising at their agreed times, Douglas Cameron spent his days alone. He walked and worked, either on lectures for the next term, or else reviewed poems that might be set to music, or songs that he might sing. He walked for miles, found quiet places to rest and work, then moved on. It was usual for him to return late.

He watched the concert's momentum mount. First Isobel and Corrine's appearance and promenade to the front of the ballroom, followed by Henry McDermott's fluster. Witnessing the transformation of those in the entrance and Gentlemen's Smoking Room into an audience - seated and attentive amidst the hum of its own anticipation - he made his own move down the side to take his seat at the piano. He listened to McDermott's first hushed announcements and noted Douglas's nonchalant absence.

The concert commenced. Twenty minutes ensued in which the two women treated the audience to the finest presentation of harp music available in Western Europe. When they finished and the applause ceased, Henry McDermott praised the spirit of Celtic music and promised more of that precious heritage in the second half. Isobel and Corrine bowed and curtsied. Helen Strachan and Nonie Sinclair exercised their descriptive imaginations at the rear of the ballroom. McDermott introduced him and Douglas Cameron in a well-rehearsed ritual montage of epithet and praise.

Aware that Douglas had not appeared, and with McDermott also giving and enquiring look and, remembering that no performance of theirs had ever gone according to plan, he started to play the nocturne that preceded Douglas's songs.

As he presented the final bars and raised his eyes to the audience in confirmation of its end, he saw Douglas at the back of the ballroom stood dead centre of the 'aisle'. Between the two breaths it took him to realise that Douglas did not intend to come to the front, he hesitated; then, with an idea of what was going to happen, commenced the introduction to the arrangement of Burn's poems and songs.

Attentive, the audience was unaware that, as they listened, the concert's proceedings were being fine tuned. He started to play and over the heads of the audience anticipated the entrance of his partners voice, which appeared at once in every corner of the ballroom and with no immediate focus in the figure at the rear of the aisle. Some in the audience turned, others remained still. Some closed their eyes and listened. Nonie Sinclair closed hers. During the third verse, while he sang, Douglas began to walk in the phrases of the melody to the front of the ballroom. The effect could never have been anticipated or achieved unless carried out in as an impromptu fashion as Douglas had made it. He played his accompaniment as if he were in Douglas's head, so attuned was he to the innuendo of the other's thoughts. The audience applauded, and applauded, and he knew that for a while the pianist had lost them. They continued into the strains of, *Summer's a Pleasant Time*, then *Green Grow the Rashes, O*, that Douglas delivered with lustre.

As it was the first time he had heard Douglas perform in his own medium, he listened and was again thrilled by his friend's voice. Soon he would write more music for him.

In the intermission Douglas disappeared to the gardens and walked the short distance to the shore to breathe the sea air. Nonie followed him and he watched her go. She had said that she was thrilled with the performance. He presumed she felt it admissible, with every presumption of privilege and right, to be able to disturb his seclusion at that moment. Isobel and Corrine joined those in the lounge and accepted the garlands of praise showered upon them. They were well known in Nairn and everyone wanted to give their congratulations. He stayed in the ballroom.

Hilda Strachan basked in reflected glory and gave potted biographies of her lodgers. She looked as though she enjoyed the attention. Helen sipped a pink gin given her by Henry McDermott and quizzed him on his appreciation of the concert so far. In the smoking room, whisky glasses were drained and replenished and a fair measure of gin and martini cocktail was imbibed - as a special liberty and to celebrate a fine occasion, as many were heard to say. Henry McDermott was slow to recall the audience to the ballroom and finished his third malt. It was, in the end, a longish interval. Douglas was back and waiting well in time to start to second half.

As the concert recommenced, the sun cast an orange glow across the panorama of the Moray Firth. The setting was perfect and admired in the minutes before Henry McDermott stood, with arm outstretched, to quieten the audience.

The concert seemed to them to have moved up a notch. The clarsachs were more vibrant, the songs more lively and the piano more resonant than before. He played extracts from, *A Scottish Summer*, as McDermott introduced it. The audience satisfiers, the old chestnuts were there, but also more serious and contemplative pieces. All were accepted with grand applause. As a finale Douglas played the flute and, with the accompaniment of Isobel and Corrine, played a medley of jigs, reels and airs that rounded the evening into a triumphal fanfare of all that is splendid in Scottish traditional music. The concert did not so much finish as adjourn to the lounge and smoking room. It was well past mid-night when the last of the concert-goers left the Golf View Hotel.

They had seen little of each other all evening and Helen was still in overdrive when they met in the aisle amidst the audience's ragged dispersal. 'David, it was wonderful,' she said and kissed him on both cheeks.

'Thank you,' he said, still standing by the piano.

'Are you pleased? Everyone was bubbling with compliments during the interval.'

'Yes, very pleased. Isobel and Corrine were marvellous. They looked so elegant. Douglas lived up to all expectations.'

'Come and have a drink.'

'In a minute.' At that moment he was not fully paying attention. 'What about you; how has your evening been?'

'Busy and there are more people I need to talk to. The review for tomorrow's Telegraph has gone: the boy took it an hour ago.'

'That's good...'

'You will come and meet Uncle Kenneth and Aunt Marie. They'll leave soon and you must say hello.'

He stalled her. 'Alright, give me a few more minutes here. I'll be along soon.' He remained in the ballroom and was glad to be engaged in conversation. When the crowd thinned, he ventured forth and met Douglas in the lounge. 'I don't know how you manage it,' he said, and took some water from the bar. 'There's new expression in your voice. The audience loved you.'

'You as well.'

'Thank you.' He smiled. 'No. I am no great pianist, but I hope they gained something from my music. You are the star and rightly so. We must set some more songs for you. I'll get onto it next week.'

The social merit of the time spent in the bar after the concert was lost on him. His thoughts stayed in the ballroom, trapped in the music that they had made there.

THE NEXT day, alone at home, he did jobs for Hilda Strachan in her garden. Douglas joined him. 'You're getting on alright with Helen, then?' he ventured.

He nodded, but resisted an answer.

Douglas seemed to catch the nuance. 'You don't seem, er, over enthusiastic, if I may say so.'

'No, I am,' he insisted, but found it difficult to express such feelings. He gave Douglas a glance to save answering further.

'You seem somewhat distracted.'

'No, well partly, it's just the concert. It was better than I could have hoped for.'

'Me too. Tell me, talking of Helen, how's your old friend Alex?'

'What's got into you?' he said, and shook his head. 'Heaven knows.' *Alex*. Just the reminder of her and there he was straight back to the village, straight back home.

'Helen's pushed her right out I presume?' Douglas kept his eyes on him.

He shrugged and wondered for a moment, then said, 'Alex was only ever a dream.'

Douglas scoffed. 'If my memory serves me right, she was more than a dream two years ago.'

'No, still only a dream then.'

Again, Douglas laughed. 'I remember the time I met her. You were not the same for days. I remember thinking how proud you were of her.'

Why was he bothered enough to remember. 'Proud?' he muttered.

'Yes, you were, like brother and sister. She had a lot of power over you.'

He shifted and looked away and then back at Douglas. 'Alex is like a picture on the wall that you see every day. She is on my wall. I see her every day, but I could just as easily take the picture down and throw it away. She is an old dream.'

Douglas sang, '*Laddie, ye dinna ken the danger you're in…*'

AFTER DOUGLAS'S comments that afternoon, he wrote a letter to Alex. It contained the response to a sentimental memory, in the dormancy of which he had slipped away to Scotland. He wrote it in the ballroom of the Golf View Hotel and when he read it, wrote it out again. Despite his efforts, he put the letter away and did not send it.

Chapter 17
(Day 8 - May 1992: Isle of Skye)

JODI SAT opposite in the saloon of the ferry to Skye. It was a quick crossing to Armadale, with just enough time for a sandwich on board. While Jodi fought with a sticky piece of fudge shortbread, on the table their coffee cups shuddered. Giggling like girls, they threw crumbs to the seagulls. Then, as the sun fell to the west, they traversed the southern part of Skye and progressed towards Broadford.

'You know,' she said, when she thought of the photograph that Jodi had taken earlier, 'when you took the picture of me on the ferry, history repeated itself.' She looked across at her travelling companion. 'It was so strange that you did it like that, with me against the rail.'

'Really?' Jodi replied, and turned sideways in her seat as far as she could and wedged herself to face her. 'Why was it strange?'

'Well, you will think this sounds silly, but it is because of a picture similar to the one you took that I have come to Scotland. A picture and some reminders of the past associated with it.'

'A picture?'

'Yes, of my husband and some of his friends.' She hesitated. 'I should explain that he died a few weeks ago.'

'Oh, I'm sorry,' Jodi said, and her face softened to a look of concern.

'No, it's alright, you weren't to know. It's good to be able to talk to someone about it.' The ease she felt with Jodi seemed to make it alright to confide in her. 'A few days ago, my daughter found some of his things from his early life. One of them was a photograph with friends on a boat going to the Isle of Lewis. He stood against the rail, just as I was. So it took me by surprise when you took the picture. That's all.'

'That's a little coincidence, isn't it?' As they drove on, Jodi relaxed and let her recount the build-up to her adventure.

She nodded. 'I think I have achieved something already, though

I'm not quite sure what it is. I am solving problems about the past. I think I have begun to know what my husband experienced at that time. Ever since I crossed the border at Gretna, I felt I have been catching up and, in some ways, catching up with myself as well. He talked about his past and of an empathy with things that he described in the background notes to his music.' She talked as though Jodi was an old friend. 'You must think this all sounds very strange.'

'You keep saying that.' Jodi smiled. 'No, I'm fascinated. What do you mean, catching up with yourself?'

'I'm a bit frightened of it to be truthful. It has something do with our knowledge of past lives I think. As if you can listen to what the mind tells you without words. I am always too busy to really listen and, to be honest, I don't really understand.' She drove along the narrow roads and all the time, as they talked, the two women kept their eyes on the scenery around them. 'One of David's pieces of music from Scotland was called, *Themes of a Nation*. All I know is that he said it was about the spirit of ancient peoples and his interpretation of the music he found on his travels. Crazy, isn't it?'

'Hm, difficult, I know,' Jodi replied. 'Those must be the Cuillens over there.'

She followed Jodi's gaze. 'Oh, yes,' and she looked at the mountains that rose in a relief to the north-west. Their grandeur fitted her mood. 'It would be nice to walk in them.'

'Many people feel their mysticism, but some people find them sinister. I'll go walking in them sometime.'

She smiled across at her travelling companion. 'It's so nice to have you with me.'

Jodi picked up the threads of their conversation. 'I guess all our pasts are somehow interwoven. I think we all have knowledge of the past.' She kept her eyes on the hills and waited for her to tell her story.

'Really? I'm surprised you say so.'

'It's not surprising. We inherit behaviour, which is our brain telling us what to do, so why can't we inherit knowledge to go with it?'

'Some theories say that is rubbish and that memory is wiped clean as a tape recording or a computer memory when the germ cells are formed. It's only electrical coding, after all.'

'Well, it's not wiped clean of all information, otherwise behaviour wouldn't work.'

'Rather controversial, but it's interesting what you say. You're very knowledgeable…'

'Thank you.'

'I've been thinking about it as I've driven along. My husband thought our characters and memories read back through generations. No-one's mind is an entity separated off from the stream of history. He went as far as to say that he thought our minds are connected to mythologies and legends, but I haven't taken much notice until now. I think he described resonances such as these in his music. Listen.' She took a cassette tape from the glove compartment and put it into the player.

'Wow.' Jodi's eyes widened. 'He was a real composer.'

They listened as they drove along. 'When he had finished his Scottish music, some years later he wrote another piece that contrasted it, based on his background in rural England. That's this one, look.' She showed Jodi another cassette.

Jodi read what it said on the back about the music and the composer. 'And this is why you have come to Scotland?' She looked enchanted by the idea. 'To find out what it was all about?'

'Yes, in a nutshell.' As they drove along, she continued to reminisce and to tell her patchy stories. Every now and again they stopped and got out to look at the views.

'You have a beautiful accent, Jodi. Where are you from; I should have asked you? You said near Edinburgh.'

'Hmm, a place called Roslyn. I will go back when I finish here. I love it there.'

'Why didn't you like college?'

Jodi pulled a face. 'It was yuch! I just didn't feel good there. The town was horrible and everything was so unfamiliar to me. I'm sorry, but I don't really like England.'

'You like Edinburgh though?'

'Oh, yes, it's fantastic. I love the whole area around where I live. My Dad was a miner. So was my Granddad.'

'I hope you manage to go to university. Para-psychology sounds fascinating. Edinburgh is a very good university.'

Sooner than expected the sign for Broadford appeared and she had to bid Jodi farewell and all the best for the summer.

As she prepared to continue, Jodi stood by the car. 'Will you call in on your way back next week?'

'I'm sorry, Jodi, I'm going on to Lewis and then on the ferry from Stornoway to Ullapool. I am going in a circle. I'll telephone you though.'

'Yes, please do.' Jodi gave a parting grin. 'I think I might need someone to talk to by then. Good luck.'

'And to you...' They waved to each other as she drove away.

THE ROAD meandered along the eastern seaboard of Skye and took her with it into the evening over expanses of moor land with moist uplands and bare rock exposed in misty summits. That morning she had woken with one desire on her mind: to achieve the job she'd come to do, to discover Scotland. Those thoughts had rested uneasy with her. Now, in the afternoon, while still determined to make progress, the day's journey had calmed her. Being alone was no longer high on the list of concerns and sleeping in a dormitory with other women the night before had helped. In the company of Jodi, she had relaxed and when she arrived in Portree, after an enchanting day of hills, lochs and the sea, had enough energy to smile. Her mind was a kaleidoscope of the images of everything she had experienced: a day with a girl and an unexpected unleashing of her emotion.

She called Anna to give her news. 'Hello Darling. I've made it to Portree. It's breathtaking.'

Anna giggled. 'How are you feeling now, Mummy?'

'Fine, just fine: met a girl called Jodi. I gave her a lift most of the way. She was lovely.'

'That was nice for you. I was so worried when you called this morning.' Anna gave her own news. 'I'll go down to see the solicitors tomorrow. They have the manuscripts and other things that Daddy stored in the bank. I'll let you know what there is. Where will you be tomorrow night?'

'On Lewis, Insha'Allah,' and she allowed a hint of anxiety to enter her voice. 'The weather is fine so it should be a good crossing to Tarbert. Only two hours.'

'You sound much better now Mummy, despite your panic in the morning. I really worried about you. But anyway, take care. I look forward to hearing how you are tomorrow. Hope you sleep well.'

'I am sure I will and you Darling,' she said, and hung up. She's moving on already, she thought.

As she stepped out of the call box into the square in the centre of Portree, with a slight spring in her step, she laughed and walked back along the street amidst the granite shops and houses. Now what? Find the guesthouse just off the harbour. It was easy. At six thirty she surveyed the streets that led from the square and decided to take a quick walk. The woman had offered supper at seven o'clock and she had accepted.

Chapter 18
(July/August 1939: to Ullapool)

AFTER THE CONCERT the warm weather continued and helped him to relax. Should he post the letter to Alex? He was caught between the past and the present; between the old and the new, and settled in neither.

Like smoke on a gentle breeze, on Sunday a mist swept in from the sea and wafted over Nairn. Inland from the town it hung in pockets across the farmland and engulfed the hamlets in a chill summer gloom.

After they had met him at the concert, Kenneth and Marie Strachan broadened their invitation to make a more elaborate event of the occasion and lunch became a banquet by any standard. It was early evening when Kenneth Strachan drove them back to Nairn and stayed for a while to chat with his mother.

Since neither had anything pressing to prepare for the next morning, they walked to the harbour. He found it difficult to isolate a moment when things had altered. Like a water lily that opens each day in the light and is closed again by dusk, as the light varies, you cannot see the changes happen.

They sat and, while he looked into the swirl of the waters that ebbed across the firth, she looked at him and said, 'I didn't forget you know, after the Burn's Supper. I waited, but you didn't contact me.'

He did not answer, but continued to gaze across the firth and caught the outlines of two warships that lay at anchor. Then he turned. 'I think too much happened earlier in the year, and anyway, I didn't expect that you were interested in me.'

Helen gave her usual spirited smile. 'I looked at you all evening; I gave you enough hints.'

'Maybe I didn't want to know just then.' He hesitated and took her hand. 'I'm sorry.'

She looked at him and then away and he let his gaze return to the waters of the firth.

AT THE OTHER end of town Nonie unhooked the ties of the curtains in her room and allowed the drapes to fall across the window, then turned into Douglas's embrace. He put his hands beneath her hair and folded his arms around her neck so that the long locks flowed over them, and kissed her.

Nonie whispered, 'I fell in love with you the first moment I saw you on the train, believe me, it was instant,' and she kissed him.

'I think I fancied you quite a lot the first time I saw you as well,' he replied, and with his arms about her waist fell back with her onto the bed and let her hair tumble over him. He breathed her in. 'I couldn't have imagined you were here waiting for me in Nairn.'

She kissed his face and his closed eyes. 'We are so alike,' she said. 'I feel you match me.' They were aware of the gentlest of contacts, each caress that held the threads between them.

THROUGH THE week he worked on the concerto and pushed the first part near to completion. The song sequence that he had started still lay in the back of his mind. In a gust of spontaneity one afternoon, he managed to complete one song entitled *Culbin Sands*. He sang it through to himself:

> Gentle love, come hold my hand
> walk with me now by Culbin sand
> and in the morn, walk by the sea
> take your first steps beside me.
>
> *Blow bonnie breeze over the bay*
> *blow gentle wind soft and warm*
> *as the first light at the break of day*
> *our love will grow in the morn.....*

Did Helen get in the way of his work? It was hard to tell. He would be able to write for her later. Now he must finish the first job. He remembered Martin Taylor's warning; set one task at a time, then head for the horizon.

On Friday evening the second concert commenced in Inverness, and though less intimate, it was as well received as the first in Nairn. Henry McDermott, true to form, to augment his already impressive introductions, boasted a detailed knowledge of the musicians.

With that concert completed they were ready to continue the itinerary to Ullapool and Lewis, and on Sunday evening made their farewells to Hilda and invited her out for supper at the Havelock Hotel. On this occasion she accepted and, in an evening of music and entertainment, everyone celebrated their time with her in Nairn. The locals stayed on in the hotel bar and lounge and joined in. Others arrived when the word spread around town of the festivity.

AS HEATHERED slopes receded behind the bus David relaxed into a reverie. Amongst the landscapes beyond Inverness, nothing spoke to him of any past experience. In the early morning sun, as the bus laboured in its westward peregrination along the single-track road, he tried to absorb the changes and keep with them. The journey was not long, and soon the driver called that they would arrive in Ullapool in five minutes.

Malcolm Ross met them at the terminus. By his dress and the way he acted he could be recognised as many things: as a fisherman, as his father was; as a rebel, as David deduced him to be; and as an artist, which his personality conveyed and he professed to be. He was clean-shaven, but had not shaved that day and his hair was as if he had that morning swam in the sea and let it dry in the wind and sun.

All four warmed to the man and, by the time they reached his mother's house in the heart of the town just above Shore Street, all chatted together. 'This is my mother, Eleanor Ross,' he said as they passed through the gate into the garden at the rear. The washing was on the line with Eleanor taking in the dry clothes.

'Good day to you all,' she said, and shook everybody by the hand. 'We have three rooms in the house, so one for the women and one for the men.'

Eleanor spoke with a mild and warm accent. 'Ross is away in Iceland and will be back in three weeks. So it's just us at home for now.'

'Ross is my father,' Malcolm explained.

Beneath a bright sky, a fresh breeze blew over Loch Broom and through the town. The smell of the sea swept along the streets.

Malcolm was hard to tie down and almost immediately on their arrival vanished. It seemed that from dawn to dusk he had something to do for someone, somewhere. When they alighted from the bus Malcolm gave him a hand-written booklet of his poems in Gaelic and in the translation as he called it.

He read them that evening. They were poems evocative of a community where the sea and all to do with it were central to life there. Malcolm wrote with a fierceness that could be reconciled with the man he had met that morning. It was lyrical poetry, with deep involvement and an agonised isolation.

What worlds met there?

When Malcolm returned, they talked. Shy and reticent about his work, he said, 'The poems come as they will and if they will, and that's all I know.'

'I would like to use some of them, to set to music,' he replied, and searched in the book to show him. 'Some are perfect as they are; poems such as, Western Loch, Columba's Shore, Spring Come, Harp Rock and Fishing Ketch.' The words seemed to emanate from a mythic potency of the past. 'These are perfect.'

Malcolm wagged his head from side to side and rolled his ever smiling eyes. 'Do whatever you want with them.'

He asked if Malcolm could write a special sequence about the people in western Scotland to describe the harmonies in their lives.

'I could try, but it won't happen in the next week.'

'What about the music around here? Where do you think it comes from?'

'That I couldn't tell you; you'll have to ask someone else.'

He nodded. 'I will.'

'I know that many tunes have only survived because they have words,' Malcolm said. 'So tunes with words are probably older than those that don't have words.'

He raised his eyebrows. 'Hm, that's an interesting thought...'

The next day Malcolm went away, and his mother said that he had gone to a bothy in the hills to write. He guessed the reason and felt an empathy with him.

WHEN THEY had been in Ullapool four days and when he had returned from his bothy retreat, Malcolm suggested he take them for a visit to Lochinver on the coast to the north. He borrowed a car and after lunch they drove west to the coast.

First they headed for the isolated home of one of Malcolm's friends.

'We have to go along that track and then come back,' he said, so you and Helen can walk on from here and we'll meet-up further along the coast. Just keep near to the road.'

With the sea to their left and the road to their right, they walked on alone. The weeks in Nairn had given way to a relaxed pace. The group was thrown together and camaraderie grew between them. Helen and he spent more time with each other and he could not isolate her from other emotions.

Further along on the cliffs they sat for a while. 'You've made love easy for me,' he said, and, with the sun on her face, looked at her and thought too long so that the words came out more like Malcolm's poems.

She did not say anything, just smiled.

'I want my love to be free for you.'

'That's a lovely thing to say. Thank you. My love is free for you as well.' They walked to the end of the cliffs that overlooked the stretch of water they call the Minch, where Malcolm had told them to look out for Lewis on the horizon. 'I think you have given me new words for the things that I feel,' Helen said when they stopped.

'I know I have been slow.'

'Don't be silly. I've been the same. We've grown together.'

Looking back towards the road, as they came towards them, they saw Nonie, Douglas and Malcolm. Malcolm's friend must have been at home, as there was a fourth person with them, and a dog. Dodging the rocks, with Douglas and Nonie trying to find the same energy as their companions, the group ran down the hill. With face flushed when he arrived, Malcolm said, 'This is Alistair Sadler.

You must talk to him about Lewis. Amongst other things he digs and will know the answers to all your questions.'

'You'd better wait to see about that I think,' Alistair replied.

Malcolm took them along the coast, with Skelp the dog at their feet, even more squashed in the car now. 'I want to show you the bays further round, near Culkein,' he said. 'We can go in a circle.'

IN ULLAPOOL he wrote each day, working in the room in Eleanor's house he shared with Douglas with a view of the fells that rose behind the town. His responses were highly charged. While work in Nairn was never onerous, here his creative energy flowed freely. In Malcolm's absence he set some of his poems to music for Douglas to sing.

'Six all have the sea as a theme,' he told Douglas, and gave him them to look at. 'I thought we could call them, *Water over the Sand*, the first line of one of the poems.'

'They look fine to me,' Douglas said, and pointed out another that he liked and suggested should be included, then left him to get on with the first scores.

When they were ready, he presented Malcolm with the fledgling settings of his poems. Melodies that came from the rhythms of Malcolm and his mother's voices and from lines of songs sung by a woman on the first evening, anchored the compositions. Douglas sang them to a violin accompaniment.

As Malcolm's first experience of his poems set to music, the effect was unexpected. 'I need time to think about it,' he said, and went away to spend the afternoon on the heights above the town in thought about the songs. On his return, looking bemused, he said, 'My words have grown beyond me. I'll never read the poems again as they were.'

It disturbed him that Douglas could not sing the words in Gaelic, and he wanted to find a singer who could learn them. He brought Sheenagh Galbraith to meet him the next day and asked him to teach her. First she sang with Douglas, then set the Gaelic words with him.

'What do you think now you've heard them in Gaelic David?' Malcolm asked.

'In some ways it must be the same as your first experience of the poems set to music. It's something I didn't expect, another understanding with new richness. Gaelic is so unlike English, with the long vowel sounds and the soft roll of the words. The language seems to have evolved in harmony with the sea and the hills.'

THE TOUR moved at a pace. With Gavin Brink due to join them the next day, Nonie prepared for his arrival. 'He'll be here late tomorrow and wants to do his own article. He has arranged a lift with the harbour master, of all people, another of his contacts from Inverness.' Since it was the evening of one of the performances, Nonie waited for him. He arrived just in time to catch the last quarter of an hour of the music.

Malcolm had arranged two venues and, with local musicians and poets invited, presented an evening of music, song and poetry. The first was on the Friday. With an impact on Malcolm as profound as ever, Sheenagh sang the Gaelic songs. David played extracts from his compositions and explained the background to them.

Now with Gavin, Nonie and Helen pursued their own goals and documented musical traditions. With all the characteristics of a detective trail, Malcolm searched out people that might help them. They listened to stories and the mythology.

News came over on the ferry from Stornoway that the posters were up and the tickets sold out. Other news spread less quickly. Letters from his mother echoed her concerns again, and the local newspapers gave news of world events. He read of the build-up of pressure on the port of Danzig on the Baltic. If Poland felt obliged to use force to maintain the *status quo*, Chamberlain told the Poles that Britain would go to her aid. He sensed a reticence in people to talk as much as they had before. They waited in silence.

At the end of two weeks a dozen or more songs had been set and Douglas was pleased that he had added new Scottish songs to his collection. 'These will go down well with my students in St Andrews,' he told Malcolm. 'Hot off the press and from Gaelic roots; your name will be in common parlance around St Andrews, Malcolm.'

On the last evening there was a fair turnout at the local inn.

Everybody sang, most with no accompaniment, and danced when the fiddle played.

Afterwards, walking in the northern night to the harbour, he and Helen stood beside the ferry that would take them to Lewis in the morning. The novelty hadn't worn off. Helen's drive forced the pace and her agenda underpinned each step. The rest fitted around her.

'So, tomorrow we go to Lewis,' she said, and looked across the harbour.

He could only see shadows on her face. 'Yes, we are on our way again. Are you excited?'

'Of course, but more than that, intrigued by the next musical delights that await us.' With their eyes cast to the horizon, they watched the last vestiges of light from the vanished sun. 'It's the same as the step onto the train the first time in London. I didn't know what to expect then, and it feels the same now, with Lewis a short stretch of water away.'

Helen mused about their other friends. 'How are Nonie and Douglas do you think? She looks very self-assured.'

'She certainly has had a profound effect on him.'

'Of course; he on her too. When I returned at five o'clock yesterday, they'd locked the door to our room, and wouldn't let me in. I didn't tell you. They shouted that I should come back later.'

He just laughed. 'As Douglas's song says, *Summer's a pleasant time*. This has been a great one.'

'We've gone as far as we can go from London.' Helen said. 'You cannot do much more with a summer than that.'

'There speaks a true Scot. What will the next seasons bring, I wonder?' He shivered. 'It looks as if my mother's fears are coming true, though. The country is sliding into conflict again. It's been coming for years.'

Helen looked across Loch Broom into the night. 'We'll face it together.'

EIGHT HOURS later Malcolm was at the harbour early and laughed and chatted with the ferry crew while he prepared for the crossing. Arriving with Helen, David felt the breeze blow from the west onto their faces and greeted Malcolm on the quay.

'This is Ounagh,' Malcolm said, and introduced a woman with a black crocheted shawl over her shoulders. 'She'll come over with us to stay for a few days with her aunt.'

Then Gavin brink arrived and leaned on the harbour wall to inspect his new camera. 'It's been provided by the office in Nairn, and as far as I am concerned, is still in the experimental phase.' Gavin was part of the team and made everyone laugh with his antics, engrossed now in his camera. He remembered when they first met at the Shore Inn near the harbour in Nairn and how he stood out from the crowd then as he did now. He called himself a lowland Scot. For David, he was the everyman, lowland or highland, it didn't matter.

'They want me to become a real reporter,' Gavin said, 'with action photography as well. I still have to learn how to take interesting pictures of groups, so that I don't chop the legs off, or skim the hair-line.' He snapped them as they stood there.

To the chorus of herring gulls, they boarded the boat to Lewis, seven of them now, and then during the crossing, Gavin made everyone line up for photographs. David smiled at the pranks Gavin used to animate them. It was his other side, the clown which hid beneath his more sober countenance that Gavin had showed once or twice before. The party had grown. There were many people now and he looked around them all.

'Come on David, smile. Put your arm round Helen. That's good.' Gavin clicked the camera.

After the first pictures, Gavin was less demonstrative. He tried more subtle angles. 'I've decided I quite like to take sneaky pictures of people from the rear,' and he hovered in the background. 'You get a different mood from behind.'

'Saves us having to perform antics for you as well,' Douglas said.

David stayed near to Helen, her closeness still a novelty, a shape the contours of which were still unfamiliar to him. 'Last night you said we have come as far as we could,' he said to her. 'I've come much further than that now. You have changed everything,' and he held the rail in the sway of the boat and just looked at her.

Alex. He should write and tell her. Where was she: Birmingham somewhere? Why should he feel guilty? His whole life had changed now.

Helen smiled and he smiled back at her. 'I could so easily have missed you,' he said.

'Davy, all I know is that I love you and we are together; this is the summer that started it.' She kissed him and pulled him to her. The breeze blew through their hair and touched their cheeks.

Malcolm came over to them and stood by the rail. He turned his face into the wind and looked towards Lewis. 'We could spend a year on Lewis and still there would be more people for you to meet and things to see. We have a lot to do.'

Helen returned his glance. 'Just give us a taster this time,' she said, 'to make us want to come back. We want to know what people think and how that shapes their music.'

'I'll try to find the mystery for you,' Malcolm said.

'I hope that it's going to be different here to Ullapool and Nairn.'

Malcolm gave a confident nod of his head. 'It is different,' he shouted. 'You can be sure of that. Whether you will feel it, remains to be seen.' And his look seemed to challenge them.

It was the beginning of the second week in August and summer was at its height. The ferry neared Stornoway and coasted into the bay that lay to the south of the town. The fishing boats in the harbour were impressive with the quay rising before them.

Malcolm spoke as they tied up. 'The herring fleet trebles its population at the height of summer. This is called South Beach where we will dock,' and he pointed over to the three wooden-pile wharves that formed the main part of the harbour.

Filled with boats, most of them steamers or motor driven, he caught sight of two old sailboats, and turned to Malcolm. 'What are those boats over there?'

'What we call *Wherries*,' Malcolm replied. 'There are only a few still active now. We see those two often in Ullapool. The *Muirneag* and the *Paradigm* are their names.'

Once they landed, a sense of expansion engulfed him. 'How often do you come over?' he asked Malcolm as they stood on the wharf.

'Every month at least,' he said, his arm around Ounagh. 'There's always something going on, so we come often.'

'It must feel like home here for you.'

'I suppose as much as in Ullapool, yes. I'd never given it any thought.'

Malcolm explained what was going to happen. 'You will stay with a man called Sandy MacClellan. He is a friend of my father and is often over in Ullapool. The house is along the front and looks onto Goat Island and the bay over there.' He pointed to the eastern peninsula.

He looked along to the houses that viewed the sea and then with the rest of group followed Malcolm. They walked for ten minutes until they stood in front of one of the houses almost at the end of the row and at the edge of the town. 'This place is well chosen,' he said to Malcolm as he looked out over the bay.

Malcolm grinned. 'I thought you would like it. I stay here with Sandy often. I find it a good place to let my mind open and my thoughts unravel.'

'It looks perfect,' Helen agreed.

'There isn't enough room for everyone, as in Ullapool, so I'll stay with other friends,' Malcolm said.

For David, the setting of the house had everything needed for him to relax and work. Language was a barrier, but that could be overcome.

Something came to mind, and he said, 'Have you come across an English poet called Auden?'

Malcolm shook his head.

'You will, I'm sure; he says that an artist must live either where he has growing roots, or where he has no roots at all.'

Malcolm raised his eyebrows and waited for him to explain.

'I always thought I needed to be at home in my village to be able to work. Like you here, where you have living roots. Then I went to London, as here, where I have none.'

'We must be equal then,' Malcolm said.

'Full history and no history: an interesting dichotomy, isn't it?'

After their arrival in Stornoway that morning, he spent time alone, walked into the town and then wove a route back to the house. At other harbours at North Beach and at the Cromwell Street quays, work continued into the afternoon and he imagined the activity that must have been the scene earlier in the morning to unload the herring and the women on the piers and the gutting stations nearby. Crates and creels stacked high and nets ready for the next sailing adorned the quays.

He settled into the final phase of their visit to Scotland. There would be concerts in the Summer Mod - the festival of Gaelic song, art and culture - and the concerto to finish. He had plenty to do and all looked set for an eventful few weeks.

Chapter 19
(Day 9 and 10 - May 1992: Skye and Lewis, Scotland)

SHE AWAKENED on the Isle of Skye. Gulls' cries and the sounds of boats and the sea replaced the cooing of doves at home in Maklam. She got up and, in the green light of dawn, peered through the window to the harbour and stony beach. A tint of phytoplankton and the refracted hue of oily wrack hung in the water at the shoreline.

She dressed, went out and followed the cobbles to the harbour and into the view from the window. A woman with a basket, a fisherman at the quay and one or two others observed a Carthusian silence. They gave just a nod and a smile as they passed. Even their movement was subdued, as if in awe of the new day. On the shoreline she looked to where sky and water fused. It was all part of the music. *This was better.*

Over the surfaces of the rocks she placed careful steps. When she looked up it was into eyes that watched her, of a seal only metres from the shore, with just its head out of the water. It bobbed and disappeared again. Down on her haunches, she waited. Then it came towards her, ripples on the surface until its head popped out again to inspect her and sniff the air. She laughed at its cheekiness and stared back. 'Hello.' She waited until it bobbed under again and disappeared.

After breakfast, as grey clouds can carry away the promise of a sunny day, she had lost the confidence of that early start, but although the power of the associations had gone, it did not matter; when her thoughts hardened, she hoped she would still remember. She did remember Jodi and hoped she had enjoyed her first night in Broadford.

The ferry from Uig to Lewis would depart at twelve fifteen. She set off at nine and drove through the open fells along the narrow roads. It was lucky she did. With no time to spare, five minutes before departure, she arrived in Uig and sat with the roof down, warmed by the sun and cooled by the breeze.

The photographs were on the seat beside her. She looked at one of David, with his arm around the dark woman. What was it they were saying to each other and who was she?

She looked around and, rather than solid structures, saw frailty and decay: the skeletons of things. It made her laugh - the frenetic struggle for life. Blue and black fishing boats lined the quay; her vision went beyond them and she pictured rotted, rusted hulks washed ashore. A fatalistic pessimism saw through the new paint and efforts to survive.

To distract herself she pressed in a cassette of songs that she remembered from the time they were recorded and knew they had been written during David's time in Scotland. Yes, the name of the writer was Malcolm Ross. One song, called Western Lochs, she listened to over and over again.

On a calm sea, the crossing to Tarbert - situated on the narrow isthmus between Harris and Lewis - took two hours. In the sheltered bow, the sun compensated for the cool breeze that brushed her face. Around the boat, the air and sea abounded with birds: Guillemots, in the water someone told her, and Shearwaters as well as seagulls that followed in the wake. She found a log of her journey easier to write than her earlier attempts at reminiscences. It's magical, she wrote. The sea has never smelt as good; so fresh and I don't even mind the whiff of diesel oil - rather heavy at times on this boat, but otherwise just superb. Clear bright skies and cold sea spray. Now the hills of Harris ahead.

Back on land, as she progressed to Stornaway, she felt a flare of empathy with the island. The warmth of small hope, that kept her going when she had departed from the village, now blossomed around her. Lewis made her feel at once a long way from home and yet close to something from David's music. Part of a picture she had constructed in her imagination materialised before her. Skye had presented a ruggedness; from the ferry she had seen peaks to the south on Harris and now Lewis opened as expanses of lower fells.

Through the tourist board, Anna had found a guest house in Stornoway - capital of the Western Isles - at the eastern side of the island. Curving around the town, the road from Tarbert entered from the north. With the harbour on her right, eventually she found herself in Cromwell Street, and then, following the road round, came to the front of the bay where larger boats were tied at two wharves. She stopped to ask the way to James Street and two minutes later parked next to a guest house built from red stone with bay windows either side of the front door. It felt good. The name on the brass plate above the doorbell was MacCrimmon. She pressed the bell.

A woman answered and took an instant interest. 'Women don't often come to stay alone,' she said.

She reminded her of a nurse and said her name was Rachel. 'No, I don't expect they do,' she agreed, and returned the woman's smile.

'You've driven all the way from London, you say.' She was in no hurry to complete the registration details.

'Yes, well, Kent to be precise, which is an hour further on.' She listened to the accent.

'You must be keen to see the Western Isles.'

She remembered the photographs and the concert programmes that they had found. 'My husband came here a long time ago. I'm following his trail.'

'Well, you're most welcome,' and Rachel handed her a piece of paper to sign. 'Just let me know if you need anything else.'

She hesitated, then said, 'I wondered whether I would be able to find anyone who might remember. He wrote music here and held some concerts in Stornoway.'

Rachel gave an enquiring look.

'It was a long time ago, I know,' she said, 'but you never know, someone might remember him. He was a composer.'

'They might,' Rachel agreed. 'When did he come here?'

She hesitated again. 'In 1939...'

If Rachel was bemused, she did not show it. 'Hmm,' she said, 'that was before my time, right enough. I really don't know. A composer, you say?'

'Yes,' she nodded. 'I'll ask around. It is such a long time ago.'

Rachel showed her to her room and left her to settle in. She telephoned Anna and told her about her day. 'I'm not sure what I'm meant to think about Lewis; it's such a contrast to Skye.'

Anna made encouraging noises at the other end of the line.

'The crossing was lovely, the boat and everything. Just as I imagined; I love it. I was almost crying at one point - with a sense of joy. I got all hot and bothered. We passed some islands called the Shiants.'

'You could be telephoning from Australia,' Anna said. 'I can't imagine the places you describe.'

'Skye was so lovely in the morning. I walked along the beach. It was peaceful and I saw a seal. I understand Harris is attractive. The hills looked dark and foreboding from the ferry. I may go tomorrow. And it's been raining a little today. The guest house is perfect,' she said, and finished her call, settling again into the excitement of being in Lewis.

Drizzle, which had started earlier, continued as she looked from the window. What should she do? Maybe go for a walk if the rain stopped later. Downstairs again, she looked around the sitting room, hoping to find some information about the town. Rachel came in behind her. 'I asked my mother if she remembered anything about a composer, and she says she does. She's in the back room, if you want to go to ask her.'

She followed her through and met Rachel's mother, Alice, who, with a blanket over her knee, sat on the couch reading a book. She greeted her with an expectant expression on her face.

'I'll put the kettle on,' Rachel said.

She told Alice about her visit to Scotland and, while Rachel bought them a cup of tea, Alice listened politely. Then Alice talked to her about Stornoway and described what she remembered of 1939, laughing quietly to herself when she remembered that time in her life. 'I was no more than a girl and we danced to gramophone records in a hall near the harbour,' her eyes lighting up while she cast her memory back. 'All that American music,' she said, and, in a quiet voice, she started to sing: '*Somewhere over the rainbow,*' and chuckled to herself. 'That was Judy Garland. Then there was Glen Miller's *Moonlight Serenade* and Louis Armstrong's *When the Saints Go Marching In.*' She hummed a little of that tune and then stopped and continued in her memories of the past.

'My husband came here then and was involved with some concerts.'

Alice nodded. 'We had so much music and there were concerts, yes; they filled the hall I was telling you about. Everyone in town knew about them and they were the talk of the island, I remember. There is someone you could talk to. He lives not far from here, called Alex, the same as you,' and she told her about him and where to find him.

AFTER HER evening meal in the guest house, despite continued squally showers, she decided to venture out. Why not walk, even though it was raining. As she walked into town, with streaks of evening sun breaking through the cloud and a rainbow curving into the trees near the castle, memories of the dawn accompanied her.

Without intent, she wandered along the front away from the town and then made her way in the direction that Alice had indicated to her. Ten minutes later she came out behind the hydro-station and stood between the barrels of two large naval guns mounted either side of a bench with a plaque to commemorate the naval training base that once had been situated there. Then, now that the rain had stopped, she retraced her steps and examined the houses around her until she found the number that Alice had given her.

She waited. Should she knock? Instead, she walked a little further along the road. A man, older than her with silver hair and beard, a stick in one hand and a pipe in the other approached ahead of her. 'Good evening,' she said as he passed.

He slowed and kept his eye on her. 'Can I help you, Madam? You'll no be from these parts, I think.'

'No, you're right there.' She laughed. 'I was just admiring the houses.'

'Thank you. Once, a long time ago, before they built the row opposite and the power station that spoilt it, we had a good view.'

She raised her eyebrows. 'Do you live here?'

'I do and have done man and boy for nigh on eighty years, at twenty two across the way.' His voice had Rachel's intonation. She guessed he was a Gaelic speaker as well.

Number twenty two. Was this her namesake, Alex? 'Oh, really,' she replied, and looked out towards the sea between the houses and let her thoughts wander with her eyes. The man caught the questioning nature of her silence.

'Is something worrying you?' he asked. 'The name's Sandy, by the way?'

Sandy. Ah, yes, Alex. 'Oh, no, nothing in particular,' she said, her mind still distracted. 'No, not really.'

'You could have fooled me.'

'No, I'm sorry; I'm Alex.'

'Alex?' He chuckled.

'No, I was just thinking, my husband visited here many years ago. I'm following his trail, but it's so long ago.'

'The place probably hasn't changed very much, except for along this street,' Sandy observed.

'Yes, I'm sure. I was more interested in what he did here.'

'Sounds a bit of a riddle to me.'

'Hmm, he was a composer; came before the war. He never told me anything about his visit, but he wrote some music here. I still play it now.'

Sandy raised his jaw and looked at her. He squinted, as though he was looking back in time. 'What is his name, if I might ask?'

'Whellans; David Whellans. He died a few weeks ago.'

Sandy lowered his head. 'Ah, I'm sorry to hear that,' and now he looked out past the houses to the headland, as if he pondered something also. He took a step to her side and continued to look into the distance.

She did not speak and Sandy brought his gaze round to her again. 'It's funny that you should be standing here talking to me, because I remember a young man who stayed with me in the house across the way a long time ago who was called David Whellans. It was 1939 sure enough. We have all got to know him since then from his music of course. He was not here for long, a week or so, but I do remember him and his friends from the time they stayed with me.'

She frowned. 'Really? He stayed with you?'

'Yes, he did, but afterwards, I never had direct contact with him. He never came back. But others have…'

She looked at him and tried to grasp the significance of what he said. 'Well, firstly, I must say that I can't believe my luck to meet you, and secondly, that I am sorry that he didn't come back. That is why I have come; to find out why.'

He returned her gaze and seemed to ask the questions about her that she asked about him. While they unravelled the past, neither seemed to mind the other's silence. Sandy broke it. 'Yes, I remember the time well. We made a fine catch of trout, as I recall, but don't raise your hopes too high, because I doubt if there's much I can tell you. It's been a long time.' He turned towards his house. 'Come in anyway, I'll make some tea. Would you like a cup?'

'Hm, of course, thank you,' and now she admitted to him that Alice from the guest house had recommended that he might be able to help. 'What a coincidence to meet you along the road.'

While Sandy made her a cup of tea, she sat at a large kitchen table that looked as if it had been sanded and re-waxed. He talked to her as he did so. 'I remember the visit; we had some heated discussions; not David, but the others, about politics and the like. I remember David though, in particular, for one thing: his ideas about what I think they now call folk memory. He believed that we brought knowledge and music with us when we were born, that we have a sense of the past. That is what he liked about the local poetry and songs.'

A look of surprise came into her eyes. 'He talked about that did he?'

'Yes, the idea fascinated him.'

'Really? I'm amazed that he discussed that with you. He talked to me about that as well.' She looked around her at the kitchen. 'Did he like it here in Lewis?'

'Oh, I think you can be sure of that. It struck me as peculiar in fact. He talked a lot about it, said he felt in resonance with the place. It seemed odd, because he had never been anywhere near Lewis before.'

She smiled and nodded. 'He's very rooted in Kent I think; by resonance, he probably meant contrast. So you say he stayed in this house with you?'

'Indeed he did.' The words rolled off Sandy's tongue. 'In the room at the front on the left. Would you like to look? Go up if you feel you would.'

She hesitated.

'Go on, feel free.'

She went from the kitchen through the door he indicated and up the stairs to the front of the house. The room was large with little furnishing. She walked to the window and looked across the street to the sea - obscured now by houses and the power station.

So David was here, in this very house just before the war and just before she had gone to India. Her mind flashed to those times, still unable to rest long on the events that so disturbed her memories of those years.

In the few moments, she tried to fix the feel of the room in her mind, then descended again to the kitchen where Sandy sat at the table ready to pour the tea. 'It's lovely.'

'I didn't hear much after they left. I went into the navy and after the war travelled most of Africa for twenty years doing fisheries development.'

'That sounds interesting.'

'Aye, it was sure enough. Then I retired back to my own home and have rested here ever since.'

She warmed to Sandy. 'What of the others?'

Sandy puckered his lips and furrowed his brow as he recalled. 'There was Cameron, a tenor with a fine voice, from St Andrew's; a fine man. Then the two lassies - a bonnie pair they made - writing their reports and the like for the newspapers. They were in the room at the back and Cameron in the attic. They seemed to get on well together, the group of them.'

'What were they like?'

'Who, the lassies? Oh, both career types if I remember. Reporters. Fine lassies, one with fierce red hair.'

'Red hair?' She took out her photographs and gave one to Sandy.

'Aye, that's them.' He went through each by name and told her what he knew about them. 'That's Helen and that's Nonie, the red haired one.'

She looked at the black and white photograph. 'Ah, so that's red.'

Sandy nodded.

She smiled. *Red hair.* 'What happened to them after the war?'

'I couldn't tell you. I went overseas in forty-six to Malawi - Nyasaland as it was then - and I never heard of them again. I heard

David's music of course on the radio and it often reminds me. It was a long time ago.'

She and Sandy chatted on and he provided more fragments of information and told her about the concerts that were held there. He told her also that, when she went over the next day, she should visit Malcolm Ross in Ullapool. He tried to telephone him for her, but there was no reply. She listened to his reminiscences and, until she felt it appropriate to go, enjoyed his soft-spoken words. She said goodbye and, walking back towards the harbour, could see the red and black funnel of the ferry that had just arrived.

THE NEXT day, at Callanish, to the west of Stornoway on Loch Roag, with the water beneath her and the group of standing stones behind, she stood on a promontory that reached out into the loch. There was nothing remarkable about the journey, and except for the stone circle, Callanish offered little to differentiate it from the fells that surrounded it. The circle was smaller than she had expected.

As other people approached, her concentration was broken. It was a man and a woman that she recognised from the guest house. 'Hello,' she said as they approached. 'Isn't this beautiful?'

'Sure is,' the woman said. She had an American accent that she found appealing. '*Celtic or pre-Celtic* the guidebook says. *1,500-2,000 BC.* Say, didn't we see you in the hotel this morning?'

She nodded and feigned surprise: 'Oh yes, I think I caught sight of you after breakfast. I'm Alex.'

'Pleased to meet you; I'm Tracey and that's Len my husband over there.'

They stood together and looked over at the stones. 'Did you see the *black houses* on the way?' the woman asked and, putting her camera to her eye, searched for suitable images.

'Yes, those with the roofs held down by nets and stones you mean? I didn't know they were called *black houses* though.'

'Hmm, *little dry stone and turf bothys*, the guidebook calls them. They look so awful to live in.'

She nodded.

Tracey twirled round and let her gaze sweep the landscape, then she giggled and gave a small shrug. 'Anyway, we must be on our way.'

She nodded and, as they parted, walked back past the megaliths. Along the road there were two other groups of stones that she had missed when she first drove by and now she returned to them. The first group of five stones left her mystified as to their meaning, but the next of twelve had more attraction. There was a circle of eight stones, with four stones inside the circle. The leaflet she had found in the guest house said that three of the inner stones represented the Celtic perception of the triple goddess; the white stone for the maiden, the redder one for the mother and the darker one for the old woman. *Mothers of mothers of girls that become mothers*: the idea intrigued her. She was alone and for five minutes stood amongst the stones. *Anna, me and my mother*.

Women held the secrets: the mothers of mothers of girls that became mothers, with concentrated knowledge in their genes. Girls stay with their mothers and most turn out good; boys are cast out to the male group and it's often touch and go with them; some fair better than others. 'I tried hard with Jonathan, but nothing seemed to work,' she said to herself. Boys that keep good contact with their mothers seem more stable. David was like that. Why do women want to be like men; men have nothing to offer women. She stared into the distance behind the stones.

Sandy had told her of the time that he had visited Callanish with David. He was there as well. *What had he been doing when he was there?* She continued her musing as she drove on.

Twice again during the drive through the island, the Americans crossed her path. After the narrow isthmus at Tarbert in Harris she continued further to Rodel where she found them in the car park when she pulled in. She admired the view together with them. 'Let us have dinner tonight,' Len said. 'Oh, I'm Len by the way.'

'Yes I know; your wife told me this morning. I'm Alex.'

'I missed having a cooked breakfast. It took us by surprise them not making one,' Len said. 'It was because it is Sunday.'

She smiled. 'Yes, Sunday. That would be very nice. About seven thirty?'

THE NEED to explain had begun to irritate her and made her wary of the questions so that she parried with bland reasons for her tour. That evening it was difficult to keep up the pretence and her resolve broke down. 'I have a sort of quest and ulterior motive for being here. I hardly know why myself...'

'Sounds intriguing; tell us more.' Tracy probed her defences.

She paused. *What should she say?* 'Well, I am searching for hills. I have just had the urge to go to the hills and so it has brought me here. Well, partly that anyway. It's strange, I know.'

'Hm, well, there are plenty of hills here,' Tracey said.

'Yes, there are so many things. My husband, who died a few weeks ago, was a composer and some of his early work was written in Scotland. At that time I didn't really knew much about his work and so this tour is to try to put the situation right and to find out why he never wanted to come back.' *And then there are the hills...*

Len looked over his spectacles at her. 'I'm sorry to hear that. Did he compose here on the Isle of Lewis?'

She hesitated again.

What did she know to tell? 'I wish I knew. He played in a concert here. All I am sure of is that once he came here. Part of a concerto was written in Lewis.'

Len made his words stretch twice the distance. 'When was that?'

'Oh, before the war; I think what I am doing is, laying ghosts. My husband always told me that was what he had been doing all his life, but he was reticent about Scotland. When he died I found I just had to come to find out for myself.'

Tracey lent over the table and put her hand on her arm: 'I think that is so touching; did he record any of his music?'

The question took her by surprise. 'Yes, of course, but you've probably not heard of him.' Having to explain heightened the loss. 'He's quite well known over here; his name is David Whellans.'

'David Whellans?' Len's vowels rolled across the table. 'Why didn't you say. Not heard of him? Of course we know of him. We have some music by him in the car. Had to when we were coming here to Lewis. We have Mendelssohn's as well, you know, *The Hebrides*, and his Scottish symphonies; bought them in a shop in Skye.'

She gave a puzzled smile. 'Oh, really, yes,' and again she was surprised at the recognition and reeled a little. 'I'm never sure these days whether people listen to classical music.'

'He is sure well known in the States. Not as well as your Queen, but getting there.'

'I'm sorry, though.' Tracey leaned nearer. 'We hadn't heard that he had died. You must be devastated.'

For the next hour the momentum of the revelation of David's name carried the conversation forward.

Despite the thoughts and experience of the day, as they talked she felt a sickness that collapsed the weeks around her. There in the dining room with her new acquaintances, the thoughts exposed her loneliness. Meeting Sandy MacClellan and being so near to something and yet so far from it, did not help.

DURING THE night she woke with a start from a dream of her grandmother, of the image she always had of her now, the serene woman with straight ash grey hair that visited the village for the last time before she went away to London. The image fused with the other images of her day, of Callanish and images that welled from lower levels of her consciousness.

Inert in the strange dark room, as though the memories were hallucinations that flared behind her eyelids, she searched for their meaning. Turning on the light, she got out of bed and, from the open window, looked into the dark town. How strange. Then she thought of Anna and muttered to herself, 'I wish you were here, my dear.'

As the sounds of the night from the still air played in her ear, she remembered Jodi. 'How are you settling in?' she whispered, and remembered what she had said about her attachment to her home town. 'Not too homesick, I hope.'

Her thoughts swirled around her. Tomorrow she would go to Ullapool and then to Nairn.

Chapter 20
(August 1939: Lewis/Ullapool/London)

SANDY MACCLELLAN'S kitchen in the house on Seaview Terrace had an oak table that acted as the surface for all culinary activities. In the evening, after the table was laid for supper, those not cooking sat around it. Beer and whisky were on the house and while Gavin Brink attacked the malt with Sandy, Douglas Cameron was into his second beer with Malcolm.

'Glad to see you're keeping up Helen,' Douglas said, and topped-up her glass from his third bottle. 'Here you are Nonie my love, a drop more to keep you with me.'

For days, the discussion had been about things, western Scottish. 'It's all about language,' said Malcolm. 'The people in the west have a tradition of independence based on their purer roots. Those in the east are such a mix and have been so politicised by the English. The basis of independence is language.'

David looked up. 'Politicised? Why by the English?'

'Well, who else?' Douglas interjected.

Remembering Douglas in his London days, he wondered how the conversation would go. 'Well, the Scots themselves for one thing,' he responded, to which Douglas scoffed and Helen smiled.

While he grilled fresh mackerel, Sandy kept an ear to the talk, and said, 'The history of these islands has been one of friction and short-lived victories for forces that ravaged their neighbours for control.'

He listened to the intonation in Sandy's voice.

'If you are asking me, it has been about egos, influence and charisma,' Sandy continued. 'Mind you, that's what all politics is about.'

Supper intervened and everyone sat around the table. With steaming vegetables, Sandy served mackerel. The discussion turned to present-day politics and then to Malcolm's plans for the week. He told everybody again about Callanish and encouraged the group to accompany him on a visit.

Malcolm brought the discussion full circle. 'I like the idea that we have knowledge of the past within us.'

Sandy looked interested. 'What do you mean by that?'

'We were talking about it earlier,' Malcolm said.

'I'll give an example,' David added. 'People respect poets like Malcolm. I think it's because they know that poets bring something to us that is deeper than the present.'

'People's shared ideas you mean?' Sandy asked, pouring another whisky.

He shook his head. 'No, not quite that; I think that is different. Poets are a good medium for patterns of times past to come through to us today, because poets listen to their minds and produce a summary of what it says to them. They have a sense of the past. They write their response as a poem and report it to people now.'

Still in his striped apron, with a fish-slice in one hand and a glass in the other, Sandy stood up: 'That sounds reasonable, if it works in that way. More mackerel, anyone?'

He continued. 'Here in Lewis there are families with ancestries that go back undisturbed into history. What their minds could tell us, if we listened, might be very informative. When Malcolm listens to his mind and writes a poem, something raw comes down from the past. The clearer he can listen, the more raw it is. That is why Malcolm's poems have an impact.'

Looking at Helen, he tried to explain further. 'Remember when we talked on the train going back last time, Helen, about patterns and the music of particular people? Poets tap into patterns which they find in their own minds. They might not know what they are or what they mean, but they just respond and write.'

She thought back. 'Yes. *You have to listen to what your mind tells you without words,*' she said, and précised his description.

'Precisely. You say you like towns such as Edinburgh and London. Why? If you listen to your mind, you can learn a little about why you like them. Some people say you should listen to your heart. It's the same. It's what your mind tells you without words.'

'I'd never thought about it that way,' said Sandy.

'The mind throws out messages all the time; pictures, ideas, likes and dislikes, patterns of emotional response that tell us something about ourselves. We might think they are 'thoughts', and not recognise them as something more significant from the past. I think it's in our genes, like Darwin's finches, part of the process of evolution.'

Resting her chin on her hands with her elbows on the table, Helen said, 'And you think the patterns shape the way we develop and grow?'

'They must do - by the responses that people make to the world around them.'

Helen rolled her head on her hands. 'What do you listen to, if it's not words?'

'The emotional responses to things; how you feel. Then you put that into words. That is why I feel at home in my village in Kent, because I feel a response to all that goes on there. Where the emotional response comes from is the question.'

Gavin was not convinced. 'Seems a bit farfetched to me,' he said, and slurred his words. 'Sounds more like meditation.' He took another gulp from his glass.

'Well, I'll give you another example.' He turned to Nonie who had moved away from the table and sat in the only other chair in the kitchen, a large armchair. 'Nonie wants to be a journalist. Why?'

She looked up from her book: 'You talking about me?'

'Yes. Why do you want to become a journalist?'

'I like the idea,' she said, and burrowed deeper into the chair.

'Do you see what I mean? No reason, she just likes the idea. Where did the idea come from? Something must make us respond to some ideas and reject others. Why does one person accept the very ideas that another rejects?'

'I've always enjoyed writing,' she said.

'Yes. If there is some information locked in your memory, from your ancestors, who may also have been good writers or reporters and gatherers of information that might come through into your desire now to be a journalist.' He finished, drained his glass and stood up and waited for a response. When no one continued, he went over to help Sandy who was busy clearing up.

'You've talked yourself out, then?'

'Yes, I think so,' his voice now subdued, and while the rest chatted on, he said, 'I think we have done enough for one night. Douglas will no doubt want to keep going until the morning.'

When Malcolm and Ounagh said it was time for them to go, the discussion was still intense and the feelings running high.

'There's malt in the bottle enough for another each,' Douglas jeered, as Malcolm opened the door.

'Save it for tomorrow,' Malcolm said. 'We'll see you all bright and early.' They waved goodnight and closed the door behind them.

IN STORNOWAY, as part of the summer Mod, two concerts were performed. An early following was gathered and people responded to Malcolm's penchant for publicity and leadership in the community. Douglas played and sang, but their presence was not so much the focus as a part of a wider activity. The concerts became free-for-alls. It was what Malcolm had said when he spread the word: the bringing together of poets and musicians. The first was on Monday and the second on Thursday.

Between the concerts, for two days, while he drew together what strands he could from Ullapool and now Lewis, he left the rest of the group. The stream of inspiration that had been running in flood in Ullapool still ran in Lewis, and might see the concerto finished sooner than he thought. In order to finish other compositions and to give the first performances on the soils that inspired them, it began to look certain that he would have to return later in the year.

It was planned that Malcolm would take them to Callanish on the inlet where the standing stones mark the landscape in defiance of the passage of time. He had talked about the place for days. 'It's a pre-historic time clock, an astronomical observatory. The site dates from 1,800 BC. If you look along the stones over the great menhir you see the pole star in their line. Then there are four other stones that give an alignment with due west and indicate sunset at the equinoxes. Some authorities think certain stones point to the Pleiades or other constellations. It tracks the cycles of the moon: quite remarkable.'

'So we'll have to go at night, shall we?' said Gavin.

'We could, if anybody's a mind to. I've done it myself.'

'That might be a good idea,' David said. 'Why don't we do that?'

'Agreed, then,' Douglas said. 'What about tomorrow night?'

Malcolm finalised the decision.

'There is a good moon at the moment, and so it would be possible. You can see well on a cloudless night,' Malcolm said.

So it was, that late on Friday evening they arrived at Callanish. From a distance the group of stones rose as a surreal forest against the sky beside Loch Roag. The central menhir, a pillar about fifteen feet high dominated the ring. Two lines of stones led off to the north. Malcolm was correct and the moon provided light to see everything with unusual clarity.

'So who built it and what did they use it for?' Helen asked, when they had walked around the stones for half an hour or more in the silver light, to anyone who might answer.

Douglas replied. 'No-one is sure; must have been some sort of religious centre. It shows the directions of certain stars and points of the meridians and can be used to indicate the eighteen-year cycle of the moon, apparently.'

'Was it used as a calendar?'

Now Malcolm answered. 'Probably not: if it was, it cannot have been very accurate. The stones today cannot tell you the exact day of the summer solstice for example. They are too crude and too near together to give an accurate line.'

From the shadows behind Malcolm, Gavin asked: 'So what was the point of them then?'

'Maybe as a sign of religious authority and to mark annual cycles. Until recent times, some families here on Lewis have been held in esteem as, belonging to the stones. No one knows why. Local people congregated at the stones on May Day and mid-summer morning.'

'I wonder how they worked out the astronomy, four thousand years ago?' said Douglas. 'Must have been geniuses.'

'They knew an awful lot,' Malcolm replied. 'Probably taught the Egyptians a thing or two, as well.'

'Really?' Surveying the night sky, listening to the calls of the gulls in the dark, he stood back and wondered about time. The moon: he remembered what Paul had said years ago. Rhythms of the moon, and here they were in the moonlight at an ancient moon clock. How did this fit into the patterns. How far back could he go?

The stones were not as he had imagined, not as his classical idea of the impressive and foreboding circle at Stonehenge. Nothing like that at all, more in the shape of a Celtic Cross with a small central arc, then with arms to the east and west. It was difficult when you were among them to discern the shape. The stones were uncut and retained irregular shapes. All were different and stood like people at prayer. Two lines of stones ran in a corridor to the north. It was much smaller than Malcolm's description had led him to imagine. He stared into the central altar and tried to imagine the past.

Douglas came up and gazed in the same direction - into the midst of the stones. 'Inspirational, isn't it?'

He nodded an agreement. 'If only we had a better grasp of the past. It's hard to imagine the people who once lived here. Who were the leaders and thinkers behind this?'

'I imagine they were very similar to us,' Douglas said. 'Don't you think? The area was much more fertile in the past.'

Surveying the mysterious circle of stones, he said, 'I wonder what those who, *belong to the stones* remember in the patterns that they have inherited.'

Douglas squinted into the moon. 'I've no idea, but it's good to know that educated people did exist here and that the west is littered with monuments to them.'

What he wrote in Lewis were reactions. He absorbed the energies and could hear music in his mind, an ocean-swell of vibration, drone and polytone that flowed from the wind and echoed on. Flat time of the past picked out on the breeze. A drone, like a car you watch drive towards you that passes and continues until it disappears from sight. Even the people on Lewis had forgotten the reason for the stone's presence.

Or had they? How much was trapped in their knowledge and minds? Did any of Malcolm's poems signal these roots?

He sketched as many of the themes as he could before distraction blurred them. On the evening at Callanish, he wrote with fluency. Something in the pattern vernacular was different from that of Ullapool. Here he tried to catch what seemed to pull away from him. The eddies were strong as an aversion is strong.

AFTER THE visit to Callanish, news came that within a month or six-weeks it seemed inevitable Britain would go to war. Pressure was building on Poland: *War Clouds over Europe*, the Saturday Daily Express headline read in Stornoway. Still no-one really believed it.

A telegram left a few days later at the post-office was for Helen from her editor in London. She was needed and was requested to return the next day. Britain's Auxiliary Fleet had been mobilised in Weymouth and they wanted her to go to report on the event. Her time sojourning in Scotland had come to an abrupt end.

The news was as he had expected, but still came as an irritation. His work had just begun. How would the concerto be finished now? Because of the forces that began to control his life, unease settled in him. Could he stay and let Helen return by herself. No, that would never do.

On the morning of their departure, he looked from the window of his room in Sandy's house across to the waves smattered with white crests. Even when it rained the sky was bright. A breeze drove the squall and clouds raced in to a day of silver and white. He put his pencil in his pocket, rested his hands on the window ledge and stared out. He would return, he had no doubt of it.

His impressions were coloured by shades of the real and the unreal. What he saw in the rain was real, and this was a place of real seclusion that he longed for. Yet his presence in it was artificial. He was not part of the peace of this place and it felt as if he were in a side street, a two-week space that he had filled with an out-flow of imagination. Now they must leave, the visit curtailed by events elsewhere. *Damn them.* He picked up his holdall.

Sun broke through the clouds and the quay warmed. The concerto's third movement, as it was then formed, eddied across his thoughts. That was real. He felt as if he carried a burden that no-one recognised or even knew about. How could they; all his music was in his mind.

Now distractions returned, and with them the responsibilities to the real world. He adjusted to departure and to the demands of his friends. Maybe he could snatch another day in Ullapool. That now seemed uncertain and he relied on Helen to arrange activities as the tour fragmented.

They crossed back to the mainland and stayed in Ullapool another night. Douglas, Nonie and Gavin departed the next morning for Inverness. The harbour master had come to their aid again. Then they were gone.

'Farewell friend,' Douglas said. 'It was a good road that you set us along; until we meet again.'

Helen and he remained until mid-day when they took the bus to Fort William. The opportunity to return by the western route was one they could not miss. Gavin had recommended it.

What had he achieved? The sonata was completed and performed. The first two parts of the concerto were complete and, if he could get down to it in London, the third part would not take long. A whole string of Malcolm's poems were set to music and many others from Douglas. Some of his own songs were included.

They had been productive weeks.

Scotland: Helen Strachan's vision had turned out to be inspirational. The combination of the two of them and the group of friends had worked well, with so much achieved: whole compositions, strings of songs and great performances that entered the hearts of people. And all accomplished so easily. What more could he want? He had tapped into folk memories of people's minds, through the rhythms of their voices and language, their words and poetry, the melodies of their music, and drawn his own creative thread from them; found harmony with the people and places he had visited.

Now he should go home, back to Maklam, and begin to work there again, stronger and more resolute from his time in Scotland. Could he do that now? Yes, he could, and yes, he would.

In Fort William, they caught the train to London.

Chapter 21
(Days 11, 12 and 13 - May 1992: Lewis, Ullapool and Nairn, Scotland)

RAIN CAME in squalls as she stopped and looked back toward the guest house in Stornoway, then drove down to the ferry point. The drenching gusts kept drivers in their cars on the esplanade. She shivered and kept the engine going to keep warm.

Nairn on the east coast was the day's destination, but first, at the end of the crossing, Ullapool awaited her. The ferry docked at 11.15, and fishing, what was left of the industry, spoke to her from the quays, where crab pots lay stacked and stub nose trawlers bobbed on their ties. The day warmed and the first real sun she had felt since Loch Lomond burned through the shoulders of her fleece. As the ferry tied up she shaded her eyes.

Now that she had crossed from Lewis she turned to let her gaze linger on the grey waters. What she had come to Scotland to do was almost done. Some of it no doubt was lost to her and gone forever.

Beside the harbour she parked her car and followed the old man Sandy's directions to find the Ross's cottage. It did not take long for her to come upon the house in a street behind Shore Street that circled the town on the loch's edge. A woman opened the door and she asked for Malcolm. She was told he was away in Edinburgh, to read his poetry at the Poetry Library of Scotland. The woman looked kindly and smiled at her. 'But do come in anyway. You must be Alex. Sandy telephoned last night and told me he had met you.'

With Malcolm not being there, as she crossed the threshold she felt unsure about her visit.

'I'm Ounagh,' the woman said, 'Malcolm's wife. Sandy told me about you.'

She smiled and acknowledged her and guessed her hair must once have been Nordic fair. Then, while Ounagh boiled the kettle and offered her tea or coffee, she recounted how she met David.

'I have only faint recollections. I've heard David's name over the years, but then Malcolm has many friends.'

A number of books were laid on the coffee table where they sat. 'I found these to show you.' Ounagh pointed to them. *Poems and Songs of Malcolm Ross*, she read on the front of one. Underneath it said, Musical arrangements by David Whellans. The others were later anthologies.

She smiled. 'What about the rest of the group?'

Ounagh cast her mind back: 'There was Helen, David's friend, and Douglas and Nonie.'

She waited, and so Ounagh continued.

'Douglas sang; he sang Malcolm's songs beautifully. I heard him when they were here. He had a wonderful voice. I didn't have much to do with them, or Helen.' She sounded apologetic. 'Helen worked with a man called Gavin. He took photographs on the crossing to Lewis and made us all laugh. In fact, that is one of my clearest memories of them all, on the trip over to Lewis from here in Ullapool, with Gavin playing the fool and taking snaps of us.'

Nodding, she opened her handbag and took out a photograph. 'Do you remember this one?'

Ounagh gave a high pitched giggle. 'Oh, I only saw some of the photographs he took. Yes. It's strange to see this one now after all these years. Look at me.'

'This is one my daughter found amongst David's things.'

Ounagh nodded. 'They had to leave sooner than expected I remember and there was some argument about whether David could stay for a few more weeks. He did want to stay longer, but Helen was against it. The war and her work forced her back to London.'

'Why did he want to stay?'

'His writing I think. He was getting on well and Malcolm was working on a long poem which he finished later. It was called, *Ancestors*, which David had asked him to write. It's in one of those books.'

She nodded. 'And what was Helen like?'

Ounagh delved into her memory. 'She seemed to be in charge. She wrote to Malcolm. A little distant I felt, I must say.'

'Why was that?'

Ounagh looked apologetic again. 'I think she was very

ambitious.' Her voice had a singsong Scots accent. 'At that time I hadn't been out of Ullapool. I didn't understand high-falutin people like her.'

Ounagh told her everything she could remember and described Malcolm. And then, when it seemed polite to do so, she thanked her and said she needed to be on her way.

She said goodbye and Ounagh waved before she closed the door. The knowledge she had gained did not mean much, nor did it solve anything, but she had talked to people who remembered David. At least she had tried and followed her feelings. One more piece of the jigsaw puzzle had been added in.

The turn of the car south was like waking from a trance, the click of fingers that awoke her. The terrain was as wild as ever. Almost as far from Kent as she could be in Britain. In fact, her plan was to drive north and then east to Inverness, not to take the direct route. She wanted to divert to Lochinver on the coast, to the place named on the notes with the photographs. All it said was, *Today we came as far as we can, to Lochinver and looked west to Lewis.*

As she drove along, a single track gave her spectacular views of the mountains and lochs. From Lochinver she took the coastal road to the headland at Achmelvich with beaches below. She looked out across the Minch to the Butt of Lewis that she had left behind that morning and which now was a faint line on the Atlantic's margin. Her link with the music waxed and waned.

What had she found? Glimmers. This was her last chance. She wiped her eyes. There had been no great revelation, but she was a little wiser.

On the headland in front of the sea she began to weep. 'I've almost lost it forever,' she murmured through her sobs, 'and nothing is settled. I cannot go home.' The idea began to prey on her mind and for the first time she wept for David. 'I'm sorry,' she said. 'I want your blessing my love. I love you. You never gave me the chance to say goodbye. Now I've lost you and there are things I will never know.'

She called Anna. 'Anna, it's turning out to be so awful. I need you here to let me cry and you are too far away.'

'Come home, Mummy,' Anna said, then made one of those instant and free decisions. 'I'll come to meet you.' The words sounded distant in her ears. 'I'll leave now.'

'No, don't be silly,' she wailed.

'Yes, I'm coming. Where will you be next?'

'Nairn.'

'I'll meet you there. I feel I need to get away sometimes as well. Call me again later if you can, or I'll leave a message at the hotel.' Anna's voice disappeared.

She had not known how low her spirits could be until those moments. Her heart was low. How could she drive in that wretched state? She breathed in, slipped the gear lever and pulled back onto the crown of the highland road.

In less than an hour she had crossed half the distance from the west to east. The wind dried her eyes and her skin was cold. She stopped at a high point where no sign of human habitation could be seen between the horizons. She walked to dispel her emotion. Grief for the searching spirit brought tears again: grief for human strength belittled by death, the smiles and anger, frustration and elation that had been levelled.

Had any of this been worth it? What was her part in it now? She moaned to the rugged moorland, 'What is left?' The Dornoch Firth, where the road swung round towards Inverness, opened in front of her. She drove on and then through Inverness where she did not linger, just drove on and on. With a despondent heart she drew near to Nairn.

The town put on no airs. Neat houses after the sign gave the briefest of introductions; then into the High Street and a minute later Harbour Street and down to the quay next to the River Nairn where it entered the Firth. She drove around to the seaward side and parked with the expanse of the estuary before her and the town behind.

Had she missed something?

After the isles of the west there was no show, none of the bravura of some of the stops on her trail. Nairn seemed to apologise for its modesty. The majestic firth, its water unlike any other she had seen, was active with colour, blue and green, slate grey and abalone, flamingo and dun in the sun. She got out and walked to the end of the seawall. It seemed a step to the other side of the Firth where gorse on the steep hills cast yellow sparkles on the water. A man with binoculars pointed. 'Dolphins. Bottlenose. See them? Over there: here, use these.'

She took the binoculars and looked while she focused, found them with difficulty. 'Yes. One, two of them surfacing every few seconds.'

'Yes, maybe a few more; they're playing.' He looked like someone who would know.

'Isn't that thrilling,' and she smiled at the man. 'Thank you for showing them to me. I've never seen them like that before.'

'No, you wouldn't. Not many people have. They're only here around these coasts.'

She should get to the Golf View hotel. 'Thank you. I must be off.'

The leaflet with the name of the Golf View Hotel had fallen out of an envelope on the studio floor, one of the first worn and faded pieces of paper she had looked at, something normally to be thrown away without further thought. Now it had brought her there, to Nairn. She took it out of her bag and, while she sat beside the harbour, read through it again. *Festival Concert,* it said, *in the ballroom of the Golf View Hotel, Nairn, Friday 15 July, 1939.* More than fifty years ago.

On the edge of the Firth, where the houses stopped and the golf course started, she found the hotel. 'I've put you in a room that overlooks the river, Madam,' the receptionist said, and beamed, sticking out her chest in her neat suit. 'And there is a message from your daughter,' she said, and handed her a note.

'Oh, thank you.' The note was scribbled in the receptionist's handwriting. She read it: "Caught the train in Grantham; Max is fine, he understands. I'll be on the train to Edinburgh and will find somewhere to stay tonight. I'll be there tomorrow around mid-day. Early train to Nairn. You stay put and relax. Will call later."

She folded the note and put it in her purse then showed the receptionist the concert leaflet. 'I've come here to find my husband's past.'

'Oh,' The girl said, and looked impressed. 'Can I show this to the manager?'

Soon, she had quite a crowd around her.

'My goodness,' the manager said. 'David Whellans. I never

knew that some of his music came from here.'

'Yes,' she said. 'I don't know much about it either.'

A porter carried her bag to the stairs and they made a fuss of her. This was one place that David spent some time. Going down again, she stood at the ballroom window and looked across the Firth. Below her, people played on the tennis courts. The ricocheted noises of balls on rackets rose from the courts. A concert was performed in this room with Douglas Cameron. This was part of the unknown past.

She looked around, tried to imagine how it had been, looked at the leaflet again and imagined the concert goers and David playing. The Scottish music that had haunted her, the sonata, was rooted here. Now she knew. The obituaries mentioned it.

The receptionist came up and stood beside her and looked out of the window. 'Is it all a mystery to you?' she asked, a touch of intrigue in her voice.

'Yes, it is really. More than fifty years and yet the leaflets and photographs and being here make it seem as if it could have been yesterday.'

'Weird, isn't it,' the receptionist said. 'No-one knew he ever played here.'

'No, I know. Yes, it is uncanny. People don't usually do this sort of thing, do they?'

WHEN SHE saw Anna alight from the train the next morning, she edged her car forward and pulled up at the kerb. Anna ran and lent over and kissed her, then threw her bag behind the seat. 'Oh, Mummy, look at you, you've been crying.'

She drove to the Golf View Hotel, parked the car and pulled the hood up. Then they walked through Fishertown, through the rows of neat cottages and grey-stone houses. She chatted about the previous days. 'At first Lewis was moving, but then I lost it and on the second night I felt so desperate.'

Anna smiled and nodded as they arrived at the harbour. 'I don't see any fishing boats.' She surveyed the fleet of small yachts, thirty footers mainly that were tied in rows across the harbour. 'They are all pleasure craft. I've always wanted to go sailing. The whole idea is such a challenge.'

While she let her gaze wander around the harbour, she continued her account of the journey. 'In Lewis on the first evening, a coincidence occurred: I met someone who remembered your father. He owned the house they stayed in. I was looking at it and then he walked past.'

Anna linked her arm with her mother's. 'Hmm, that is a coincidence. What did he have to say?'

'He wasn't able to tell me much. It was too long ago and they were only there ten or so days. His name was Sandy.'

At the shop on the harbour, they bought some smoked salmon. 'No fishing here now then?' Anna asked the man.

'No, not for a long time. It stopped when they couldn't export to Russia any more in the Sixties. They tried trawling for prawns, but now they've all gone.'

They continued through the town and then along Seasalter Road on their way back to the Golf View Hotel.

'What else did Sandy have to say?'

'He put me in touch with someone else in Ullapool, a man called Malcolm Ross. I went to see him, but only his wife, Ounagh, was there. She was with your father when he was in Ullapool. It was nice to meet her, but she didn't remember much.' They passed Coulter House and she stopped to look at it and admired the grand bay windows on each side of the impressive front door. 'Isn't that a lovely house,' she said as they looked over.

'I like the stonework,' Anna replied, and smiled at her mother. 'All the houses around here are impressive.'

'I wonder where your father stayed when he was here?'

'Hm, I wonder…'

They walked on.

Anna seemed to feel pleased that she had made the journey. 'So you have managed to achieve some successes.'

She knew she was trying to be encouraging and remained silent. No-one understood. Not Anna, not anyone. 'Well, possibly a little, yes.'

Anna was still smiling. 'I'm really excited to be here. I know it is sad, now that Daddy has gone, but to be learning about parts of his life that we haven't known very much about, is, as you say, so moving.'

She nodded.

'Let's have a good day today and then get you back home tomorrow,' Anna said.

AT THE hotel they entered into the lobby area, with the bar on the right. 'I want to show you where the concert was held, the one that we found the leaflet for. It was in the ballroom of the hotel.'

'Okay,' Anna replied. 'We can get some lunch as well.'

'Of course. I'm sorry; you must be hungry after such an early start.'

In the dining room during lunch, Anna remembered something. 'I have a letter for you that I found in Daddy's things. It doesn't say much, but it's to you.'

'To me?'

She waited for Anna to search through her bag and accepted from her a cream-coloured envelope with a letter inside. It was just a page in David's handwriting. The sight brought a wave of nostalgia over her and for a moment she couldn't read it.

My Dear Alex,

it started and she looked away, then brought herself back and read on,

Surprise greetings from Scotland and apologies for neglecting to let you know that I was going away. This letter comes to you from Nairn, a small fishing village on the Moray Firth, a world away from London. This is my second trip. I came in June for a few days to sample the local music. Now I have returned to attend the Nairn and some other festivals. I came with a friend, Helen, who I met in London at a Burns Supper earlier in the year.

Tonight I am taking time off after what has been an arduous, but rewarding few weeks of work. Last night Douglas - remember? you met him in London - and I presented a concert here in Nairn that I think was very successful. You would have appreciated it, not because of anything that I did, but for the sheer joy of Douglas's

voice and the music of the harpists that played - two
women from Nairn.
    It would be good to hear from you. We have been so
out of touch. My fault I am sure. Did you receive my last
two letters, back in April and the New Year, if I
remember? Your work seems to fully occupy you now. I
often think it's strange that we lived so close together in
London, but saw so little of each other. Anyway, I hope
you are well and coping with all that's new.
    With fondest wishes and of course much love to you.

She folded the letter and, as she looked at Anna, for a moment was unable to speak. Then she said, 'He never sent it because I hadn't answered his earlier letters. Look, he says so. I was so frantically busy, and always tired.' She felt distraught. 'It's my fault. He's crossed out something about this woman Helen.'

Anna nodded. 'Maybe that is why he didn't send it. It was written here in Nairn. I thought you might like to see it while you were here.'

Upset now, she said, 'It solves nothing. Yes, thank you for showing it to me, but nothing is solved by it. I even meet people, but they don't know anything. At least he was thinking about me when he was here. It must have been the concert in the leaflet in this hotel that he refers to in the letter.'

Anna continued to be positive. 'It does help; you are learning more about what happened. Each piece of information explains something. I think it's great to come here and learn about all the places. I will do it more myself, I think, in future, sometime.'

She tried to agree, but said, 'I wonder what else still lurks in those trunks.'

Anna's voice was calm. 'We'll see. I am pleased that I came to see you here. It's filled in some gaps for me too.'

'I seem to feel even more lost now. I'm glad I have seen the places where your father came to and wrote his music, but they seem remote to me. I don't connect with them.'

Anna lent over and took her hand. 'We need to slow down now and stop thinking about it so much.'

IN THE afternoon, from a shop near the harbour, Anna hired a bicycle and went off to investigate the town as best she could. In her absence, she walked to the shore of the Firth and watched the waters lap over the rocks. Still nothing was complete. Her emotions formed a landscape inside her as variable as the sea, driven high by gales and low by the under-tow of the deep. Was she dreaming? Yes, maybe she was.

While she grappled with the threads and clutched the ends as they slipped from her fingers, she nodded and smiled to herself. She knew now where the music came from, why he loved it here. She had learnt a little of what it all meant. Anna was right; the letter brought her closer to the past. She remembered and felt shock and regret.

'I know I let you down,' she muttered to herself, 'but we made it in the end, didn't we?'

The next morning she and Anna departed from Nairn and Anna drove them home.

Part II

Chapter 22
(New Year, 1940: The River Humber, Yorkshire)

'WHAT'S A winter without frost,' Sergeant James Fenton said as the men, with shovels on shoulders and a day's work clearing sand ahead of them, marched in close file past the guardhouse. 'Move it on, stop your complaints,' he rasped, and, as the squad continued along the spit, thought - *it's going to be difficult to keep them at it today.*

A hundred yards to the left, the North Sea pitted its strength against the shore. A hundred yards to the right, in the lee of the wind and the curve of the land, the Humber lay at low water. Between them stretched a three-mile peninsula of shifting dunes, three hundred yards at its widest, a precarious prominence between water and sky.

The squad walked along the spit on a concrete road, newly laid and already partially covered by wind-blown sand. The war began with a flurry of preparations: blackouts against air raids that did not come and evacuations of children from London and other cities. On the Yorkshire coast they built defences: concrete on more concrete. For the men posted there it seemed unreal. Through the sun's glare he strained to see the swirl of the Humber that stretched south from the spit, a water line that churned beyond pockmarked mud. He scanned the flats, exposed as the water receded at low tide and that stretched away into the sun in the crook of the peninsula. From the guardhouse you could see it all, right to the opposite bank that marked the edge of Lincolnshire five miles away. The silhouette of Bull Fort stood black beyond the mud on the river's back. Two double-barrelled Bofors protected the approach inland along the estuary to Hull.

Near the base of the peninsula and positioned at a place where the headland narrowed, the guardhouse controlled movement of vehicles and personnel. A barrier halted traffic. Where a powder of frost covered the matted turf that grew through the sand, he stamped his feet on the frozen ground. Snow from a week before Christmas left drifts along hedge bottoms and below the bank that protected the land from the sea. As the men continued along the spit, he brought up the rear and hurried them along.

The new life there had begun to grow into him. At first, unsettled by the contrast to home, he worried, but then wrote to tell his wife how he had begun to adapt to the solitude, to the aqueous margin between sea and river beneath a big sky, and how he had taken to looking at the stars. At night he stood outside and gazed into the firmament. She sent him a book about stargazing with maps of the heavens and the moon. Some of the younger men had not adapted so well and found the isolation hard to endure.

Work progressed on reinforcements for the railway and up-grading the track that would take supplies the three miles to the main installations by the point. The squad cut through the dunes, ripped at the marram grass and shovelled sand.

A lorry pulled up at the guardhouse and was given permission to continue. As it moved past the squad he watched it progress along the peninsula on the concrete road and further on force a solitary motorcycle off the road into the dunes as it passed without slowing down.

He forced a wry smile: *that spelt trouble for the lorry driver.*

Five minutes later he watched the lorry reach the magazine tower at the end of the road. Other than Shelduck out on the flats and the marram grass that shuffled in the breeze, it was the only movement on the spit.

THE FIRST days of 1940 were hard for the men on the East Coast. Captain Lynch looked tired and stared across the guardhouse. 'Thanks for getting here so quickly,' he said, and stood up from the desk. His tone was formal. 'I want you to go over to the dyke defences and get things moving there again.' No emotion showed on his face. 'You'll probably have to get tough. I want the stops finished by the end of the week: I don't care if they work all night - just get it finished.' The rise of his eyes before he turned back to the other officer indicated the end of the instructions.

Outside the guardhouse the weather turned worse. For two weeks nothing had changed. It had been bitterly cold: each day the same. Now the sky looked subdued, but a subtle stiffening of the breeze told more. The motorcycle gathered speed to a limit gauged by the rider's expectation of losing control on the icy road. He opened the throttle and handled the machine more easily now after three months of practice with numerous near misses on the pot-holed roads. An icy wind seared beneath his chin into the crevices around his ears.

Further inland, at the dykes, a dismal scene presented itself. A makeshift shelter rigged beside the blockhouse offered some protection. In front of a tarpaulin that flapped in the breeze, smoke from a brazier shimmered. Concrete-encrusted shutter boards that lay heaped on the edge of the dyke and tools abandoned next to a mud-spattered lorry told of the current state of work. There was no sign of men.

Cursing beneath his breath, he did not dismount, but rode past the blockhouse and along the dyke until he caught sight of a group of soldiers standing beside a line of six-foot concrete tank stops. The line ribboned across the hinterland beside a mound that had been constructed two hundred years earlier to protect the land from flooding from the adjacent narrow canal that fed to the Humber. This was the edge of Sunk Island, which over the centuries, like the Polders in Holland, had been reclaimed from the river. With the blocks, the canal formed a formidable defence. When he was sure they had seen his approach, he stopped and found a level patch to leave the motorcycle. He strode over to them. Frozen grass cracked beneath his feet.

'What's going on, Lance Corporal Maplebeck?' he rasped, his voice as cold as Lynch's had been earlier to him. He stood before the group and waited for an answer.

Maplebeck, the natural leader with the right combination of confidence and physique and all the forbearance that his peers lacked, turned and spoke, a note of resistance entering his voice. 'We're just taking a well-earned break, sir.'

He surveyed the men and, although he understood what they were going through, knew enough to keep a tough stand and how to handle Maplebeck. Something about him, a suspicion that he could turn nasty, told him to take care. The man was like a spring that gave more resistance as you pushed. He gritted his teeth. 'Looks to me as if nothing's well-earned around here,' and he let his eyes rest on Maplebeck.

The lance corporal resisted. 'The ground's like iron, sir, slowed the digging for the footings to a standstill. We're carting sand more than a mile.'

He spoke slowly. 'I don't care how hard it is Lance Corporal, the job's got to be finished.' He walked past the stops to where he could survey the length of the completed defences, then, as the soldiers watched him, looked back at Maplebeck. 'There's a gap of about two hundred yards in the line and it needs filling. I want it done by the end of the week.'

One of the men, who he recognised from the broad East Yorkshire accent, shouted from the group: 'Yer think Jerry's goin' to come an' land up here then, do yer Lieutenant, and this lot's goin' to stop him, eh?'

He looked around the group. 'It's not my business to think anything, Boseman. Nor yours.' He waited to see if they had anything more to say. As he turned his attention back to Maplebeck, they looked at him, an air of unease amongst them. 'What do you need to finish the job, Lance Corporal?'

Maplebeck was quick to respond. 'More men, some new gear and a break in this weather. It's worse than Siberia out here, sir.'

He countered with sarcasm: 'You should be used to it Lance Corporal, and you as well Boseman. You've been keen enough to remind us of your origins in these parts. This is your patch.' He turned away and looked across the winter fields to the eastern sky that darkened by the minute. 'You're here to defend it.' He turned again to look at the line. 'You'll have your men; I'll get another section here, but I can't control the weather.'

Another voice called out from the group. 'It's all a damned waste of time, if yer asking me, sir.'

He looked around, at the faces of the men, but did not answer. They remained silent under his gaze. Instead, he turned to Maplebeck: 'Come on, show me the line.'

The two men walked along the dyke, a short way, so that they could view the defences formed by the tank stops. The line meandered across the farmland towards two tents that marked an anti-aircraft emplacement on the river. It had been moved there a few weeks before, one of the few movable gun units they had. The others were in concrete emplacements that made flexibility impossible. The place was full of concrete. He looked at it. Most guns had been sited badly and could not be moved.

As he'd told himself before, and would tell himself again, it was just lousy foresight and lousy planning; and the saddest thing, it was too late to worry about it now.

Arriving at the blockhouse where the equipment was stored, he stopped and turned to Maplebeck. 'Make sure you clear out all that gear and set up a camp across the road. Then start work on the other side.'

Maplebeck's gravel voice almost hid his irritation. 'Yes, sir.'

He felt the resistance. 'You'll be on night-shift if things don't show progress today. Now get your section moving. I shall be back this afternoon.'

He started towards the road, but then turned: 'Oh, and Maplebeck,' and he looked him in the eyes, 'get a shave before I see you next, and smarten yourself up. You look a mess.'

SINCE THE middle of October, when he arrived by train from London, five weeks after he was called up, he had been in Yorkshire for three months. His fourth journey north in as many months showed the change in the country.

Wedged in a compartment and unable to move, with packs and cases at his knees, he shook his head. The hope that was germinated in the same journey in July with Helen, now was dead. *Damn them*, he thought, but wasn't sure who he was damning.

When he departed from Scotland, and went home, his writing stopped. A week later he joined the Royal Artillery and it felt as if he would never write again.

Khaki-clad passengers filled the train and on every station platform along the way, military uniforms transformed the population. Nobody was easy with it and the novelty had not worn off. For some, the uniforms brought memories of the horrors of twenty years before. To everyone, they drove the message home that the country was at war. Changing trains at Doncaster, he watched the transition of countryside along the curve of the Humber after Goole and smelt Hull before he saw it, the breeze from the fish docks heralded the city. Then a bus ride along a road that twisted east through undulating farmland and villages delivered him in the late afternoon to a place called Easington, where a lorry and James Fenton were waiting for him.

So he reported at Spurn, his second duty station in the 75th Anti-Aircraft Regiment Royal Artillery. Memories returned of the weeks before at Gaston in Kent, where he was given 3.7-inch gun practice, and of the two weeks in Northumbria where he had been for officer training.

Now he buttoned his tunic at the collar and lowered his goggles.

The catalogue of actions that needed to be taken before the end of the day assembled in his mind. There would be more orders from Lynch to add to the list of work that occupied the days. Attention to the list was a distraction from his inability to write - even to play - music, and from his separation from Helen. She was in the words he spoke and the commands he gave to the likes of Maplebeck. Still she was in the background of the scenes he acted out and in the views of the landscape he saw. Four months into a war and nothing had happened. They had built defences and waited.

Setting off again on the motorcycle, he throttled up and sped along the concrete road back towards the spit. Though poorly defended, and surely there would be little resistance, nobody believed invasion could happen on this stretch of the East Coast. Invasion would be easy on the low-lying terrain a few feet above sea level. It was too far, they said; too much sea to cross and Kent was the obvious choice. In the dreary days and nights when they waited and watched the skies, the men had debated it many times. Others, though, did believe it would happen there. With the Humber a perfect entry for ships, it would be a better choice, they said, for at least a secondary wave of invasion forces. So the uncertainly hung over them: was the war real? It unsettled the men, who did not take it seriously. What was going to happen; would there be an invasion? The officers were ambivalent and the uncertainty cascaded through the ranks. Maplebeck's squad had constructed hundreds of concrete blocks in three months. As well as being cold, they were bored.

Everywhere it was the same, a war in which nothing had happened, except in Poland which had borne the first brunt. Britain's expeditionary force spent the months entrenched beside their French allies, motionless along the eastern borders of France.

Across the fields, the breeze gusted harder and the chill penetrated his leathers. Squalls came in from the east, from Holland and Denmark and beyond, probably all the way from Siberia. Maplebeck's comparison was not far from the truth. More snow was on its way. The sea tossed spray over the dunes behind the garrison quarters at the base of the spit. Pulling up before the end of the headland, he walked to the top of the dunes. The sea smashed into the beach and dragged shingle in its undertow. Three miles out, a cluster of ships - trawlers, merchantmen and naval vessels - waited for the tide to turn to let them enter the Humber.

He continued his ride and soon parked the motorcycle next to the guardhouse. At the door, as the barrier lowered behind him, he called to the soldier on sentry duty.

'Yes, sir?'

'Find the name of the driver of the lorry that arrived this morning. Get him to report to me at the guardhouse at two o'clock.'

'Yes, sir.' The corporal saluted.

HE CLOSED the door behind him, removed his gloves, unbuttoned his coat and waited. Captain Lynch sat at his desk and finally looked up.

'Good afternoon, sir. I'm afraid they need more men up there. Conditions aren't good.' His lips narrowed before he continued. 'I've promised they'll get them.'

Lynch nodded a few times, and then, looking at the surface of the table in front of him, at first remained silent, but then shook his head: 'Well that was mighty kind of you.' He spoke as if it were a preposterous suggestion. The chair hit the wall as he got to his feet. 'Where do you suggest we take them from?' While he continued to show his exasperation, he stared at him: 'The railway or the batteries at the Point; or maybe you'd like to volunteer yourself?'

He listened. The men at the dykes were demoralised and their work had become slipshod. They had become careless and there had been accidents. The easiest way to inject morale was with more men. He knew Maplebeck would respond to an increase in his squad. 'When you've got the stops finished, you can pull the whole squad back to the cuttings.' He stopped and watched Lynch, who gave no reaction. 'It makes sense; finish one job to help make the rest easier, sir.'

Echoes of what Martin Taylor had said before he went to Scotland, such a short time ago and now he had to put up with this.

Lynch looked desolate. 'Do you think I haven't considered that? How long will it take them?'

He unclenched his fists. 'I told them a week. I reckon a day or two more. Give them the men, they'll have no excuse. You can't push them any more in these conditions.'

Lynch seemed to have no energy to argue debatable points. He made his decision. 'Alright -' He walked to the window and, as he appeared to calculate the costs, gazed into the river's distance: '- Take eight men; take them from where we need them least: none from the cuttings.'

He nodded.

Lynch looked bad, pushed himself too hard. If leadership by example was needed, Lynch didn't provide it. The initial panic to complete the defences had been too much. Lynch fought authority, yet wanted to impress. He could not take the responsibility. He hesitated. 'I am sure you'll tell me it's none of my business, sir, but you look as if you've had enough for one day. Why don't you turn in? I will finish the shift. There's nothing else to be done today.'

Lynch sat down again and reclined into his moroseness: 'I'll let you know when I need your help, Lieutenant.'

Turning to leave, he worried about the weather, but doubted if Lynch would be interested. 'It looks like more snow, sir. Could delay things.'

Lynch did not look up. 'We'll worry about that when we have to.'

He nodded again. 'Could be sooner than you think, sir.'

'I don't care,' Lynch hissed, and still looked down at his desk. 'It can't get any worse; the weather's the least of my worries.'

He left him, doubting whether that was true, and now went along the spit to inspect the newest gun emplacements. Batteries all along the spit, with increasing frequency, engaged aircraft out to sea that attacked convoys along the coast. They were not easy to handle and included 6 and 9.7 inch guns from World War One ships that had been brought there and mounted in the coastal defences. Successes, were few.

Further up the coast, beyond the line of tank stops, lay the Kilnsea anti-aircraft battery, an emplacement of four guns. In the early afternoon he inspected three emplacements there and arranged practice schedules for the next few weeks. Then he returned to the Guardhouse; Lynch had departed, but the lorry driver was there.

He looked at the man. 'What's your name, private?'

'Perfect, sir.'

Had he heard correctly? 'Perfect?'

'Yes, sir.'

This couldn't be true. His mind searched for a line and he held back a smile. Was this the first hint of humour in months? 'Well, Perfect, you've got a nerve…'

'Yes, sir.'

'You know why you're here?'

'Yes, sir.'

'Good. Where are you from?'

'Easington, sir.'

He smiled. '*Easington?*'

'Yes, sir.'

'Well, there's nothing *easy* around here Perfect, and there's nothing *perfect* either. In fact, everything is bloody awful, and so pushing me off the road this morning only made things worse didn't it?

'Yes, sir.'

'And that wasn't very considerate, was it Perfect?'

'No, sir.'

'And it wasn't very bright, either, was it Perfect?'

'No, sir.'

'Do you know why?'

'No, sir.'

'Because if ever I see you drive like that again, you'll be mixing concrete with the men of 17 Corps. Is that clear?'

'Yes, sir.'

'And that won't be easy for you will it Perfect?'

'No, sir.'

'Good. Dismissed.'

The man saluted. 'Thank you, sir.'

As the man left the guardhouse, he sighed and looked across at the duty corporal, a man called Michael White, who now tried to hide a grin. He always smiled and he laughed back at him. 'If we ever do a Review, corporal, remind me to include that little sketch in it,' and he laughed again.

'Yes, sir. We should do that, sir, a show for the men.'

'Hm. We do need something to brighten up our lives. I'll see you later corporal,' and he followed Private Perfect out of the guardhouse.

INLAND FROM the spit, the northern sector was where Maplebeck and the tank defences were located and now he rode in that direction to inspect progress. Seven gun emplacements lay between the peninsula and Welwick five miles away. Morale was low and conditions were bad. Even in good weather the men suffered discomfort. They lived in tents and makeshift shelters by their gun emplacements. The temporary camps allowed some flexibility, but since mid-December the weather had worsened and the men were not used to the harsh conditions. If there had been more sightings of enemy planes along the Humber - rather than just out at sea - they might have felt some justification for their misery. The initial enthusiasm had evaporated long ago.

In bad weather the river margins seemed even more remote. Canada geese grazed the grasses behind the raised levees which protected the land from flooding. His passage along the grass dunes disturbed some swans before he stopped at the dykes. A newly shaven Maplebeck, his hands red and swollen by the cold, stood by the shelter.

'You'll have another section over here, tomorrow,' he said, and kicked sand off his tyres.

Maplebeck saluted and nodded his approval and he accepted his thanks.

'They'll bring their own gear.'

'Thank you, sir. It's going to snow.'

'I know; it's building up for tonight.' He was not going to let up. Maplebeck eyed him.

'You've worked on the stops in the snow already.' *You can't make concrete when it's freezing, though.* 'This is your God-forsaken patch of Christendom. We need to protect it. You can prepare the foundations.'

If he felt like replying, Maplebeck did not; somewhere to the south, beyond the spit, a noise distracted them. With the resonance of thunder, the sound seemed to come from underground. As the noise repeated like some kind of detonation, the earth shook. Seconds later a plume of silver fire erupted beyond the spit, followed by the report of an explosion.

The puzzled look in Maplebeck's eyes spoke for them both. 'It's the ships at anchor, sir.'

He strained his ears and waited for more blasts. 'I think you're right.' Starting to run along the line towards the road, already the rest of the men had preceded them. Some stood on top of the blockhouse and peered into the distance. Two were on the lorry roof. 'Can't tell what it is, sir. Must be the ships.'

'Only thing it can be, sir,' another said.

Men clambered onto the blockhouse and lorry to get a better view.

'I'm sure you're right,' he replied. 'Come on, let's get down there. Take the lorry ahead; I'll follow.'

Two miles from the dykes the road turned left at the riverbank. As the lorry approached the bend, the quick-firing anti-aircraft guns on Bull Fort opened up. The lorry stopped and he pulled up behind. Ten or more large aircraft streamed in formation past the Fort, then headed up the Humber and turned back towards the point and came in to bomb the gun emplacements.

'What the hell are they?' someone shouted, as they jumped onto the shingle.

'Must be Dorniers,' another answered.

'Dorniers?'

'Yeah, and Stukas, those: dive-bombers. See the cranked wings.'

In the wake of the bombers, and above them, more aircraft followed. The destroyer's guns could be heard and the heavy coastal batteries at the Point opened-up to join them. Still they could not see the ships.

'Come on Lance Corporal, get your unit down to the Point.'

He set off before the lorry and opened-up the throttle as much as he dared. The road led east towards the coast then turned right to the peninsula. He stopped at the place on the dunes where he had seen the ships earlier in the day and ran to the top. Despite the poor light and swell of the waves he could see enough. Four merchant ships were enveloped in smoke and flames. A naval vessel had been hit and exploded as he watched.

Behind him the confusion on the ocean was countered by the screams of the aircraft in the sky. He turned to see the bombers return, almost overhead, harassed by fighters.

Hurricanes: must have come from Leconfield.

The bombers returned fire from the upper turrets. There were bursts of anti-aircraft fire like grey balls of cotton wool that burst in the sky, but they were all behind their target. The aircraft attacked the ships again and Hurricanes wheeled like wasps around them. They left their vapour trails: a calligraphy of combat in the sky. It was too much to take in. One bomber was engulfed in a cluster of grey cotton wool, then shattered into pieces.

Without warning one of the aircraft broke away and headed northwards along the railway track towards the lorry and guard house, with him in direct line of attack. The nose gunner started to fire and bullets bounced off the concrete road around him. He scrambled for cover in the dunes and then watched the plane bank to the right and away over the sea as a Bren gun opened fire on it from a carrier that arrived along the road from Kilnsea. Bullets impacted on the rear gun-turret of the aircraft as it flew on. Well done, whoever you are, gunner; he would find out later.

Another explosion ripped through the air. It seemed too large to have been caused by the bombers. He stood up and looked towards the end of the spit. *God, were there U-boats?* Out to sea, a Stuka circled and came back in low to dive-bomb a merchant ship, which like others was heading away from the scene. Some of the smaller craft made it to the estuary and, as they proceeded up river, clung to the far coastline. Two cruisers headed out to sea. *Could they hunt U-boats?*

The sky turned blacker over a sea that was ablaze with oil. Waves crashed hard on the beach as the lorry passed along the road and brought him back to his senses.

'Close thing, there, sir,' Maplebeck shouted.

'Too close,' he agreed, and turned to run to his motorcycle. 'See you at the end of the Point.'

He sped on behind the lorry and at the guardhouse the sentry scrambled down from the top of the sentry box to raise the barrier. With no luck, he telephoned to find Lynch. The anti-aircraft fire became more spasmodic. As he followed the lorry, at the observation tower at the centre of the Point, he abandoned his motorcycle.

On the eastern side where the sea merged with the river's waters, the beach drew his attention. He knew that out on the ocean men had died and that more would be dying as he ran. What he saw and heard was real; ships had sunk. Bombers circled again to deliver final blows to their quarries and anti-aircraft guns on the peninsula fired and gunners tested abilities gained from too-brief instruction. Their intervention in the conflict had been too little and to no avail. Eyes and reflexes were ill prepared. On the highest point of the peninsula, he stopped at the first heavy anti-aircraft emplacement and crouched beside the sandbags.

'How is it,' he shouted to the first crewman he saw.

'Bloody awful, sir; can't get the distance right. It's hopeless.'

'I saw one bomber go down, so tell the rest of them. It is possible. Keep it up and keep trying. Take it slow and don't panic.' He left the emplacement and ran down to the beach.

The crippled destroyer had drifted nearer to shore and lay about a mile away. It looked massive when it sank in the winter dusk. The force of steel that on land would have crushed buildings cut a swathe deep through the water that could only have been equalled by the ship's virgin impact at its launch. Like the roll and dive of a seal, the vessel fell through the waves. Only when explosions from its hull drowned out the drone of aircraft and the noise of the ferment of the sea and wind did eyes turn to watch the boat's final collapse into the ocean. A cloud of steam erupted at the place.

Two rescue-launches headed out through the swell. The lifeboat was out as well. Yellow dots on the water identified stricken seamen. Through the spray that whipped from the wave crests, he could see rubber lifeboats approach. A seaman swam ashore and, through the waves, fell head down on the beach. Things happened too quickly. He ran towards the man and pulled him up. 'Well done.' The words sounded ridiculous. 'Come on.'

The man staggered to his feet, then collapsed again. He was white with cold and, holding him upright, he dragged him up the beach. The shingle shifted under his feet and gave no grip and he stumbled under the weight but managed to stagger on. Another soldier grabbed the man's free arm and he felt the weight lighten as they surged forward. He stumbled again in the shingle and then his grip steadied as they came to the edge of the dunes.

'Take him on and get him warm. I'll go back down.'

The beach was in turmoil. He caught a soldier by the arm and told him to tell the search light batteries on the Point to sweep the water and beach.

He called out: 'Lance Corporal Maplebeck, arrange search parties to patrol the beach all-round the Point. Take any seamen ashore and get them warm fast, or they'll be dead from exposure in this cold.'

The sky cleared of aircraft and as the RAF fighters departed to the west, they tipped their wings to the coastal defences of Yorkshire. As the bombers disappeared in the darkness of the eastern sky, the drone of their engines faded. All attention then focused on the boats and the calamity at sea. Thirty minutes of action at the most, not much more than the time it had taken for them to drive to the Point, had caused all this.

Where was Lynch?

On the river side of the spit, where the waves were calmer, a rescue launch came in close to the beach. He ran over with some others and waded out thigh deep to help take off three seamen. The water felt as if it had just melted from an ice flow and his muscles flinched. Lynch was in the boat with them, hardly recognisable beneath a brown army cape and rubber cap. Of course: where the high action was; he looked haggard and desperate.

'Get this lot back, Whellans. We'll keep searching. Send a message to get any boats out here they can.' Lynch steadied himself against the low rail of the launch as it rocked in the waves. 'And make it quick. Tell them to shine a search-light around each of the rescue boats.' His voice disappeared, though he seemed to want to speak: 'Keep them well lit.'

'Yes, I've done that, sir...'

The launch reversed again and groaned into the waves. *Take it easy, you fool.* He nodded into the spray.

Helping drag the hapless seamen up the beach to the dunes, he handed them to others to take on to safety. Then he ran to the control tower, mounting the wooden stairs which zigzagged up the outside and relayed Lynch's messages to the duty officer. At the windows, his eyes were drawn to the view of the sea beyond the peninsula. Here he could see the whole panorama, magnified into detail by the sweep of the searchlights that gave the dunes and the sea a luminescence beneath the black mantle of the sky. Six lights raked the waves. The ships had gone, scattered, or vanished into the estuary. How many had been sunk? From the tower he could see that men could be carried by the current, perhaps miles across the estuary, and many would have been carried back along the spit. 'We should get a call out to the coast guard on the other side and tell them to search the beaches for survivors,' he said to the duty officer. 'I'll get parties out on this side.'

He left the tower and ran back to the beach to find Maplebeck. A voice called out, 'Take care, sir, running like that on this sand; you'll break your leg.' At the water's edge, Sergeant Fenton stood in the half-light.

'Thanks for the advice, Sergeant. If a broken leg is all I get in this war, I'll think myself lucky.' He took the opportunity to enlist the Sergeant's services. 'Will you get a squad together, Sergeant, and head up the spit. There may be seamen washed up for miles.'

'What about down here, Lieutenant?'

'I'll sort out down here. Maplebeck's around the Point somewhere with a squad searching the beaches. There could be men freezing to death on the seaward side. Send a party right to the top and leave no stretch of beach unsearched.'

'Right you are, sir.' Fenton turned to the men around him, and rasped out orders.

The launch with Lynch returned and brought more sailors plucked from the sea. Lynch sat in the cockpit looking as though he'd had enough. He caught Lynch's eyes, narrowed in a grimace and shouted into the cockpit. 'How are you, sir; what have you done?'

Lynch clutched his right forearm. He appeared to shiver as he squinted back at him. 'Fell over. It's nothing.'

Fearing the worst for the man and trying to get into the launch, he shouted, 'Get out of here, sir. You're pushing yourself too hard. You've done enough.' Lynch shouted for him to get back.

'You're exhausted, sir. You can't take any more. Get out.'

The searchlights danced across the water. One hovered over the same spot and picked out the yellow of a lifejacket. The launch droned out again to collect the sailor.

He had been away from the beach for ten minutes and now turned away and looked inland where he could see at the top of the shingle, beneath the dunes, a line of twenty or more bodies. He stood and stared and it took time to level his mind to the narrowed dimensions of the world around him. He had been a long way from the war; now, with no warning, this.

The destruction continued into the evening and no-one knew when to give up the search. How could they know? The search parties waited and continued to search until the only ones found were long dead. Even then, no one knew whether all hope had gone. Reason said twenty minutes in that frozen hell was enough. Only the toughest survived longer. Some had made it to the beach, only to die with the frozen wind on their backs before help arrived.

'What now, sir? What else do you want us to do?'

It was Maplebeck, returning with his squad. 'Have you searched all the leeward beaches?'

'We have, sir.'

'That's good. Would you do one more sweep of the seaward side; you never know. Then report to the Ops Room.'

'Will do, sir.'

He watched him run off down the beach with his men and wondered at human nature.

When most of the men had left the beaches and returned to the bunkhouses, conversations were subdued. Some posed questions they found collaged in the chaos of their minds. For many, silence disguised embarrassed shock at being caught unprepared. The attack had come and they had lost, been made to look foolish. Some covered their dismay with innocent chatter.

'What sort of aircraft were they?' One man asked.

'Who cares,' someone answered. 'They thrashed us anyway.'

A crewman looked at his booklet. 'The bombers I think were Heinkels. They are those with the upper turrets. You can tell by the outlines.'

He showed the drawings that had been issued to anti-aircraft crews. 'The dive-bombers were Stukas. The smaller fighters probably Messerschmitts. They call them Bf 110s, the only ones that can get this far.'

'Then there's Dornier 111Ks,' another man added.

They had seen how easily destruction could be wrought. How easily a landscape could be broken. They had paid the price; the cost of ignoring what they knew, but had disbelieved.

'If they'd sent an invasion force, we'd all be dead now,' someone said.

What would come next?

JAMES FENTON did not enter the bunkhouse at the base of the spit, but stayed outside, with the collar of his greatcoat turned to the wind, and gazed at the stars. Someone came alongside him next to the bunkhouse, a silent figure in the blackness, who he guessed was Lieutenant Whellans.

'Is that you, Lieutenant?'

'It is, Sergeant.'

He turned his head. 'How are you, sir,' he asked, then turned back into the darkness of his own vision. Although he'd known the lieutenant barely three months, despite the differences between them, he felt he had started to get to know him. Despite doing his job better than many, his mind seemed to be somewhere else: on his music and things he did not really understand. Sometimes he heard him play the violin.

Although five years the lieutenant's senior he hesitated before he spoke again; the lieutenant didn't speak, either. 'Today's been our first test, hasn't it, sir. I know now is not a good time, but I'd like to talk about it sometime if I could.'

'Of course; we'll all need to talk it through.'

He waited, but all he could hear was the sound of the lieutenant's breathing in the darkness beside him. 'We always knew that wars killed people, but until today we'd forgotten that meant us as well.' He waited again.

'True,' the lieutenant said. 'Until now the war deadened our minds with its monotony and we only half believed it would come to us.'

He stared into the night. 'Going mad with boredom while we mixed concrete to defend the country. Then today - this happens.'

'We'll have to get better at defending our country,' the lieutenant said.

As he nodded his reply in the darkness, he thought of his family. 'My father had a heart attack a few weeks ago, from too much strain running the timber yard, with me not being there to help him. He's alright, but won't be able to continue working. He'd have been fine if it wasn't for all this. We're all the losers.'

For a while the lieutenant was silent. What was he thinking about? Then he said, 'You're right, sergeant; the war has many ways to change lives.' He went silent for a moment and then added, 'Captain Lynch has a broken arm and looks in poor shape. He's done too much and is going down with something - probably a fever.'

Many more out there took much more than a broken arm. 'How many of our men are injured, sir?'

'Two killed and seven injured.'

'We didn't expect that this morning, did we, sir.'

The lieutenant's voice was quiet. 'No, we didn't; it's taken us by surprise. Anyway, I'll need your help tomorrow to comb the beaches. I'll arrange some others to help at first light.'

He stood with his back to the wind and his eyes on the sky. They'd have to pick up the bits; all move on. 'I'll be pleased to help, sir.'

'Thank you,' the lieutenant, said. 'I'll see you later.' He

disappeared into the darkness and, as he continued to look on into the night sky, where the stars shone bright, he heard him enter the bunkhouse. For many more minutes he stayed there, thought of his wife and children, and for the first time during the war was frightened. They were in danger; they were all in danger.

Like a ghost, the lieutenant's presence remained beside him. All the lieutenant wanted to do was write music; all he wanted to do was cut timber at home in the yard. The lieutenant hadn't settled yet; was even less settled than him; as lost as any of them, and concerned about Lynch when he should have worried about himself.

That evening he wrote to his wife and told her about the day.

AT DAWN the arc of the spit's eastern flank caught the new light. It had snowed, and flakes were still falling. After only half a mile they saw the first body. A soldier raised his hand to point into the distance. 'There's one,' he called, the grave tone in his voice an acknowledgement of the inevitability of the task and that they would bear witness to the aftermath of the conflict, tossed up fragmented and bitter on the beaches.

With eyes set on the patch ahead, they walked towards the one scar on the otherwise unblemished landscape of the peninsula. Before they reached the body, their minds had adjusted to its unfamiliarity. What struggle had there been? When had death brought an end? Who was he? Surf splashed on his bare feet that lay splayed into the tide line. The clothes were naval, the skin washed white by the sea, as pale as the flecks of ocean that spattered on it. Stubble on his chin looked black. Snow settled on the sand and on the seaweed; flakes melted on the man's hair where they landed. He might have been asleep, and it was unnatural not to speak to him, not to shake him, not to want to help him. For a while they watched and wondered.

'Alright, in your own time, take him up the beach,' he said, the words fell like a final prayer. Three of the men carried him up and over the dunes to the road. He told one of them to go back for the lorry. 'Tell the driver to continue along and keep with us.'

On they walked in silence through the shingle. Although the

second body looked much the same as the first, the repeated image of death was harder to take. The man, a big man, maybe from a fishing boat, looked gaunt. The question was the same: who was he? The lack of answers seemed more devastating than for the first. They realised they would never know; this was a seaman's death. The sea had killed him; what of a soldier's death?

The lorry stopped on the road behind them; they delivered the body to it and then walked on. 'What do you reckon our chances are then, Lieutenant?' It was a question from one of the men as they clambered over the next breakwater.

He shook his head. 'I really wouldn't know? We are isolated, as if these sailors and we were the only people in the war. Yet we haven't even fought.' He looked ahead along the coast. 'Who knows what's going on elsewhere. All I know is we are stuck in this wilderness. Nobody knows about us and nothing happens for months, then this.' They listened to the sand that gave way under their feet.

'What about those Bren guns you said were coming, sir; we need more guns?' the soldier asked.

'You must be joking; there aren't any Bren guns. Carriers yes, but no guns. The country's on its knees. We need more than guns.'

'Maybe we should all be on our knees then, Lieutenant?'

They stopped and, across the sand, met each other's gaze. He nodded. 'Maybe we should; it has started now though, and prayers always come as an afterthought. God and soldiers are popular in times of strife, but, afterwards, are soon forgotten.'

'Most people wouldn't know what to pray for anyway, Lieutenant. Don't you think?'

He looked at him. 'Would you?'

'I think so, sir. What about you?'

'Good question. I've spent half my life in church. Not praying, but in there all the same. I don't know.'

In silence they trudged on.

Nearer to the Point the shoreline was littered with the first wave of flotsam from the sunken boats. Material that could be carried easily by the sea was deposited first: wood, clothes, rope, boxes, paper, logbooks and a host of other items. At the shoreline, the water was laden with half submerged debris, waiting for a wave to flip it the final length onto the sand. Later the deeper currents would drag up still more material from the boats.

The men stopped to look over the wreckage and fragments, lingered and stared, let their imaginations stray back into the heart of the misfortune of the previous day.

'Over here, Lieutenant,' someone shouted. Two men stood with their eyes cast to the sand. It was an arm, severed at the top of the humerus, which protruded under a gash of bloodless flesh.

'Where's the rest of 'im's what I'm wondering, Lieutenant,' one of them said, and they both looked out across the swirl of the waves to where the ships had been anchored - to the empty sea.

There were no ships to look at now; none would anchor there again. He stared as well, while the soldier's question wandered like a gull over the wave crests. 'Best not to think about it too much, Cuthbert,' he said, and looked again at the piece of human body. 'When you're ready, take it to the lorry.'

He trudged forward and shouted across the slope of the beach. 'Come on, let's move.' The heavy sky of the previous afternoon had cleared. The peninsula, blanketed with snow, lay immaculate in the light of the low sun. Snow cleansed the land, mirrored the seclusion that had fastened onto the men.

For five minutes they walked and then Fenton's voice broke the silence. 'We've been stripped of everything,' he said, and then stopped to look into the vapour of his words, starting to walk on as his thoughts hung in the air.

He'd been broken by all this; maybe they all had.

Fenton seemed to work through his own sequence of events. 'Stripped of every feeling but loss, every emotion but fear. It's bloody ridiculous.'

He looked at him and silently acknowledged his comment on the tragedy. It took them four hours to walk all round the spit checking for bodies. Lunch that day in the canteen was a sombre event.

In the weeks that followed, the men who had served on the peninsula returned to a routine while they waited for the next attack. Although they believed now that invasion on the East Coast could happen, still they could only wait.

He waited also, not for the war to end, or for the next attack, but for his mind to settle and for it to be able to find the equilibrium that he knew could exist in him that would allow him to create music again. Even after this, in the aftermath of the attack, even though attention to duty occupied him and took all his energy, surely he could write. He wrote to Helen, sometimes managed to telephone her, and wrote to his mother. That was all.

NEAR THE end of the peninsula, where it was widest, the operations room formed the heart of the military installations. Walking past the observation tower alongside a high wall that edged the dunes and retained the encroaching sands, by a concealed entrance, he saluted a sentry on duty. Another body had been washed up. What should he do? Best deal with it himself; call the lorry and take a couple of men. He stopped and waited for a few minutes, then went in.

Beneath the dunes, at the end of a forty-yard passage and where the air had the stench of damp plaster, the operations room was located. He entered and nodded to the communications officers and the duty sergeant. Captain Lynch, who, if he hadn't known better, he might have thought had been in the room all night, stood by the stove. It was difficult, but he tried to sound cheerful. 'Good morning, sir.' He nodded his greeting across the room.

At first, Lynch did not reply, but lifted a kettle from the stove and poured water into an enamel pot. When he did speak, his voice was flat. 'Would you like some tea?'

He hid his irritation: 'Yes, please, sir.' While the duty sergeant studied his log book, he waited until he caught Lynch's eye. 'You look as though you could live in this dungeon for ever, sir.'

Lynch scowled. 'Just as well as in that other flea-ridden pit.'

He almost shook his head, but instead said, 'There's another body washed up past the breakwaters; I'll go and bring it in.'

Lynch shrugged. 'Rather you than me. Send Fenton.'

'No, I'll go,' he replied, and putting his knapsack on the floor, unbuttoned his tunic. 'It's beginning to cause problems for the men.'

Lynch kicked a chair from under the table and sat down. 'Bugger the men.'

He stared past him and at the sergeant: 'In January more than five hundred men died off the coast, sir, torn apart in shell blasts, burnt in the ship's blaze, or drowned.'

Through increasingly nervous eyes, Lynch stared. 'Don't you think I know that; that's war?'

He stepped over to the filing-cabinet and, taking out the daily log of incidents, opened it and started to write an entry. He paused and looked at Lynch. 'There have been more than two hundred bodies washed up on the beaches from that one action. The men need help to cope with it.'

Lynch ignored the comment.

The soldiers on the peninsula watched and, in their minds, scaled the devastation. Now, a month later, when bodies were washed up on the shoreline they were fish-eaten carrion. For the men that found them, the experience broke into whatever understanding of life they may have had. It was the stuff of horror-fiction and, becoming hardened, the hardening was a protection that made some of them callous, less human than they had been before.

Lynch talked in the background. 'They're soldiers…'

He half listened.

'They're beginning to dwell on things too long,' Lynch said.

'It's not that; there's too little to occupy them, sir,' and then he thought that maybe it was time to do a review, a show for the men, as Corporal White had suggested.

Most days they waited for something to happen. The men on the coast could find no answers that made sense to them. Questions that were asked in the bunkhouse found no recourse to reason and no defence. Any quarrel between the events that had happened and what might have been was unresolved in those months as they watched and waited.

While he drank his tea, he called the guardhouse. 'Morning Corporal; would you ask Sergeant Fenton to bring the lorry down to the breakwaters, please? Tell him I will meet him there in half an hour. Ask him to bring a tarpaulin and two more men.' He listened for a few minutes to the corporal's voice, smiled, nodded once or twice, and then put the telephone down on Lynch's makeshift desk.

'Thanks for the tea, sir. I'll be back at ten.' He left the room.

Although the snow had gone, in early February, the ground

remained frozen. Bushes were picked out in frost around the observation tower and the motorcycle needed care to manoeuvre it on the iced roads. He drove a mile along the peninsula, to where the breakwaters started, and headed for the place where he had found the body earlier that morning.

CLIMBING DOWN from the cab of the lorry, James Fenton saluted Lieutenant Whellans.

'How are you today, Sergeant?'

'Under the circumstances, remarkably well, sir. And what about you?'

The lieutenant took a deep breath and looked out over the sand to the ocean beyond. 'I wouldn't say I was remarkably well; fair maybe, but pleased to hear that you're well anyway, Sergeant.'

He followed the lieutenant's gaze. 'Thank you, sir.' The lieutenant was quiet, as if he had questions in his mind that he never asked; things he wanted to say, that he never said. He turned again to him. 'Been too quiet from the east since the last attack, don't you think, sir?'

'It has; it's very ominous.'

Two men in the back of the lorry threw down a tarpaulin. He dropped the tailgate and they jumped into the sand and unhooked a stretcher from the side of the lorry. The lieutenant pointed again towards the breakwaters. 'Alright, over there.'

Adjusting his woollen hat, and waiting for the lieutenant to catch up, he set off behind the men. Relaxing, as the lieutenant caught up and started to walk by his side, he noticed a weary look on his face; he seemed to be struggling more than usual. He laughed: 'I've wanted to tell you, sir; I've written an account of all that happened and sent it to my wife. I had to get it out somehow. That seemed the best way.'

The admission seemed to amuse the lieutenant and brought relief to his face. 'Really; that sounds interesting; what did you write?'

'Thank you, sir; a sort of description of the attack; to get things off my chest.'

'It sounds as if it worked; how much did you write?'

Now he hesitated; he had been doing it every night and, in the secret way he had done it, felt dishonest, as if he'd done something sordid or grubby. 'Pages...' he replied, '...twenty maybe; I had to do it twice, to get it right. It's taken me all this time.'

'I hope you'll let me read it,' the lieutenant said.

He nodded. 'I will, sir.'

It wasn't so much a sigh, but more with a sound of regret in his voice that the lieutenant said: 'I wish I could write some music...' but then, before he could reply, he changed the subject. 'How are your wife and family getting on?'

'Oh, they're fine, sir. My wife's joined the WVS. Says she's never felt so important.'

The lieutenant smiled at him and then turned to look ahead to where the salt-washed timbers of the first breakwater rose along the beach. The breakwaters stopped sand being washed along the coast. It built up on the north side so the sand was higher there. Even at the top of the beach there was a drop of five feet that deepened to seven or eight feet lower down. Massive rusted bolts stuck out from the middle of each stanchion.

'I hope you will be able to start writing again, sir,' he said, and wondered what the lieutenant meant by, *writing music*? 'I keep a diary, now,' he added, as he climbed over the breakwater, and pulled himself up against the diagonal holding-brace as the lieutenant followed him.

'Your wife will be better informed than most people about what's going on out here,' the lieutenant said, as they started again along the beach.

He echoed the comment. 'I suppose she will. That's the trouble; the rest of the world hears the news and reads the papers. I like to let her know what's really happening. I give her the gossip in my letters.'

Lieutenant Whellans nodded. 'I thought of wars as being big things. Now I realise they're not. They're a series of cryptic incidents, when men die. The battles are a small part; soon finished, but the war goes on. The same as here.'

He stopped and looked out to sea again. 'Did you read the new Hornblowers last year, sir? *Ship of the Line* and *Flying Colours*.'

'I did, yes; I really enjoyed them.'

As he looked out to sea, he said, 'All the stories I've ever heard about battles, even sea battles, were never like the one we saw here. It started and finished before we knew what was happening.' He let his words carry on the breeze.

Although the lieutenant listened and nodded, he seemed lost in his thoughts. The images were still fresh. 'And now out there on the bottom, there's a cruiser with fish in the engine room,' he said, and started to walk on with the lieutenant beside him.

In front of the next breakwater they came to the body, washed up and left below the high-tide mark as the waves receded. The lieutenant had found it earlier when he inspected the beaches.

'How long does it take you to run to the end and back, sir?'

Lieutenant Whellans pondered: 'Forty minutes on a good day; depends which way the wind blows. I don't hurry and the sand slows you down.'

Without looking too much, they threw the tarpaulin over and rolled the body inside so that they could lift it onto the stretcher. They looked at the rolled mass. 'We've even got used to this now,' he said, and shook his head. 'We don't think about it too much anymore.'

Each man held a corner of the stretcher as they started back to the lorry. First they went up the beach beyond the shingle to where the sand was harder, then to the top of the breakwater where the difference in levels was smallest. They pushed the stretcher over, and trudged through the soft sand at the top where the beach merged to the vegetation of the dunes.

A few minutes later the lieutenant skidded out of the siding on his motorcycle and pulled away along the road. He climbed back into the lorry and, looking through the cab window at the two soldiers sat behind, felt alone, holed up there on the coast with a bunch of men he didn't know, telling them what to do, and with officers he didn't understand. Poor buggers! As he pulled the lorry out onto the road and crossed the new railway track to follow the lieutenant, his mind returned to his wife and children, two hundred miles away, seemingly safe enough with his and her family around them, but also in danger. The war had taken away their freedom as well, and for what? For nothing.

He drove to the mortuary to deliver his load.

THE GUARDHOUSE was on the way from the breakwaters. Corporal Michael White watched for special packages and it was a notable day that passed with no communication. A letter or a package, with that careful handwriting, arrived every day. 'Interesting looking package today, Lieutenant,' the corporal said and pointed at the parcel on the desk as he entered the Guardhouse. 'Photographs again, d'you think, sir?'

The corporal was the happiest looking man on the station, always with a smile. Black hair cropped short and black-rimmed spectacles gave him a startling appearance. 'Could be; let's have a look.' Sure enough, with a thick sheaf of newspaper cuttings that he guessed described them, photographs spilled onto the table.

'Where is she now, sir?' the corporal asked and waited while he inspected the writing on the back of a photograph.

'This one says, Folkestone harbour.' He handed it to the corporal.

Helen Strachan witnessed the war from the cliffs of Dover and the harbours of the south coast. She made new friends; Virginia Brightman and Rachel Fitzgerald were reporters for the New York Tribune and the Chicago News. Together, they toured the batteries and coastal defences and witnessed the broad picture of the escalation of Britain's war, watched it in the skies and the seas off the south coast. Helen observed from a distance. There were many others - reporters for a hundred newspapers and journals - all who watched the clock-tick sequence of events escalate into the hours of history. They sent their news to a world that watched Britain. Three or four times a week or more Helen wrote to him and in between, telegrammed and telephoned from wherever she was, sent her reports and thoughts, snippets of information, the lockets of her joy shared daily in the unbroken thread of emotion that started and continued from when they first met.

'There's another one here,' the corporal said, and handed him a letter. 'Looks interesting, as well. And here's one from your mother.'

He laughed. 'You'll have to meet her one day, and my mother.'

He took the two envelopes, and immediately recognised the

familiar handwriting on the other one. On the outside it said: BFPO Rawalpindi. He smiled. The message was clear and was not a surprise: from the far-flung reaches. Alex had gone already; always said she would. 'It's from an old friend of mine,' he said to the corporal. 'A doctor in India.'

'An Indian doctor?'

'No, a woman from my village in Kent.'

'Ah,' the corporal replied.

I'm in northern India... she began. The rest of the letter, although it was seven pages, told him little more than that. She was in India, with the Indian and British forces that made preparations to protect the subcontinent.

Must be the longest letter she's ever written.

She wrote paragraphs that described her experiences of life there, with many anecdotes and cameos of the novelty of such a new and special environment. *And what better place to be than India*, she wrote. *It is wonderful: such a fascinating country.* The people are warm and life is so rich and the places so enchantingly beautiful...

Throughout the day, to grasp all the details, he read the pages again and again.

TIME PASSED: the up-grading and expansion of the old railway track was completed and new rolling stock brought in. Three box vans and three open wagons arrived, as well as old coaches that survived from earlier days. The crowning glory was an engine that was nicknamed *Black Sapper*, which came under its own steam from Hull to Patrington station and then was hauled on a low-loader to Kilnsea.

On May Day he counted seven months of service on the Yorkshire coast. On his night off, for want of something better to do, he went to the Crown and Anchor, one of the pubs near to the peninsula, which had benefited from the influx of servicemen. The white-painted building stood alone on the edge of the river. Beyond it, the line of tank stops formed a ribbon across the fields next to the dyke. The pub served a dispersed community of fisher and farming families. After seven months, when he walked in, he no longer felt a stranger.

The publican, a man called Chas, saw him enter and started to pull a pint before he got to the bar. 'Now, then,' he said.

'Evening,' he replied, and put his money on the bar.

The publican had seen a quick turn round of servicemen over the months. 'Still 'ere then, are you?'

'Yes, for better or worse.'

The solitude encapsulated in the peninsula appealed to a certain sort of person. In May only a minority of them had been there longer. Many had applied for transfer, but like Fenton, he rose above it. What had happened to him was bad, but a festering familiarity with the place helped to overcome the hardship. While he could not come to terms with the fate that brought him there, that had stopped his work, stolen his freedom and broken his contact with Helen, he feared more the prospect of a move.

He looked at Chas, who handed him the pint: 'I'm starting to be inspired by the wildness of this place.'

'People 'ere just want to get away,' Chas retorted. 'Can't stand the boredom.'

'How long have you been here?'

'All mi life; father and grandfather before me.'

'Are you bored?'

'Nah, this is where I belong.' He pulled another pint. 'What d'you do before then?'

He laughed: 'I'm was a composer.'

The statement usually stopped conversations. The publican raised his eyebrows, so he continued. 'I wrote music; the war has put an end to that.'

By Christmas, he had survived by telling himself it would be short-lived. Now, in May, little had changed. Lynch, at least, had gone. The January attacks heralded nothing more than a further period of inactivity. The inertia of inaction was as entrenched as the east wind. They waited and watched from the side lines. The routine blanked out any opportunity to write music.

'We don't get many composers here,' Chas said.

Another man at the bar entered the conversation: 'What sort of things do you do, then?'

'I've done many things: music for theatre and films, music for songs, some orchestral pieces and some classical pieces, which I wrote in Scotland.'

The man nodded: 'A bit difficult doing that sort of thing here, I should imagine.'

He laughed again; he didn't know how true that was. 'When I had the chance last year, my mother wanted me to go to America. A friend of mine emigrated in August, when it was obvious we were going to war. My mother forwarded a letter from him. Now he plays with an orchestra in Cape Cod in New England. Maybe I should have gone.'

The man lifted his eyebrows in acknowledgement. 'That would have been running away though, wouldn't it.'

He shrugged. 'Yes, I suppose it would, but if he had stayed here and joined the army, as I did, he would never have played again. Not as well as he does now. He would have lost the spark of greatness that he has. I think he did the right thing to get away. Now he's made it to the top and will be there when this is all over. I haven't worked on anything since September.'

The publican added: 'See there's more happening down south.'

Another man at the bar agreed. 'Attacks on shipping routes from London to Plymouth.'

Each morning, the newspapers arrived from Hull, and every article was read and reread by the men. The newspaper clippings from Helen complemented the information. One told of a convoy of twenty colliers attacked as they carried coal to southern ports. Despite its destroyer escort, only a handful made it to Plymouth.

'They're getting a pounding in the Channel,' he added to the conversation and stayed at the pub, spending the evening with the locals. Later, until closing time, he played dominoes.

By the end of winter, most of the construction work on the spit was finished. By early summer he had begun to settle to the environment, to understand the balance between sea and the narrow coastal margin. He learnt to live in harmony with it; in some ways had started to know it better than London.

Each day, with growing assurance, he snatched minutes from other agendas, forced out a strand of mental energy. Then, slowly, he began to compose again. Small, but fragmented pieces of music condensed onto the pages of his manuscript book. They came as a relief.

At the start, the strain caused disharmony, but it improved, and he opened his mind to emotions. The strand was like a candle that flickered in the corner of a chapel. He reflected on the war. What he wrote was a response to emotion. Its boundaries widened.

IN THE EARLY days of May the war had taken a turn for the worse. When the call came the previous October, Douglas Cameron had joined the 1st Queen's Own Cameron Highlanders - his father's regiment. In mid-October, 158,000 conscripts went to support the French efforts. Douglas was with them, stationed east of Brussels on the line of the River Dyle. Not unexpectedly, since they parted company in Scotland in August, he had received only one or two letters.

Unlike for himself, it seemed that the events had not affected Douglas so much. In his letters he said that he sang every day, often to the amusement of the men, until it became an accepted part of life in the unit. France was a pleasant stroke of luck. Douglas took it in his stride. The push west would come.

The storm of war broke over Holland in the early dawn of May 10. He listened on the radio to the news, gathered from reconnaissance aircraft, that armoured divisions had rushed the frontier bridges on Holland's borders. Parachutists had landed behind the Dutch lines. Defeat came to the army five days later. Simultaneous attacks occurred into Belgium and France. On the night of May 12, after only two days, tank divisions reached the River Meuse near Sedan, ten miles inside France. The Belgian army retreated to the River Dyle where it joined the British forces. The fighting was fierce.

In the bunkhouse on Spurn, and in the Crown and Anchor, they read the news with horror. His mother wrote of the noise they could hear in Kent in the silence of night from across the channel; the sound of guns, she said. People in East Kent could hear the war in Holland, Belgium and France. The Allied line along the Meuse broke on May 14. The Teutonic deluge continued. Thereafter, the Allies were in retreat. A quarter of Douglas's unit was lost on the Meuse.

He telephoned his mother often and listened to her distress: 'Last week, in the middle of the night, Chilham was bombed,' she told him. It was the first he had heard of any bombing on the mainland of Britain. 'Just out of the blue,' she continued. 'Why Chilham of all places?'

The news from the forests of the Ardennes grew worse. Stuka dive-bombers instead of artillery supported the invaders and allowed them to advance at a speed that took the defenders by surprise. A gash tore through the allied line that severed northern and southern forces and left only open country ahead with no fortifications on the most direct route to Paris. A massive attack through the forests of Ardennes was well underway. By May 20, Panzer divisions spearheaded their way to the French coast at Abbeville.

On the East Coast, newspaper cuttings covered the walls in the bunkhouse. It seemed to everybody that, almost before anything had started, the beginning of the end was in sight. In the bar at the Crown and Anchor he chatted with the new Captain, a man called Andrew Stephenson, who studied the progress of the war. The British fought on the northern section of the front. Stephenson propped up the bar. 'We think we've had it bad here; conditions are desperate in France.'

For one with no more real information than anyone else, he spoke with remarkable authority. 'You seem to know a lot about it, sir,' he said.

'That's the historian's eye for detail.'

'Ah, I wouldn't have placed you as an historian.'

'There you go you see; I wouldn't have placed *you* as a composer.'

'No, I suppose not...'

Stephenson continued: 'Supply lines have been cut, food and ammunition are in short supply, and all routes lead to the sea. Three days ago the British forces fell back from the River Dyle.'

He drew together a fragmented picture. 'I thought the intention was to march south to Amiens and to reunite with the main body of French forces?'

Stephenson shook his head. 'No. The line of the River Scheldt was held with difficulty and the southern push never happened.'

The British, French and Belgians retreated to the Scheldt. It had become clear to everybody that, in a corridor that stretched 70 miles inland and was 25 miles wide, they were trapped. The squeeze occurred on all sides so that the order to evacuate on 26 May came with relief. The next day troops withdrew to a perimeter around Dunkerque. Ostende fell and Boulogne was lost on May 23. *The eyes of the world now are on the defences of Calais*, the newspaper headlines read. Each day that Calais could survive allowed time for troops to be lifted from Dunkerque. On 25 May two British divisions retired from Arras towards the Channel ports. Calais's forces fought until the end. It came on the afternoon of May 26. Those that survived were taken prisoner. The town was reduced to rubble.

For all his superciliousness, Stephenson had a sensitive streak. 'You're worrying about that friend of yours, aren't you?'

At the question and its unexpected intimacy, he blanched and could feel his face remain strained. He nodded: 'Each day as I read the newspapers, I think about the progression and then move to the next day's unfolding of events. We'll never know the finer details.'

What was true for the soldiers on the East Coast was equally true for those in France. No-one would ever know what happened. Stephenson waited for him to continue. 'I have a friend in Scotland, and received a letter from him.' His words came slowly. 'He's a poet and sent me some poems; last year, I set some of his words to music. On the grounds that it would affect the welfare of his family, he's been exempted from the army. He fishes with his father.'

'Fishing? He'd better take care.'

'I think he fishes the inshore waters.' He re-focused. 'He told me he'd received some news from Douglas in France a month ago.'

Further south on the Dunkerque bridgehead, the fury of the attack on the forces that held the twenty-mile front along the La Bassée canal fell on the second Division. La Bassée formed the southern anchor of the canal defence system. The forces were compelled to fall back, strafed by Stuka bombers at low level. Throughout Sunday 26 May, the second Division, subjected to artillery fire and infantry attacks, held its position. Then in the evening, on the extreme left of the Division's line, the forces that included the Cameron Highlanders came under heavy shellfire. Company after company was overrun. The Cameron Highlanders were left to hold the town all night. On the morning of the 27th May the town was stormed and Panzer Divisions crossed the canal. Before noon the British sixth Brigade had been overrun and wiped out. Rommel's seventh Panzer Division set about enlarging the inroads. Kilt-clad Scots fought in the rubble for every inch of their territory. La Bassée was engulfed in flames and smoke and was lost by nightfall.

Day by day, prospects deteriorated. News came of the Belgian army's cease-fire at 4.00a.m. on 28 May. After incessant days of bombing, the demoralised army gave up. For the previous few days, the King's personality had held it together. The newspapers complained that the British Commander received only a few hours' notice of the cease-fire.

At the bar of the Crown and Anchor he joined the usual speculation about the war's progress. 'There's more going on than can ever be told in the papers,' Stephenson said.

'We can only imagine most of what happens.'

'Now that the Belgians have capitulated, you can forget British troops in the north ever re-establishing communication with the French in the south,' Stephenson said.

'The best thing they can do now is to bring everybody and everything which can be rescued home,' another man added. 'The papers reckon that 50,000 troops might make it.'

'Too bloody right,' someone added.

The talk of an evacuation had continued for weeks. The almost daily infusion of hearsay and gossip from Kent that was delivered on the telephone by his mother kept him better informed than many of what was happening in the south. After the first hint, on the 5 May, that evacuation might be necessary, an incredible succession of events had unfolded.

His mother telephoned: 'Apparently Mr Churchill was in Dover yesterday. Our neighbour's brother, who works in the docks, saw him arrive in a special car.'

By 28 May a full-blown evacuation commenced from Dunkerque, the only Channel port that remained open. The newspaper descriptions of efforts to lift the beleaguered men grew in detail. On June 1 it was reported, incredibly, that 34,484 men had been landed at Dover the day before. A flotilla of every type of boat imaginable had been involved: destroyers, transports, drifters, minesweepers, paddle steamers, trawlers, motor yachts, Dutch Scoots, hospital ships and many foreign vessels.

When they landed, the troops were exhausted. The whole of Kent was ransacked to collect food and clothing, and at stations such as Tonbridge and Faversham, collection centres were set up. His mother had volunteered to help at Maklam station and then went to Headcorn to help there. She told him that they estimated 60,000 troops passed through on 31 May in one day alone.

It was pandemonium.

The trains stopped for twenty minutes to give food to the men. Tin cans were used to serve drinks. When the time was up, the cries of *sling them out* resulted in a shower of cans thrown onto the platform, all to be washed before the next train arrived. There were ambulance trains as well, with nurses and doctors on board.

By the 4 June, more than 240,000 British and almost 100,000 Allied troops had been evacuated from France.

Sometimes the newspapers portrayed events with comic book simplicity. It made the stories of suffering on the Dunkerque bridgehead hard for the reader to assimilate. The carnage and tragedy were not confined to the beaches at Dunkerque. Many boats were sunk during the crossings. The destroyer *HMS Wakefield* sank after torpedoes from an E-boat struck her on a return journey to Dover with a load of troops.

While he read the newspaper and wrote to his mother, he sat in a sheltered part of the dunes and looked out to sea. Scenes described in the channel overlaid his memories of those on the Yorkshire coast. The drifter *Comfort* sank after being the victim of a terrible mistake. She was mistaken for an E-boat and attacked by a British minesweeper. After 2 June, evacuation was only at night because of the pressure of daylight air attacks. By 4 June the Dunkerque perimeter collapsed and evacuation ceased.

After Dunkerque, throughout the country, plans to counter the threats of invasion were strengthened. At the beginning of June, the expectation of invasion attempts was high. It seemed the logical next step. There were stories of the possibility of forces leaving from Norway to invade Shetland or further along the eastern Marches. The earlier attacks on the Yorkshire coast heightened this expectation and lent credence to the stories. On the telephone he learnt from his mother that they had removed all the road signs in Kent. 'Can't see what good that will do,' she said.

Now it had started they would need all their strength to resist. The newspaper headlines echoed his thoughts. In the shoreline batteries on the East Coast the men waited in fear of the unknown.

The good weather painted the peninsula in new colours and vitalised the natural world. In the quiet lacunae of the summer days, he found a shallow self-possession that allowed him to make some sense of his feelings.

What themes? What could he write about? A cycle about war? It had been done before. Not to worry… He wrote sketches, more like musical poems, and became even more attuned to the environment.

Attacks on Channel shipping increased and Helen travelled from port to port to chase the developments by the hour. No news came from Douglas. The remaining British forces were cut off in the south and moved west. Helen was in close touch with Nonie.

On the 17 June, and the day before, the radio was on all the time. A piece of trumpet music, the Trumpet Voluntary, was played between announcements. He could only suppose that it was intended to boost morale. At 12.40, the French army announced its cease-fire. It had been six weeks since the first wave of invasions swept into Holland.

The battle of France is over, they said, and now the battle of Britain begins. Two days later he went off duty at mid-day. Helen telephoned soon afterwards and he was called back to the guardhouse to take the call.

'David, my love,' she said, 'Hold tight.'

He heard the words, and in her voice heard the tears she tried to hide from him.

'David, my love,' she repeated. 'Douglas has been killed.' He listened and still heard the words long after they had been spoken.

Then he heard himself say, 'Alright,' and, 'I'll telephone later,' before he replaced the receiver.

Leaving the guardhouse, along the turf ledge at the side of the river above the stony beach, he began to run. With tears in his eyes, he kept going for miles until he found a road that cut inland and followed it through the flat landscape of fields and ditches. The afternoon was warm and the road deserted - as private as any open tract of England could be. He ran with no aim. All he could hear were skylarks in the air above him, the accompaniment to summer days that he had grown used to. He sobbed and his face was wet. Through the afternoon and evening he walked inland towards the dykes and beyond, across the fields and through gaps in the hawthorn hedges. By a pond at the corner of a field, he stopped and sat. A moorhen clucked beneath the bushes that overhung the edges. Newts swam to the surface, then hung in the water and sank and swam away, their tails flapping like pennants behind a boat. By evening, he found himself back at the coast north of Easington.

Few thoughts accompanied his wanderings. Somewhere in France Douglas had died. *Where; what had happened?*

He saw the space that Douglas once occupied and could not imagine how he would not be there to continue occupying it. He saw him one minute, the next minute vanished, as a tree rooted one day and the next cut down and gone. It seemed like a possession that had been stolen and could no longer be found. It was not there anymore, and as much as he searched he would never find it. Douglas would not grow into any future that he may have planned. While he had sat there in Yorkshire, Douglas fought to the end.

BEFORE MIDNIGHT, on the turf outside the guardhouse, Fenton found him. 'Hello, sir,' he said, and sat down. He sensed that something was wrong. He always knew roughly where the lieutenant was, and could always find him if he wanted him. For the last few hours, while he searched, he'd covered for him.

Something was wrong and he guessed he knew what it was. For weeks the lieutenant had followed the war in France, fearful for his friend there; it didn't take much imagination to realise what had happened.

'The captain was looking for you,' he said, and followed the lieutenant's gaze across the estuary. Light from a waning moon illuminated the sea behind them and the air held the heat from the day. He sensed the tension in the lieutenant. 'Almost midsummer,' he murmured. The lieutenant did not reply. Only the cry of waders broke the silence across the mudflats.

'What is it?' he asked. How would the lieutenant say the first words? Everyone learnt more about life out there on the sand spit, and through the bond that had grown between them he felt he understood some of the lieutenant's worries.

'I had news this afternoon...'

He listened.

'...a friend of mine was lost in France.'

He nodded.

'I think I told you about him...' and now he turned towards him.

'Yes, you did.'

'It's the sort of thing you know can happen,' the lieutenant said. 'I'd hardened myself against it.'

He waited longer and wondered how he would feel himself. 'Tell me about him,' he said, but knew the question might need more time than was available to give an answer.

'He was exceptional...'

He waited; then he prompted more: 'In what way?'

'All those ways that can never be described: big; noble; nothing trivial, nothing petty; just straight and good.'

He nodded. *Like we all wanted to be.*

'...He was a musician; a rare singer; knew how to harness his talent; one of those who is wholly great.'

'How long had you known him?'

'We met at college, on the first day, back in '35.'

Now he turned away and listened to the night.

It was the lieutenant who, into the silence, spoke next: 'If a person can ever see into another's mind and soul, I think I saw into his. I just can't think of him not being there.'

'Where was he killed?'

'A place called La Bassée, Helen said. I read about the town in the papers. It was three weeks ago already. Three weeks... and we have just sat here; we didn't know a thing.' The lieutenant ground his foot into the sand and kicked the pebbles. 'He was the sort of person who never ran away. All the strength of a true soldier.'

'You were close to him?'

'Of course... I felt close to him; as close as you can get, I suppose. After last summer, we had a lot left to do together.'

He nodded, then spoke in a whisper. 'Listen!'

Lieutenant Whellans turned towards him and waited.

'No,' he said, '*listen!* I'm sorry about your friend, but *listen*: over there.' He nodded towards the river. Less distinct than the cries of the waders on the mudflats, more distant than the breeze, somewhere to the south over Lincolnshire, the murmur of aircraft engines filtered through the air across the estuary. It was difficult to pinpoint, but the sound moved inland. Only minutes later, the horizon over Hull, fifteen miles as the crow flies, erupted in a glow of incendiary flares. Explosions could be heard, muffled in the night, with the resonance of a storm a long way away.

'*Bastards*: why are they bombing Hull?' It was a half whisper of disbelief as he stared at the sky. It seemed there was little time for sorrow, even less to consider the suffering that caused it.

The lieutenant stood up: 'I'll call communications to find out what's going on.'

'No, sit down, sir; I'll do it. You stay here.'

Backing up the dunes to the guard house, and expecting more to happen any minute, he kept his eyes fixed to the sky. At the guard house he received confirmation that Hull docks were under attack and coastal batteries had been alerted.

He took control: 'We should be ready for them,' he told the corporal in the guard house. 'Alert the captain. I'll get over to the units on the river. Lieutenant Whellans will do the lights.'

He returned to the lieutenant and gave him the news. 'I'll go over to the batteries.'

'Alright; I'll take the search lights,' the lieutenant agreed, and stood up again. 'Make sure they don't start too soon.'

Leaving the lieutenant, he made his way to the riverside and prepared the units. The aircraft did come, but mainly to the north, three or four miles across the hinterland of Holderness. The noise of their engines carried easily on the air. They must have crossed the coast south of Holmpton, where Maplebeck took the squad on nights off. In each battery, the men listened to the retreat until there was no sound left, only the call of seabirds again.

It was one o'clock in the morning and the air had turned chill.

Walking back along the river margin to the spit, he wondered whether he should try to find the lieutenant. Over the last few weeks he had seen him start to ease up and knew he had begun to write music again, heard him play the violin and often listened. He was good. How would the news from France affect him?

HE ASKED for six days leave, wrote a quick letter to his mother to tell her he would see them at the end of the week and, the next morning, took the bus to Hull.

From the moment he boarded in Easington he listened to talk about the raid. Then, as they approached Hull, evidence of the attack was everywhere: a railway bridge damaged and houses hit nearby. At the railway station he bought the Hull Daily Mail. Incendiaries showered on east Hull, one headline read. Incendiary Bomb sets Marfleet field ablaze, read another. They were softening them up. It was all happening at once. Why had he taken leave just when this had started?

During the journey to London, anticipation grew with the passing of each field and pasture. Church steeples and villages receded into the distance as he ticked off the miles. As the train edged south, even the light changed. It was mid-summer's day.

With a last belch of steam that rose to the roof, the train pulled in and stopped. Picking her out in the crowd, he ran across the platform and, dropping his bag, clasped her with his arms. 'Hello my love,' he said, and stood with his forehead against hers. 'It's been so long; you look wonderful.'

The embrace relaxed into steps along the platform, but still they held each other. 'They've started bombing Hull,' he said. 'Just last night. That was the northern town they mentioned in the newspaper.'

'Really? That's incredible,' she said, and then hugged him again. 'You look good, too. I've arranged the place to stay in Rochester with my friend Adrienne. We'll take the underground to Victoria. She expects us at six.'

IN THE HEAT of the afternoon, two miles from the naval

dockyards of Chatham, they walked the still streets. There was no breeze to take away the sultriness. 'It's famous for the number of pubs, this place,' she said. 'There are so many sailors.'

In London the service colour had been khaki; in Rochester it was blue and white. He had no expectations of the town, which, from visits in his childhood to the castle and cathedral, he was familiar with. They stepped out of the sunlight into the *Volunteer*. Helen had been there before with Adrienne and insisted on buying the drinks. The bar was airy and the square tables well-scrubbed. Benches in the corner offered the first privacy since Kings Cross.

'It's great to be close again; you can't imagine the emptiness of days up there on the coast.'

Helen smiled at him. 'Oh, yes, I can; my days are anything but empty, but I have been lonely for you.'

He watched her as she spoke. 'I keep you with me in everything I do.'

She wore a cream dress with short sleeves cut away almost to the shoulder that fitted close and flowed to the knee. A black jacket, she carried over her bag. Her eyes, as she recounted the things she had done over the past weeks, rested on him. They were dark, almost grey, and the skin at the top of her cheeks fluttered around them as she smiled. He took her hand and remembered as they exchanged their stories. Always Douglas occupied the corners of their thoughts.

'Tell me about Nonie. I tried to speak to her on the telephone, but could only leave a message.'

She lent and rested her head on his shoulder and thought for a moment. 'She was distraught, they told me. You can imagine. I don't think she'll ever get over it.'

He saw tears appear at the memory. She sobbed: 'I wanted her to come to London, but she couldn't, and I was unable to go to Scotland. She is stationed in Stirling now. Gavin went over to be with her straight away, and she has a friend that stays with her. Eventually she called me; just cried on the telephone and wept, and then her friend said she couldn't speak anymore. That was two days ago. Everything that's happened to us is so awful.'

He closed his eyes and felt tears come too. 'It's much more than that.'

Her voice was husky. 'I can't believe he's gone from us.'

Letting his head roll back, he stared at the ceiling. 'And what's worse, I wonder if we'll ever be sure where and how he died...'

'Does that matter?'

'I don't know; I think so. Until now, I held everything together in my mind; I'd hung on to all we did. I thought we could pick it up again.'

'I know...'

They sat in silence and then she stood up. 'Come on, let's go to Adrienne's. I can't think about it anymore.'

Outside, the sunlight made it hard to feel depressed. Following the incline through the streets of Rochester, they continued along the pavement beside the gardens of terraced houses. Each was full of flowers with bright foliage. Some had small window boxes and hanging baskets near the doors that trailed masses of petals.

Helen stopped and admired them. 'We'll always keep some flowers somewhere for him.'

Above the town, the street followed the contour of the hill. With a wooden gate and flowers in pots at the door, Adrienne's house was much the same as all the rest. She welcomed them. James, one of her friends, was with her. Later, in the garden at the back of the house, they had supper together and drank beer and filled the evening with laughter and words.

Adrienne waited until it was dark, then said that she had to be up early and so was going to bed. James departed and walked home through the un-lit streets. Only the moon showed his way.

'They've left us alone,' he said, and put his arms around her as they stood in the garden. 'Do you think she approves?'

'I think, on balance no, but she's fine.'

He leaned on her shoulder, and then, in the evening gloom, they followed Adrienne upstairs, and opening the door, entered the room at the front of the house. Both sash windows had been raised high and the scent of flowers wafted in. Helen stood by a window and looked out. The light of the sky was at that last point of twilight before it succumbed to dark. No artificial lights could be seen and slowly their eyes adjusted to the shadows. Across the road a thrush, perched beside the chimney on the roof, presented its parting song to the day, a repertoire of trills and whistles. She listened and looked at the garden beneath, where blue cornflowers grew between pink roses in the dark beds. The thrush flew off and in its wake, calls of quieter birds broke the silence: a blackbird in the shrubbery and a quiet *tswee* that she could not recognise. A bat, which at first she mistook for a swallow, flitted past. Somewhere across the town, the noise of a train diminished and an open top army jeep rolled by with four soldiers making merry.

She did not close the blind and waited for him to follow her to the window. She felt him come near, fold his arms around her, and draw her to him. She felt him kiss her hair and blow his breath through to her neck. He found the skin below the hairline and ran his lips over the surface.

'David, my love...'

'I've missed you...'

He kissed her and felt her relax.

She turned until her lips trembled and she held him as if stood in the balance of a dance-step and swayed until only her lips remained touching him. Then she came back, and, pushing him against the surround of the window, relaxed so that he held her. She clasped him and received his caresses and brought her hands round and undid his shirt. Then he raised her dress and let her under garments slip to the floor. In the sensation of love, she clung to him, pushed her hands to the wall and spread her fingers, moved around and over him.

Behind them, as they stood in each other's arms, the houses and gardens darkened. The alleys were black between the houses and her eyes rested on the roofs that caught the last light. He kissed her shoulders, let her undress him and then lay with her in the shadows of the last light. It was with a sense of freedom that she ran her fingers through his hair and down his neck and arms and kissed his stomach. Later, when they stood by the window again, the night was silent. The smell of the southern town was unfamiliar to senses tuned to air washed clean by waves. Finally they slept.

At 4.30, birds sang in the first light. He turned to look at her curled beneath the sheet and caressed her arm and felt her awaken and respond. She folded into his arms and they kissed as she drew him to her and reeled and recoiled in his passion and pulled him close to her.

Again they slept.

Later, when Adrienne had gone, there was no need for them to do anything. At nine o'clock the sun cast long rays through the window across the bed and walls. He made some tea and brought it to her on a tray.

'Isn't it a relief that we've managed to escape,' she said, 'to this lovely room? So far from anyone and anywhere.'

He did not want to spoil the moment with negative words about Douglas and so said nothing. He poured her a cup of tea. 'How did you meet Adrienne?'

She seemed to cast her mind back the two years since they had met. 'She came to visit her friend in London, whose sister works in our office. I met her then. We were all invited out one evening.'

'You're very alike.'

'Hmm, other people have said so.'

'Thank you for writing to me so often. I know you love your work; it's coming right for you, isn't it?'

'Yes, it's very challenging, and there's a lot to do. The times certainly are rich with opportunities, but I do hate your being so far away.'

'Our minds are in one place, while we are in another...'

'Could you transfer to Kent?'

'I could... but, would it make any difference? Still we would be apart most of the time. There would be the army routine. My mind shrivels more each day in its drudgery.'

'I think it would be better.'

'Yes; alright, I'll try...'

Trying to forget, in the afternoon they walked, and for a while, in the sun, succeeded, and talked about their dreams. The road went to the river and with the castle behind them, walking at the water's edge, they continued beneath the iron-bridge that crossed the river to Strood. When they could go no further they cut back past riverside warehouses and walked as far as Chatham station, then up the hill and across the common to Rochester. It was four o'clock when they found their way back to Adrienne's.

Throwing her cardigan across the banister, she went up to the bedroom. Adrienne had not come home and the house was as they had left it. He drank a glass of water and took one to Helen. Near the window she sat on the bed and, with her hairbrush in her hand, looked out. Behind her, so that the curve of her back moulded to him, he held her, and breathed the smell of jasmine from her neck.

'We are so lucky.'

Brushing her hair, he kissed her where strands fell beside her ear and moved round and let her fall onto the bed and ran his fingers from her ankles and along her legs. He kissed her and breathed on her. She pulled his head towards her and kissed him and rolled over him and made love to him until he gasped and relaxed beneath her.

The afternoon merged into evening and leaving a note for Adrienne they went out to sit by the river. Tomorrow they would part: she to London and he for a night at home before he returned to Yorkshire. It was 22 June.

First they walked beneath the sycamore and chestnut trees that edged the banks upriver from the castle and caught the last of the sun as it touched the Downs to the west. They circled round into the High Street and bought a drink at the Jolly Sailor and went out to sit on the grass beside the Cathedral beneath the castle walls.

On the grass he asked her to hold out her hand and to close her eyes. He placed something in her palm. 'I want you to have this.' It was a silver sixpence on a silver chain. 'I asked mother to send it to me for you. It was from my grandmother. I want you to have it.'

Taking it, she held it in her fingers and let the chain fall between them. 'It's lovely; how can I take a gift from you that belonged to your grandmother?'

'Because I want you to.'

She opened the clasp and placed it around her neck. 'It's just right.'

He was glad that she had accepted it.

The evening passed and neither he nor she pushed or pulled its progression.

AT SOME point the sound of rain entered his sleep and, drenched, as she ran to the station to go back to London, he saw Helen. When he awoke, drips from the gutter on the roof fell past the open window. Beside each other, and preparing to part, they lay awake.

Only hours later, seeing her onto the train was real and, kissing her one more time before the whistle blew, they did part. There was no planned follow-up, no knowledge of the next steps they would take, but when he caught his train, her words remained in his mind: *stay here another day, don't go home yet.* He had resisted, but now wished he had stayed.

The journey took less than an hour and allowed little adjustment to his homecoming. As he passed through Kent the glimpses from the carriage of orchards and hop fields blurred the images of the past two days that flared in his mind. Although the journey unsettled him, as the miles passed, the landscape lured him and lulled him. He had written to her every day, but still felt that he had neglected his mother. Some things he could not write about. At his destination, with one or two people to meet them, just a handful of passengers alighted. At the end of the platform he saw his mother and put on a bold face.

'Darling,' she said, as she rushed up to him. To see him and to receive a simple kiss on the cheek seemed enough to set her world to rights. 'David, darling, welcome home; we've missed you so much.' They walked arm in arm and, on arrival home, she put on the kettle and made some tea.

The house stood in vivid contrast to the conditions in which he lived in Yorkshire. Unlike the quarters on the peninsula, the house was well cared for. He saw things anew, larger and clearer than he remembered. His room, which was pristine as the day he left, had the strange and calming stillness he had grown up with. The piano, transported home from London, stood in the middle on its green carpet.

For the rest of the day he listened and talked. His father arrived at lunchtime and then remained at home to make the most of his son's presence; he smoked a cigar after lunch. 'Nothing much has changed around here my boy,' he said. 'It must seem rather dull to come home.'

'No, absolutely not; that couldn't be further from the truth. I was just thinking how good everything feels here.'

When he forgot himself, nostalgia completed the picture set by the surroundings of his childhood. Home was a place that he fitted, and blended into with ease. 'You, know, I haven't been here at all very much for almost five years.'

'And you have changed,' his father said. 'Over the past six months, you seem to have grown into that uniform. You look every bit the part now.'

'If that is the case, it's an accident. I don't enjoy it or feel it at all.'

'How is it going, anyway?'

'Not good I should say. Bombing started in Hull.'

Theo nodded. 'Yes, so I read and hear; it's just amazing. What about that captain fellow. How are you getting on with him these days?'

'He's gone; been replaced. I told mother. It's better now. I've learnt to give as much as I take. Found a side of my personality I didn't know I had.'

'I'd say you've hardened. I'm not sure I like it.'

'Maybe I have. The place is a wilderness. The monotony and the inability to write are the killers. Now, although in truth I find it less monotonous, I still can't do anything creative.'

'Just keep going. I think you're doing alright.'

They talked about his father's business and how they contributed to the war effort making toughened glass. Edwin, who co-managed the business now, returned in the afternoon. 'We've got another big order from the MOD,' he announced to everyone, '- it's an ill wind that doesn't blow anyone some good.'

Tea was laid in the garden and, later, beneath foliage of vine leaves and trusses of grapes, like small peas, that hung under the glass roof, they gathered for supper in the conservatory. His mother fanned herself. It pleased him to see her at ease. 'Oh, I feel quite light headed,' she said. 'That glass of wine was too much. It's such a long time since I drank wine.'

'It's good to see you relaxed, Mother, - after the stress of the past months.'

She fanned herself more. 'Tell us what you've managed to compose.'

'Nothing, really, only trivial amounts: I have done nothing. We, the whole army, have done nothing.'

'You said you were doing a little.'

'I know, but it really is so little.' He laughed when he thought how little he had done.

'You said you were doing a concert.'

Again he laughed. 'Ah, yes. Yes, if that is what you can call it. We have started a small *review* for the summer. Forty soldiers having their first go at amateur dramatics and music hall repartee - if that's what you call a concert.'

'Better than nothing...'

'That, I agree, is true. We have some fun sketches from life on the East Coast wilderness.'

The evening had the familiar feel of old times about it and for a while he relaxed into the memories.

Later, when he lay down to sleep, as if he were a marionette dandled on a string and worked by others, the present jolted him to reality. How good it would be just to stay there in Kent. That was where he should be. Maybe yes, he should try for a transfer, and get himself back there.

DRIVING TO Easington, before collecting the lieutenant from the coach, he completed the two or three jobs he needed to do. If he never saw them again, there were those he would not miss; Lieutenant Whellans was not one of them. The jobs made him late and, as he turned the corner into the square in Easington, he saw him outside the pub. 'I thought I'd come to collect you myself, sir,' he said. 'Welcome back and apologies for being late. We've had some action while you've been away.'

'Thank you; have you?' the lieutenant replied, climbing into the lorry.

'It's a pleasure, sir. How was the trip?'

'Describe the Elysium Fields to me, sergeant.'

'As good as that, sir?'

'It was.' Then the lieutenant sounded more serious. 'Well, although going home was painful, I could easily have gone AWOL.'

He laughed. 'Well then, a double welcome back, sir. We need you here. And how was Helen?'

The lieutenant cast a glance over at him. 'She's fine; really doing well.'

He waited, but the lieutenant didn't say anything else. 'You're looking well for the break, sir; and how's life at home?'

Now the lieutenant seemed to check himself and his voice told the story. 'Thank you: everything at home is good. It is where I should be; where I can work and write.'

'Hm, it's always a joy to go home,' and he thought of his own home, but, trying to keep the conversation cheerful, said, 'You started writing here though, didn't you, sir?'

'I did, but it was a struggle…'

He smiled and looked over at the lieutenant: 'Things are hotting up, you'll be pleased to hear, sir.'

'Yes, you said; what sort of action?'

'We brought down a Heinkel that was dropping mines in the Humber at the mouth of the estuary.'

'Oh, that is progress.'

'Yes. It managed to crash-land in the fields over there.' He pointed. 'I'll show you later. We had some fun with it; I'll tell you about that later too. Hull's taking a pounding. The bombing's merciless.'

As the lorry rumbled past the Crown and Anchor, the lieutenant nodded. Over the months, although everyone had struggled, he himself was in better shape and had sorted out a lot of the frustration and was getting on well. Despite the trip away, it seemed the lieutenant still wasn't winning his struggle and it worried him. As they neared the guard house he looked over at him again, now lapsed into silence.

'Anyway, welcome back, sir.'

The lieutenant nodded an acknowledgement. 'Thanks.'

Dropping him at the officers' quarters, he returned to the gun emplacements at the Point. Maybe he'd be better in the morning.

THAT EVENING, in the officer's mess, he fretted. His heart was low and so, where the breeze bent the reeds, he walked along the edge of the marshes that spread inland from the peninsula. In Hull, that afternoon, while he had walked through the streets to pass an hour before the coach departed, he had witnessed the results of the bombing and felt no sense of reason to carry him forward. In a bright sky the sun rolled over the estuary into the low landscape beyond the river. It faded in an endless decline and the night came softly.

Later, in the officers' quarters at the end of the spit, he found no comfort and sat alone on the steps of the observation tower. Before him, while the country waited for the progression of war, lay the uncertain future of summer. The fall of France had brought the invading army to the Channel coast. To overpower Britain, first they would have to deal with the RAF. Britain's hope rested on them. The conflict drifted closer and he had no doubt that it was real. Douglas had paid the price for this certainty. Now he wanted the loss redressed. His soul had hardened and he saw a job to be done. Back with his unit, back to avenge his loss, he tried to settle his mind and calm his emotions.

A MONTH later, in early August 1940, still he had done nothing but contemplate the ocean. The shoreline batteries let off the occasional round at enemy aircraft that strayed near the coast on bombing sorties to Hull and other Yorkshire towns. Otherwise, they were silent. He had to do more; Kent was the place to be and perhaps the time was right to transfer.

In the empty days he tried to compose music, but the energy that prompted it did not last. It would never work.

Elsewhere, the contrast to the lack of activity in Yorkshire could not have been greater. The battle for mastery of the skies began in mid-July. For three weeks, over England, opening blows were exchanged. 'They were just sounding out the defences this afternoon,' said Stephenson, one evening in the Crown and Anchor. 'Thin end of the wedge, if you're asking me. You wait; there'll be more next time.'

Stephenson referred to another surprise attack on Hull. The first shocks were felt in Yorkshire in the week after his return. Until then, as everywhere else, Hull had suffered only night time attacks; now the city felt the blow of the first daylight raid in the country. In itself it was not much; a lone aircraft ran over from west to east and made a few spasmodic attacks on barrage balloons, and then, at 5.30 in the afternoon, dropped stick bombs on oil installations at Saltend in East Hull. Shrapnel pierced the side of a tank that contained 2,500 tons of petrol. Despite some flames, it was sealed before it exploded. The coastal batteries watched the raider head back out to sea.

Events vindicated Stephenson's prediction. Across the country, the bombing escalated. By mid-August attacks in the south had moved into a higher gear. His mother fed him the latest information on the situation in Kent. 'Yesterday they bombed Bekesbourne, just down the road of all places,' she said, 'and six people were killed. It's just a pocket-handkerchief of a place. They've bombed the radar stations, which I can understand, but why Bekesbourne? Of course the airfields have been hit. What an awful way to spend the summer...'

'The RAF is fighting back though, isn't it?' he asked down the line.

'Well, by all accounts, they seem to be holding their own. Today your father says bombers have attacked Detling airfield. Joan Cunningham telephoned and told me she had seen them - forty or more - going over in droves. A few days ago some planes came down near Canterbury. Two of the pilots were killed.'

The newspapers were full of it. *Dogfights over Kent.*

He sat by the sea. Come on, he thought, and penned a few more lines. Then he closed his eyes. His composure was wrong; his emotions too fragmented. In August, the Battle of Britain - as it had become known - reached a climax. It looked as though the air force would crack. He read about it and listened to the news in the Crown & Anchor. The discussion and debate of events was intense.

Expectancy mounted, but at the beginning of September the raids tailed off and quietness returned to England's skies. Fighter Command had won, and it appeared to the onlooker that the worst of the assault was over.

The calm only preceded the next storm that came a few days later. On Saturday afternoon the Operations Room under the sand dunes of the peninsula received communication that, in the first daylight raid on the capital, bombs had started to fall on London. The attack appeared to focus on the docks and was heavy. Later in the evening, the radio reported the devastation that had been wrought in the packed streets of the East End. 300 aircraft dropped 300 tons of bombs, they said. The city was almost brought to a standstill.

On Black Saturday, thousands of incendiary bombs dropped in broad daylight, followed by high explosives at night, crippled industries and services. East London took the brunt of the first attacks. Miles of Thames-side warehouses blazed into the night. In Woolwich Arsenal, through the barrage of exploding ammunition, fire-fighters could not fight the flames. In the great warehouses, thousands of tons of tea, sugar and oil fed the flames, and rum and paint formed molten streams that sizzled into the Thames. The stench of burning rubber could be smelt on the south coast.

To report on the extent of the daily carnage, Helen returned from Southampton. Fewer letters arrived for Corporal White to monitor. 'Only one letter so far this week, sir,' he said to him one morning.

'Her mind's too much on her work; here we are bystanders...'

By the end of September, from dusk to dawn, bombing in London occurred every night. It became a routine. The papers coined the phrase the *Blitz*, a word derived from the German Blitzkrieg, lightning war, which is what the Germans hoped it would be, like the lightning strikes through the Ardennes forests into France, pushing all before them.

Each evening, air-raid sirens wailed, followed by the sinister drone of approaching bombers. Terrible damage occurred in Stepney and Shoreditch. Then it spread to Chelsea and Westminster. The Houses of Parliament were bombed and Buckingham Palace was hit three times. Nothing escaped. When the moon was full and bright, and the bombers had a clear view of the city, they called it a *Bomber's Moon*.

He read the Hull Daily Mail: three firemen killed and only one body recovered. Craters in the road big enough to take double-decker buses, it said.

Londoners slept wherever they could, in all kinds of shelters. Some refused to be evacuated from their homes, even in high-risk areas. Others joined the annual migration to the hop fields in Kent, which for many came as a welcome relief.

The wreckage was not only in London. A letter from his mother brought incredible news. The village had been bombed. Two parachute mines had fallen on the main street. Fifteen people were killed and eleven injured.

By now it was not boredom that confirmed his decision to ask for a transfer, but lack of opportunity to fight back. Another was Helen. He knew he must try to do something to be closer to her. Because of the distance between them, he had begun to neglect her.

He approached Stephenson who passed on his request. It had taken him a long time to settle and now he felt disquiet at the prospect of a new start at another station. The peninsula was not perfect, but it had become familiar.

At the end of September he adjusted to the prospects of the move. To abandon the place, give up on it at a time of low morale, seemed wrong. Stephenson received word that they might send him to Avonmouth! It would be nearer London, but second best to Gravesend or somewhere else in Kent. Then the news came that his request had been turned down. No reason was given. Permission was not granted and he must stay in Yorkshire.

A SPELL of calm weather followed and it was almost a year since his arrival. How could he break the downward cycle, re-find his old self, reinvent himself there on the East Coast? He talked to Helen on the telephone. 'I'm sorry. I tried.'

'No, don't worry; I'm going to come to you instead. I've thought about it already and I'll ask to be sent to Hull - on secondment or exchange possibly. So, it's my turn to try.'

He laughed. 'I hadn't thought of that. I might go there as well. Air-raid duties around the city. Good idea.'

When she hung up, he went to find Stephenson. It was already dark and he found him off-duty in the barrack hut. With his shirt sleeves rolled up, reading the daily paper and feet on the table, he made a stark contrast to Lynch. 'Evening, sir,' he said, and sat down.

'Evening, Whellans. How are things with you?'

'Good. Bit casual for an Oxford man, aren't you?'

'Inverted snobbery old boy. Don't need to flaunt the airs and graces you know.'

'Quite. I was thinking - if I can't transfer to the action in the south then maybe I could get more of the action here, particularly now that things are starting to intensify. I thought I could do more work with other batteries along the river, nearer to Hull, as we've discussed. Look at the overall defence strategy for the Humber and see what we can do.'

'Sounds good to me. I'll call Captain Collinson; see what he says.'

A WEEK later he arrived in a village called Preston, near Hedon, not far from the edge of the Humber east of Hull. He would stay for a week and use the station as a base from which to tour other emplacements and look at the overall defence strategy for the Humber approach to Hull. By the time he found the Gun Operations Room, air-raid sirens sounded.

'Evening, sir,' the sergeant said as he looked up. 'We were expecting you later.'

'Yes, apologies. Opposite to the usual excuse; I was keen to get here.'

'Not to worry, sir, you're just in time for a reception party that's arriving along the Humber - a score or so of assorted bombers,' and as he looked over, a barrage went up from the nearest battery. 'I'm Gifford. Captain Collinson is away until tomorrow and this is Corporal Barnes.' Barnes eyed the violin case that he carried over his shoulder on a makeshift leather strap. He took it off and laid it on top of his small grip on the floor.

'Travelling light then, sir?' Barnes asked.

'I'd never thought about that, corporal. Do you think I am?'

'Looks like it to me, sir. On the fiddle as well are we, sir?' Barnes replied.

He smiled. 'The old ones are the best, aren't they, corporal? It helps to while away the long hours.'

Now Barnes stopped his joking. 'Of course, sir.'

'I hear that you are quite an organist as well, sir,' Gifford said, to rescue Barnes. 'I enjoy organ music.'

'Yes. I've played at St Patrick's in Patrington. The *Queen of Holderness* they call the church. Beautiful gothic architecture and an impressive spire. Fine organ as well.'

'I know the church, sir. You're welcome here as well. We have the King of Holderness - St Augustine's - in Hedon. Maybe you could play there for us?'

'Really? Well, maybe I could. Yes, I have heard about St Augustine's. Thank you, Sergeant.'

'Try the piano out back, as well, sir; in need of a good tuning,' Barnes said.

'Maybe I'll do that, as well.'

Gifford looked sideways at Barnes, then back to him. 'I tickle the keys, myself, on occasion, sir.'

'Do you, sergeant? You can take me round to the church sometime.'

Gifford gave him the look of one who shares common interests and looked sideways at Barnes again. 'It will be a pleasure, sir.' He sounded lively and showed the confidence of a Master of Ceremonies; he gave the impression that he enjoyed his role at the centre of the stage. Preston was on a main flight path into Hull and Gifford held the station's reins.

He felt the man's eyes scrutinise him.

'Would you like to come and have a look at the batteries, sir?' Gifford offered. 'I've got to go down there anyway. The nearest is on the river. It's not far.'

'Yes, thanks, but I need to make a quick telephone call first.'

'Use this one,' Barnes said, and indicated a telephone.

He listened to the tone long enough to know there would be no answer and hung up. The sergeant looked across. 'Out of luck, sir?'

He nodded. 'Second time today. I missed her at lunch time and now the office is closed. She might call here. I gave her the number.'

The sergeant was helpful. 'I'll take a message if she does. What's her name?'

'Helen. I'd be grateful,' and he repeated their names to remind himself. That was the trouble with the army - too many names. Sergeant Gifford, Corporal Barnes, Captain Collinson...

Gifford looked sympathetic. 'You're from Kent, aren't you, sir?'

'Hmm, yes, Maklam.'

'So am I, sir. Quite close, at Wingham, sir.'

'That's a coincidence. It's good to be here with you for a while.' He felt disloyal to those who couldn't so easily get off the peninsula. Fenton, in particular. 'I hope it will be worthwhile.'

'I am sure it will be, sir. You're also quite a radio ham, I understand.'

He raised his eyebrows. 'The grapevine has been working, hasn't it!'

The sergeant's grin was inscrutable. 'Barnes will take you to the batteries, sir. I'd better wait for the lorry.'

'See you later, then, Sergeant Gifford.'

As he followed Corporal Barnes out into the dusk, Gifford made a light salute. Almost by way of an excuse for his previous remarks, he said, 'It's been relatively quiet on the coast.'

'No chance of that here, sir. This is the best weather we've had for weeks, and the moon is good, so we can expect the worst. They may come in further south over Lincolnshire, so you miss many of them out there on the peninsula.'

'That's why I'm here, to see something happening, so you can show me the worst.' The heavy pound of the guns now sounded and flak guns added an overtone.

'Even if we don't down any, we do force them to fly higher,' Barnes said.'

At the battery, the silhouettes of rows of enemy aircraft on course for Hull showed against the pale sky. As they watched them come in over Lincolnshire, he stood motionless.

'You should have been here when the daytime raids came over in early September. It scared the pants off us.'

'We saw a few at low level off the Humber, way back in January. The ships there didn't have a chance. Fishing boats as well. We found the sailors washed up weeks later. A few aircraft caused terrific destruction.' He shuddered at the memory.

A searchlight probed the sky. Barnes followed the beams. 'It's hard to get them when they are so high. Then they start to twist and dive. We got one in our searchlight a few nights ago, but still didn't hit him. It takes forty seconds for shells to reach them. Impossible.'

'Surely they can think of something to improve on that.'

'You would think so wouldn't you, sir. They need to. The docks were hit last night, and twenty one civilians killed.'

He looked at the sky and cursed. 'We must do better than this.'

As the bombers passed over and the guns went silent, Barnes glanced at him.

'You have a Radio Detection Finder here, don't you?'

'Yes, at HQ. RDF transmitter and receiver.'

'I'd like to have a look at that later. It's a long time since I did any amateur radio stuff, though. My father's very good at it, and is helping the MOD.'

'Alright,' sir, I'll show you,' Barnes said. 'I'll take you to the barrack hut now if you like, sir. It's not far, but don't build up your hopes.' The two men walked back along the road. 'Do you play football, sir?'

'I wouldn't say I was marvellous at it. I play more rugby.'

'We are playing tomorrow, so if you want a game, you'll be welcome.'

'Thanks. I'll join you.' As they walked, sirens sounded and artillery fire could be heard from across the river.

'There they go,' Barnes said, and stopped to look. 'Here we are talking about tomorrow's football, with death and destruction happening ten miles away.'

Then, only minutes later, the sky to the west flared in an inflorescence of white light followed by explosions that shook the night. The flashes continued as the glow of fires showed on the horizon towards Hull.

'It's our fault; it's our artillery that allowed them through to do that,' he said.

Barnes seemed puzzled. 'Hadn't thought of it like that, sir.'

His voice hardened. 'It's our job to stop them.'

Barnes nodded.

They walked on. 'So how many have you brought down?'

Barnes was eager. 'Two. Maybe three, four.'

From the tone of his voice, he could have been talking about a hundred.

'We are pretty certain we got one last week.'

He shook his head. 'But that's nothing…'

He imagined Barnes's shrug and look of hurt in the dark.

Then Barnes seemed to come down to reality. 'The ground defences are too dispersed, sir. There are thirty batteries each of four guns covering ten miles in the flight-paths between Hull docks and the coast. Accuracy is poor. What can we do?'

'Better than our present record, that's for sure.'

Barnes tried to make excuses. 'The crews work day and night. No wonder success rates are poor.'

'But you only had one searchlight unit working, just now.'

'We've had orders to switch on only when an aircraft was being tracked. They reckoned the searchlights were more help in guiding bombers to targets than for us to spot them.'

'No one told us on the coast. What is Captain Collinson like?'

Barnes perked up. 'He's a good man, sir; you'll like him. We expect him early tomorrow.'

Later he received a message that Helen had called and, from a box in the street, he called back. It was almost impossible to dial in the dark. Eventually he heard her voice. 'Hello, David.'

'Hello. It's a bad line.'

'Sorry I missed you when I called earlier.' She sounded miserable.

'Don't worry. It's awful not being there with you. What are you doing at the moment?'

The distance remained in her voice, as if she had been knocked down in a fight and was trying to pick herself up again. 'I'm doing more work at night; in Bexley.'

'You must be tired.'

'No, I find the work very stimulating.' There was a pause. 'There's always another job waiting to be done.' She paused again. 'Davy, it's been four months since we saw each other.'

He heard her tears, and said, 'I know; we no longer have our lives. What are you doing in Bexley?'

He heard Helen struggle. 'Something on the night life.'

'Very funny.'

'No, it's true.' Helen's voice lightened a little. 'I am just seeing what happens. Day in the life of an Air-raid Warden, that sort of thing.'

'Oh, I see. I saw your article about the underground.'

'Hmm,' she murmured. 'Look, I have to go. There is a lot of racket going on outside. I'll call again. I'm still trying to get up to Hull.'

'Alright - I love you.' He waited for the line to go dead then hung up. He walked along the streets beside houses that looked as though they were empty. Only the smell of smoke from the chimneys told of their inhabitants. What was happening? he asked himself again.

When he returned to his room the conversation still tormented him. He understood her hurt and shared her frustration. It was his fault; he should have been more forceful. Months of being apart: he should have insisted on a transfer.

He lay on his bed and for distraction put his mind to air-defences - how to improve the success rates of the anti-aircraft crews. He was even starting to think like a soldier. The war changed people. He got up and went out again and, at the battery, found Barnes. 'Can we go over to HQ and see the Radio Detection Finder?' he asked.

'Alright, sir. I'll find the driver.'

In the Barracks HQ, he watched a plot of aircraft as they approached the coast. 'So, early warning is good, but we still find it impossible to shoot them down.'

'Precisely, sir. Even if you can see them in broad daylight, it's impossible to hit them.'

'Yes, I know that. We'll have to work on it.'

CAPTAIN COLLINSON gave the impression of being a man who was in control of his affairs; there was nothing ostentatious about him, but he looked like a man who, as he approached his middle years, enjoyed life. 'Lieutenant Whellans, good morning,' he said, when he met him in the Ops. Room the next morning. 'Welcome to Preston HQ. I hear you found the coast a little quiet?'

'It is an astonishing place, sir; perfect for bird watching if you like that sort of thing. The bits the army hasn't covered with concrete, that is.'

'Yes, well, life is livelier here, as you have no doubt found out. Have they shown you round?'

'Yes, first introductions have been made, thank you, sir.'

'Good. I want you to do some morale boosting. So get to know the men and see what you think we should do.'

He was pleased at this opener. 'I wondered about the success rate you are having, what we could do to make things better?'

Collinson glanced over at him. 'Damned if I know. Give that

some thought. These guns were fine twenty years ago, but no good against modern aircraft.'

'I had some thoughts last night. We can talk them over.'

'Sure as hell. I understand they liked your ideas at Spurn.'

'If they did, they forgot to tell me, sir.'

'Hm, that's the army for you. I'll be back at lunchtime. Let's meet then.'

Later that afternoon, with Collinson's chat behind him, he went to see Sergeant Gifford. 'We are going to try something new, and you are the key to the plan.'

'Really, sir?' Gifford looked pleased. He stroked his moustache, seemed to will it ever wider across his jowls.

He looked at him. 'Clearly we need to use the guns more effectively. That's obvious to you as well as to everybody else.'

Gifford put his pencil down. 'Well, yes, I suppose it is, sir.'

He paused; his qualifications were flimsy. Any authority he had was grounded in his mathematical ability and knowledge of amateur radio operations. But he had the conviction that things should be done better.

'The crews will have to work together, and the lights as well. We need co-ordinated action aimed at the leading aircraft. That's your role.' He explained his plans to Gifford. Together they briefed the gun crews. When he had finished it was almost dark and as he departed, he was aware of Gifford's glance at Barnes as if to say, *who the hell is he to tell us*?

No aircraft came that night. He sat it out in one of the tents beside a gun unit. The nervous expectation exhausted him. The next night was better. Gifford relayed information as it came in from the sector airfields of Lincolnshire. The flight paths were almost the same as on the first night he had watched them.

'Remember the plan,' he shouted to the first gun crew in his battery. 'Practise judging the time ahead of the aircraft and go for the leaders only.' The action was over in minutes. They flew over and then were gone, heading for Hull. There had been little evidence of co-ordinated action. Beside the gun unit, he looked into the darkness and gritted his teeth.

The following afternoon he debriefed the crews. Disappointment showed in the lines on his face. 'You were all over the place.' His first words were followed by silence. He looked around the men. They didn't have a clue.

Stirred by their innocence, he said, 'Too many of you think you are in short pants playing cowboys and indians in the back garden. You didn't have a hope in hell last night. From now on, that nonsense stops.'

There was silence. Then a crewman piped up. 'Nobody has any idea of height and distance, sir. The radar is not accurate enough.'

He remained serious. 'The sound locators on the searchlights are primitive and all but useless. The radar is all we have. Familiarise yourselves fully with it and everything to do with gun operation. I expect every individual to be able to recite line and verse of the manual. Sergeant Gifford...'

'Yes, sir?'

'Any man who cannot do that will be on a charge.'

'Yes, sir.'

He looked again around the room. 'We must use our brains and the equipment we have to our best advantage.' They should know that already. 'You have the brains. The equipment is out there.' *Could this ever make a difference?* he wondered.

A despondent voice replied. 'It's impossible to get everybody working together, sir. By the time the aircraft arrive, you just have to get on and blast hell out of the sky.'

He looked at the crewman, and paused. Then he said, 'Were you at my briefing two days ago?'

The man nodded. 'Yes, sir.'

In an uncharacteristic lapse of concentration, he took it out on the man. 'What's your name?'

'Willet, sir.'

'Then Private Willet, either you were not listening or you are slow at understanding. Which is it?'

Willet hesitated. 'I'm not sure, sir.'

He paused. 'Well you'd better be sure next time I see you. I shouldn't need to say this again. 'We attack the leading aircraft, and then cut a path back through the main formation as they fly over. All guns work together; take the front of the formation first. The lights concentrate on the first aircraft. That is our chance. I want them to fly through your shells.'

'It'll frighten the lead crews, if nothing else sir,' one of the men said. 'It's worth a try.'

'Thank you for your encouragement,' he replied and nodded. 'Is that clear then? Tonight we try it my way. Put your brains where your mouths are and use them.'

The men dispersed and he accompanied Gifford back to the Ops. Room. Gifford was silent until they entered. Two soldiers stood smoking by the desk. 'Douse 'em, you two,' he rasped. The two men stubbed their cigarettes and saluted. Gifford took out the Daily Report's Book and handed it to him. 'That contains all the information on previous activities, sir.'

'Okay, thank you; now tell me a few things sergeant: firstly, how do the aircraft navigate; do they take their bearings along the river and fly on a beam?'

'Yes, that's it, sir; they do fly on a beam,' Gifford agreed.

'So, clearly we're in luck. There are two things we can do. If they're a beam, they will fly in the same place...'

Gifford looked doubtful. 'Sometimes they come in over Hedon or from other parts of south Holderness. Difficult to say where they will come from. They fly at different heights. Seven and a half thousand, maybe higher or lower.'

'Yes, but if there is a beam, then we need to work out where it is. So monitor the precise flight paths every night. Even look back over the past months and find out if there's a pattern.'

'Yes, sir. Then we can disrupt the beam?'

'Yes, and also we'll know where they fly.'

'Ah, of course...'

'Who's the wireless operator?'

'Fellow we call Sparks, sir. Corporal Johnson.'

'Good. I'll talk to him.'

Before dark, he walked along the river and looked out across at New Holland. What did it all look like from the air at night? What an odd turn the world had taken, for him to think about such improbable things.

That night the aircraft came again. They were later, and cloud blocked the half moon. A mild breeze from the land wafted through the batteries.

'Operations report ten raiders along the Humber.' Gifford spoke on the radio to the battery crews. The familiar drone announced their approach, although it was impossible to see them. Two search lights probed and for a few seconds caught sight of the slender silhouettes. It was enough to give a bearing and the guns responded in staccato bursts. Then the aircraft were gone. They had had three minutes at the most.

The crews were despondent. 'See what I mean, sir,' said Barnes. 'It's impossible.'

He thought differently. 'It is difficult, but the performance was better, even though there was less time. The pattern of attack was more compact.'

The night was busy. Twenty minutes later aircraft were reported on return course from Hull. The engine noise carried further on the breeze and gave more warning. 'There they are, sir,' Barnes shouted and, as if in confirmation, a search light cut into the dark. There were gaps in the clouds. The guns had already opened up, and sustained a barrage until the aircraft were gone. 'What did you think, sir?'

'Better. We're getting the hang of working together.' He sat out the night in the tent. One more alert came, but the aircraft were too far to the west. He slept until mid-day and was awakened by loud knocks on the door.

'Coming,' he shouted.

It was Barnes. 'Good news, sir. A Heinkel crash-landed near Lincoln last night. We must have got one on the way back. Another was confirmed. Came down over Grimsby. Probably one we hit as well.'

He smiled, and then forced himself to concentrate. 'What makes you so sure?'

'It's ten miles to Grimsby and it was going in the right direction. Who else could it have been? We were the only unit to engage returning aircraft before that one crashed. The other, who knows.'

He smiled again. 'Good. Sounds as if you are right. Tell Sergeant Gifford to prime everybody for tonight. See you later.' He closed the door and went back to bed. The afternoon was bright when he awoke, with an autumn sun behind the curtains. He was pleased to see a clear sky. They would be ready again that night.

The first reports came at 20.39: a formation approached along the Humber. The sky was clear. A searchlight observer was first to spot a cluster of bombers. Seconds ahead of the guns, the beams went up. He stood with Barnes at the observation post. 'We must get one tonight, sir.'

He watched: 'Yes, if they put up a close pattern of fire, we should.'

In silence, as the formation moved above them, they listened. 'Look, sir; something there.' Barnes pointed. It was just possible to discern a black streak that plummeted towards earth over Lincolnshire. Barnes was jubilant. 'It must have been us.'

'Call in to find out would you, Corporal, and let me know.'

The aircraft was confirmed. He had been in Preston a week, and small gratification was the reward. There was one for Douglas.

In the evening, on Gifford's recommendation, he went to the theatre in Hull. *Cheerful place, with Victorian charm; you take your chances with the bombing*, he had said. Maybe there would be none. In the interval, he had a beer at the bar. What a ridiculous way of life. Stepping outside, the evening was eerily quiet.

As if in response to the thought, the wail of a siren went up. Then a terrific crash shook the street and about a hundred yards away what had been a shop front vanished in a sheet of flame. Crouching on the pavement, hands over his ears, he wondered where he should he run to. In quick succession, other explosions occurred. He listened to the crash of stone and glass as a building collapsed. Other people appeared in the road; a man lay bleeding from the mouth. He attended to him, but he did not respond. Others had been hurt and people stopped to help them.

In a matter of minutes fires burnt all along the street. Bright flashes, like lightning, showed where bombs fell; plumes of flame shot into the sky. The sound of sirens and bells cut through the chaos. His eyes smarted from the smoke that blew towards him.

Anonymous killing. He ran to where he could hear screams from a building with the roof down and the windows blown in. He could see nothing. Still the calls for help continued and he went in through the door. 'Where are you?' he shouted.

'Here, in the back room...' It was a man's voice.

He stumbled through.

'Where?'

'Here.'

'Keep talking.'

He found the man amongst the kitchen debris and carried him out to the road.

'My wife, as well,' the man said.

With another man who had a torch, he went back in. They found the woman, who was unconscious, and took her out; then he watched as others took over the rescue operations. Air Raid Wardens, the army, firemen and everyone were on the streets to give a helping hand. He walked away. *My God.*

The next night was as bad. At the Battery near Hedon, news came in from Spurn of the approach of hostile aircraft along the river. Within five minutes, the night air was filled with drones of aircraft engines. Anti-aircraft shells hissed into the air as the bombs rained down. The docks and town took the pounding. Outside, one of the signals operators, a local man, was in tears as he witnessed the city succumb to the bombing.

Over the next few weeks, those in authority grasped at any way to improve things. Collinson recognised that the new ideas about gun operations had started to work and was quick to see a chance to further his own influence. His recommendations meant further tours to other units along the Humber to discuss strategies for ground defences and to describe the methods they had developed at Preston. An immediate itinerary was drawn up that took him around the area, often visiting four units in a day, and then re-visiting to solve problems and reinforce the methods with the crews.

ONE DAY, when he had been in Preston for over four weeks, Fenton brought letters for him from Spurn. The first was from his mother. Kent now is just a war zone, she told him.

The second, which was better, was from Helen. Brief and excited, it brought the news that after going to Birmingham for a week she would come to Hull. Could he find her somewhere to stay? She had a contact called Jane Callow at the Hull Daily Mail office who might help.

'Well done, Helen,' he whooped, then stood up, walked round in small circles for a moment and went to find Fenton who was chatting to Gifford. 'Helen's coming to Hull,' he said, and beamed at them and clapped Fenton on the shoulders. 'Isn't that great?'

Fenton laughed and nodded and Gifford raised his eyebrows. 'Let's hope she likes it here then, sir. We'll plan a welcome party for her.'

'Yes. What shall we do?'

'We'll think of something, sir. Tidy the place up a little for a start,' Gifford said.

Two weeks later, in mid-October, while he was at a gun emplacement on Sunk Island, a jeep pulled up and the driver got out. 'Sergeant Gifford sent me, sir, to tell you Helen has called; she's arrived in Hull. I'm to take you to find her, sir.'

He beamed at the driver. 'Marvellous, Rider; a day earlier than expected. Thank you. Wait here while I finish off, and then we'll go.'

OUTSIDE THE offices of the Hull Daily Mail, when he arrived, he had to pick his way over the rubble. Just a few yards from the entrance, while mess was cleared from the road, two burnt out lorries were being towed away. News was big business, and as he waited for Helen to finish a phone call, he was impressed by the frenetic activity. He gave her a small kiss when she came over. 'At work already, I see.'

'Of course. Hello, soldier boy.' The smile didn't leave her face. 'I'll never get used to you in uniform.'

'And Hello reporter-girl. You're just the same as ever.'

She took his hand and looked around the office. 'Sorry it's a bit public in here.'

'Don't worry. Welcome to the north eastern town. And a day early too.'

'Yes. I managed to get an unexpected lift to Doncaster and then caught the train. It's so great to be here.'

'Have you found your lodgings; did Jane show you?'

'Yes. That's all been sorted out.'

'I want you to come back and meet everybody at HQ. Will that be possible? I'll bring you back later. Or maybe, you can stay at

Spurn?'

'I'd love to. Drive me round to pick up some things from my room, then we can go. Being a day early, I think we can take the liberty. I'll go and tell Jane.'

On Tennant Street, where he and Jane Callow had found lodgings for her, the sun reflected on the roofs and windows and lit the last leaves on the trees into vibrant shades of yellow and red. The house was a Victorian semi with bay windows and a small lawn at the front. Their car pulled up outside.

'I hope you're going to like it here.'

'Of course I will. It's such a lovely place. Thank you for finding it for me.'

CORPORAL RIDER drove them east out of Hull and an hour later they were at the Station HQ at Spurn. 'They're not expecting you until tomorrow, so it will be a surprise for everyone to see you,' he said, as he pushed open the door.

The place bustled with soldiers in uniform and there were women from the ATS who were stationed at Spurn, also in uniform, as well as civilians who came from Kilnsea. Despite it being light outside, all the lights were on and all the blackout blinds were down.

As he entered and Helen followed, the lights went out and a chorus went up. *For she's a jolly good fellow, for she's a jolly good fellow, for she's a jolly good fel-low, and so say all of us...*

Then the lights came on again and everybody cheered. The canteen was exceptionally bright, as if spot lights had been trained on them. 'Well, I didn't *think* they would be expecting us,' he said. 'Word must have crept in on the grapevine.'

He looked around the room and Helen looked suitably embarrassed. Captain Stephenson walked up to them. 'Welcome to Spurn Point, Miss Strachan,' he said. 'We've been expecting you and it's a pleasure to meet the famous reporter at last. Rider kept us informed of your movements.'

She threw off her shyness. 'It's a great pleasure to meet you as well Captain Stephenson and to be here too. I have heard so much about you.' They shook hands and Stephenson saluted.

'Don't go over the top, sir,' he said.

'That was the First World War Lieutenant; we don't do that anymore. We've all read your articles, Helen. Lieutenant Whellans circulates the newspaper clippings every day when you send them. We get a lot of our news about what's going on down south from you, as much, if not more than from the local newspapers. You're already a household name around here.'

'Well, thank you. It's great to be here to meet everybody. I've heard so much about you all, as well.'

'So,' he said, and turned again to Stephenson, 'this is Captain Andrew Stephenson, the wisest man on the station, as well he should be. If you want sound advice - on any matter - he's a safe bet. Just make sure you have plenty of time to spare to listen to the answer. He's very comprehensive.'

'Now you don't go over the top, lieutenant,' Stephenson said.

The journalist in Helen took over. 'I look so forward to talking to the Captain, and taking all his advice, as well as interviewing him at some stage.'

'Madam, it will be a pleasure. I will tell you things about Lieutenant Whellans you didn't know as well.'

Helen laughed.

'Thank you, sir,' he said. 'If you'll excuse us, I'll give Helen a tour and introduce her to everyone else.' He led her across the room. 'This is Sergeant James Fenton, the second wisest man on the station.'

As he shook hands with her, Fenton dwarfed her. 'Very pleased to meet you Helen.'

Someone put on a gramophone record of dance band music and soon couples danced around the floor.

'And this is Corporal Michael White, who has read every letter you ever sent me and on many occasions was first to see the photographs and read the newspaper cuttings. Isn't that right Corporal?'

'Beggin' your pardon, Miss Strachan, but I have to admit that often that has been true. Not reading your letters though.'

'Yes, I know that as well. David told me, and often when I sealed the envelope, I imagined you and David opening them together in the guard house. You must show me around later.'

They sat at a table with the others and relaxed into the evening. When the music finished, the quarter master raised his hand. 'Quiet everyone. Two of the lads have a party piece to perform for you, which Lieutenant Whellans will recognise.'

They stood up, and went into a music hall sketch based on George and the Dragon. It was one of the more humorous sketches that he had rehearsed with them for the Barrack's Concert earlier that summer. Now they did it whenever opportunity arose. Then two of them did a sketch about a soldier called Perfect.

'You've made it a very cheerful evening,' he said to the quarter master. 'Thank you.'

'It's a pleasure,' he replied. 'We've got a three piece folk band next to give us some songs.'

'What else will you pull out of the hat?' Helen asked

'Oh, yes, that as well,' the quarter master replied, 'We have a magician later.'

Before he departed, Stephenson came over again. 'Very pleased to meet you Helen. We'll see more of you here I hope from now on.'

'Yes, I am sure you will. I'd appreciate a visit to Spurn and to do an article about what goes on here.'

'Good idea. It would give the men a boost. I'll clear that with Major Wheeler.'

'Yes, I'd like to see him and then talk to you and have a look around.'

'Consider it done.'

Helen stayed for her first night in Yorkshire in the only place suitable on the station, in the ATS quarters with thirty or more other women, while he collapsed into bed exhausted.

Almost a year to the day since he arrived, and now Helen was there. Something he never expected to happen...

The next day, Rider drove her back to Hull.

HELEN MADE her second visit to Spurn - this time on official business - with Jane Callow. They arrived in a car with a driver from the Hull Daily Mail. He met them and sorted out the first part of the itinerary. First they met Major Wheeler and then interviewed

Stephenson. Once the official introductions were over, Maplebeck was detailed to take them around the station.

'Give them a full tour and tell them all they need to know, won't you Corporal.'

'I will, sir.'

He watched Maplebeck drive them away.

What a change in a man in just a year. Lost all his stubbornness and grown in reliability every day.

The weather was fair. The North Sea rolled in a calm motion and the river lay bright to the west. When they set off, the water rested at low tide, mud flats glistened in the sun, waders probed and gulls pecked at the surface.

A planned tour of two hours stretched to four that included lunch in the mess. When he returned from a visit to the Kilnsea Battery and expected to find them at the guard house ready to leave, they were not there. Corporal White was.

'Miss Strachan came here, sir, and I showed her around. She saw the cuttings pinned on the notice board from her and the photographs and was pleased that you shared them with us. Now she's off to the Kilnsea Battery with Corporal Maplebeck.'

'I've just come from there. I must have missed them.'

'Said they'll be back at three, sir.'

'Alright, not to worry. Where's Captain Stephenson at the moment?'

'Down the end, sir.'

'Could you call him. I need to talk to him.'

'Yes, sir.'

He spoke to Stephenson, then put the receiver down.

'Okay, I'll be back at three as well,' he said, and went out.

At one of the gun emplacements that he had visited earlier, Sergeant Fenton and the gun crew looked perplexed. He arrived with Stephenson and they went to inspect the guns.

'What's the problem, Lieutenant?'

He showed him one of the six inch guns. 'Hair line cracks along the base of the barrel, sir.' He pointed and showed Stephenson. 'Here and here.'

'How old are these guns?'

'Twenty five years at least, sir,' Fenton answered.

Stephenson nodded. 'Yes. That was my information. Didn't they come off the HMS Cardiff?'

'Yes, sir.'

'Hmm. Think we'll have to scrap it, don't you, Lieutenant?'

'Don't think we have any choice, sir.'

'What about the rest?'

'They're alright as far as we can see. Is that correct Sergeant?'

'As far as we can tell, sir, the rest seem fine.'

'This is an important position, so we'll have to replace it,' Stephenson said. 'Heaven knows what with though. I'll try to get one of those new Titans.'

He nodded to the Sergeant. 'Decommission this now and reallocate the crew.'

He accompanied Stephenson to his vehicle and then started back to the guard house. On the way he met Maplebeck with Helen and Jane on their way to the canteen for a final round-up before their departure.

'It went well, then? he asked.

'Very, I should say,' Helen replied. 'What do you think, Jane?'

'Weird in places; a very male environment.'

Trying to figure out Jane Callow promised to take a while; she was unfathomable. Had he missed or misunderstood something? Helen seemed to get on with her. 'Yes, well…' he muttered.

'Corporal Maplebeck was very helpful,' Helen said. 'He showed us everywhere and I am sure, if we had let him, would have kept going all day. You are very knowledgeable, Corporal.'

Maplebeck acknowledged with a gracious nod.

'He's from this area and knows it well; you were a crab fisherman, weren't you, Corporal, and know all the locals.'

'Yes, sir. That's right, I was.'

'Seems more like a prison than a station,' Jane said.

'Yes, well…' he said again.

'Very bleak. What do you find to do?'

'Not a lot, to be quite honest. We've made tons of concrete.'

'And still they get through to bomb Hull…'

'Yes, well... We're making progress with that...'

'Why do you have guns down here at all?'

He paused. 'What do you mean, why do we have guns here at

all?'

'Well, to protect Hull, concentrating your fire-power into a smaller circle would make more sense. No aircraft would fly over here if they were sensible would they? They know you're here, don't they.'

'Yes, well, in some ways you're right…'

'I am right.'

'Yes, you are… but, it's not as simple as that.'

'No, it never is, is it?'

'This place is really wild,' Helen said. 'I'm surprised how remote it is, as well. The people have a distinctive character in the whole of the area.'

'They certainly do…' Jane replied.'

'Anyway, what do you think the best story of the day was, Jane?' Helen asked.

Jane had no doubt. 'The one about the jackdaw that went down the barrel of a gun and they could hear it but couldn't get it out. So they dismantled the gun, the jackdaw flew away and then they couldn't put the gun together again. It's still in bits today. How's that for competence?'

He looked at Maplebeck.

Helen replied, 'Mine was the one about the Heinkel they shot down. The gun crew saw it crash-land near Kilnsea and so went to have a look. They found the pilot uninjured, but because he looked so shaken, took him to the Crown & Anchor and gave him a pint. They chatted and asked him where he came from and then gave him another pint. It was only then that they thought to ask him for his pistol, get on with the formalities and call the Police.'

Everyone laughed.

At least they could find humour, even in dire times.

THAT EVENING he rode to Hull and lodged for the night at the house in Tennant Street with Helen. It was a formality, and though the landlady wasn't the snoopy type, they took care not to offend her by transgression of the house rules.

When he awoke in the morning, finding he was alone, he got up and, opening the door onto the landing, could see Helen in the room at the back, sat at the dressing table at the window writing. The creak of the landing warned of his approach and she turned, pen poised. 'Sorry to disturb you,' he whispered.

She gave him a good morning smile. 'It's alright. I've almost finished. Come and sit here,' and she pulled a chair closer.

He gave her a peck on the cheek. 'Writing in the chill dawn,' he said. 'You never stop.'

'I'm catching the first sun. It's lovely here, looking over the gardens and backs of houses, watching the birds. This is my dawn chorus. The fresh stories of the day.'

'Like a baker: up early to bake bread.'

She laughed. 'Yes. Stories are like dough; you need to make them and then let them rise and grow.'

'I'll make you some tea then and let you finish,' and he gave her another peck on the cheek.

'Alright, then we can think about later. I don't want to miss my time with you. Mrs Green isn't up yet.'

He crept down to the kitchen.

AT HALF past ten, Helen settled on the back of the motorcycle. She laughed and pulled her scarf tighter. 'I hate this helmet,' she said. 'I must look a sight.'

'A lovely sight and hold tight.'

The roads from Hull to the East Coast passed through twenty miles of farmland that in October was a mosaic of ploughed fields and grassland grazed by sheep and cattle. Their first stop was in Skirlaugh.

When the motorcycle stopped, Helen laughed. 'Wow,' she said, and almost fell over on the grass verge when she dismounted. 'That was exhilarating. I never knew it could be such fun on the back of an army motorcycle.'

'Thought you would like it.' He raised his goggles and rubbed his red ringed eyes. In the fields before the village, tractors and, in some places, horse-teams ploughed beneath clouds of seagulls that swooped to catch worms and insects turned up by the share.

'Isn't this a great place; so different to Kent.'

'Yes. Look at those horses. Remember the Clydesdales at

Coulter Mains in Nairn?' She looked wistful. 'So remote and incredibly unspoilt. Look at those gulls: hundreds of them behind the plough.' She turned in a full circle on the spot to take in the images of the pastoral landscape. 'I love it…' The sun shone in her eyes. 'I wonder how Grandma is today.'

He looked at her. 'Mm, yes, I wonder,' and peered narrowly to look at the horses in the fields. 'Come on, let's get on. I want to row you across the lake at Hornsea.'

'Memories of Loch Broom at Ullapool,' she said, and pulled on her helmet.

Heading for the coast, first east to Aldbrough and on through the villages of Cowden and Mappleton, the roads were empty except for farm machinery and the occasional military vehicle. The East Riding bus hooted behind and he slowed down to let it pass. All the passengers waved.

On a bench on the promenade in Hornsea they sat and looked out across the ocean, drinking tea in mugs from the last kiosk to stay open at the end of the season. The town clung to the remnants of the summer.

Helen looked to her left and pointed into the distance. 'If you keep going up the coast, and keep going - past Newcastle, past the Firth of Forth and Aberdeen - you will come to Nairn.'

He smiled and nodded. 'Don't keep reminding me.'

'I have to; it's the only thing that keeps me going.'

Taking her hand, for a while they walked along the promenade. At the slipway, where small fishing boats were pulled up onto the sand on their trailers, he turned and gave her a kiss on the cheek.

She rested her head on his shoulder. 'I love you, David.'

'I love you, too.' As the sea crashed on the beach, he looked into her eyes, her words gentle in his ears.

ON HORNSEA Mere there were rowing boats and, far off, two small sailing dinghies. At the jetty, he paid for the hire of a rowing boat, and, holding it while they got in, the attendant then pushed them off. Positioning the oars and rowing out into the mere, Helen clung to the sides and faced him.

'Don't look so worried,' he said.

'You're crazy; how did you know about this place?'

'Sergeant Fenton said he went pike fishing here. We'll row out to the middle and have our picnic while we drift.'

'We can try. *Life on the ocean waves*,' she sang.

'You can row when I've had enough.'

'I'll have a go. How big is the lake?'

'A couple of miles long I think. It's the largest in Yorkshire.'

She looked over the side and trailed her fingers in the water. 'How deep is it?'

'Does it matter?'

'No, but Lock Ness is deep enough to hide monsters.'

'Not Hornsea Mere: this is shallow.'

She looked beyond him. 'We'll soon be at the island.'

'Oh, okay,' and he shipped oars, then reached for his duffle bag.

'Careful,' Helen said, grabbing the sides.

He passed her the packed lunch box. 'You can do the honours.'

In the breeze, they ate as they drifted towards the boat house and threw bread to the ducks. 'Doesn't life go in circles? We threw bread to the seagulls on Loch Broom.'

'And we'll throw bread to the seagulls there again. Your turn to row?'

'I have done this once before, so I might surprise you.'

After a minute or two, she had made fair progress. 'You have surprised me. We'll soon be at the jetty.'

'Good. I want to get back where it's warm and just with you.'

THE FOLLOWING day, driven by the Daily Mail driver, he took Helen to the Driffield airfield where a Wing Commander John Western showed them round.

'We had 77 and 102 Squadrons here with Whitley bombers. After the airfield was bombed in August, 77 Squadron moved to Linton-on-Ouse and 102 to Leeming. When everything is repaired, we expect some of Fighter Command to be stationed here.'

'There is still a lot of damage,' Helen said.

'There is; slowly we're getting on top of it and at present operate as a decoy airfield.'

'Tell us about the attack in August.'

'A formation of about fifty Junkers - Ju 88 bombers - came; they probably flew from Denmark and might have been more were it not for interceptions by RAF fighters from Leconfield and Church Fenton that engaged the squadrons, including Heinkels and some Messerschmitts, over the North Sea. Many were diverted and poor old Bridlington on the coast received some of their bombs. But the Junkers got through.

'It was real pandemonium. About one hundred and seventy bombs fell. A number of people were killed, fourteen in fact. Hangers were destroyed, along with offices and barracks and twelve Whitleys.' As he remembered the day, he looked out across the airfield. Then he showed them round.

'I saw one of the hangers go up; watched the bombs as they left the aircraft and saw them fall. It was like slow motion. Then all hell let loose. Bomb after bomb exploded and ripped the hangers apart. It went up in an inferno; the walls and roofs collapsed like flimsy models. Smoke and dust rose into clouds above the burning wreckage as the Junkers that dropped the bombs diminished in size into the distance. I remember thinking they must be pleased with themselves. Funny how I could think about them like that at that moment, but I did.'

When Helen had finished her interviews they returned to Hull. He took his leave of her and rode back to Spurn.

A FEW mornings later, before he departed for the batteries along the coast near Withernsea, he called her and spoke to someone in the office. 'Sorry, she's not here yet. Had a busy night and still getting her notes together.'

'Ask her to call me when she gets in, please,' he said. 'It'll have to be in the evening.'

He spent less time now on night duty, but worked with the crews to find better ways to co-ordinate action. That weekend he was based again in Preston. Helen did not call and he thought he might ride into town to see her.

Over the weekend he caught up with sleep and tried to feel more at home, writing to his mother and telling her his news and about Helen. On Saturday evening, as he waited and watched, the air-raid siren sounded and the sky to the east over Spurn lit up like a glass chandelier.

'What the -' he heard someone say. Whatever it was, it was new. Lights laid to guide bombers perhaps. A few minutes later what seemed to be a single aircraft went over and then the sky lit up with a shower of sparkling flares.

He nodded. Cunning, that's what they were; incendiaries to light a path to the targets for bombers. Would it work?

A few minutes later, explosions sounded in the distance.

DESPITE BEING unsettled, in the midst of all this, on Sunday afternoon he felt relaxed enough to think of music. He played through a few bars and opened a new page of his manuscript book. Sometimes Hull could be as quiet as an East Coast seaside resort. People listened and waited; there was nothing to do but the same. In mid-November he had been a soldier for more than a year.

On Monday morning he tried to contact Helen again and recognised the voice on the telephone as one of her colleagues.

'David, she is missing. We are not sure where she is.'

'What do you mean?'

'We don't know; we are trying to find out.'

'What do you mean, missing?'

'We just don't know where she is.'

'I don't understand.'

'David, we don't know where she is. Nobody does. She is missing.'

The newspapers reported air-raids daily and significant damage made the headlines. Everybody knew that the papers sensationalised things and unless one lived in the heart of the city, experience of air raids was limited to a small part of the population. It was as all accidents, something that happened to someone else. He realised what was being said to him.

He said the words, but assumed there must be another explanation. 'You mean an air-raid?'

'Maybe.' There was a pause. 'We don't know.'

The muscles tensed in his neck and throat. His voice quietened. 'Call me when you have information.' He put down the receiver and went into the street and walked away in silence. When he returned, Barnes was making tea in the Ops. Room. He must have noticed his hand shake when he took the cup. 'What's the matter, sir; you alright?'

'I don't know,' he said, and gritted his teeth.

Barnes looked at Gifford. 'Are you sure you're alright, sir?'

'They told me Helen is missing.'

Gifford walked around the desk and stood beside him. His face muscles tightened. 'I think you should sit down, sir, drink your tea.' He paused... 'I'll call to find out what's going on. Do you have the number?'

Gifford made a few calls and ten minutes later put down the receiver. 'The fire services remember her, sir, - in Tennant Street - two nights ago. She was writing about what was going on.'

'What else?'

'Nothing, sir. They don't know anything else.'

Three firemen killed and only one body recovered. Craters in the road big enough to take double-decker buses, he remembered earlier newspaper headlines.

Two hours later Gifford intercepted a call. His face was passive. When he replaced the telephone, he glanced over at Barnes. 'Stay here. I'll go and find him.' He walked to the officers' quarters and found him in the mess. He came to the point: 'It's bad news, sir.'

He stared at Gifford who returned his look of hopelessness.

'They found a woman in the rubble in the road next to Tennant Street yesterday. Her lodgings weren't bombed, but the whole of the next street was. She must have gone round there. She is alive, but unconscious and badly injured in hospital.'

He did not move: maybe exposure to the war's realities had hardened him. He let the tension seep through his spine, to his neck and forehead. Gifford watched him and waited.

He shuddered and continued to stare across the table and out through the window. He repeated what Fenton had said before, '*Bastards*.' There was no warning and no going back, no opportunity for forgiveness. However little he understood before, he had found something he understood less.

'Call Fenton, will you, please, and ask him to come.'

'Yes, sir.'

At 6.30 that evening, in the hospital, he looked at Helen. Fenton had come immediately from Spurn and with Gifford now stood beside him. For a number of minutes he could not see her as Helen. Then his mind brought her back from the bandaged and broken person who lay before him. Underneath the cuts her beauty was whole, all that she had ever been. His mind adjusted and he saw her as before. The chain with the silver sixpence hung around her neck.

Fenton stared at her. He turned to him. 'Fenton, is this the end?'

The sergeant did not reply, but first looked at Gifford and then at him. For a few minutes more he looked at Helen, and then, as he turned to walked out, Fenton said, 'She will get better, sir. Tonight will be the worst night; but she will get better...'

Half an hour later they dropped him outside the pub in Preston. 'Not too much, now sir,' Fenton said. 'She'll get well again. I hope you'll not overdo it.'

'Thank you; thank you for coming,' he said, and slammed the car door.

Across the road from the pub, was a school. Although it was the evening, there was activity - a concert or something. Chairs and music stands adorned the stage in the hall. He sat down. The children in the orchestra took their places and when all was quiet, a woman came to make the introductions. He did not listen, but stared at her and as he stared, saw Helen superimposed on her. The children started to play, but he got up and walked out and across the road to the *Fife and Drum*.

Telephone his mother, he thought, but did not. Tell her, but he could not. Telephone Nonie Sinclair, but he stopped himself. Then he dialled and heard her voice. In the wail of Nonie's words, 'Oh, David, no,' and in the silence before she sobbed the words again, he heard the shock he had felt. He listened to the silence.

'I'll call you again.'

She spoke in a whisper. 'No, David, don't go. No, no...'

He could not listen. 'I'll call in half an hour,' and, as he put the telephone down, shuddered with the sound of her voice in his ears.

What seemed to be hours later, after he had called Nonie again, Fenton and Gifford walked into the bar and took him away.

HE ASKED for a night's leave and went into Hull. It had taken three days for her to regain consciousness. Now she was lucid.

'Hello, my love,' he said.

'I was silly David; took too many risks. Wanted the big story.'

'It's okay...'

'I'm sorry. I should have been more careful,' and she laughed. The expression appeared on half of her face. The other side remained immobile. A yellow pallor coloured the skin around her eyes.

'Give it time. You'll be fine.'

She shook her head. 'They hold little hope that I'll walk again. They have a happy way of doing that, of giving you the bad news when you least need it.'

'Then it can only get better,' he said, and took her hand.

She smiled and shook her head. 'We tried Davy.'

Now it was more difficult for her to smile and she closed her eyes.

Still wet, when he reached the hospital steps and made his way to the centre of town, he wiped his eyes. At six o'clock, at the bar of one of the local pubs, he sat and waited. Air-raid sirens sounded at eight thirty and, leaving the remains of his third pint, he went out. Not far away explosions resounded across the city and he walked towards the noise. Fire engines rang their bells and the shadows of trucks passed in the darkness. Further on, an orange sky and the smell of fire caught in his nostrils from the breeze along the streets. At the scene of the first raid an army of civil defence workers fought the destruction.

Motionless, as he looked into the chaos of rubble and collapsed buildings around him, an Air-raid Warden saluted. 'Shouldn't stay out here, sir.'

He nodded: 'Thank you for the advice. I just need to see what's happening.' As he spoke another building collapsed. Was that what happened to Helen a few nights ago?

'Easy enough to see, sir.'

He looked into the flames. 'It's hard to imagine, however many times you see it.'

'True enough, sir.'

Rescue squads tunnelled through the debris to people buried. As the noise died down behind him, he walked on. Across the city, sirens wailed again. An army lorry brought him to a new scene of destruction. For an hour he helped, but with nothing more to do, he walked away. At two o'clock in the morning, back in the centre of town, in the railway station, he slept on a bench. At six o'clock, daylight revealed pathetic sights. Crowds wandered along the pavement as if dazed.

'Our homes have gone,' one man said as he passed. This was what the air defences were meant to prevent, he told himself again.

Travelling across town, where similar sights greeted him along the way, at the docks he found more devastation. Before heading home, he went again to see Helen, and then, back on the street, found himself racked by soundless sobs. Finally an army lorry took him east and out of the town.

On the telephone, his mother listened as he told her everything that had happened. He had not talked to her about Douglas, but this time was different. He told her all there was to know.

'David, I'm sorry,' she said. 'I'll come up; I'll be there tomorrow.'

'No.'

'Yes, I will. I'll stay at Helen's lodgings. Ask the landlady for me.'

ON THE train the next day she came to Hull and in the afternoon walked with him along the river. 'I have worried about what has happened to us in Kent, but I have forgotten about you. The devastation here is much worse.'

He remembered when, as a boy, he would tell his mother everything. Now it was more difficult. 'Everything was good a year ago. Now it is such a disaster.'

'It's a pity I have never met her,' his mother said. 'Or Douglas: you should have told me; you have been so secretive.'

'I knew you would meet them one day.'

They passed the ferry terminus and walked on along the river side. After her experience of the war in Kent, his mother seemed resigned. 'I am concerned about Helen, of course, but I'm concerned about you. I know it sounds trite, but you could channel all that feeling into music.'

'Yes, I could, but not with everything else that's going on.'

She spoke with a mother's calm. 'It will come back.'

He shook his head. 'I have no time; I don't feel what I want to feel. Others control my life. It's impossible.'

'Will you be able to visit Helen?'

'That won't be a problem; Stephenson is very understanding.'

She stopped and looked across the river, and now sounded at a loss: 'I'm sure you will be able to write again; be selfish, start to put everything you do into music - every experience.' She threw her head back and gave him a defiant look: 'You'll get over these setbacks.'

He set his jaw and tried to rise to his mother's encouragement. 'It sounds easy, but I will have to change now, before I can do that.'

His mother stayed in Tennant Street and the next day went with him to see Helen.

BY MID-NOVEMBER in Yorkshire, the weather deteriorated. High winds from the north brought storms that lashed the peninsula. A grey sky and greyer sea merged so that the horizon was lost in them. One night at high tide waves flooded the spit. Next morning, with the storm at its height, every soldier was called out to protect the exposed shoreline with boulders. The torrent of the waves dwarfed their efforts, and everyone watched and marvelled at the force of the sea. By the afternoon fears were raised that the spit would be breached. Vehicles were brought to the landward side as waves flooded the road. Two hours later they would not have made it.

Sand and the clay that underlay the road were scoured away and the waves broke through the concrete of the road and railway track. For two days thirty foot waves battered the spit. The storm continued through the third night and by daybreak a breach appeared. It was impossible not to be impressed by the damage the sea had caused. When it abated, fifty yards of land had been carried away, and transformed the peninsula into an island.

Lorry loads of hard core and boulders were brought to fill the gap. Every available man collected boulders in parties of ten for each lorry. It was disappointing to see the small impact that a lorry load of hard-earned rocks had on the gulf between the two strands. Local builders assisted with heavy hard-core brought from further afield.

Throughout the period, by taking the bus and walking to the hospital, he saw Helen every other day. A month after the air-raid near Tennant Street, visits became routine and they found a bearable balance. Sometimes other visitors were there too. Nonie arrived and stayed and the three of them sat one evening and talked. It was the first time he had seen her since the news of Douglas's death, and it was difficult to know which was more unbearable.

One evening on arrival at the hospital, he found Helen sitting up in bed and chatting with the duty nurse, a Sister Smith.

'You're looking better,' he said, and it was true.

'Yes, she does,' the Sister agreed.

'It's an illusion,' Helen replied.

He gave her a small box. 'I bought you these.'

She looked at the pair of ear-rings that he had bought. 'Davy, thank you.' Tears filled her eyes.

For a moment, neither could say anything. She looked at him.

'David, they are taking me to another hospital. They say I'm strong enough to be moved. They have suggested London. Tomorrow or the next day.'

He watched her pull herself to a more comfortable position, had learnt not to try to help her. 'I won't be able to come to see you.'

She gave up the effort to move. 'Davy, I know; but I'm helpless now.'

'I'll come to London.'

'Yes, I would love you to,' she said, looking uncomfortable as she lay there, 'but it will be difficult.'

'I will get a transfer. Call me; tell me as soon as you know when you will go. They won't refuse me now.'

Something was being taken away. Whatever he may have felt, the choice about the future was not his any more. Choices he may have had were something of the past.

The next day, Nonie called. 'David,' she said, 'Helen is going to London tomorrow. Can you go to see her this evening?'

He was on duty. 'Nonie, it's impossible; there is no-one else; Collinson is away.'

'Try,' Nonie said.

'I will,' he replied.

He stayed in Preston that evening, but rode into town at seven o'clock the next morning and was in the hospital at eight. Approaching along the ward, he saw her head turned away and her eyes closed. Surprisingly she looked younger and he stopped and for a moment was unable to continue. Sister Smith came over.

'It's difficult, isn't it,' she said. Her voice was subdued.

He nodded.

'You look shattered,' she said.

'Yes, I've been up all night, like you; air-raid duty.'

'Yes, I know. You heard that she leaves today?'

'Yes…'

'I'll tell her you're here.'

She turned with tears in her eyes. 'Thank you for coming. I'm sorry I'm leaving you.'

'Don't worry; I'll come to London.'

'No, I mean it. I'm so sorry, but I don't want you to see me like this anymore. So in some ways it's good that I'm going.'

'I don't want you to go.'

'No, Davy, don't say that.' She turned away.

'But I don't; I can't bear it.'

'Davy, there will always be problems now. You will have to forget me.'

He looked at her. 'Don't be ridiculous.'

'I'm not being ridiculous, Davy; it's what I know.'

'Remember Nairn and all we did. You need to get back to work. We'll get through this.'

'I can't move David. Without my arms, I'd be helpless. I can't move at all.'

'But you will…'

She smiled, and tears filled her eyes again. 'I'm sorry. Now I'm feeling sorry for myself. I've been so silly.'

He took her hand.

'Nonie came down yesterday. She'll go with me to London.'

'Yes, I know.'

'She's on her way now.'

For an hour they sat together and when Nonie arrived, he watched her talk to Helen and make her comfortable. He stayed until she was taken to an ambulance and said goodbye. Then they drove away and he watched Nonie wave from the rear window. Her mother and father would meet them in London.

AT THE END of the month, on Christmas Eve, he travelled to York to meet Nonie Sinclair on her journey north to Scotland. She had gained compassionate leave and would transfer to the south. He planned to do the same. Compared to Hull, where the signs of damage remained everywhere in the streets, with rubble that needed to be cleared, roofless buildings and barrage balloons hanging over the parks and open spaces, York looked unscathed. They met at the railway station and sat in a bar for two hours before Nonie had to catch the train home for Christmas.

He returned to Hull and, to his parents' dismay, stayed there. On Christmas day he volunteered for extra duties; he manned the observation tower and watched the horizons.

JAMES FENTON went home and returned on the twenty-eighth of December. Then, on New Year's day he took advantage of a lorry set to go to Easington to get a lift with the lieutenant and go with him to the 'Bell', the pub in the village. Later they walked across the farmland a few miles inland from the peninsula.

In the preceding weeks, he had started to carry some of the burden for the lieutenant. It was a fragile relationship; how could he help pull him out of this?

The lieutenant spat his words. 'This year has done for me,' he said, and stumbled as he walked. 'I don't care anymore. I've lost too much.'

'I think you have to stop thinking about it, sir.'

With hands thrust in his pockets, the lieutenant threw a glance at him. 'It is not just thinking about it. I've changed. I don't feel anything now. My mother is hurt by my inability to talk to her. I try, but it's impossible.'

'It's early days yet. Give yourself a chance; and, if I might say so, sir, stop drinking so much.'

The lieutenant turned and stared at him, the look in his eyes, hostile; one of disbelief. 'Don't be so trivial. Do you think I care?'

It was dangerous ground. 'I know how black it looks, sir, but you just can't give in. You're made of better stuff.'

'Don't be so bloody patronising.' His eyes fixed him in a mocking stare. 'I can do without that.'

'I'm sorry, sir; but you are.'

'What can you say that I don't know already? Tell me the purpose.'

'It is to survive; as simple as that.'

His grunt was derisory. '*Survive*? For what?'

'To prove that you are strong enough to survive,' and he tried to emphasise his words. 'That's all; to prove you are strong enough.'

'You're crazy.'

'You have to survive to prove that it was worth it.'

'To prove what was worth it?'

'To prove that what other people have done and suffered was worth it. You have to survive for them, for Helen, so that you can remember what they have done.'

The lieutenant stopped and looked at him; the words had hit home. 'Thank you, yes... Survive? I am not sure I am even strong enough to survive.' Then, in silence, he walked on.

He was lucky. His family were fine and so far, except for the hardships of army life, the war had not affected him. It had taken a greater toll on the lieutenant.

THE FIRST week of January brought cold winds and clear days. In the past he had trusted continuity, sought it, but now, if he had progressed, it was because of the shove of the crowd. At the end of 1940 he came close to losing his grip on seriousness. It seemed that those who said, don't take things so seriously, might have been right. Like a cat that had lost a life, one of his faiths had been broken - his faith in continuity. He no longer struggled to be as he had been, no longer struggled to force the pace, but accepted loss of control, gave into the will and movement of the crowd.

Once the road and railway were re-laid, life at the Spurn station returned to normal. Helen moved to another hospital. He wrote and imagined her propped in her bed and with the help of nurses replying as best she could.

In Hull, little of note occurred in the continued onslaught of the war. The stimulus of the New Year might have been the turning point but in the days of the fledgling year he found barely enough reason to continue, *to survive*, let alone write. People needed to be shocked.

Surveying the forces around him, he began to respond and find a fragile balance in which he started to work. Tenuous threads evolved from the provocation of war and from the turbulence of upheaval. He had no hesitation to show his anger at futility. He felt his grip tighten and abandoned hope that he could return to where he had been before.

In fits of torment, he wrote music of denunciation and for a while managed to keep going until the strain on his emotions became too great. Then he turned to easier things and looked to what he saw around him. For weeks he wrote music descriptive of the solitude of the reaches of the River Humber. The description was therapy for the more turbulent expression of anger that welled in his consciousness.

In those first weeks of the year, work fitted between the daily routines of army life and the uncertainties of what the next day might bring. He remembered when, years ago, his father had visited Wales. Fear then was of the rise of fascism in Europe. Look at it now; how right he was. He revived the ideas and added a turbulent passion to his views.

Usually, once a month, his mother visited and brought him gifts. She stayed in Tennant Street with Mrs Green and they became friends. Sometimes she visited Helen in hospital in London.

To legitimise time spent on music, he put together another review and gathered a group around him which, in the best spirit of amateur dramatics, mastered the script and score. A review meant that a piano had to be installed in a Nissen hut next to the officers' quarters. After that no one seemed to mind how much time he spent at the piano or with a pen in hand at the open page of a manuscript book.

As time progressed he performed his work with a small orchestra that played for the Cottingham Choral Society. Gifford had introduced him to the conductor and, through his interest, the orchestra started to grow and attract more musicians. At the end of 1941, at a concert in the town hall, he performed a number of his compositions. It was a renaissance: a new beginning.

AT OTHER times he lived in isolation and alternated between the artillery stations at Spurn Point and in Preston near Hull. And always he ran, today away from the sun, first along a crest of turf above the inner bend of the river Humber and then through shingle that edged the mud-flats. The river curved into a bright strand of water, with somewhere in the distance, the open sea and the peninsula's arm.

To his familiar eye, it was evident where the camouflaged installations and gun emplacements interrupted the contour of the land. His life had dimensions as narrow as the shorelines on which it existed. He had changed his shape to fit the mould and in so far as a place could instil itself into a person's soul the peninsula had done so into his. The pattern of the place had etched itself on him, forced him to adapt to its demands. A capsule of water and sky entrapped him; air that was never still and sands that moved were as natural as anything he had accepted before. The Humber was a constant companion.

Ignoring Helen's wishes - that he should not go to see her - when he could gain leave, he went to London. In May, she left hospital and went back to live with her parents who had moved from London to a new home by the sea in Brighton. In doing so, she isolated herself. He suspected that her pride would not allow her to accept his care or concern. It seemed that she confused, or pretended to confuse, his love for her for pity. Nonie had transferred to Bracknell, so that she could be near her.

Though less easy to go to Brighton, when he did, their favourite place to sit together was at the windows of the first floor lounge that overlooked the sea. And though she could not walk, she had recovered some mobility. When the weather was good, he pushed her along the promenade and to the end of the pier. 'You look as well as when we first met,' he said.

She laughed. 'Flattery will get you everywhere, but you know it's not true.' She wore a mauve beret and a mauve scarf that she adjusted as they went.

He spoke behind her as he pushed her along and said, 'I want us to be together as soon as we can. The war will all be over soon and I want to come to Brighton.'

Helen turned her head to look at him. She never relented on her rejection of their past and tried to make him seal it away also. On the one other occasion he had tried to return, when he tried to gain a transfer, she had rebuffed the attempt. She smiled and, while she turned away, nodded twice in response to his words. 'I'm glad you still want to; you could probably start to write again down here.'

'I'm sure I could.'

'But, Davy, another part of me says no, you shouldn't come.'

'How can you still say that?'

With her eyes set on some distant object, she said, 'because I know it's the best thing...'

He laughed. 'It's ridiculous to talk this way.'

Helen's face hardened. 'Once my dreams were with you; then one day I threw them away. Strange how an event can change one's dreams and vision of the future. Fate played its hand. Please don't let us go through that any more David, for both our sakes.'

He waited, and at first did not speak, then said: 'I will come though; I will come to Brighton.'

'Alright, yes, come. Yes, of course I would love that. Part of me will always want that, but I do not want to hold you down. Not now or ever. Yes, come to Brighton...'

THROUGH THOSE months he continued to write and again became ambitious. His first symphony carried much of his anger from the time that most tested him in 1941. Its writing extended over many months and, because of dissatisfaction with its initial narrow and bitter outlook, had to be re-drafted numerous times.

The fourth concerto for oboe and flute followed and carried a further burden of sadness. The two works began to expunge his loss. Afterwards, sometime in the future, when he could compose properly again, the struggle would be easier.

News came that Helen's brother Gordon had been killed in the retreat from Burma. It seemed the final catastrophe. He could not confront the pain that he knew the news must have brought to Helen, and sealed it away in his brain.

The war continued and he travelled to other coastal defences of the northeast of England. After periods of little or no bombing, despite the landings in Normandy, air-raids started again and in some ways intensified. London took the brunt of it.

Then the first flying bombs, the *buzz-bombs* or *doodle-bugs* fell on London. Initially no-one knew what they were and the observers on the coast were in consternation at the sinister sound. At first there were a handful, but a sustained bombardment soon got underway and caused serious damage. The V2 rockets were worse. They gave no warning of their approach and caused greater damage throughout the winter of 1944 and into 1945. In the north, all remained quiet.

The war spanned a period long enough for him to have forgotten when it started. The period lasted longer than any single event he had experienced and forced him to conform to patterns that were not his own. Many lives, not only his, were destroyed or damaged. For no-one would the future be the same.

A POINT occurred when he knew he had turned, when anger had been washed away, blown out of him by the incessant breeze. By the summer of 1945, hostilities had ceased and for every child born in that summer, the war belonged to an earlier time. It had finished and, for a while, euphoria replaced the deprivations of war. Life could be described again as normal.

Horizons widened, but his horizon remained modest. He placed it at Christmas and set a target to close the present chapter. What about Helen? He felt an unthrottling of energy. As the Humber's waters receded and the tide went out, he looked across the mudflats. In the New Year, he would go to Brighton. That was that; it was final. He would not be deterred.

Work had to be finished and ideas needed to be grown. He resisted the temptation to make quick changes, but decided to watch and wait. At first, the transition from war to peace did little to change life on the peninsula. He ran where he had run for years through a cobweb of tracks at the river's margin, as just another creature on the dunes.

His mother wanted him to return to the village, but that was impossible. How could he tell her? Maybe she suspected that he might go to Brighton. First he would go to London; make it a half-way stage.

PART OF THE consolidation focused on the Fantasia Orchestra in Hull and came in the summer. In a devastated city, the newly established mid-summer concerts of the orchestra were a triumph of optimism over tribulation. Having returned from the USA in 1945, fortune, and encouragement from him, brought Paul Spiers to Hull to join the Fantasia as its leader. He added strength to the much weakened orchestra. After all this time, he had never met Helen.

Now, in July 1945, on the morning of the day of the first performance of the Fantasia's summer concerts, with the sun in his eyes, he ran back from the sea.

Ten minutes later he opened the door to the room he had occupied for more than four years - one of the converted stables that formed part of a terraced row of wooden sheds that were built for the ponies used in the construction of the railway line. They were reclaimed for officers' quarters when the ponies had been sold. Dry and airy now in the early summer, as his tenancy drew to a close the knowledge of his imminent departure seemed to hang like a premonition over the room. Soon everything would be gone. Parts of the station already held the torpor of dereliction.

Lieutenant James Fenton was there too. He packed his bag and went to find him to take him to Hull. They were going to the theatre, Fenton as well. Fenton had seen his work grow as much as anyone and now would be rewarded with a seat amongst the special guests at the concert.

STANDING BACK from the main street, the theatre steps rose from the pavement to a colonnaded entrance. The foyer boasted a red carpet and gold ornamentation on the walls and ceiling.

In the front stalls, well attended by the acting Director of the Royal College of Music, Martin Taylor, on one side of him and the Mayor on the other, Hans Bergsland took his place again. Forty or more dignitaries, including Fenton, Collinson and Stephenson, occupied the front two rows. Bergsland found it difficult to sit in the small seat and shuffled to make himself more comfortable. At the beginning of the performance, the announcer informed the audience that in his heyday Hans Bergsland - for five successive years - had been the Norwegian cross-country skiing champion. But that was not the reason for him being the guest of honour at the performance; what explained that was his long standing role as the conductor of the Oslo Philharmonic Orchestra. To appeal to his national pride, Grieg's Piano Concerto and an arrangement of his folk tunes had been performed.

At the beginning of the second half, Bergsland seemed surprised to see the youthful appearance of the conductor who mounted the rostrum, a man with whom he was unfamiliar. David Whellans was thirty, and for almost six years had served his time in the army on the East Coast.

A short sonata for pianoforte came before a longer concert overture that consisted of a descriptive symphonic poem entitled, *Margins*, which interpreted the coastal landscapes of the east of England. The evening's programme concluded with a presentation of the first two parts of the composer's second Violin Concerto, which was one of his most poignant works that more than any previous work plumbed the depths of human spirit and described the loss of a dear friend.

Gratifying for the seated dignitaries, and for the conductor, the Norwegian visitor's mind appeared to be distracted from his discomfort in the narrow seats by the music, and he sat still for the best part of the performance.

Afterwards he went to the foyer where Bergsland waited to meet musicians from the orchestra. The visitor was easy to pick out; he stood head-and-shoulders above those around him - even Fenton.

When Bergsland saw him he broke from his group and stepped towards him as he approached.

'Yar, that was an excellent performance,' he said, and proffered his hand in greeting. 'I liked it all.' By nature, and with the visage of a Nordic god, he appeared hyperkinetic.

Not expecting the sudden burst of praise, he thanked him. 'It's been an honour to perform for you.'

'All your own work, heh?'

He nodded. 'All my own, yes.'

'Yar, for one so young, if I may say so, this is excellent work. With all due respect to the founding fathers of this city, I didn't expect to find such new and, should I say, youthful music here.'

He searched for right responses. 'I'm pleased you enjoyed it.'

'There is good melodic phraseology, dare I say it sometimes daring harmonic variation and idiom, and - much colour: I liked it. Very angry sometimes,' he said, and gave a manic stare.

Having been trapped in a backwater for so long his work had received little comment and now he would have discussed it all night. 'The pieces were performed here for the first time last year,' he explained, 'so the orchestra was familiar with them, but I think they were far more confident with the Grieg.'

'That is why you conducted the orchestra yourself?' Bergsland asked.

'Yes; it seemed the easiest way.'

Bergsland was unquenchable. 'When you come to Norway, will you conduct as well?'

He continued to keep up with the string of pleasantries of the conversation. 'If I ever have the pleasure to visit to Norway, I will be very pleased to conduct my work, yes.'

'No, no. You will come soon, please? We will make arrangements. When can you come? For the New Year, I hope. That will give us time?'

What was Bergsland trying to say? 'Are you inviting me, Mr Bergsland?'

Bergsland made a dramatic flourish of his hand. 'Hans, Hans, please...'

He nodded, 'Yes, Hans, of course; are you inviting me to come to Norway?'

'Of course; it must be. What else do you think?'

'I'm not sure what else, but if you are serious, I accept.'

'Yes, good...' He put out his large hand again, and shook his. 'We have a deal then - I think you would say?'

'Yes, of course.'

Before they could take the discussion further, the Mayor shepherded the guest away. 'We will talk again tomorrow -' Bergsland said and, turning as he left the theatre entrance, said, 'Will you be here at lunch time?'

He smiled and nodded his agreement. 'Surely, yes, tomorrow: I'll be here at lunchtime.' He disappeared down the theatre steps and he watched him go. 'Yes, tomorrow at lunch time,' he muttered to himself.

While it appeared unconditional, the invitation had been delivered so quickly that he did not know whether or not to take it seriously. *There's many a slip between cup and lip*, would have been his mother's cautionary response. Whatever the outcome, the invitation had immediate impact. As he stood there, the vision of opportunities it created started to close an era. If only Helen could have been there.

Paul Spiers caught him in the foyer. His own delight at the performance showed, and he tossed back the hair from his forehead. 'Satisfied then: the composer from Maklam has arrived?'

He nodded. 'Hmm, and in no small part thanks to you,' and he embraced his friend. 'Thank you for being with me.'

Behind them, with his mother on his arm, and his father and brother in tow, Stephenson approached. 'Well done, Whellans,' Stephenson chanted, partly mocking the way he spoke to him in the army, and shook his hand. His mother gave him a kiss and everyone else congratulated him.

Behind them, Martin Taylor homed in on the group. 'Mr and Mrs Whellans,' he said, 'I think we met some years ago, when David first came to the College. I'm Martin Taylor.' He too shook hands. 'Congratulations, David.' He turned to his mother. 'I have seen many remarkable musicians over the years. I am pleased now to add David to my list. There was a time - I must admit - when I didn't think he would make it...'

She smiled. 'Thank you,' she replied, and gave him a gracious smile. 'I never doubted it...'

With a slight bow of his head, he returned the compliment.

'If we're quick, there's time for a drink,' Stephenson said. 'Come on, shall we all go across the road?' And, so saying, he led them out of the theatre.

Afterwards they walked the short distance to Paul's flat - a few streets away in the Drypool area of the town. It had become usual now for him to stay there on his visits to Hull. On this occasion, Stephenson stayed as well.

PLANS WERE in motion for more performances with the Fantasia Orchestra. The invitation he received from the Norwegian added impetus to this work. At lunch the next day, Hans Bergsland lived up to his promise and made a formal invitation that he should visit Norway to work with the Oslo Philharmonic and to present a series of concerts of his work. He suggested Easter and he accepted.

More success followed: a request to write music for a radio documentary on rural and urban life, was followed by a collection of Yorkshire songs, *Summer Sky Lark*, and four piano sonatas called, the *River Suite*, which depicted rural life of the area's he knew. Four string quartets with a similar theme also saw completion.

The stimulus of new work precipitated moves to leave the army. Parting came at the end of August, but he chose not to leave Yorkshire. When he departed from Spurn Point, it was with the honour of being the longest serving soldier on the station - five years and eleven months. Stephenson - now Major Stephenson - remained to expedite the final withdrawal and closure.

For the rest of the summer, he went to Hull and stayed with Paul, whose flat in the heart of the urban port lent itself to his need to draw strands together. Sketches were started for the documentary series and another work, *A Peninsula Life*, was completed.

As summer turned to autumn, the impetus to return to London became irresistible and at the end of September, on an early train that pulled out from Hull and into the curve of the Humber, he departed from Yorkshire. As he crossed the river at Goole, the autumn sun rose behind him and, four hours later, he walked along the platform at King's Cross.

STEPHENSON, WHO soon would return to London, offered lodgings at his flat in Swiss Cottage, which had survived the bombing, and now he headed there.

Alone through October, for a while the gaps between activities were greater than the time spent on them. He reflected on new shapes and it took time to adjust to their patterns. A first focus was the machinery of trains and railways. For an urban documentary series for radio he worked on an image of dirt under the fingernails.

Helen's father offered him a flat in Brighton - with a studio where he could work. He agreed, and started to make arrangements, but Helen maintained her stance: she did not want to burden him and while not negative, was not positive at a time when he needed her support. In those weeks, when he spoke only to shopkeepers and bartenders, some of the impetus of the previous months was lost. As autumn closed around him, the optimism of the summer dissipated.

Each day he searched the stone environment of London and sketched ideas. Themes centred on technology - the form and function of urban life. The process was speculative since no certainty existed that anything would result from it. To begin with he spent days in stations where he watched trains and walked around them, stared at them, looked under and listened to them. It was a long time before his mind connected external shape with internal function. Only then could he translate understanding to music. The steam engine epitomised the energy of engineering.

Sometimes, in the evening, Stephenson would be there. 'How are you, my boy,' he would say.

'I've spent the whole day along railway lines with the sound of trains Doppler-effecting past me.'

Stephenson humoured him and listened. 'I don't know what the hell you're talking about to be honest, but if it ends up with a decent tune, you can listen to as many trains as you like, old boy.'

'Sometimes I don't know what I'm talking about myself...' he replied.

One evening by midnight he had scored a hundred bars that could have been trains, or horses' hoofs, or the sea across the shingle in Yorkshire, by then he did not know. He heard the lines as notes from a lute and would not try them on the piano for fear that he would disturb the association before it had settled. The next day it would sound new to him. The images were not translatable to the words of any conversation he felt like having. He would have to describe a vapour of half-thoughts that to him were as solid as girders in a factory superstructure, yet to others invisible and flimsy as gossamer. Even when he had finished, most of the message was lost. Like an iceberg, only the exposed island of ice would melt in the listener's ears. He closed his manuscript book and threw it on the armchair. There were no words in the sentences before him; only a full stop some way off that he worked towards.

He put water in the kettle, poured Camp Coffee in a cup and drank it as he looked out of the window and listened to the night. It was past full dark. He wanted assurance that he knew enough to have a clear picture. At that time he lived in the no-man's land between doubt and surety. The knife-edge cut into him. It seemed the move back to London had wounded him again.

Later, Stephenson met him at breakfast. 'Hell's teeth man, you look rough.'

'I only had three hours sleep...'

'Go back to bed then,' Stephenson said, and made him a cup of coffee. 'I thought you were bad in Yorkshire, but this is ridiculous.'

'Don't worry; it's just the change. I'm not settled.'

Stephenson was not the sort to offer sympathy. 'I've been in a new job at the British Museum for a month and feel as if I've been doing it a lifetime.'

He resisted the sort of explanation needed. 'It's not quite the same, is it.'

Any minute he expected Stephenson to tell him it was his *artistic temperament*, but showing a rare streak of understanding, he said, 'No, maybe not; anyway, good luck old chap, I've to be off. See you this evening.'

In a job for which there was no job description, the place and surroundings needed to be secure. Not only were his present surroundings unfamiliar, they were temporary. He found it hard to focus his attention.

IN NOVEMBER, Helen wrote:

> *Davy,*
>
> *I do not want you to come to Brighton. I'm sorry, but I have made up my mind that it is the best for us both. I think it is through love, and not through lack of will or longing. I know that I wasted our chance. Accept this now and so let me live my life, and you live yours...*

He stopped reading. 'I must go to her,' he murmured, and could see her in Brighton as she wrote the letter, even imagined the look on her face as she did so. How alone she was. 'I must go to see her,' he said again.

It was an anxiety that came many times, each only to be rejected by the force of rejection that he felt from the letter. He wrote to her and called her and talked to Nonie, but he did not go to Brighton. There was no change in her determination. She had said no, and she would never say yes. He had waited for the close of the year and welcomed the psychological curtain-drawing that it brought.

At Christmas he returned to Maklam. Could he work there again? Paul Spiers was home. He stayed into the New Year when he began to look forward to his visit to Norway, and then returned to London and stayed with Stephenson.

First January, then February passed; then March. He returned to Maklam and walked the Downs, went to the Royal College, returned to Stephenson's flat and tramped the streets of London. Eventually a time came when he knew it was too late to hope for Helen to change her mind. With no need to remain, he gave up his lodgings with Stephenson and went back to Maklam, which again became his home.

Then, in mid-April - Norway. In his absence his symphony was performed by the London Orchestra and a month later his war concertos were performed in a May Gala in Bristol. In the summer, the Northern Symphonia performed his works in Leeds. The BBC put out a programme that synthesised work from the war years and provided a commentary on the composer. Most of the press were kind and it felt strange for his work to be performed without his presence. He talked to conductors and orchestras and then they worked alone.

THE YEAR passed and in the autumn shards of an earlier period were re-aligned. On an evening in November that allowed him no time for preparation, Alex stood on the doorstep of his parent's home in Maklam. His mother told him to answer the door and at first he didn't recognise her. She looked tired; the fatigue from ten years of study and work through the war years was written on her face.

They both laughed.

'Alex.'

'David.'

His brain, which was slower than his senses to react, found him nothing to say. First it had to respond to the involuntary signals across every synapse that tightened muscles. He blinked.

She filled the gap. 'Welcome home.'

Now he saw that the woman in front of him was bolder and stronger than the one he remembered. 'No, welcome home to you; you are the one who's been away.'

She laughed as well. 'I guess we've both been away. Welcome home to us both then.'

With a dramatic gesture, he ushered her through the door. 'Come in, come in,' he said. 'I think everyone was expecting you, but me.' He took her coat and, showing her through to the drawing room, called his announcement of her arrival: 'A visitor, everybody; Alex is here.'

When they came through, his father and mother greeted her. His father said, 'Sorry, David, yes, it was all a bit 'spur of the moment'. What would you like to drink my dear?'

She looked around the room. 'The vase on the mantelpiece is lovely, Elizabeth.'

Elizabeth? How much contact had there been between them? Alex had returned to Maklam much less than he, only when on leave from India. Whenever she had done so, she must have called to say hello. They sat down together. 'Apologies for sounding abrupt at the door,' he said. 'I've looked forward to seeing you, but

I didn't expect to see you at that moment.'

'It's my fault; I telephoned an hour ago to ask when you would be home. You'd been in London for the day and Elizabeth said to come now.'

'Well, I'm pleased you did.'

She had spent five years in India and two years in West Africa and returned only weeks before. First she had served in Rawalpindi where she became affiliated to the Indian Medical Corps. In no hurry to talk, she sat and waited and at first he took her quietness for reticence. She was simply tired and now that she could relax, she did.

'I've tried to contact you,' he told her. 'Mother told me you were back in England, but of course that did not mean you were contactable any more than you ever were.'

'Well, you should have kept trying shouldn't you? She cast dark eyes at him and smiled again. 'But it is true, I have been very busy since I returned. I've been on the move a lot.'

A shadow came over her face which he tried to fathom. She seemed saddened by her memories or inhibited about talking about them. Then she smiled and looked at him and he remembered her as a girl, years ago before she went away. He thought he had known her, thought he had known his mind about her. Like the slipper discarded after the ball, here was something that fitted. He looked at her and saw Helen. How often had Alex interfered with his thoughts about her?

The revelation came that for years he had lived in the obscurity of his mind. Beside Alex he felt he had not made the best of his opportunities, that fate had cast him into insignificance. She had blossomed, was older and wiser, still intact. Even more than anything, despite her fatigue and sadness, she seemed optimistic. Was she naïve; maybe she was.

Then, when, in an instant of lapsed concentration, he caught her eye, he changed his mind. As she listened to his father, her head was bowed and she looked over through eyes which held knowledge, of a person who had grown and knew much. For the first time he acknowledged her as a doctor. She knew as much as any army medic, probably much more. He saw himself beside her and felt empty. Eleven years earlier they had departed from

Maklam. He realised that he could never tell her what had happened to him. It would be churlish, would sound like an excuse. Putting on a brave face, when she asked him to tell her what he had been doing, he simply said, 'I've been a soldier.'

For a moment Alex spoke as if she chatted to pass time with a patient. 'Yes, I know, but what have you been doing?'

'I've been doing what soldiers do, soldiering,' and he remembered Douglas. They had grown too far apart. How could he explain to her?

She nodded and searched for other entries: 'What about music?'

He smiled. 'I've done a little.'

She smiled also, and as she looked saw shadows around him as an aura. He looked haunted. Where had he been; stuck in army barracks for six years. It must almost have killed him. 'Tell me.'

His mind reeled back to when she had asked the same question years before: *Tell me*. She turned keys... For a moment, he hesitated; she had grown bigger than him. It was more than the old awe. She had succeeded. Her worth was clear.

Before he answered and considered the work he had done, he looked down and remembered all the non-acclaimed works that had been performed at forgotten premiers in the war years: 'I've done enough, if truth were known, but that's the trouble - it's not known; it's all waiting for the public. I've done a war cycle.'

When they talked, she knew she heard only half a story. 'That's good, and you achieved it while you were in the army; you've done well then.'

'It's not been easy.' How could he start to recount all that had happened.

How haunted he looked. She sharpened her mind and began to concentrate. It was not straightforward and would need care. 'I saw something about you two years ago in the Times.'

He looked puzzled.

She took out a piece of paper from her bag. 'Here, I kept it.' She handed it to him. It was an article about a concert in Leeds, in which his third and fourth concertos had been performed. He had not seen the article and it seemed unreasonable that she should have it.

'You can't hide, you see.'

This was extraordinary.

'I always knew you would be famous, Davy.'

He felt like a boy who is complimented by his aunt for doing well in a school poetry competition. 'It was only like a village concert...'

She heard bitterness and read a thousand messages. 'This article is real and complimentary; soon I want to hear it played in London.'

His father came in from the kitchen. 'Supper's ready; what about another drink, Alex? Same again?'

She handed him her glass.

'Beer, David?'

He nodded. 'Thanks. Did you ever see this?' he asked and showed his father the newspaper clipping.

'Think so. Your mother keeps them all.'

The performances in Leeds were small, very parochial, amateurish. True, he had not been very communicative about them; who had there been to communicate with?'

The space between them at that moment felt too wide to breach. As he thought this, Alex tried to bridge the gap. 'What else have you been doing?'

His defences came up and, for a moment, he cracked. 'I've been cooped in bloody army barracks and guardrooms for six years of hell. You've been in a lot more *theatres* than I have.'

She balanced on the edge of the conversation. Something seemed to have gone wrong. 'At least you've got a sense of humour,' and she became more serious. 'But now the cooped-up part is finished; now it is the time to get back on top.'

Still something worried her, something was hidden. She sent out the lifelines. 'There is too much to talk about now; what are you doing tomorrow?

'Nothing special.'

'Why don't we go out, and then you can tell me about everything. And I'll tell you about India and Upper Volta?'

Still feeling downcast, he nodded: 'Yes, that's a good idea. I'll come to call for you shall I?'

They agreed.

After supper, his mother sang. 'Come on; you play David and

I'll do some old favourites.'

HE RETURNED to London and visited Alex at her flat in Hampstead Heath not far from the flat he lived in before the war. The closeness allowed him to return to where he had been, to start to bridge the years.

Must talk to her, he thought, but the wounds had healed too much and to open them was unthinkable, even to tell Alex. So he edged forward. The documentary series demanded descriptive themes and soon he saw his way to completing them.

He met Nonie Sinclair on one of her visits to London. She had remained in the WAAF, where she had been a driver, and now carried out literary work. One evening in the West End, on her way back to Bracknell, they met for supper. For a few hours, they chatted.

On the occasions he needed to visit London he stayed in Alex's flat in Hampstead. Much of the time she lived in the hospital and while he may have stayed for a week or more, he seldom saw her. On arrival home at those times the flat was how she left it, usually not a thing out of place. She might notice a re-arrangement of cushions on the couch, greens together, browns together, patterned Indians along the top; or that a flower vase had been moved, a manuscript book forgotten on the chair. Otherwise, it was as if he had not been there.

THE PLAN for marriage was a women's affair in which he was involved least of anyone. A date was set for 1 May in 1947. She told him that she had always believed in him. Could that be true? Yes, she had always been part of him, as a sister; innocent, chaste, not to be harmed. It was what he had once imagined would happen.

In its intimacies, she took him as a blank sheet to which her ink fused so that paper and words were something new. He fulfilled her desire. Had there ever been a choice? Yes, there had: things could have been different, and she would never know. They were together again.

She was so different from Helen. His moves mirrored hers, each step, reflections of senses that danced between them. She awakened knowledge in him of her, as water and light are to a seed. Her senses responded in an unfolding of passion.

One weekend when they were together in London, he resolved to tell her about Helen and Douglas, to share those events in his life. It was impossible not to do so, and yet, seven years had begun to seal the past and the taboo he felt at any approach to the topics remained strong. At the end of the weekend, he had failed. Silence had become easier than openness and at one level had always been the intention.

When they married, Alex moved out of London back to Maklam where they bought the cottage. He knew it was where he wanted to be. There was never any suggestion of turning back. The marriage was made in the security of home and community. Old threads were re-joined. He returned to the earth of his ancestors and re-found his boyhood.

Part III

Chapter 23
(Days 14, 15 and 16 - May 1992: Cambridgeshire and Kent)

FOR WHAT seemed too long, she listened to the breeze in the branches of the trees. The wind eddied around the open patio doors and a chainsaw, or was it a strimmer? rasped somewhere in the distance. It was ten o'clock in the morning, Anna's husband Max was at work, the children at school, Anna in her study and the murmur of the breeze in the trees after the appliance stopped...

Had she already started to forget? Only three days since Nairn, but the tour of Scotland had started to blur. Since arriving at Anna's she had done nothing. What were the headlines? Mystery of composer's Scottish tour revealed; ferry crossing photos give up their secrets. There had been glimpses into the past that explained some of the questions; but nothing about the greater picture, nothing about the future.

As a place to stay, Anna's house had everything going for it: a perfect situation in the heart of the village, daily help and a separate wing with its own entrance through patio doors onto the garden. High walls screened the house, from its often noisy, neighbours. Behind them, silver birch and sycamores stood taller than the house and added to the screen. In a village of individual house design, where the minimum age was at least two hundred years, the house was not ostentatious. In the lustreless light of the wet day, as she looked out of the window, the ochre walls appeared dull. On balance, she hated it, the house and the whole village.

The room was the only redeeming feature. Windows opened to the garden on both sides. Beneath one of them, with a white counterpane and a throw that looked like a meadow in summer with poppies, was the bed. Next to it stood a shiny chrome music stand with a book of Beatles' songs open at Eleanor Rigby. It had been like that for as long as she could remember. On the opposite wall, a print of Van Gogh's cornfields with crows looked down on her. It seemed an odd combination, Eleanor Rigby and the crows, though she appreciated them both. The room could have been somewhere else - in France perhaps. It had the feel of summer inside, with polished parquet and white walls. A yellow curtain over the recessed space acted as a wardrobe. Even in miserable weather the room retained its brightness. Anna's guitar gathered dust next to the cupboard: a still life, and a violin case lay on the floor. A ewer in a corner for show and a delicate chair completed the arrangement.

She sighed.

Now, along the corridor, she heard Anna approach; her voice preceded her. 'Is everything alright?'

She waited until Anna's head popped round the door. 'Yes, thank you. I think so.' She smoothed the counterpane on the bed around where she sat. 'I think I will just go out now for a walk.'

'Okay. How long will you be?'

'Oh, I don't know. I'll see how the weather holds. I won't hurry.'

'That's good.' Anna gave a thumbs up look and turned to go out.

'Are you alright, my dear; you looked miles away just then.'

Now Anna gave one of those, *who knows* looks. 'Just moping over my work, I guess.'

She suspected something deeper. How was Max behaving these days? 'The last few weeks must have exhausted you as well.'

'Yes, they must have done.'

She waited, and sensed there was more. 'Anything else?'

'No, not really. I just feel a bit deflated that's all. I didn't realise how beautiful Scotland was. It made me feel restless. I was just thinking about everything. It's lonely now without Daddy being here.'

'I know. I'm sorry, I've neglected you and only thought about myself.'

Anna had cared for her mother and now expected her mother to accept the simplicity of her explanations, to be simple and to get on. She had suffered too, but had managed to hide it. The acute phase of care had passed. It was an inevitable outcome. Life had to move on.

A glance in the mirror, and a flick through her hair with the comb, finished her preparations. That would do. She twisted the top off the toothpaste and brushed her teeth. It would be wet along the river. Where should she go? She sat on the bed and laced her boots.

'Oh, dear,' she said. Was her judgement flawed? The old fool just took off to Scotland with no aim, she imagined them saying. She's confused. Give her time.

'Over and out,' she said; no amount of breast-beating was going to change anything. Maybe time would be the solution after all. She doubted it. Give it a few days; then that would be that.

Somewhere in the blank of the future, she saw things stop. But there was no end. There was always something beyond the end. *Time*.

She daydreamed. If we had no memory, it would be easier. How easy it was for the past, or our memory of the past, to colour our image of the future. Why did what had happened make any difference to the future? Life let you down. Everything else would no doubt change; David had gone. It was naïve to expect anything. She'd been a fool. Not wise enough to see. What of hope and optimism and enthusiasm? All those impostors. What momentum they gave us; sent us off to our futures, carried us along; until now - anyway, until now...

Out into the lane, she walked towards the river.

Into the ashen sky, the twelfth century Castle Keep protruded above the trees and a flag flew from a pole on top. She had often climbed the tower and looked down from the windows, as though she could look down the ages from Norman antiquity. Soon she passed the farm and walked in the direction of Cox's wood - about a mile further on. Could she remember the way around? From the rise beyond the farm, the route went past Selby Hall and led down into the village. Walking slowly at first, eventually she sat for a while in the sun at the edge of a copse where she could look across the farmland.

A couple walked past; they had not seen her. Then they did and nodded a good morning. Standing up, she nodded back and walked behind them until she came to a lane.

Her decision was to do nothing, to think nothing, make no effort, but just to walk. If nothing else arose for her to do, she would continue to walk. When she was tired, she would rest. If something attracted her attention, she would respond. If not, she would walk. She'd give it a few days. She had only two aims - not to be looked upon with pity and to avoid inward reflection. If that was the case, she'd failed already.

The hedge bottoms along the muddy lane were rich in the remains of cowslips and primroses that were battered by the rain. She cut through a farmyard to Cox's wood. Yes, even without a map she could remember the names. The route through a field with heifers took her over to a stile that led into the trees. The footpath meandered between horse chestnut coppices towards the road to Minton.

Her watch said 11.15. 'Lord, what must I do to keep going,' she muttered to herself.

When she reached the road, she stopped and said hello to a woman at one of the cottages. The woman dumped her shopping bags on the path outside the gate and acknowledged her with a smile. 'We're lucky the rain has kept off, aren't we?' she said, as the woman slowed down and wiped the mud from her boots on the grass verge.

'Lucky for me,' the woman said and fumbled in her bag for her keys. 'Missed the bus and decided I'd walk rather than wait another hour; I never learn.' She opened the gate and went through into the garden.

She smiled and walked on.

A short distance further she turned down a track with a sign that simply said *Farm*. She guessed she was half way round the circle. Mustn't be too quick. Nothing exceptional struck her about the arable farmland north of the village. *Toads Crossing* a sign said. Like the village at home, this was not her place.

Slowly she walked, but soon would arrive back at Anna's, so decided to make a detour. The lake at the castle crossed her mind. She remembered the benches. She could go there and sit for a while; that would do. Her first swallow of the year flew over. For a while she watched the ducks.

Down to Dartford and a dash along the M2: less than two hours to Maklam. She couldn't go yet. Why not? She put the thought of her own cottage out of her mind.

Through the trees from the bench by the lake, she saw Max's car pass and turn down the lane. Back for lunch. Perseverance had paid off. Better go to buy the mushrooms for Anna. As she stood up, the ducks squawked and flew across the pond.

LATER, AFTER supper, at seven thirty, she sat alone in her room. It was a long time until seven thirty in the morning. She was tired, but not enough to sleep for twelve hours.

Jodi came into her mind, that lovely girl, and she remembered the journey to the Isle of Skye, and the crossing on the ferry. *She should call her. Yes, call Jodi.* She dialled. 'Hello Jodi. How are you?'

'Great; it's lovely here. Thank you for telephoning. How are you?'

She remembered the day she had just passed. 'Fine as well.'

They chatted. 'Jodi, I've been thinking about something since we met, which I want to talk to you about. I would like to help you, so that you can do the university course and not have to worry about money. I hope that I don't embarrass you, but I would like to.'

Jodi seemed to hesitate. 'How do you mean?'

'Well, you told me that you had used up a year of your loan already and would have to work to support yourself. I don't want you to have to work while you study. You said that your Mum and Dad haven't got enough money and so, well, I thought I could help you - with the financial side of things, if you see what I mean.' She felt that she was not making a very good job of her offer. 'Will you think about it?'

Jodi still hesitated. 'Yes, okay, thank you, Alex. That is so kind of you.'

'You don't mind me offering?'

'No, not at all; it's just a bit of a shock. People don't offer things like that.'

'I know, but I really mean it. Please accept the university course and do what you most want to do. We can sort out the details later. I'll help with your maintenance somehow. Pay the rent maybe?'

Jodi's voice sounded more confident. 'Yes, okay, I'll ask my Dad.'

'Alright. Think about it first yourself.' She gave Jodi her telephone number. 'I'll call you to see how you are in a day or two. Alright. Bye.' She hoped she hadn't offended her.

A few minutes later Anna came. 'I've found a book you might like to read.'

A book? She didn't need books.

'I've just called Jodi, the girl I met on the way to Skye. She is getting on well with her new job in the hotel.'

Anna nodded in response. 'Would you like to read a story to Dan before he goes to bed? He would like that. Caroline is doing her homework.'

After she read to Dan, she dozed off. It was dark when she awoke and a blanket covered her that Anna must have thrown over when she found her asleep.

THE NEXT day, after a quiet lunch on the patio outside the French windows, and against her better judgement, they departed and Anna drove her home. In the fields of Essex, red swathes of colour cut through the green. 'It's good to see so many wild flowers again,' Anna said. 'I love the poppies, even though they are weeds.'

'*Weeds?* I never think of them as weeds.'

Anna squinted in the rear mirror and let a car past. 'Penny for your thoughts.'

In a kind of histrionic exasperation, she shook her head, and Anna turned to look at her, caught her eyes in her quick glance. 'I don't seem to have solved anything.'

'What else is there to solve, Mummy?'

'I don't know.' Her voice undulated. 'Some things worry me. Yesterday I just walked - aimlessly, quite aimlessly. My mind was blank, still is, wiped clean of everything that occupied it before, you know, such as work, friends, society; they've all gone and, anyway, leave me cold. And all that is left is this feeling of restlessness and images of faraway places like Monet landscapes, gentle meadows and quiet hills. It's crazy, but so strong. Everything about your father and Scotland just irritates me now.'

'It sounds odd, doesn't it?' Anna agreed.

She nodded, 'Do you remember at the funeral, there was a

woman there, with red hair? I didn't know her. I see her in my mind every now and again, for no reason.'

'Yes, I remember.' Anna changed gear. 'She didn't stay long.'

'Who was she?'

'I don't know. I could find out.'

'And I still see the pictures in my mind of patchwork hills.' Her words came quickly. 'I cannot let go. Who was that woman with your father on the boat? Why were they all together? The letter you found said he went to Nairn with her. I never knew that at the time.'

'Do I detect a hint of jealousy?'

She gave the barest laugh. 'I thought you would say that. No, well, yes - perhaps.'

Sandy told her one of the women had red hair. She became pensive. 'I am just perplexed; who was she? The woman with red hair?'

THE VILLAGE shop in Maklam closed as the sun dipped away from the afternoon. Children ran from the bus stop and women walked behind with pushchairs. They looked as if they had been to the beach for the day somewhere along the coast. All movement had the feel of going home.

Anna turned down the lane towards the cottage. It was three weeks since her father had died.

As she arrived, she felt exposed. Mr Joseph, the gardener, was at the gate and moved out of the way so that Anna could pull in. The top of the car was down. 'Hello, Mr Joseph,' she called. Leaving silence in the driveway, the engine died. 'It's nice to see you; I'm surprised that you still working though. You're just on your way home are you?'

He nodded, gave her a smile and then opened the car door. 'Just on my way,' he said, and offered his hand as she pulled herself out.

Her glance took in the small changes that two weeks had brought to the gardens at the front of the cottage. 'Everything looks pretty; the peonies are so pink and you are looking well, Mr Joseph. Has everything been alright?'

'Alright,' he nodded.

She gave a reassuring smile. 'Good. Well, don't let us keep you. We can catch up with everything tomorrow.'

He stepped behind the car and then turned back towards her. 'Plenty of flowers to pick,' he said.

She smiled. 'Thank you, Mr Joseph. That's very kind.'

'Until tomorrow then.' He turned and walked off along the lane.

Was Mr Joseph looking at her differently? Yes, of course he was. She was different now.

A path led around the cottage to the garden at the rear. The garden was perfect, nothing out of place. Mr Joseph had worked hard; he must have come every day - some extra devotion he felt he needed to give?

Although she did not want to go into the house, she forced herself to put the key in the lock of the French windows and turn it. It was not hers any more. In the living room, the sun fell on the arm of the chair through the window. She felt it: hot to the touch. It was a good house, smelled clean.

Here she was again - though not to stay.

In the kitchen and upstairs in the studio, all was as it had been. Anna seemed to know to hang back. In the studio were the piles of papers from the trunks that Anna had left on the floor. She stepped around them and looked at the paintings on the walls. Her eyes settled on the large picture of the view down the winding streets of *Senlis* in France that David had commissioned for her and brought back one summer many years ago. The frame picked out the colours of the painting: the stone in the walls of the houses, the slate and tiled roofs and the neatly laid cobbles of the street itself. Shadows and sunlight mingled on the stonework, in delicate sandstone yellows and flaking greys. Her eyes followed the street down into the painting, to the roofs of the church that rose beyond. Music played in her mind - melodies switched on by the memories. As a door in her mind, the music opened, as the street itself opened into the painting.

'*Bonjour, Senlis,*' she said.

Though she had not visited there as a girl when her grandmother and grandfather were alive, she knew that it was the street near to where they had lived, and now the painting and her knowledge of the town from more recent visits caught her attention. On the opposite wall hung a smaller picture that she inherited from her grandmother and also showed the town. Hearing Anna unpacking, she looked along the corridor towards her room, but then turned back to the paintings and let her thoughts rest on them.

Later she played music from the early years of the war. It was one of the symphonies; how David managed to write it while serving in the army remained a mystery to her. The contrast of the symphony with the music from Scotland could not have been greater. It showed anger and harsh feelings. The emotion disturbed her and the desolation in David from that time still touched her. Through the more turbulent strands, the violin carried a theme of sadness. She knew that Paul Spiers played the piece. It called beyond her into passion and talked of David's anger and loss from the war.

Outside, the dusk closed in.

David was difficult to pacify then, when they came together again, and now she laughed bitter laughter. How often he went away, on retreat, she remembered. A thousand ghosts haunted him that he could never find rest from. He struggled with his ghosts.

Didn't she also? Ghosts from India and those same years that spanned the war? Those terrible years: she shuddered when she thought of them. The years in India she had buried and she hadn't returned. Why had she never talked to him about them?

Everything reminded her of how she felt when she met David again and how he had changed since she knew him as a girl. What he had done during the war had been of no consequence to her. That he wrote music was enough. It was how she had known him, and was all she expected.

Now she was home again. *Home?* This place was not home. Home had been a person not a place. If ever home could be a place the place was not here. She smiled at the reaffirmation. 'I'm secure with you,' she said. 'My heart is with you, but it is not here.' And a small part of what was broken is mended. It must have been me that changed; and if I haven't, then I've never really been in tune with everything in the cottage or in Maklam. I am only here because my mother came here. 'So, that's alright, then,' she muttered.

The cottage is where a woman lived with her husband, who has now gone. She nodded to herself.

The night was quiet. While Anna worked, she walked into the garden and, as Mr Joseph had suggested, picked flowers. On the kitchen table, she put them in a vase, then went to close the French windows.

'Your friend Jodi has just telephoned,' Anna told her when she came inside again. 'You've just missed her.'

'Oh, thank you. I'll call back.'

Jodi came to the telephone. 'It's good to talk to you Jodi.'

'I've written to accept the university place.'

She smiled: 'Oh, that's good,' she said. 'I'm so pleased.'

Jodi's voice bubbled. 'My Dad said we would find the money from somewhere.'

'That's the best news I've had for a long time. You have my offer as well; you must accept it. Think of me as a doting aunt or the wealthy actress that you imagined I was when you first saw me.'

Jodi laughed. 'Okay. Thank you. Will you come to see me?'

'Of course I will; of course I will, Jodi...'

WITH ANNA, on the train, she made a visit to London, and at first, as they linked arms, they walked through Covent Garden and chatted. 'I'm glad you came with me,' and she squeezed her daughter's arm. 'I know you're busy. I just want to visit my old haunts again.'

'You haven't given up, have you, Mummy? I mean, given up trying?'

As she twisted locks of her hair in her fingers, and Anna looked round at her, she shook her head: 'No; why do you say that? Other things have changed, but I haven't given up.'

'I thought you seemed resigned, whereas it is possible to start again, don't you think? We're always starting out on something, and there are so many things you don't know and could do.'

She raised her eyes. 'You make me sound like a school girl and you an old maid.'

'You are, in some ways, aren't you? You are all there has ever been, Mummy. I've thought about it. You are the same now as you were when you were ten years old. If life mattered then, it must matter now.'

'That's different; we move on, don't we,' and looking around, she said, 'Fancy a coffee; shall we stop somewhere?'

They found a café, and chatted for another hour, and then caught the tube. For her, a visit to the Royal Free Hospital was the aim for the afternoon. 'I want to see it again, walk around again, around the Free, walk the streets and say goodbye.' Which was all true and, an hour later, they walked along Pond Street past the Royal Free Hospital.

When she turned the corner, the view she gained of the street seemed on a different scale and dimension to her memory of it. Although the traffic had trebled, she felt good to walk amongst her memories and in surroundings that were hers and could never be taken away. The hospital had given her all she wanted as a girl - to be a doctor - and she owed it most of what she had achieved in her life. For ten years she had given every ounce of energy to the hospital - everything - and then, from a distance, continued to give for the rest of her life. It was still hers. She had shared the vision that the hospital had given her with many like-minded women.

Remembering an occasion when she and David were students and she had visited him, she stopped and looked along the road. He had shown her his flat and given her tea, then taken her to the Royal College of Music and showed her around. Later, she had showed him the hospital and, in the evening, had eaten in a restaurant and he took her home by taxi.

'We'll walk up East Heath Road into the street where David lived. We walked this route together when we visited years ago for nostalgia's sake.' It was so close to the hospital. David had told her that he had come to live in Hampstead because she was there and the only person he knew in London. *Could it have been different?*

Looking along the terraced row, they stood now by the door of David's old flat. Then she turned and they walked towards the station and up Rosslyn Hill where her own flat had been. Grey London: well-hewn stone, but grey. Good Welsh slate, still grey, red brick and grey. It had grown to be part of her.

While Anna clung to her arm she retraced her steps and at three o'clock, stepped inside the hospital entrance, with a smart modernness about it: glass where she remembered solid walls. Slowly, in her mind, the layout started to return to the one she knew.

Taking an envelope from her bag, she gave it to the receptionist. 'It's a letter for the Dean. I want to make a bequest to the School. They can write to me.'

They left the hospital and walked away.

Before she lost sight of it, she turned and glanced once again at the building. 'That's for all my memories and all I owe you,' she said, and she smiled at Anna.

Chapter 24
(Summer of 1954: France - Senlis and Paris)

SEVEN YEARS after they were married, they made their second summer visit to *Senlis*, a town near Chantilly, not far from Paris.

When the festival had been brought to his attention, he might have ignored it but for the family links that Alex had with that part of France. Her mother was born there and had met an Englishman and moved to Kent. When he told her about the festival, she was excited. 'We can go together with the children and have a lovely summer.'

One day they looked at a map and made plans. As a girl, she had never visited her grandmother, but remembered times when her grandparents had visited them in Kent and talked about their home in France. Her response to the idea set in motion plans for her and the children to accompany him for part of the time. After he contacted the organisers, arrangements blossomed. In each of the first two years, they spent three weeks together in *Senlis* and then he stayed on.

This year, in advance of the festival, a hazy sun greeted his arrival. Alex would travel with the children in two weeks' time. He took up his attic residence in a house in the Rue Chantilly. The owner was Dominique Blanc, a retired merchant who had made his fortune bringing oysters from Brittany to the restaurants of Paris. His wife Marie-Louise offered a warm welcome.

Having grown used to the busy town of the festival the previous year, now he found it still before the influx of visitors at the beginning of July. Each day he wrote to Alex or sent a telegram of the highlights of his day. As Helen had done for him all those years ago, a thread of continuity and contact stayed between them.

Paul Spiers was there too, and, at the beginning of July, took up new accommodation next to the Chapel of Saint Therese in a street avoided by most traffic in the town. The change moved them closer together. Days were varied, usually busy, one seldom the same as the next. Paul settled in and began to give music classes. Mornings and evenings saw him in performances, then at the end of each afternoon, they would meet at a bar near the cathedral.

AT THE END of one afternoon, having packed away his violin and closed the lid of the piano, he waited for Paul. Watching from the window, expecting to see a single man, he ignored a group of three that approached. Only when they were at the entrance below did he recognise Paul. After a few minutes, when they had not come up, he went down to the vestibule and heard Paul's voice with those of two women. The trio were still occupied in a conversation they had brought with them, but parted as he approached and, as was Paul's way, he made quick and noisy introductions.

'This is Colette and Martine,' he said, and added, 'You don't mind if we go together do you, David?'

The question seemed irrelevant and in the street they retraced the steps the three had taken and headed for the cathedral. He walked beside Colette.

'Paul has told us a lot about you.'

'Only good things I hope.'

She smiled. 'Most of it; he says you're a great composer.'

She was attractive, bright and artistic, with colourful jewellery and expensive taste in clothing. She could have been a model. 'By that I hope he means, *good*?'

'No. I think he means you're great. He says you have known each other a long time.'

'We're from the same village; known each other forever. What about you and Martine?'

'Only since the Sorbonne. We have done a lot since then.'

Three or four paces ahead, Martine's voice flowed uninterrupted, so that Paul's contributions were heard only when she paused for breath. He turned often to look at Colette.

'I think it's important that people talk,' Martine was saying. 'People do not talk enough, don't you think? They stay all day long in their own place and can spend whole days without talking to anyone: musicians especially. I know it is true. I have known people like that.'

'She makes up for anyone who does not talk much,' Colette said.

In the wake of Martine's words, until they came to a bar close to the cathedral, *Notre-Dame de Senlis*, they chatted. Outside, they sat and drank beer. After that encounter, the group began to meet together each afternoon. Paul fell in love with Colette and the bond between them grew from those days.

One evening they played in a concert together. After the performance, the group stopped by the Café Marc and sat on the pavement and ordered beer all round with Pernod and green chartreuse. It had become a habit that when the occasion suited, this band would play wherever they were. They did so on this occasion. Paul started with some Breton tunes that could not have contrasted more to the concert they had just performed. He brought the stillness of the countryside into the streets of *Senlis*. Those on the pavement listened. Then Colette played traditional French tunes to which he added some English. With much improvisation all were adapted to the moment, caught in its gaiety and laughter. It was a lively evening that drew a crowd to the café. They played until midnight.

The festival aroused feelings of hope. Colette seemed to be swept along in the furore of its current. 'Whoever called this a festival of light was right; it is so exhilarating, don't you agree? Everybody you meet says it is.' She talked as the group departed into the cooling night.

'Yes on both accounts, yes,' Paul replied. 'If music can create light, then this is a festival of light.'

'It's so divine.' Martine threw her head back and breathed in the night air.

DRIVING HERSELF, by road from Calais, Alex and the children arrived in *Senlis*. The journey from Kent was easy: one hundred and eighty miles door to door. She drove so that she would have her car and spend the time sightseeing with the children. Anna was six and Jonathan four. She was reminded of how David had been before they married. Compared to then, his work occupied him fully and the periods of inactivity had ceased. The progress brought relief to her.

In the house on the Rue Chantilly, the sound of children

delighted Marie-Louise Blanc, who treated them as part of her family. Marie-Louise was enchanted by the young English girl and boy who spoke French and by their mother as well. To have them in her house seemed to be a pleasure that transported her from her own life into another. Marie-Louise imagined the house in England that she described and the differences in lifestyle compared to *Senlis*. She inspected their clothes and asked about the shops. She quizzed her about food and cooking and showed all the herbs and spices in her cupboard.

On the first evening, to discover the town, they walked the streets. Passing through the square near the cathedral they walked beneath the trees, and marvelled at the ancient buildings. The evening sun shone between houses and into tenements that led away from the cathedral spire.

One afternoon Marie-Louise and she walked into the town and she was shown the best shops and special places for women to find what they wanted for their homes and families. During the week, Marie-Louise constructed menus that showed off France to its best. Her husband said he had never eaten so well. She talked to her neighbours and brought them to meet her guests. It was Marie-Louise that organised the family outings and arranged cars to pick them up and young men - the sons of her friends - to be their guides. It was as though on first meeting, a trigger had touched her maternal instincts that made her cherish every moment of caring. Marie-Louise had not fussed or enjoyed herself so much for twenty years. She knew that parting would be an emotional time for them.

In the weeks before the visit, she had planned and daydreamed about how she would use the time; it would be a pilgrimage to the home of her grandmother. In the hills and meadows around the town they walked and found a place to stop for a picnic. In some ways the landscapes were reminiscent of England; in others very different. Hay dried in swathes across the hillside and swifts circled, lifted on the currents that swept them upwards over the lines of trees that edged the fields. She felt at peace there.

Afterwards, Anna asked, 'Can we go to find some wild flowers to take back to Madam Blanc?'

While she walked with them, David, with Jonathan on his shoulders and Anna running before him, searched for wild flowers.

She let her eyes wander through the colours and the tones of the fields. On the brow, struck by a familiar scene, she stopped to take in the panorama of the hillside.

'Look,' she said, as she turned and called to David and opened her eyes wide in amazement, 'there it is.' She ran to him and then turned and gazed up the hill where his eyes rested on a small church beside an arbour of cypresses, its pointed spire rising against the undulating background.

'That's the church on the hillside...'

'Which church?'

'The very one, exactly as I have seen it, ever since I was a girl.'

She started to walk up the hill, away from David and the children, and stopped to look again before she continued, all the time with her gaze fixed on the church ahead of her.

'Come on,' he said to Jonathan and Anna, 'let's go with Mummy to the church.'

They found her in the porch with her eyes fixed on the inscription over the door, painted in fading letters on the stone lintel.

'What does it say, Mummy?' Jonathan asked.

'There are many doors, but few will open. Find the door that opens for you,' she read and translated.

'That's what you always say, isn't it?' David replied.

'Yes, it's just incredible, but I have never been here before. First I see the church, just as I have always seen it in my mind, and then here is that saying, in French, that I have never seen before, and yet have always known and said.'

David raised his eyebrows. 'Hm, well, that certainly sounds curious, doesn't it; let's have a look inside...'

SOMETIMES HE rented a studio from an artist called André who, with his brother, owned the building that stood at the highest point of the town. Within the ancient town, the windows looked out onto the expanse of tiled roofs across the slope of the hill. When the sun shone, the roofs sparkled against the stone of the cobbled streets and houses. Noises that entered the opened windows were those of birds and subdued chatter from the streets. At times André's whistle and the tap of his mallet mingled with the trills. It was a fertile compost in which his work flourished. For others who listened, a piano and violin also might break the silence of the progressing day. *Senlis*, and concerts at the Chateau of Chantilly, formed the foci of those summers.

'I want you to choose a subject for André to paint for you,' he told Alex. André had completed many canvasses that showed the town through scenes of its cobbled streets. His studio occupied a commanding view on the upper side of the square that typified the town and conjured views down streets that wound into the old quarters.

'I think I would like a view of the street that leads down from the square,' she decided, and André painted it for her.

AT THE END of their stay he accompanied Alex and the children to Calais and then on the return journey spent a day in the region to the south where he wandered the countryside and wondered about Douglas.

Part of the attraction of *Senlis*, was its proximity to the region of Douglas's death, which meant that pilgrimages to the battlefields of the retreat to Dunkerque were part of a parallel agenda to his summer programme. He embarked on the search he had decided to make long ago - for the place of Douglas's death.

Over the years, since the war had ended, he could have made this visit at any time; it would have been an easy journey from Kent. The possibility, an intention to be fulfilled when time allowed, had rested in his mind, and the Summer Season in *Senlis* provided the opportunities.

First he drove on the *route de Furnes* to the east of Dunkerque, to see the area, and then south towards Saint-Omer. Where a church rested in the lee of the land he stopped surrounded by colonnades of trees beside the agricultural landscape with sharpened definition in the afternoon sun. Little sound disturbed the scene, but he imagined what those caught in the rear-guard actions might have heard, and conjured images of the past. The land, with the sureness of growth, had healed its wounds. Only the cemetery remained, defiant of the forgetful.

Getting out of the car, he stood in the rank grass beside the road. After two months in *Senlis*, amidst a frenzy of activity, now he was alone, uninterrupted in his thoughts. The moment was a step into the frailty of his expectation. What he wanted to see no longer existed. The places of history had changed and the energy from that time had dissipated, as if some mystical judge had decreed that all trace should be erased in a scramble to hide the evidence. Douglas Cameron was one of the soldiers listed as missing. His body had been buried and was now folded into earth. Wherever the place had been, as in the open fields of Dunkerque and Saint-Omer, no part remained. He dwelt on the dilemma of death, and could not reconcile the man he knew with a simple description of earth. Explanation eluded him. All that flowed from the human spirit had no denominator in the substance of agricultural landscapes. The dried stubble of wheat fields could not account for it.

The longer he stood there, the more the earth drew him away from his memories. He admitted that time had robbed him of the sharpness of his feelings. He could not say anymore whether his memory of Douglas was accurate. He saw his face, but the memory blurred into what he saw now in photographs. He knew that songs and music were scrapbook fragments. He remembered a fervent pride in Scotland, an insatiable wit. The assumption, that harmony would prevail over conflict, with which Douglas faced life, he now adopted as his own. These were the elements, surely of no chemical origin, that would never return to the earth.

Continuing on his way, he stopped at the town of La Bassée where Douglas was killed, not far from Bethune, a town forty miles south of Dunkerque in the heart of mining country. Pigeons flew over the fields and swooped to the copses between them. He stopped to walk along the canal outside La Bassée.

This is where you were old friend, and he stepped onto a concrete road the colour of sand. *I will always remember.*

Course grass overgrew the edges and gravel scraped on its surface beneath his shoes. He walked on the verge until he found a position to look across the landscape. Haze shimmered above the scattered trees at the limit of his vision. A breeze blew across the fields and wafted on his face. In front of him fields of dust-laden crops waited for the harvesting gangs to arrive.

His gaze raked the fields. Pictures formed in his mind of what they might have been before the innocence of the present scene, when they had been trodden over by the feet of one army in retreat to the sea, followed by those of another that advanced upon them.

Then he returned to *Senlis* and in the house in the Rue Chantilly worked on the last movement of the violin concerto that he had started in 1941. The seeds that had been sown all those years earlier in Yorkshire now started to grow. With effort the composition unravelled. If he closed his eyes, he could hear the calm of the music's theme that he had first written on the coast of Yorkshire. Throughout the writing, Helen returned from the corners of his memory and broke into the music. The longer he concentrated, the longer he held and distilled, the richer the theme grew, purified by the stillness. He heard the emotions that arose from the calm, was able to hold them and pick up the strains again and continue. His work was easy, easier than it had been for years. There was no struggle and a succession of ideas rewarded his efforts. To complete the work, he would need to go one more time to La Bassée.

FOR SHORT periods, for stimulation and a distraction, he took leave from *Senlis* and lodged in Paris. Colette stayed there with Paul Spiers for part of the summer and found him lodgings in Montmartre. The quarter's pavements were enlivened by an abundance of street performers who formed the catalyst from which music precipitated in his mind. Dancers, musicians, jugglers and painters worked from dawn to dusk. The unconventional acts were a law unto themselves, moulded more by the performers' hybrid tastes and inclinations than artistic purity and adherence to originals. Once he got to know some of the artists, their mix of colour and character provided a fusion of stimulation for his work. When it rained or at the ends of days, the artists met in the Café Bleu in Montmartre. They paid little, but sat next to those who paid more. The balance of economic forces worked for the proprietor and in their favour.

The Café Bleu was patronised by the faithful and the rich. The proprietor chef, a man of intellect and personality, spent as much time waiting at tables as he did in the kitchen. His apron covered a paunch that was as much part of the fame of the establishment as anything else. He steered his way around the room with his specialities, *steak au poivre*, *cassoulet* or *filet mignon* and later *flambéed crêpes suzette*, carried four plates at a time above his head. Flattered with individual attention, his guests delighted in the morsels of information he provided about the cuisine: a spice here and a cooking method there as intimacies to the women, or the precise origin of the *fromage de chevre* or better still - the brandy - used in the sauce, for the men; a repartee for the clients as rich as the menu.

One evening, at nine o'clock when it was already busy, he pushed open the door of the café and Paul arrived ten minutes later. They prepared to play to a packed house.

In an alcove near the windows at the front of the café, first they played a set of tunes that he had entitled, *Danses de la Rue*, which in parts were fast and flowing and in others slow and suggestive.

'You should compose more like these,' Paul said.

'Do you think so?'

'Hm. Why not add some Breton tunes?'

'Good idea. Let me have some.'

'I remember your first major composition, *The Downs Overture*,' Paul said as they settled into the evening. 'Remember? I still play it.'

'We've moved on a little since then, haven't we?'

With barely enough floor space, two women stood to dance and tables were moved back by precious inches to allow them. Their attire was peasant, but their accents unashamedly Parisian. The origins of the dance were French, possibly further east in Europe, bourrées and mazurkas. The stamp of feet and swirl of skirts told of the traditions. They clapped as the tempo rose and laughed at the unexpectedness of the sequences. In a slow movement a man danced with one of the women, a duet of pass and turn in which their eyes remained locked through the slow and sensual crescendo. The three performed by day in the streets of Montmartre. The music, as much theirs as the composer's, came from the streets. Its inspiration had been their performances and the music that accompanied them. Rightly the clientele did not know which they should appreciate most: the proprietor's wit, his food, the music or, at this moment, the dancing.

The full cycle of street music was entitled *Pavane* and throughout the evening they played each part of the cycle. The subject of the music lent itself to descriptive passages. Circus, dance and mime were transposed with ease. Street music was incorporated into a patchwork of traditional and contemporary tunes and a more reflective passage brought the canvas and palette of the street painter to the cycle. It was the first time that the whole composition had been played in the café. Colette Lafait accompanied them to form a powerful trio of violins. This evening she arrived from a performance with a friend, both still dressed in concert attire. Once her friend had had a drink and removed his bow tie, he performed the fourth movement of Vivaldi's Four Seasons, with extensive pizzicato in the largo, as a cello solo.

Such evenings brought much pleasure.

'I was thinking that it would be great to record a concert here, but then I wondered if the sound equipment and cameras might ruin the atmosphere,' he said.

'They're a great audience,' Paul added. 'We should try. I'll talk to Colette; she knows the right people.'

The spontaneity of the dancers was the magic on this occasion. That they recognised and could dance to the passages and appeared to enjoy them, provided the music with the only seal of approval that he looked for. This was the music of Paris: light and unashamedly commercial. For the music he composed in *Senlis*, he sought only approval of himself, and wrote from stimuli within him.

AFTER THE festival in *Senlis*, when people had departed, he sat alone in the Café Marc. In sympathy with autumns that he recalled, leaves swirled in the roads and filled the gutters. Then the trees were bare again and streets less golden. In the café he sat and jotted notes in his book, wrote to his mother and to Alex and to Anna enclosing wild flowers he had pressed for her.

He never found another singer to compose for. At the end of that second summer, with no real knowledge of the segment of country, again he tramped the canals around La Bassée and gained a greater insight into the area. Though he had no knowledge of events in 1940, he felt he had found the place where Douglas died and that in some part at least he had fulfilled a commitment to his friend.

One thing now remained for him to do: complete the missing movement from the violin concerto started in 1941. The work was planned and drafted out, and he intended it to be finished with a piece of music grown from the place where Douglas died.

He departed early from *Senlis* and drove north in a car that he had borrowed from his artist friend André. The beauty of Picardie rolled away from the road on either side as he drove, and then undulating countryside replaced the pine-forests. At ten o'clock, beside the road where it crossed the canal south of the town of La Bassée, he locked the car and walked west towards Bethune along the edge of the black strand of water. Green rushes grew in fresh patches in places at the edge and at others the unprotected banks fell in eroded gullies to the waterside. After a while he stopped where the vestiges of the walls of a building showed through the turf beside the canal bank. A line of yellow foxgloves meandered away behind the overgrown outlines where buildings used to stand. He sat for an hour while he listened and watched. Then at the village of Cambrin, where barges were moored to wooden quays, he crossed the canal and walked north through Givenchy, past Violasses and back in the direction of La Bassée. He walked through fields of sugar beet and harvested barley and approached the town from the open countryside near Lorgies.

As he traversed the landscape of fields and woodland in which La Bassée nestled he worked on the missing third movement. Although it was difficult to imagine what happened in those fields in May 1940, the movement became one that portrayed the silence and healing of the passage of time.

Back in the town, at the main hotel, he ordered supper and sat down to write. For three nights, between further excursions into the local countryside, he completed the movement.

THEN HE returned to *Senlis* and finally, with Paul, travelled to Calais to return to England. The ferry skirted the coast and turned away from the headland and away from France. In the middle of the Channel he watched the cliffs of Cap Blanc Nez narrow to the horizon behind him. They talked about the summer in *Senlis* that had caught their imaginations. In front of them the cliffs of the south coast of England grew more visible as those of France diminished.

Leaning on the ferry rail, Paul gazed to the line of the French coast. He seemed sad to leave. 'Here's to *Notre-Dame de Senlis*,' he said, and lifted his glass in the direction of France.

'And to the Chateau at Chantilly.'

'God bless all those who sail in her.'

At nine o'clock each morning an ensemble had played to audiences that came in from the streets and then went on their way again. He caught Paul's look of nostalgia: 'You should have stayed, you know.'

'And played all summer in the cathedral. It was a pity that we only played there for three weeks.'

'We did enough...'

'Maybe I will go back soon...'

'You should.'

Paul looked wistful. 'I remember the church each time I went there. If I could spend my days with the equanimity of the last few weeks I would be very happy.'

'Don't you think you would become bored after a while? Too much of a good thing?'

'Oh, I don't think so; it suited me. Reminds me of the church in Maklam.'

'True, but music needs to create its own atmosphere, don't you think?'

Paul clasped his hands behind his head. 'Of course: but if to achieve that you have to perform in isolation from your surroundings, then that would be difficult. The surroundings also make the music.'

In the evenings, when the air was warm, they had played to audiences that filled the cathedral so that people stood in the aisles and recesses. It echoed to Bach and Pachelbel, Elgar and Borodin. At those moments, the elements of musical beauty came together as much as anyone could hope for. Musician and listener enjoyed a feast of sound. At the ends of the performances the audiences sat in their seats and chatted. No-one wanted to leave.

'I just found it superbly invigorating,' Paul said.

He nodded. 'You know, I've been wondering, would it work in England? A festival such as that, in Kent, or somewhere else?'

'It might. Something was right in *Senlis* though. I take my hat off to the organisers.' Paul smiled and took another mouthful of beer.

A Summer Season of Music: the summer had seen them take part in a frenzy of workshops, practices, virtuoso performances and lectures. Between all of these, every opportunity had been taken to sit in the cafés around the town. Paul had given classes in a room of the Chateau of Chantilly. He played in a string quintet and travelled to perform in Paris. A mix of activities made the individual at once a performer, teacher, student and appreciator. Paul had played and he had composed. They were days full of music with little time for other thought.

As they crossed the Channel, they agreed that the festival had worked. The town itself, the weather and the will to strive for perfection, all contributed. A mood of relaxation prevailed. For him a sunlit room at the top of the house and the lack of distraction made life very bearable. For Paul the spiritual uplift found in the churches scented his appreciation. It recalled his choir-boy youth in the church at home and the Cathedral in Canterbury. A hundred or more musicians from seventeen countries brought a novel atmosphere to the town. The stimulation and interaction could not have been more complete.

The ferry rolled a little and he clutched his glass as it slid towards the edge of the table. 'I take it you're not looking forward to getting home then?'

'In part, I must admit that I'm not. It'll take me time to settle down again.' There will be the tour of the north of England later in the year. 'What about you?'

He nodded. 'I might miss *Senlis* for a while. I worked well there, but there is plenty planned for me at home.'

Paul mused on the summer. 'Do you remember the village we visited one Sunday, where lunch lasted from eleven o'clock in the morning until seven in the evening?'

'Impossible to forget,' and he made a face that did not suggest he fully enjoyed the experience.

Paul had revelled in it. 'You weren't very well, I recall.'

He nodded.

'Every half-hour another course was brought in. Stuffed limpets: do you remember those?' Paul said. 'Brought down fresh from the coast.'

He groaned. 'All too well. I can't say I was over-thrilled. It got a little out of hand at times.'

'Oh, I wouldn't say that: all the cheeses and local dishes.'

'Yes, and the over-powering saucisson.'

'The women spent so long in the kitchen, we hardly saw them. They just kept coming out with more courses; it was a dream.'

He withheld criticism of the amount of food he had been expected to eat that afternoon. 'The most memorable part for me was seeing the shooting stars, when we relaxed in the garden after dark, and drank the last of the wine.'

Paul nodded. 'Yes I remember. Long live France and long live French cuisine.'

'Well, with any luck it will all happen again next year. You can start to look forward now.'

'I am.'

He turned towards France where the coastline diminished to a slender ribbon. 'Just imagine what it must have been like here in 1940.'

'Where?'

'Here, mid-Channel, during the evacuation from Dunkerque.' *When Douglas was defending the retreat.*

'Mayhem, by all accounts.'

He nodded.

Chapter 25
(Days 17, 18 and 19 - May 1992: Kent)

DEW GLISTENED on the grass; she trailed her feet through it across the lawn, watched the fish in the pond and threw some pellets from the plastic bag that she kept hidden behind a stone at the edge. The black and golden fish fought for the food and thrashed in small ripples at the surface. In the silence of the garden, she waited and then returned to the cottage. Anna had departed the previous evening, and in her solitude, she sensed every step and every breath she took.

Inside, from the studio window she could see the trail of her footprints through the dew as dark patches in the silver sheen. On the studio floor the piles of papers and manuscripts that Anna had left lay scattered in small islands around the piano. She planned her day around them, would look through them slowly; there was no hurry. She had nothing else to do.

When she looked again from the studio window the dew had vanished with the rising of the sun. The traces where her footsteps had been were gone. What about her past, where her footsteps had been long ago? *What had she forgotten?*

Beneath the painting of *Senlis*, and beside a pile of papers, she sat, ready to continue her searches. The string fell off the first bundle and spread the contents on the floor. They were large photographs in paper frames. Despite herself, as she remembered again familiar scenes, the images pleased her.

This must have all been in the fifties. There was David with other people she recognised, garlanded at concerts, all smiles to the audiences. They were the special times; she was back with them in events long gone, back with the applause and cheers. It made her laugh. She relived David's and, to some extent, her own past.

The thought came to her of when she stood in the ballroom in the Golf View Hotel in Nairn, when she had wondered about the concert there. Had David felt as good then, before the war, as she remembered he had at the time of these photographs?

On the floor, seated cross-legged, she smiled at her memories. For a while she forgot everything. More packs were opened and the items turned over to be examined. The supply seemed endless.

Through all the years there had been no times of hurt or deception in her life. The years had been lived in harmony. She chose the next bundle, which contained letters, all in standard envelopes tied with string. There must have been fifty at least. It was not that the contents were shocking, or that there could be any cause for recrimination, just that she did not know, until the moment she saw them, the things the letters told her. The effect was, as any revelation to the unsuspecting, dreadful, a total shock.

Letters from Helen Strachan to David Whellans in 1940 and his to her. Though there were many, the first few were enough, and wove a path of havoc through her reason. She read and became more upset as she did so. Then she opened them only and glanced through, more and more. The words poured out in such a neat hand-writing. Many were full of newspaper clippings and photographs addressed to David in Yorkshire.

'*Oh, God,*' she said and in final desperation, threw them down. The sense of violation caught her unawares. Its impact sickened her. This is what her premonitions had been about, something years before their marriage.

There seemed little place for reason and logic at that moment of her crisis and she turned and ran from the studio. The door banged and her breath came in gasps. Her legs trembled as, in the hall, she grabbed her cardigan from the chair and ran into the garden. Thoughts slotted into place; the realisation probed like a jagged knife.

The woman on the boat to Lewis, yes, her; the language of the letters was intense, not the words of a mere friend, but deep and soul searching, not written to hide feelings but to express them in detail. She understood; there was no doubt. They were words that revealed intimacy and sincerity. The dark woman that he had his arm round. More than just a pose for the camera. Why had she been so stupid? Was this what it was all about?

Now she ran into the lane and towards the church. She checked herself, turned and went back towards the village. Then slowed to a walking pace and kept going past the pub and the butcher's shop to where a footpath cut back from the railway crossing to the fields. She took it and progressed towards the woods. Nettles stung her ankles. *What was she doing?*

She kept going. Someone was up ahead, a man with a dog. 'Good morning,' he said as they passed each other. She stepped along the narrow path worn to bare earth between the fields. The grass in the shade at the edges was wet with morning dew.

Woodland fringed the fields and she stopped suddenly, now frightened. 'Where am I running to?' she muttered. 'I thought it was over.'

Beneath the trees there was a gate. She stood beside it for protection and rested her hand on the top bar. She felt safe; it was only a short walk home. In her fear, she felt her smallness in the world. If she had ever believed in her own God, it was then that she asked for help.

Half an hour later she walked back, cold despite the sun, but her disbelief was colder. She had suffered pain enough. Now pain born of anger and of not being able to talk to the person she loved about something she desperately needed to talk about.

Why didn't you tell me? Why didn't I tell you? The words returned and revolved in her mind. '*You should have told me. Why did I find out like this?*'

She locked the cottage door behind her and went to her room, closed the curtains and lay down on the bed. 'Enough,' she wailed, and with closed eyes, tried to calm her mind. When she awakened, still shocked, her head ached in the confusion. How long she had lain there she was not aware.

Letters. Letters. David's letters from long ago. Her confusion turned to anger, not directed at him but at herself, and guilt. At least David wanted and tried to tell her. She got up and rushed to her wardrobe and took out a box. Inside lay a bundle of letters, the same as David's. For a moment she found it difficult to breathe. Then she touched them, but drew her hand away and tears came to her eyes. *Oh, God*: a bundle of letters from her past, a captain in the army who she had met in India. He never knew he had been a father. She should destroy them now, but she shook her head and returned the letters to the box, closing it away again behind the wardrobe doors.

She must tell Anna.

THE NEXT morning, after only two days, when Anna returned to the cottage, the flood of her mother's misery confronted her.

'I'm really sorry you've had to come back so soon. I'm really leaning on you too much.'

Anna nodded. 'Yes, I know, but it's alright. You sounded so upset. We're both learning about father. I don't mind.'

'Thank you,' she replied, and then told her about the letters. 'They're abandoned where I left them in my panic.'

While Anna went upstairs, she distracted herself in the kitchen, washed the dishes and cleared up. After a while, when Anna did not return, she became impatient. *What was she doing?* She must have read them all by now, surely. Then she heard the piano. *What on earth was going on?*

After more than an hour, she went upstairs. Her entrance startled Anna. 'Oh, I'm sorry,' Anna said, and saw the questions in her eyes. 'I was wondering about the letters and what they meant. I thought I would play for a while.'

She looked at Anna. 'You don't seem too concerned; don't they mean anything to you.' She looked around the room. 'You've cleared them away.'

'Yes...' Anna seemed confused. 'I am concerned. I'm sorry Mummy. Come on, let's go downstairs.'

She saw her daughter's eyes and knew she had been crying, and regretted her words. 'Yes, let's go down.'

'I don't know what to say,' Anna said, and hung in the living room doorway. She seemed to barely understand the impact that the letters had had, and said, 'Sit down and I'll make us a drink.'

'There is nothing to be done now.' The waiting had made her embarrassed. 'I don't want to talk about it anymore.'

'Yes,' Anna replied. 'Mummy, I know how you must feel, but I don't know what to say.'

A pang of compassion rose in her for her daughter. 'It's not your problem, my dear. I'm sorry.' She turned away. 'I just wonder why he never told me.' Speaking as though to herself, she said, 'It makes me think there must be more to it.'

And then she looked back at Anna, as panic rose in her again. *She needed to tell Anna things, as well.*

'I have read the letters,' Anna said, 'letters that were once the possessions of my father. Have I pried? It seems so.' Her words were almost a whisper. She sat down. 'He must have meant them to be read, don't you think? Otherwise he would have destroyed them long ago, wouldn't he?'

She shrugged. 'Who knows?'

Anna was emphatic. 'He would. I'm sure he would not have wanted to hurt anybody. Remember when you had your anniversary party you said Daddy wanted to tell you something.'

Her mind went back, just those few weeks ago. *There's something I want to tell you, something I've wanted to tell you for a long time*, he had said to her. 'Yes, I've wondered what it was about.'

'Well it fits, doesn't it?' Anna's look suggested that she thought it might be a real possibility.

'Why would he have wanted to tell me then though, after all that time?'

'Who knows,' Anna repeated. 'I have seen another part of his life.' She smiled at the revelation. 'He had once loved someone else, who had returned his love. You know, the passion of the letters was more than I could bear, more than I have ever felt or had someone feel for me. He was human, had loved and lost and surely had known hurt and pain as me. How did the love that I read about compare with his love for you? They are things that I have never known about him.'

Now Anna wept, and she watched her. This was not the time to tell of her secrets. It would be too much.

'They are tears of joy for my father, tears of celebration,' Anna said, and laughed through them at the trees and sky outside the window and threw her hands up in a gesture of triumph for him. 'I'm sorry, but I'm glad as well.'

She said nothing.

'I only skimmed through and could grasp only part of what they said. One day I hope I will know everything. Why were both father's and the woman's letters there? I want to read them again, so I'll keep them with me for a while.'

She was not sure what to think, and for the rest of the morning stayed by herself, and left Anna to continue in her wonder. At lunchtime they came together again and peeled vegetables and made soup.

'When I went back on Monday,' Anna started to say, 'a thought occurred to me of how we might solve some of the mysteries.'

She looked puzzled. 'Which mysteries?'

Anna waited. 'Well, those surrounding Scotland, and now this.'

Her tone was irritable. 'Oh, I really don't want to think about it anymore.'

'Hmm,' Anna nodded. 'I know the letters have upset you, but I decided to try to find out more about the people in the pictures?'

She looked at her and frowned. 'How on earth could you do that?'

'I phoned Thomas Sperring, who wrote one of the obituaries.'

She repeated her stare. Possibly her eyes hid a look of worry. She felt panic at the thought again of the unexpected. 'You did what?'

Anna continued. 'Yes. I think you know him. It was a good place to start, it seemed. We talked for a long time and there is someone he thought you should meet.'

She cast her mind back over the last few weeks. *What more could there be?* 'Yes,' she said, 'I know Thomas. He was one of your father's friends. Who should I meet?'

'His wife,' Anna said, and waited.

'His wife?'

'Yes. She's a woman who we would know as Nonie Sinclair.'

'Nonie Sinclair? She was in Scotland.'

'Yes. It turns out she was the one at the funeral; the woman that you've been asking about, with the red hair. It's her, Thomas Sperring's wife.'

Now, with the spoon from stirring the soup still in her hand, she sat down. 'Yes. I've never met his wife. How strange.'

She closed her eyes and joined the threads. Panic took over. 'Oh, I don't think I could.' She stood up and walked through to the living room. She remembered how futile the discussions with Sandy and Ounagh had been.

Anna called after her. 'There are others who could help. There is

Malcolm Ross of course, who you know you could contact by telephone, but this woman Nonie is the best. She is often in London.'

She called back through the hall. 'Anyway, we would have to contact her. It would be impossible.'

Anna came through and sat down next to her on the couch. She looked at her. 'I have contacted her; it wasn't difficult.'

At first, while she considered, she remained expressionless. 'Anna, this is too much.'

'After the energy you put into the trip to Scotland, why not a little more?'

She laughed. 'No, no, it's impossible...'

'You tried to meet Malcolm Ross. This would be the same, but better: woman to woman. She came to the funeral. That tells you something.'

Anna coaxed her along.

She felt a flicker of pain cross her face. 'What does it tell me?'

'Well, if nothing else, that she has kept in touch,' Anna replied, and trod carefully. 'The trouble is, she's going to Scotland herself at the end of the week and can only meet you tomorrow.'

Fatigue dulled her mind. 'I suppose that would be alright. Oh, the soup,' she said, and rushed to the kitchen to turn it off. 'I think it's burnt,' she said, now sobbing.

'Not to worry,' Anna said. 'Come on, let's go out. We'll go to the pub and I can have a glass of cider.' They walked through the village, more relaxed than she had been the day before and Anna recounted what she had learnt from Thomas Sperring.

Chapter 26
(May, 1992: Kent)

ON THE first of May he cut back the unwanted strands of clematis that had woven a mesh over the porch and attended to the newest shoots of honeysuckle that projected into space with nothing to cling to. Some he pruned away, others he tucked back into the mass of their origin so that, later in the summer, their flowers would hang at the right height over the door and scent the air with their fragrance.

He watched Alex as she busied herself with the fabric of their lives. In quieter moments, when her energy waned, she visited friends or took flowers to the sick on a rota of devotion organised by the vicar. Since it was May for her that meant, 'borders'. A calendar was kept in her mind of all that should be done throughout the year. It forced order into her life. May was a time of anniversaries. Today was one of them; they had been married for forty five years.

Some weeks before, when she had been asked what she wanted to do to celebrate their forty fifth wedding anniversary, she had been helpful in her response, almost to the point of encouragement with her suggestions. He had taken her at her word and followed up on an afternoon tea party on the lawn - if the weather turned out fine - and a quiet supper for some friends in the evening. Over the weeks he had mended decaying garden chairs retrieved from a pile at the back of the shed, touched them up with varnish and glued the loose joints. He made seats from tree stumps around the garden and nailed planks onto large logs for benches.

In the early days of April he had put the anniversary out of his mind. The latter years had seen a consolidation of many strands of his work, a convergence and coalescence of ideas that had replaced the destructive themes that dominated the decade after the war.

The chances of the weather not being fine for the anniversary were slim. Even before March was out, spring seemed set to break new records and, by mid-April, the forecast for a summer drought seemed well founded. The weather suited him and he managed to nurture ideas so that preparations for the anniversary did not erode his thoughts. Ideas that he liked, but could not devote time to, he handed to student composers from the Royal College.

On the morning of the anniversary it was not with thoughts of music or of the anniversary on his mind when he awakened, but of a reckoning with his past. For the hundredth time - 'Forget it,' he muttered to himself; the memories were best left in the closet of forgotten events. Was it a betrayal that he had never told her? Equally, would it betray her now to tell her? What was there to tell? That he had never forgotten a man and a woman he knew long ago. Yes, it would be a betrayal, because for him some parts were as yesterday. Would she understand?

During the garden-party, throughout the afternoon, he moved from one of his makeshift benches to another, from shade to sun, from conversation with others to his own contemplations. Likewise, through the dinner party in the evening, he wondered. Old friends did not demand formality, and familiarity allowed them to depart early with no offence. Paul Spiers and Colette and two of Alex's friends from the village left at ten o'clock. In the kitchen, Anna was occupied with the last pieces of clearing up.

He closed the door behind them and turned into the hall and to Alex. 'Happy anniversary, Darling.' He put his arms around her and gave her a kiss. Still with a glass in one hand, he folded his arms around her waist. 'It's really the anniversary of a whole lifetime,' he said, and swayed a little as he spoke and steadied himself against her. 'Seventy odd years we've known each other.'

Old thoughts and memories came to mind; memories about the beginnings of events in life, which had not been remembered by their own formal markers. He shrugged and looked at her as she steadied him.

'You've had too much champagne.'

'Hmm, I suppose I have; good, isn't it? Come on, let's go out and sit in the garden, there is something I want to tell you that I've wanted to tell you for a long time.'

As the air cooled, they sat at the bench near the edge of the garden in the scent of lilac and in the shadows cast by the light of an old street lamp that was hidden in foliage near the rear drive.

She pulled her shawl around her as she waited. With the light behind him, she could see his profile in its glow. He wore a green cotton shirt and she felt the goose flesh on his arm beneath the short sleeve. His mind often threw up notions and ideas he wanted to share with her, but in the passage of time he might forget, only to remember later.

'There is something I have never told you,' he said, and turned towards her. 'Something I have never been able to talk about, that I have never talked to anyone about. Only one or two people have ever known.'

Her eyes narrowed. If she frowned, it was lost in the shadows.

'It's about something that happened when you and I were in London, after college, and you were still at the Royal Free. When we met again after the war, you put my moods and depression down to the aftermath of all that had gone on in those years. You were right, but that was only part of the explanation, in many ways the least of the reasons.'

He stopped and retraced his steps through the events of those times. She seemed to sense a struggle in him and kept her silence. Then he felt the moment pass and the tension weaken and knew that he was losing the struggle with what he wanted to say to her.

He turned to her again. 'I'm sorry. I'm not doing this very well.' Through the shadows, he looked at her.

Relaxing her grip on the arm of the bench, she brought her hand back onto her knee. 'That's alright: the words will come when they want to,' she said, and he heard her breathing grow deeper and felt her shiver as she waited.

'The champagne has gone to my head. I can't think any more. Let me tell you tomorrow.'

She leant forward and put her cheek against his. 'No, go on, you can't stop now.'

Anna's call from the French windows distracted them. 'Telephone, for you Mummy.'

She stood up. 'Don't think this gets you off the hook; I'll make it brief.'

Despite her intention, she was on the phone for ten minutes. The call returned her thoughts to the responsibilities of work that started early the next morning on the first day of the Association for Medical Education conference.

He went into the kitchen, where Anna had finished clearing up and where no trace remained of supper or the preparation that had gone into it. She closed the windows and drew the curtains. 'All ready for tomorrow; done for another day. Mummy can get off tomorrow morning without worrying about it.'

He nodded. 'Thanks, you've been marvellous Darling.'

When she finished on the phone, she came back to him. 'Come on,' she said, and led him back to the garden.

'I wanted to tell you about something which happened…' He looked at her, and smiled.

'Yes, go on.'

'It's funny; you want to say something but can't.'

'Well, there's no hurry…'

'Yes, it's too late now, and it's waited long enough anyway, another day won't matter. Tomorrow: I'll tell you tomorrow.'

UP EARLY the next day, she collected a colleague from her home and drove to the conference venue. An hour's drive saw them there by eight. Lunchtime arrived before she managed to get a moment alone.

Plush maroon chairs lined the walls of the foyer and she sat on one and closed her eyes. Around her two hundred charged conference-delegates unleashed their energy in conversation about their ideas for medical training or for social agendas later that evening. *What a highly sexed lot they were.*

Now, with her eyes closed and torn between the attraction of a quiet walk in the park and further dedication to the cause in the main hall where a buffet lunch awaited, she felt the stress ebb away and sat on. As President of the association, she knew where her duties lay.

Opening her eyes, she stared into the curtain of suits and black skirts. To her left, Gerald Swanson manoeuvred towards her between the crossed legs of those seated at the edge of the foyer and the knots of people stood next to them. As he threaded his way, a shadow of concern on his face, he stared towards her. At first he did not speak. *What new crisis had arisen?*

It was his look at her for too long, as if he searched for what to say, and the grey pallor in his cheek, that gave him away. The realisation vibrated through her mind that there was something he had to tell her that he struggled with.

'Alex, David's had a heart attack,' he said.

As she continued to look at him, her brow furrowed and remained so. She caught her breath and her stomach started to throb. 'Go on.'

'He's in the County. The Air Ambulance is coming to pick you up. I asked them.'

She did not move, still looked into his eyes. He seemed to know that she asked for more information.

'It doesn't look very good.'

She nodded her acknowledgement and thanks for his honesty and now her chest shuddered as she breathed slowly in. Her inhalation released a wave of energy that flowed through her spine and dissipated in the small of her back.

'Come on,' he said. 'I'll drive over after you. Bridget will look after everything this afternoon.'

Even as they spoke, the Air Ambulance touched down on the lawn outside. Gerald waited for her to stand and walked behind her as she led the way through the crowded delegates and out of the main entrance. She looked ahead, did not notice that the volume of conversation lowered in the few seconds it took her to walk to the entrance. As she became aware of the noise of the helicopter outside, she felt exposed. Eyes turned to follow her and by the time she had gone through the doors, the hall was silent. Bridget Conrad made a simple announcement. Ten minutes later the helicopter landed on the pad at the County Hospital.

She held David's hand.

At two fifteen that Monday afternoon, she knew that his life had gone. She sat in thoughts, made a telephone call and drank the cup of tea that the nurse brought to her. She accepted Gerald Swanson's guardianship in those first hours.

Though far from composed, her mind was clear. What flowed through it was a chronicle of parts of her life, and then a sensation of panic that none of it mattered.

'Gerald, I want my car,' she said. 'Will you ask somebody to bring it, please.'

'What are you going to do?'

'I'm going to go to Eleanor in Walmer.'

'Good idea. Let me take you.'

'No, it's alright. I want to go by myself. I'll be alright.'

He spoke softly. 'I think it will take too long to get your car. Take mine. I'll bring yours later.'

She looked at him and weighed up the suggestion. She agreed and thanked him.

Gerald gave her his keys. 'What is her number? I'll call you and let you know when I'll be there.'

She gave him Eleanor's number and then stood up. 'I think I'll go now. Here are the keys for my car.'

ELEANOR LIVED on the coast, a hundred yards from the waves, in a house that looked across to Belgium. With the telescope on the upstairs veranda, you could see Calais to the south. It made good sense to go there; Eleanor was an old friend, but that was not the reason for the decision. It was because she lived on the coast. In the midst of the knowledge of David's death came images of hills and meadows, like a dream, a place conjured from her subconscious thoughts that she couldn't explain. Eleanor on the coast came to mind by association. To go there seemed to offer comfort.

Anna would already be home in Cambridgeshire.

On the way she stopped to think. Many things troubled her. For the moment, it was not David's death that was the focus, but things to do with her responses. She could not help it. The events sparked a catalogue of introspections about her life, about David and, what she found most surprising, about what she was going to do. *This isn't right*, she thought.

She did not hurry and by the time she arrived at Eleanor's house, was still a long way from the point of break down. She had shown no emotion for five hours, as if she had paced herself until the car stopped outside the house.

Eleanor was there. She must have stood waiting for ages. Often she gave the impression of being a more serious woman than she was, but on this occasion, with her hair allowed to flow freely, she looked relaxed.

Staying in the car with the window down, she watched Eleanor as she approached. She knew there was no need to smile and so did not. Eleanor did, but that was all. She stood by the car and then said: 'Come in when you're ready, there's no hurry.' She turned and left her with her smile of support.

For a few more minutes she waited, then got out and walked across the narrow strip of dune and shingle in front of the house that grew wild fennel and horned poppies. She did not find the path, but walked through the sparse cover of coastal vegetation. The flint and pebble shingle that dipped to the tide covered her shoes and after a few steps got in between her soles and the leather. She looked out to sea towards Belgium and France to her right, and, for the first time of many, told herself she was being absurd.

At the front door, she heard strains of an aria she did not recognise. Eleanor made tea and she sat and drank it.

'Do you want to call Anna?' she asked. 'I can call her if you want me to.'

'No, I'll do it. I wanted to leave that until I got here. I need you to be near me when I do it. She was at home with us this morning. Jonathan will have to come from Mali.'

'Okay,' Eleanor said. 'The telephone's there. I'm here to do anything you want. The room's ready, the one at the front.'

She nodded and gave her thanks with a smile.

'I'll make some supper at about seven,' and she left the room.

From the moment that Gerald Swanson came towards her in the conference hall, to the moment Eleanor left her alone, she could not have described the state she was in. She knew it was not what people said should happen, or what she imagined they expected to happen to her as they watched. What should have happened had not happened in those hours. She had held on and now, alone and secure at Eleanor's, closed her eyes and let the shock settle in her, and tried to understand her reactions.

A few hours of her life had changed it all. *Who was she now? Who had David been?* She looked back over their life together. Her vision funnelled to a narrow period after the war and to things she did not understand from that time. *What should she do?* The urge she felt to move, remained, and feelings that she could not explain or tie down, welled through her.

THE NEXT morning, knowing that difficult days lay ahead, she gritted her teeth. What had happened had happened and the time for quiet reflection had gone. Within hours, Anna would arrive and Jonathan later in the week. They would take over and do what they thought they should. They would talk to her and say what they thought they should say. She had told Eleanor as much as she could think of and Eleanor had listened. Now she would stick it out until it was through.

Chapter 27
(Days 20 and 21 - May 1992: Kent)

THE CATHEDRAL gardens were at their loveliest. She met Nonie there and recognised her as the woman she had seen at the funeral. As she watched her approach, the woman seemed sure of herself, walking with ease and grace beneath the trees, wearing a plain summer dress, just darker than her complexion. She guessed she was the same age as herself. Why shouldn't she be? And, yes, she was taller.

The images of her in the photographs returned and now she saw the hair red and not dark as the photo suggested. Nonie smiled and shook hands and sat beside her on the bench.

She composed herself: no need to speak first; no hurry. She did not know what she expected to happen. The person who sat beside her could have been an old friend. She could not help but relax next to her.

Nonie started to speak: 'I feel I know you well,' she said, and turned sideways as far as she could so that she could look at her. 'Over the years, I have wanted to talk to you many times on the occasions we have been together.'

She listened, the soft Scottish accent of her voice lulling her and, conscious that her own breathing had quickened, she raised her head and tried to breath more deeply.

Nonie seemed to sense her confusion. 'I'm sorry, it is going to take a while to tell the story.'

She nodded. 'Yes - when have we been together over the years?' Nonie's opening comment had sent a shiver down her spine.

'Oh, usually at concerts and social gatherings.'

She looked at her in wonder. 'And you knew me?'

'Of course...'

'And yet we were never introduced?'

'No. I know it sounds strange.' She let her gaze wander across the lawns towards the cathedral. 'David did not want it that way. He put it off, me also; I've done the same. We both agreed to bury the past.'

It felt as if she had not grasped the subject of the conversation, as if two strands of dialogue had started. 'Look, I'm terribly sorry...' and she turned to stare at Nonie, '...I am confused; is there something I should know that I don't?'

Nonie smiled. 'No. It is something that has happened alongside you, but there is nothing especially that you should have known.'

She drew in her breath. 'Tell me something else to begin with.' *Was the question relevant?* 'When did you last see David?'

Nonie nodded as though to acknowledge a misunderstanding. 'In November.'

She moved uncomfortably on the bench.

Nonie continued. 'If he had still been alive we would have met at the end of May.' She looked at her. 'We have met twice a year ever since the war, every May and every November.'

She shivered, listened to the tones of Nonie's voice, as those of a radio presenter or the reader of a *Book at Bedtime*. It became softer and the words sounded distant.

'Now it can finally end,' Nonie said. 'We agreed that it should, but David died before he could tell you. So I have waited too. It is only because of your daughter, that we can close the book.'

She brought herself back from the words, which both distressed and distracted her. 'Whatever it is, whatever it is that you have to tell me, could you start now at the beginning. I feel that I am only becoming more confused.'

Nonie nodded her head. 'Of course, yes, I keep forgetting that you know virtually nothing.' She waited for a while to gather her thoughts.

'David and I agreed on Christmas Eve in 1940 that we would bury the past and keep it between us. That is what we have done.'

Her mind raced. She regained her composure. 'I think David did start to tell me; it was the night before he died.'

Nonie murmured. 'Oh yes, of course; on your anniversary.'

She looked at Nonie. 'Yes, how do you know that?'

'Well, as I say, I feel I know you very well. I will explain. I think it will become clearer. What did he tell you?'

'Almost nothing, just that there was something he had wanted to tell me for a long time. Something he had never been able to talk about, that he had never talked to anyone about. It must have been about you. Then he found it difficult and stopped. He didn't tell me anymore. I said it would wait until tomorrow. Then it was too late. There were things I needed to talk to him about as well...'

'Good. It has nothing to do with me, though,' Nonie said when she had finished, and then started her story from the beginning, from her first encounter with David and Helen and all that followed.

She told of meeting Helen an David together in Nairn, and then of Douglas, of how she fell in love with him at first sight on a train from Inverness and of their time in the summer of '39 with David and Helen, and of what followed.

'What we buried were dreams and memories and the love that we had for two people. They both died, one literally and the love of the other, in effect, for David, in 1940.'

She shuddered and bowed her head. Tears came to her eyes. 'Douglas Cameron, yes, I know the name. I think I even met him once. I've read all the letters from Helen. I once knew someone who died too...'

Nonie showed surprise, but continued: 'I waited in June for news, only to hear of Douglas's death in France.'

She looked at her, into eyes that could remain dry now after all the years, and said, 'I think I'm beginning to understand.'

'Helen was my greatest friend,' Nonie continued. 'We had much in common, she being from Nairn as I am. When David telephoned to tell me she had been injured, I think it almost killed me. It could well have killed us both.'

She sat in the silence of Nonie's words. 'How was she injured?'

'In the bombing of Hull at the end of 1940.'

She nodded. She remembered the time when she had worked in London hospitals through the blitz before she went to India. Nonie did not need to say any more, but she waited for her to continue.

'It was made all the worse because her brother Gordon was killed in the war as well. He died in Burma in 1943 and that brought more grief to the family.'

She nodded again, then stopped. '*Gordon?* What was Helen's name,' she asked.

'Strachan,' Nonie, told her.

She didn't reply, but looked past Nonie to the lawns and borders set with flowers behind her. *Gordon Strachan. Captain Gordon Strachan.* She stared into the distance beyond Nonie.

'Are you alright?' Nonie asked. 'You've turned very pale.'

She shook her head. *Gordon Strachan? Why had his name suddenly dropped into the conversation?* 'Yes. I'm alright,' she replied, but her attention was no longer focused on David and Helen. 'I'm just confused, that's all...'

'This is too much of a shock for you,' Nonie said. 'You look cold now.'

'Yes, despite the weather, I feel a little feverish.' It would take longer than the next few minutes to understand what she had just heard.

'Shall I continue?'

'Yes, that's alright.'

So Nonie continued to recount her tale. 'David met Helen in London. She brought him to Scotland and she grew to love him. Later, after the accident, she pushed him away. It was a terrible time for us. The period was brief. Helen tried, but eventually saw that it was no good and started to close herself off from the world. David has talked to me about it so often since then as he struggled with himself to understand.'

'You mean she did not love him?' Her voice trembled.

'Oh, yes, she loved him, and he loved her. It was because she loved him that she would not burden him with herself.'

She did not really understand, but Nonie continued. 'I met Thomas after the war, and grew to love him.'

'Yes, Thomas Sperring,' she said, and nodded. 'I've met him on and off over the years, but never you.'

'David and he were old friends. They met during the war.'

'I didn't know any of this.' She looked away and shivered again.

'It didn't matter, not until now.' Nonie smiled at her. 'David always loved you, in a deep and eternal way. You know that; in quite a different way to Helen.'

How could she speak like this? And again she looked at Nonie. 'Yes, I always knew he did.'

Nonie continued the story. 'He went to France to find out where Douglas died. So much of his best music came from there. Thomas always admired it greatly.'

She pictured the painting in the studio. 'Yes, I have always thought so too.' As she spoke, she let her eyes rest on Nonie. 'He thought his music here in Kent to be his deepest, from the soils of his origins, but his music from *Senlis* was some of his best. I didn't know about Douglas though.'

'Douglas's death affected David, if anything, more than his despair over Helen. It was earlier, in May and we heard in June. The interruption of the war started David's depression, but Douglas's death broke him as a composer at that time. That he ever wrote again was a miracle.'

How could Nonie speak with such authority? Slowly she began to understand. 'The war hurt David in a way that I have never understood,' she said. 'I can see now that my explanation at the time was superficial.'

Nonie's voice continued. 'David searched for the place where Douglas was killed. I never went myself.'

She cast her thoughts back to France. 'My grandmother came from that part, a little further south. We have a lot in common with the area. She and my grandfather were from Picardie. I didn't know David went there to find out about Douglas. I imagined it was because of my associations with *Senlis*.'

Looking into the pages of her past, to things she had almost forgotten, she hardly heard Nonie telling her about them, and telling her more than she knew.

'He did go because of you, but David couldn't miss the coincidence that it was so near to where Douglas was killed, with the chance to visit those places as well.'

She breathed in, and nodded her head.

'We don't know where he was buried.' Nonie's voice was distant. 'We just know the town where he died. David wrote the last part of a violin concerto there.'

'I'm sorry,' she said and immediately regretted the words.

Nonie gave the slightest shake of her head. 'Afterwards, after we'd heard, David and I met in London on Christmas Eve 1940 at the station in York. We always laughed afterwards when we looked back at that meeting. We didn't know what to do. We wept and sat in silence and held each other's hands. I was in the WAAF and went back to Scotland for Christmas. I had stayed with Helen when she was transferred back to London. David returned to Hull. We met again each year of the war.'

She closed her eyes and tried to let the knowledge settle in her mind.

'Afterwards... Well you know much of the story yourself. I met Thomas at one of David's concerts after the war and we were married, at the same time as you in 1947, on the same day, in fact.'

Now she looked at Nonie in disbelief and Nonie read her thoughts and smiled. 'Forgive me, yes,' Nonie said, 'I know it sounds incredible.' In a gesture of acknowledgement, she waved her hand. 'I know so much about you. The things that David did not tell you, I also never told Thomas. Perhaps now, I can.'

'But why didn't you talk about it; it seems so unnatural, so - unfair?' Then she hesitated; *was this any different to her secrets?*

'Yes, I've often pondered upon that myself. David at the time was very near the edge. His anger got the better of him at times. So much had gone wrong. In Scotland in July and August, immersed in his music, he could have stayed there for many months. I remember his energy and love for his work. Everything was going well. The war put an end to his equilibrium and all that he wanted from life. He suffered terribly for those years. At the time for both of us, it was right to bury our memories. We buried the pain and the past as though it never happened. It was a way to cope with the events, the war and the loss.

'But later, why not later?'

'Later? Yes, why not later?' Nonie paused and thought and closed her eyes, then turned and looked at her. 'I think David would have told you, except for one reason.' She looked away again. Her voice seemed more distant. 'It was a final tragedy. Helen did marry - a man she met at the hospital - who had been injured in the war. He cared for her and she found some happiness with him. Then in 1960, she died.'

She shivered and shook her head. She thought back. 'It must have been when I came back from a course, in the spring; I remember he was not himself for weeks.'

Nonie nodded. 'That sounds right.' She paused. 'So we continued to share the memories alone. We feared that it might destroy something if we tried to tell others. It seemed alright to do that.'

Again, at the revelations, she shook her head and accepted Nonie's explanation. Now her voice was calm. 'Tell me of the others. What has happened to them?'

'Gavin Brink became an author. He wrote historic novels about Scotland. He died in 1980. Malcolm Ross lives in Ullapool still. We both kept in touch; David more so. He still used Malcolm's poems, even recently.'

She nodded. 'Yes, I was in Lewis a few weeks ago and tried to meet Malcolm.'

'Hmm, Anna told me. You must have had a great insight to make you want to go.'

'I don't know: it just seemed right. Now I understand why.'

'Did you learn anything?'

'I told myself I had learnt very little. Now, after what you have told me, I think there was more. I have a lot of thinking to do now.'

For the first time Nonie looked distracted. 'I hope one day you will forgive us.'

'Of course, and you me; I've been so selfish.'

Nonie stood up. 'I think I have told you everything. I hope we will have a chance to meet again.'

Together they walked through the gardens to the car park beneath the city walls where they said goodbye.

Before Nonie got into her car, she opened her bag and took out a small box. 'David gave this to Helen. She told me at the time. Helen's mother gave it to me at Helen's funeral.' Nonie took a chain with a silver Victorian sixpence on it from the box. 'I have had it all these years. I didn't have the heart to give it back to David. It was from his grandmother. Perhaps Anna would like it?' She handed it to her and then drove off.

EXCEPT FOR the briefest comment, she remained quiet when she returned from her meeting with Nonie. She went to her room and asked to be alone.

Later, as she picked flowers in the garden, she watched Anna and saw how she inspected each inflorescence with care so as to only choose the best. An observer would have said Anna looked content. As she bent amongst the flowers, she moved with ease and lightness. When she had gathered enough, she took them into the cottage and up to the studio where she arranged them in a vase on a small table near the window. Already the piles of papers had been cleared from the floor and the trunks pushed back to the wall. Except for the piano, his old armchair and the flowers on the table, her father's music room was empty.

For her, there had been a change. As easily as events had caused disruption in her life, so had the feeling been reversed. She felt she had been released from the whirlwind that had carried her in its vortex. And yet, even now, some things remained unfinished.

In the sitting room in the evening light, she sat with Anna. 'It's still not over by far, but at least the events in Scotland have been explained. I suppose I should be grateful for that small mercy.'

'Are you sure it is sorted out?'

'I think we have answered the riddle of your father's time before the war, and about his state of mind afterwards. Strong and steadfast as always, but with so much else to cope with.'

'What about you?'

'In some ways I feel simple again.'

'That's good.'

'In others, even more perplexed... I still struggle with the games my mind plays - with, for example, the recurring images of hills. They were not Scottish hills, but still they return, and slowly I think I am beginning to understand why.'

'I think it has been another exhausting week for you Mummy. I hope you feel a little happier now?'

'Yes, I do,' and she got up and walked to the window. 'I feel clean, less alone.' Her thoughts wandered. 'I think it's going to be alright now. I have something to look forward to.'

Anna gave a smile. 'Have you? I hope so. Whatever you do, don't do anything in too much hast.'

She could give her no assurances; she was just tuning into who she was. 'It turned out that I got full marks for intuition when I went to Scotland, so I think I'll stick with my intuition. And what about you, what have you to look forward to?'

'Oh, the children, Max, work...'

She looked at her daughter. 'Yes, but what about *you*?'

Anna squirmed, and, in a heaven knows what sort of response, shook her head. 'That's a very male sort of question - *what about you?* - as if I haven't enough already with my family and home? They are enough, aren't they, my home and my family? I neglect them with all my work and research.'

Perhaps they were. 'Yes, I suppose you're right; that's how I have always felt, but I wonder now about other things that give us reason - much simpler things.'

'Like who we are?'

'Yes, who we are and where we come from.'

'Where we come from?'

'Yes: your father was lucky; he knew where he came from and stayed where he belonged and thrived...'

'We'll have to try to do the same then,' Anna said.

PERHAPS IT was the sun that glinted through the trees, or the sound of birds that broke her concentration. She looked at the untidy patch of grass at her feet that had not yet settled. Dew glistened on new shoots and bare earth showed in places.

'I hope you don't mind,' she said. She sat down beside the grave and let her mind wander back over all she had done and found out over the three weeks since the funeral. It was 27 May and, in new leaves and petals of flowers and trees and some of the first roses that she had placed in a vase on the grass, the colours of summer grew into the fabric of the village.

Unlimited choices lay before her. 'I hope you don't mind,' she said again. Her sandals lay beside her and she dug her toes into the earth, made holes through the turf, and let the soil blacken the nails.

Are we the same? Yes, we are; we have not changed. You are as you have always been and I am as I have been. We, the first person, the joined 'us', are still here, and always will be.

She smiled at the conclusion. 'Hm, yes, we are alright,' she said, and standing up, started to walk back through the village to the cottage. As she walked, tears filled her eyes.

In the hall, her over-night bag lay unzipped on the floor.

Although not large, it contained everything she needed. In the kitchen she had left a note for Mr Joseph. Please water the plants and make sure there is nothing in the fridge to go off.

The sight of her bag beside the front door made her laugh. So inadequate. A book and a small framed picture from the table in the sitting room she threw in for good measure. Then, looking around and imagining the accumulation of belongings scattered throughout the cottage, she knew nothing else mattered.

We don't need any of this, and again she laughed. When did we begin? At a choir practice in church on a Tuesday night. That was when it started, the first time I saw you, that was when our lives together began; when I was eight years old. We began then and we still are…

Nonie's story had corrected the mistakes made when she read the letters on the studio floor. It had set her as near to normal as anything could. The explanation left her with herself.

She thought of *Senlis*, her grandparent's village in France. The temptation to go to the studio and to look at the picture of the town was too great to resist, and quietly she climbed the stairs. It drew her as always, trapped her imagination in the crevices of masonry and the lives she imagined behind the walls. She let her eyes rest on the canvas until she heard music. She remembered David when they had stayed in the house in *Senlis* those forty summers ago. Then, with the music in her mind, she went down to the living room and played a cassette, some of David's compositions from Paris, but mainly those from *Senlis*. She put it in her bag.

'You live on my darling.' This is all part of us; we did most of this. How much of the music is in me? The idea still amused her. Not you and me, but we; still we…

'Now -' she said to herself, '- anything I've forgotten?'

Picking up her bag, she locked the cottage door and after a last inspection of the garden, got into her car and drove away. 'Over to you, Mr Joseph.'

EVEN AFTER driving slowly, the journey to the coast took less than three quarters of an hour. Was she being foolish? No, it seemed right. 'Trust your instinct.'

Three hours later her car pulled off the ferry and across the port esplanade at Calais. The rolling landscape of northern France passed on either side as she drove south. A quilt of greens and yellows with avenues of trees and wooded hilltops stretched into the distances. She drove through the edges of Flandres past St. Omer, Bethune and Arras, then through Artois and into Picardie. An hour later *Senlis* was signposted thirty-six kilometres away.

At three o'clock, she approached the village of Fleurines. What she saw pleased her. Most of the houses were a shade of cream either from paint or the natural colour of the stone they were built from. It gave them a uniformity of appearance that to her eye was un-English, as yellow stone is a novelty when you drive into a Cotswold village. Some of the eroded roofs appeared as undulating seas of tiles.

Then on through a forest of majestic trees that presented a shield of green along the road that took her to *Senlis*. She knew she had arrived when she came to a roundabout with a bronze stag mounted at its centre. She stopped in the first car park she found.

'Here I am, in the town of the gentle hills.'

How slowly she had come to realise that the thoughts which had worried her since David's death pointed her there, to the place of her mother's birth, the village of her grandparents and the place of her ancestors. Now she knew that nothing could be more certain.

It was an hour before she arrived at the address of a place to stay given to her by the tourist office, in a street called Rue de la Tonnellerie. She enjoyed the search along the narrow pavements and found it easier to walk up the row of cobbles in the centre that she guessed channelled rainwater. After ten minutes she stopped for a rest and turned to look through the streets. What did she feel; safe? Yes, safe. She had left this place behind, but it had never left her. She mistook being lost for loneliness.

She walked on. Above her, red geraniums in pots and small boxes perched on the edge of upper windowsills. She found the address and knocked on the door. The sound of footsteps coming down preceded the noise of a key and the door handle being turned. A woman greeted her. Both smiled and in their own ways made the other feel at ease. She spoke French and the woman, who introduced herself as Chantal and led the way up the stairs to a flat on the first floor, said 'hello' in English.

At the back of the house, Chantal showed her to a small room with wooden floor boards and white plastered walls, bare rather than cluttered, with the simplest of furniture and white curtains with a pattern of blue flowers at the window. She listened to Chantal's explanations, smiled and nodded and was content with their exchanges.

It did not take long to unpack and she did not hurry. When she looked out of the window, at peace now with herself, she gazed across the town and further to the hills beyond. In that moment, she had a sense of looking behind herself, at her uncertain self and then forward to sureness.

Later, when she returned to the kitchen and sat down, Chantal gave her a cold drink. She watched her prepare supper and listened while she chatted as she worked. First she took a lettuce from a brown paper bag and placed it on a wooden board on the table and began to cut it up. She inspected each leaf and discarded blemished pieces, then cut along the main stem with her knife and folded the leaf in two and cut it three or four times. Every now and again she glanced over and smiled. In this way she cut ten or more leaves until she filled the bowl. Then she cleared the remains and wiped the table.

When Chantal turned towards her, she explained that her grandparents were from *Senlis* and that once, when she was a girl, her grandmother had visited England and told her that from her window in *Senlis* she looked down from the shadows of old walls onto green hills and meadows and watched the spring grow into summer.

'I have come to do the same,' she said.

RICHARD MATTHEWMAN

Photo: Helen Brown

Acknowledgements

My thanks to Helen Brown, Martin Dixon, Chris and Renee Grier,
Trevor Laming, Isabel Senior, Elizabeth Storey and David Wheatley,
amongst others, for comments and encouragement during the writing
of this story.

Thanks to Trevor Laming for the cover design.

RICHARD MATTHEWMAN